KT-501-365

Also by Barbara Dunlop

Chicago Sons
Sex, Lies and the CEO
Seduced by the CEO
A Bargain with the Boss
His Stolen Bride

Gambling Men
The Twin Switch
The Dating Dare
Midnight Son

Also by Susannah Erwin

Titans of Tech
Wanted: Billionaire's Wife
Cinderella Unmasked
Who's the Boss Now?

Discover more at millsandboon.co.uk

HUSBAND IN NAME ONLY

BARBARA DUNLOP

EVER AFTER EXES

SUSANNAH ERWIN

MILLS & BOON

First Published in Great Britain 2022
by Mills & Boon, an imprint of HarperCollins*Publishers* Ltd
1 London Bridge Street, London, SE1 9GF

www.harpercollins.co.uk

HarperCollins*Publishers*
1st Floor, Watermarque Building,
Ringsend Road, Dublin 4, Ireland

Husband in Name Only © 2022 Barbara Dunlop
Ever After Exes © 2022 Susannah Erwin

ISBN: 978-0-263-30374-2

0222

MIX
Paper from
responsible sources
FSC™ C007454

HUSBAND IN NAME ONLY

BARBARA DUNLOP

For my niece Chloe,
who's off on her own northern adventure!

One

My best friend and fellow Cal State graduate, Katie Tambour, stood on a chair in my compact dining nook, running a stud finder across the saffron-yellow wall.

"There's not much point in hanging it," I told her, not sure whether to hover up close in case she lost her footing or to stand back and mitigate the damage in the event disaster struck.

"I hung mine up this morning," she said. "I'm a pro."

My newly minted and grandly framed PhD parchment sat behind her on the small, round kitchen table. I was officially a doctor now, Adeline Emily Cambridge, doctor of philosophy, architecture and urban planning.

"You won't be moving away," I pointed out.

Katie had been offered a position here in Sacramento, lecturing on physics and astronomy at the Cal State campus. It was only part-time, but her parents lived in town, so her expenses would stay low while she built up her résumé.

"You'll be here awhile longer," she said.

"Maybe." I wasn't in any particular hurry to leave California. I'd spent the past nine years enjoying the silky air and sunshine of the state, immersed in the laid-back lifestyle and secure in my sense of freedom and self- determination.

"Found one," Katie called out in obvious delight, her fingertip marking a spot between the white kitchen cabinets and the blue and sea-green blown-glass sculpture I'd picked up at a local arts festival three years ago.

I was settled and happy in my little off-campus apartment. Only a block from the river, its balcony caught the fresh breeze on warm summer days. This far into May, my tan was golden brown from hours spent reading, researching and writing outside on my favorite lounger.

"Hand me the hammer," Katie said, reaching blindly behind herself.

"I'm not supposed to put unauthorized holes in the walls."

"It's a very small hole."

"You know I put up a damage deposit on this place."

"Nobody'll notice one more." She canted her head meaningfully toward the glass sculpture on her left. It was true that the piece had taken three hooks, and they were bigger than the ones Katie was using for my degree.

"Fine," I said on a mock huff, handing her the wood-handled claw hammer. "Go ahead, vandalize my walls."

She laughed at that, traded me the stud finder for the hammer and lined up the nail with its dangling, kinked metal hanger. "You're going to love looking up and seeing this. And you should take the credential out for a test drive—sign something *Dr. Cambridge*. I know I'll be signing everything *Dr. Tambour* for a while."

"If you do that, people will ask you for medical advice."

She tapped gently on the nail head then harder to anchor it into the stud. "I'll tell them it's a physics degree and start explaining Planck's constant. That'll stop the questions."

"I imagine it would."

Hanger secure, she twisted around and bent over to lift the framed degree. Then she felt her way to the catch at the back of the frame, slipped it over the hanger and eyeballed the whole thing to level.

She hopped down from the chair and stood next to me. "Perfect."

I couldn't help wondering how long it would stay up there before I packed it away in a moving box.

"I got a weird job offer yesterday," I said. I'd been trying to push the unsettling letter out of my mind since it had arrived. But I knew ignoring it wasn't the answer.

"Weird how?" She stepped up and made a final adjustment to the angle of the frame.

"Surprising…concerning. I don't exactly know how to respond to it." I crossed to the kitchen counter and retrieved the crisp ivory paper from my cluttered wicker mail basket. As I handed it over to Katie, my gaze skimmed the stylistic tricolored letterhead of Windward, Alaska.

Katie folded herself into the mocha leather tub chair beside my open balcony door, next to the glass of merlot she'd abandoned twenty minutes ago, and started reading.

I could tell the second the words sank in.

"Seriously?" She looked up at me, eyes wide as the evening breeze lifted her blond hair.

"I didn't apply to it," I said. "I don't even understand how they know about me."

"You published your thesis, and the graduation ceremony was livestreamed. You're hardly a covert urban planning operative."

She read her way through the project description—to design and build an arts and culture complex for fine arts education, gallery space, retail and recreational opportunities for the third-largest city in Alaska.

I sat down on the two-cushion sofa and picked up my own glass of wine from the little coffee table between us.

It was my dream job, there was no doubt about that. And I didn't kid myself. Under normal circumstances I wouldn't get near something like it without at least ten years of experience. But there was one thing that qualified me above anyone else—I was an Alaskan.

"But…" Katie looked at me in consternation. "You said—"

"That I'd never, ever go home," I finished for her. That sentiment still held. I had no intention of going anywhere near Alaska.

"So, you'll just wait for some more offers," she said more briskly, glancing at my dining nook wall. "I mean, you're all decorated up and everything."

I could wait for more offers.

I should.

I would.

"Or you could reconsider Tucson," Katie said.

"Residential subdivisions?" I couldn't hide my grimace at the thought of doing that day in, day out.

"The salary's good, and the weather's awesome."

I plunked my head against the sofa back, closing my eyes

and giving a loud snore to indicate my level of excitement about the job.

"Reno?" Katie suggested. "You'd be close enough to drive down here for the weekend."

I lifted my head. "Incorporating hotels and casinos into the community plan?" This time I gave a little shudder. "Pass."

"You better not tell me you're going to the Keys. There are snakes down there and alligators and all kinds of creepy-crawly things. I feel like you wouldn't get out alive."

"Well, there are bears in Alaska."

Katie straightened in the chair. "You're considering Alaska?"

"I just said there were bears. Does that sound like I'm considering it?"

"It's not as if the bears stroll down Main Street," Katie said.

"In Windward they do." Grizzlies could be a genuine danger all over Alaska. "Remember how you were taught stranger danger in elementary school? Well, we were taught bear aware."

Katie polished off the remaining wine in her glass and rose. "So, you prefer snakes?"

"No." Snakes scared me down to my toes. Also, alligators ate people. Bears mostly wanted people to stay out of their way. Big difference.

"Casinos aren't looking so bad now, are they?"

"I'm not excited about designing a flashy casino."

She refilled her glass at the little breakfast bar then rocked the merlot bottle my way in an obvious question.

"Please." I held up my glass. "I need to get back to them all one way or another."

I could turn down the offers and stay another month in California, hoping something better came along. Budget wasn't a problem. But I found I wanted to get going. Now that I'd defended my thesis and officially received my degree, I wanted to get started on the rest of my life.

"I find liquor is always helpful when making life-altering decisions," Katie joked as she walked my way with the bottle. "It sharpens the brain, tees up the old synapses."

I lifted my glass for her to pour. "Here's to teed-up synapses."

We said, "Cheers." And then we settled back into our seats.

"It's not going to be Reno," I said, even though I loved the idea of being within driving distance of Katie.

"Well, going to the Keys will give you perpetual night-mares, not to mention giving me perpetual nightmares wor-rying about you."

"And designing the Tucson suburbs would have me climb-ing the walls within weeks."

Katie drank thoughtfully. "You see what you just did."

I knew I'd eliminated the competition. I took a hearty drink.

"It sounds like you're going to Alaska," she said.

"My very successful father's in Alaska. My very success-ful uncle's in Alaska." I let out a groan of despair at the mem-ories of growing up in the Cambridge mansion. "All of those prominent family expectations and pressures are in Alaska."

"Well...how far is it from Windward to Anchorage?"

"Not far enough."

"But there's no road, right?"

"My brothers have corporate planes."

"How will they even know you're there? Are you wearing a tracking bracelet or something? Chip in your arm?"

"My uncle Braxton will feel a disturbance in the Force." Katie laughed.

"You laugh," I said with heavy sarcasm and a dire expression.

"Because you're funny."

"Uncle Braxton's got a wily sense of what's what and who's where."

"Your uncle Braxton's a psychic?"

I swung my glass in an arc. "My uncle Braxton's a schemer. So's my dad. And they've had their eyes on me for years as a potential asset to the family dynasty."

"You're twenty-seven years old."

"I know."

"They can't make you do anything you don't want to do."

"I know that, too." I did know that.

There was always the choice of saying no. I'd done it in the past. But that simple tactic didn't account for the guilt I'd feel when I had to turn them down for something they swore was in the best interest of the family.

I reached across the coffee table and picked up the letter again, rereading paragraph four.

Katie spoke up before I finished. "I could be your wing-man—*person*...doesn't sound right that way, even though it is."

"Wingperson for what? Are we going out tonight?"

"I could come to Alaska."

I did a double take, trying to craft an amusing comeback, assuming she had to be joking.

"I'm serious," she said, looking serious. "Classes don't start up until September. I can do the course outline from any-where."

"You're planning to run interference with my father and uncle for me?"

"Or the bears. Don't forget about the bears."

"No offense, Katie. I'd *love* to have you with me anywhere I went. You're the best friend I've ever had, but it wouldn't help. Those two are a force of nature."

"And I'm not? You can't have missed my PhD in astron-omy. It's hanging on my wall now. And let me tell you, na-ture doesn't get anymore forceful than a supermassive black hole." She jabbed a finger in my direction for emphasis. "I've studied them. I know as much as anybody about their gravi-tational collapse, accretion of interstellar gas and active ga-lactic nuclei."

"They suck the living energy out of anything that happens by, right?"

Her face scrunched up a little at my simplistic description. "At an astronomical level, yeah...basically."

"That's my dad, Xavier, and Uncle Braxton all over the place."

Katie looked confused. "I can't tell what you mean by that. Am I coming to Alaska?"

The midafternoon air was warm and clear as we stepped from the plane onto the tarmac at the Windward airport in Alaska.

"Can you smell that?" Katie asked in wonder.

"Smell what?" I detected a little jet exhaust hanging in the air but nothing noteworthy.

"Nothing! It's clear and pure, like the bubbles coming off expensive champagne. My lungs don't know what hit them."

"Champagne gives off carbon dioxide. What kind of a scientist are you?"

Katie linked her arm through mine, our backpacks tapping together. "You didn't tell me Alaska smelled so nice."

"There's no heavy industry up here." Like Katie, I inhaled deeply, reminded of the pureness of the air. "To the west, there are miles of ocean—over four thousand of them until you hit China. To the east is northern Canada—not exactly a hotbed of industrial emissions. Straight north are three national parks."

We entered the terminal building through sliding glass doors, leaving the sound of the runway behind. The decor was fresh, updated since I'd last been in the city, but the concourse was tiny compared to the international hub in Anchorage.

Katie spun around. "It's exactly what I pictured."

"That's because you searched the airport online."

"Sure, but you can't get a real feel for something until you're standing in the middle of it. This is how I thought it would feel."

People moved past us in both directions, casually dressed, most in work clothes or outdoor wear. Windward prided itself on being independent and unpretentious. Alaskans were like that in general.

As we made our way to the baggage claim—one carousel, no need to figure out where our bags would come out—I caught sight of a photo on the wall, a mural, really, since it was so big. It was clearly a dedication ceremony, maybe for the airport renovations.

Congressman Joe Breckenridge smiled knowingly down at me, and a wave of anxiety rolled through my stomach. I told myself it was just a photo. The real Joe Breckenridge was far away in DC. He spent most of his time there, the rest in Anchorage and Fairbanks, where a majority of the voters lived, or on his family ranch on the Kenai Peninsula. Still, I couldn't shake the feeling that the Alaska walls were closing in on me.

"Well, that was fast," Katie said, spotting her small suitcase and darting toward it. "Yours is here, too," she called over her shoulder.

Like the rest of the Windward passengers, I sauntered over, secure in the knowledge there was no hurry to claim my bag.

"How do we get to the hotel?" Katie asked, our bags now standing at our feet.

"It's the Redrock. They'll have a shuttle." I pointed to the ground transportation exit only steps away.

Sure enough, as the glass door slid open for us, the Redrock Hotel shuttle was waiting at the curb.

The driver approached, no suit jacket or uniform, just a clean pair of black jeans and a gold golf shirt with the hotel logo embroidered on the pocket. "Adeline?" he asked.

"They know you?" Katie whispered in my ear with an excited lilt.

"That's me," I said to the driver. To Katie I whispered, "My name's on their reservation list."

"Hi, I'm Jackson. Welcome to Windward," the man said, shaking our hands before taking charge of our roller bags. "You want your packs up front with you?"

"Yes," I said, since my wallet and phone were inside.

"Go ahead and hop in." He took the bags to the back end of the small shuttle.

"This is great," Katie said, going for the door. "No waiting."

"You have to stop being so excited about everything," I told her.

"Are you kidding? If this was LAX, we wouldn't even be off the plane yet."

There was an older couple in the front seats of the shuttle bus. They smiled and nodded to us as we passed, heading three rows back.

"We weren't even the first ones on," Katie said, sliding her pack under the seat in front of her.

"Small means fast," I said. "Well, sometimes. Other times, remote means slow. And lots of times, *we don't have any reason to rush* means things take forever."

Katie laughed. "I like it so far."

"You've been here five minutes."

The driver entered and shut his door.

"And I'm already on my way to the hotel. Is that service or what?" She looked out the window. "I love the mountains. Look at all those trees."

"Coastal rain forest." I was feeling like a tour guide, but I didn't mind.

"There's snow up on top!"

I saw the woman in front of us turn her head to look. She was probably amused by Katie's southerner reaction.

"That's a glacier," I said. "The mountains go up over three thousand feet."

"So, it never melts."

"It never melts."

Katie sat back in her seat as the bus made its way along the coastline on Evergreen Drive. "I feel like I'm on an adventure."

"I feel like a time traveler." I thought about the photo of Joe Breckenridge back at the airport.

I couldn't help remembering the last time I'd seen him with my family in Anchorage. His brown eyes had been warm on mine, quizzical and searching, like he was trying to read me without scaring me off. Well, I had news for him. He couldn't read my mind, and I wasn't the least bit interested. Wary, sure, but only because I knew what was up.

He wasn't looking to find out if I was intelligent or funny or if we shared the same ethical and moral leanings. He'd wondered if I was like my dad and my uncle, if I could be co-opted for a common cause—the common cause of my family's business, Kodiak Communications, and Joe's political career.

Longtime friends of Joe's rancher father, my father, Xavier, and his brother, Braxton, had supported Joe's political candidacy from the start. They'd praised him to their business and social contacts, securing endorsements and propelling him to a win. After the election, he'd joined their effort to find federal money for a northern undersea cable to open the company infrastructure to European data traffic.

Afterward, they'd set their sights on me—deciding Joe needed an Alaskan bride from a notable family, and the Cambridges needed a connection to an up-and-coming politician. It was a mutually beneficial arrangement. Too bad the bride was unwilling.

"Your family's all the way across the Gulf of Alaska," Katie told me reassuringly.

"Kodiak Communications has an installation in Windward."

"Do your brothers ever work here?"

"Rarely. And the Kodiak offices are outside town."

"There you go," she said, as if it was settled.

I believed I had a decent chance of keeping my presence a secret. If I didn't think I could pull it off, I wouldn't have considered the job. I was meeting in person with William O'Donnell, who was the director of the Arts and Culture Collective of the Chamber of Commerce, and Nigel Long, from the governor's office, first thing in the morning to finalize the details.

The shuttle bus pulled under the front awning at the Redrock Hotel, and we walked out, tipping the driver as the porter took over with our bags and led us to the front desk.

"Checking in?" the woman behind the counter asked us. Her name tag said Shannon.

"Yes," I answered. "I'm Adeline—" My gaze caught on the television screen in the lobby, showing Joe in blue jeans, a plaid flannel shirt, Western boots and a Stetson. My brain cried out, *not again*. I felt like his image was stalking me.

"Ma'am?" Shannon asked.

"Cambridge," Katie finished for me.

"I have you with us for three nights." Shannon's voice seemed a long way off as I stared at Joe Breckenridge on the flat-screen television.

It was archival footage of Joe walking through a field with Governor Harland. The yellow-lettered chyron beneath the footage read, Meet and Greet Tonight. Congressman Breckenridge to attend a meeting at the Windward town hall.

"Are you *kidding* me?" I mustered.

"It's not three nights?"

Katie nudged me with her elbow.

I quickly shook myself back to the present.

"Leaving on the twenty-third?" Shannon asked.

"Yes. That's right." I pulled out my wallet to hand her my credit card.

"What's up?" Katie asked me in an undertone.

"Is there a hair salon in the hotel?" I asked Shannon.

"Yes, there is." She pushed a business card my way. "Through the lobby and past the elevators. It's next to the spa."

"Spa?" Katie asked with immediate interest.

Shannon smiled as she ran my credit card through the reader. "The spa hours are 7:00 a.m. to 10:00 p.m. They'll take walk-ins, but I'd advise a reservation. The hair salon hours are nine to six."

"Are you going to spruce up for the interview?" Katie asked.

"I'm thinking about it," I said.

"Is it a job interview?" Shannon asked pleasantly.

"Yes," Katie answered. Then she pointed my way. "For her."

"Well, good luck with it." Shannon handed me back my card. "I hope you'll end up staying in Windward for a good long time."

I wasn't all in on the idea yet. I was excited about the project, but the risks were starting to make themselves known. The last thing I needed was to run into Joe or have someone from Kodiak Communications recognize me.

"You look like a totally different person." Katie peered at me across the table at the upscale-rustic Steelhead Restaurant off the lobby of the Redrock Hotel. Cushioned in comfortable chairs, we were surrounded by wood accents with a beautiful light-laden mosaic of tree branches in a canopy above us. All the lighting was muted, and the windows were sparse and narrow to filter the long Alaskan daylight.

We'd ordered wild salmon citrus salads and a California chardonnay.

I wasn't convinced I loved my new hair. But I didn't hate it, either. I'd never been a blonde before, never been anything other than auburn haired.

"Bold," Katie said, leaning to one side.

I turned my head so she could have a better look and felt

the short wisps at the back that no longer covered my neck. The style was parted at the side, swooped across my forehead and just a little bit spiky.

"It'll grow back if I change my mind," I reassured myself.

"Might take a while. What's with the glasses? Are you going for an intellectual flair to balance off the blond?"

Taking out my contacts was simply another way of changing up my looks. "You're blonde," I pointed out.

"I sometimes think I should go brunette, have people take me more seriously."

"People take you plenty seriously." Katie was a bona fide genius. Everyone at Cal State knew that. Hence the offer of a teaching position only minutes after she'd received her PhD.

"At Cal State, sure." She gave a dismissive laugh. "Your glasses look really cute, by the way."

They were mottled burgundy frames, slightly rounded with a tiny crystal beside the hinges.

I adjusted them on my nose, thinking it would take a while to get used to wearing them all the time. I'd used contacts consistently since I was a teenager.

"It's a decent disguise," Katie said as the waiter dropped off our wine.

"You think?" I struck a pose.

"I barely recognize you." She took a sip of her wine, and I did, too.

"Adeline?" a deep male voice intoned.

By the shiver up my spine, I knew exactly who it was.

"You're in Windward," Joe said unnecessarily, leaving his party of three other men in suits to come to our table.

I instantly regretting having cut off all that hair. "Hello, Joe."

He was dressed in a suit today, not like a cowboy. But he had the kind of frame that could pull off any style.

He looked to Katie before saying anything else, polite and friendly as always, since there was a chance she could be a voter.

"Dr. Katie Tambour, this is Congressman Joe Breckenridge."

Katie smirked at my use of her title. She nodded to him. "Congressman."

"Very nice to meet you, Katie. Do you live here in Alaska?"

And there it was.

"California," Katie answered. "Adeline and I went to school together."

Joe turned back my way. "Are you here on vacation?"

I kept my answer vague but truthful. "We're at the hotel for a couple more nights."

"Then off to Anchorage?" he guessed.

I could tell he was probing for information.

"It's not a family trip. Just me and my good friend Katie, this time."

He was clearly not satisfied, but I didn't offer anything more.

His glance back at his party, who were now seated, told me he couldn't hang around much longer.

"We won't keep you," I said.

His frown was all but imperceptible and immediately disappeared. "You're both more than welcome at the town hall tomorrow night," he said. He smoothly removed a business card from his breast pocket and set it on the table. "Or let me know if there's anything else I can do for you."

Katie lifted the card. "Thanks."

With a nod to both of us, he left for his table.

Katie leaned forward and read out loud, *"Congressman?"* as soon as Joe was out of earshot. "Look at you hobnobbing away in Alaska."

I let out a low exclamation of intense frustration.

She blinked. "What?"

"That's *him*."

"Who?"

"He's the guy."

"What guy?" Katie's brow went up, and she looked over to their table.

"Don't," I barked out.

"What?" She quickly looked back.

"I told you my dad wanted to match me up with an Alaskan."

"You did?"

"You remember—that day in the park. The café by the river. After you broke up with Andrew."

"Yeah, well, Andrew was a dud."

"I *know*. And we were talking about hometown men."

"But you said…" She paused to think about it. "Your dad picked a *specific* Alaska guy?"

I nodded.

Her gaze slid to Joe's table again.

"Don't—"

"He's not even facing this way. Your dad picked a congressman?"

I grimaced, annoyed that fate had brought Joe to town and into this restaurant tonight.

"Wow," Katie said. "Your dad aims high."

"Depends on how you look at it."

"How should I look at it?"

"He's a *politician*." I had opinions on the morals and motivations of some politicians, and Joe had never once done anything to make me believe he was any different.

"He's a tall, good-looking, successful guy," Katie countered. "And he seemed nice."

"Whose side are you on?"

"Yours. Always yours. I'm just wondering what it is you don't like about the guy."

"How about that he's open to making a deal to marry Xavier Cambridge's daughter?"

"You're exaggerating."

"I'm not."

"This isn't the 1700s."

"They're not even hiding it."

"What does he do to make you think this?"

"Okay, Joe's a little more subtle. But he's always smiling at me, friendly, trying to draw me into corners, engage in intimate little one-on-one conversations, make me laugh. And he's got these eyes, dark, espresso dark, and you can just tell he's trying to read me. He wants to know what I'm thinking, figure out how to get past my defenses and sucker me into something. Like going out on a date."

"Maybe he just likes you."

"Ha! He barely knows me."

"Okay." The skepticism was clear as day in her tone.

"I'm not imagining things. Joe Breckenridge is at the beginning of a political career. He stands a better chance of success with an Alaskan wife with deep family roots. The Cambridges want an influential politician in the family, both for soft power and to ensure a smooth regulatory framework for the expansion of the technology and telecommunications industry."

"You have it all figured out." Katie looked slightly amused.

"*They* have it all figured out. I've been hiding in California."

The waiter arrived then with our salads and sprinkled them with fresh-ground pepper.

After he left the table, Katie looked dejected.

I checked out her salad. "Your salad doesn't look good?" Mine did.

She picked up her fork. "I'm bummed you're not taking the job."

Now that the idea had sat with me for a few days, I really wanted the Alaska job. In fact, I wanted it badly enough to rationalize a reason for staying. "Joe will only be here for a couple of days."

She brightened. "And then you're in the clear."

"He does think I'm only here on vacation."

She waggled the fork. "I saw what you did with that question. Brilliantly executed."

"I didn't lie," I pointed out.

"You gently misled him."

"Yes." I gave a sharp nod, spreading my napkin in my lap

and preparing to dig into the delicious-looking salad. "No law against gently misleading."

She grinned. "He's looking at us."

I speared a slice of avocado. "Well, we're not looking at him."

Two

I met with Nigel Long and William O'Donnell at the Windward Chamber of Commerce. William's office was a former second-floor bedroom in a historical house downtown. The more I listened to William, the more excited I grew about the project.

He explained they needed someone who understood Alaskan culture. Their last urban planner was from Chicago and had been a disaster. Now they had to simultaneously secure funding, draft the plans and also engage the community to garner public support.

I was absolutely up for multitasking.

Where William was all business, Nigel from the governor's office seemed more interested in me personally—particularly my years in California and, oddly, my future plans. It was hard to get a read on him. He acted laid-back Alaskan, but his words seemed very carefully chosen.

After the meeting, we drove out to the construction site, and I grew even more excited seeing the mountain views and the ocean so close by. I kept my enthusiasm under wraps. We hadn't finalized the details of my contract, and I didn't want to impact my negotiating position by letting them know I was dying to take this on.

The building site was far from flat. It was on a steep slope at the base of a mountain rising just north of the downtown core. I was fine with the topography. It was more interesting to design for multilevels, especially with the opportunities for ocean views.

A theater was sure to be part of the plan, and a theater didn't need any windows, so, right up front, there was a potential use for the mountain side of the site.

I craned my neck, thinking that if we went straight up a few floors, the views out front would be beyond spectacular.

"You'll be at the town hall meeting tonight?" William asked me.

I must have looked surprised by the suggestion, because he frowned then.

"Sure, of course," I quickly said. "I saw the ads after we landed."

"I'm on the panel. I probably won't say too much since the congressman's in town."

I tried not to smirk at William's acknowledgment that a congressman was sure to take up all the airtime. Politics were politics—always.

"The governor is occupied in Juneau," Nigel said. "But I'll be there to monitor and report back."

"I can formally introduce you to Joe Breckenridge," William offered.

"No," I said quickly—too quickly. The last thing I wanted was for Joe to hear that I might be staying in Windward.

"Premature?" William asked with a lift of his eyebrow.

"Yes." Agreeing with his assumption was the easiest way out.

He squared his shoulders and widened his stance. "Then let's get down to it, shall we?"

I didn't see a way or any point, really, in putting it off. "Sure."

"Does the project meet your expectations?"

It did. "Exactly as advertised," I said.

"And the site?" He looked around us. "You can see the potential."

I scanned it again myself. "I can."

"And you know what it takes to live in Alaska. I don't have to give you that spiel."

"You don't have to give me the far-north spiel." If anyone understood the challenges and advantages of living in remote Alaska, it was me.

"Any questions on your side?"

As far as I was concerned, it was down to the fine details. "Can I assume the salary will be commensurate with my education?"

He smiled at that and tossed out a very attractive number. "Plus benefits, of course, a northern living stipend and housing."

"Housing?" I was surprised by that but tried not to look it.

"The chamber owns a furnished heritage house over on Rampart Street, and we've freed it up for you. It was built in the '20s but has been updated several times since. It's the former residence of Paul Pettigrew, a fishing boat captain and one of the founders of Windward."

"He was also a bootlegger," Nigel added. "He and his bride, Rosie Jane, came from Seattle. Not that anybody believed that was her real name."

The story had me intrigued. "Why not?"

"It was rumored that she had quite a wild past before they met and married." There was a thread of judgment in Nigel's tone. "The ladies of Windward had their standards."

I found myself coming down on Rosie's side. "Sounds like she was probably just independent, given the times. I'm assuming you didn't intend to seem uptight and judgmental, right?" Actually, I wasn't too sure about that.

Nigel's pinched expression all but confirmed my thoughts.

"It was difficult on the children," William said.

That prompted another question in my mind. "Does she have descendants in town?" I wondered why the Chamber of Commerce would own the house instead of the family.

"They moved south years and years ago."

I could understand that. Who wanted to hang around a small town that had treated your mother badly?

"Back to the core question," William said. "Are you accepting the position?"

I couldn't help one more glance around the building site, thinking of a hundred ways to utilize its topography. A storied heritage house to live in for free was the icing on the cake.

I smiled and offered him my hand. "Yes. I'll take the job."

He grinned widely as we shook. "That's terrific news. Just terrific."

Nigel was a little slower on the uptake. He smiled, too, but there was something off about it. Again, I couldn't quite put my finger on his attitude.

When he spoke, there was a touch of irony in his tone. "Welcome aboard, Adeline. The governor's office looks forward to working with you."

"Thanks." I searched his expression as I shook his hand, but I didn't find any more clues.

"So, an announcement tonight?" William said.

I faltered. "Can we hold off?" I struggled to come up with a reason. "I need to talk to a few friends, family members first."

"I understand," he said. "No problem."

"I'll let you know as soon as I've settled everything on the personal side." It would be approximately the same minute Joe Breckenridge stepped on a plane out of town.

Joe was seated in the center of the panelist table on a low stage at the front of the town hall's main meeting room. The three panelists had microphones, notes and glasses of water in front of them, while an MC stood behind a podium to the right. Joe was flanked by William on his left and a fortysomething woman on his right.

Katie and I slipped in the main doors, taking chairs near the back on the left-hand end. The room was about half-full, with citizens continuing to stream inside as the clock ticked down to the start time. I had no intention of asking any questions, only gauging the perspective of the crowd about the arts and culture complex plans.

The meeting was to cover three topics—the arts and culture complex, improvements to a nearby national park, and the potential for a road linking Windward to Skagway to provide access for the panhandle city to mainland Alaska.

Katie leaned over to whisper in my ear. "He spotted you."

My gaze immediately went to Joe and, sure enough, he was looking my way.

He smiled, and I curved my lips up in return. I guessed it was too much to expect to merely blend in with the crowd.

"He's looking at you like you're made of ice cream," she said.

"Ick," I said, getting a sticky feeling.

"You're fussy for someone who hasn't had a date in six months."

"It hasn't been—" I did the math inside my head. "It's five... okay, five and a half."

"He's a really good-looking guy."

"I didn't mean ick about Joe. I mean ick about being ice cream."

Joe *was* a good-looking guy—there was no disputing that. Most women would say he was great-looking. He was tall, fit and just cowboy enough to avoid being classically handsome. He was obviously intelligent—too intelligent for his own good, I often thought. I'd sat through conversations with him and my family members—seen his eyes light up and his lips twitch with dark or irreverent humor that others didn't seem to catch.

I considered that smart, but it might have been a personal bias, since I'd caught the humor, too.

"I'd probably let him lick me," Katie said.

"Double ick!"

She laughed. "Wait, he's coming over."

"No, he wouldn't—" But I saw it was true.

He was up from his seat, had stepped off the stage and was headed our way.

"Maybe he sees someone else—" I looked behind us, hoping...

But he stopped at our row. Katie was in the end seat and he looked over her. "Curious," he said to me.

"About?" I held my breath and waited for him to elaborate, wondering what he meant and how much he knew.

He nodded to the front of the room. "Are you curious about the meeting?"

"Oh. That was a question?"

He tilted his head, looking once again like he was trying to read my mind.

"The road," I answered to throw him off. "I'm interested in the road extension."

"For Kodiak." He gave a nod of understanding.

I didn't much care if Kodiak Communications had road access to Windward or not. They'd done perfectly fine with plane and boat access up to now. But I played along.

"Will they build the road?" I asked.

"Possible. There's still the problem with the steep terrain on some sections of the coast."

I nodded to that. I did know it had been a barrier for years now. But people kept hoping the federal government would step up with enough money to shore up the hillsides and provide them with a land link out of the city.

I caught the MC's concerned look directed Joe's way, and I gestured to the stage. "I think they might be waiting for you."

Joe turned to see. "What are you doing after the meeting?"

"I'm…" A lie didn't immediately appear in my mind.

"Taking me sightseeing," Katie chimed in—great wing-person that she was.

Joe glanced at her serene expression, his jaw tightening just a little bit. "We should talk, Adeline."

"About?"

"You know what about."

"Joe—"

"Good evening, ladies and gentlemen," the MC said.

"They definitely need you up front," Katie said.

Joe gave me a look that said we weren't done talking, but then he left, striding swiftly to the stage.

"Wow." Katie blew out a breath and sat back in her chair. "That is one intense man. What do you think he wants to talk about?"

"Probably picking out names for our grandchildren."

Katie laughed.

The MC introduced the panelists.

"Have you guys ever talked about it?" Katie asked as the crowd applauded.

I joined in. "You mean sat down and said, *hey, you know how my dad wants me to marry you—what do you think of that?*"

"Yeah. Just throw it on out there."

"No." I couldn't imagine such a cringeworthy discussion.

The MC opened with a question about the national park.

"You should tell him you're not interested," Katie said.

"He knows I'm not interested. Good grief, how many broad hints does a woman have to drop?"

"Seriously? He's a guy. Some of them aren't too bright when it comes to hints."

"Joe's bright."

"You know this because?"

"I've watched him in conversations, debates, jokes."

"Jokes?"

"He gets humor." I thought back to a few specific instances with my uncle Braxton. "He's got a very dry sense of humor."

The woman sitting on stage next to Joe was talking about an interpretive center in the national park. I caught Joe's gaze on me again. It was intense, heated and almost sexy.

I silently groaned. The very last thing I needed was to start thinking Joe was sexy. I had enough on my mind at the moment.

"You should get it over with," Katie said.

"Get what over with?" I was afraid she'd guessed my sudden wayward attraction.

"Tell it to him straight. Tell him you and he are never going to happen. Tell him to find some other perfect Alaskan bride to marry."

I grinned. I couldn't help it. Joe would be stunned to silence if I was ever that direct.

"You're smiling," she said.

"It's an entertaining image."

"He's smiling back."

I focused and saw that he was. I was instantly sucked into the invitation of his open expression. I shouldn't react this way. He might be sexy, but I wasn't going to be swayed.

I quickly sobered, and his expression turned cajoling.

I realized we were having a conversation across the crowded room.

"It might work," Katie said.

"He'd only take it as a challenge." That was my fear.

Joe could tell I didn't want to pursue a relationship, but it hadn't deterred him for one moment.

"Do you have a better idea?" she asked.

"Stay out of Alaska." I knew I hadn't taken my own advice.

The MC invited Joe to speak, and he leaned slightly toward the microphone, his deep voice resonating through the hall, stilling the crowd. It was easy to see how he got people to listen to him. People should listen to him—about his ideas, at least. But not me. And not about whether or not to date him.

"Adeline?" Kate asked.

"Hmm?"

"You sure it's not something else?"

I turned to her. "What else?"

"Are you afraid you might be attracted to him?"

"No." My answer was instantaneous even as I felt a hot little rush go through me.

"Uh-oh," Katie said.

"There's no uh-oh."

"Oh, *you're* not attracted to him, not one tiny little bit."

I wanted to flat-out lie again, but I didn't lie to Katie. "He's physically attractive. You said it yourself. He's physically attractive, but that's all. That's it. Most of the time he annoys me."

She considered me for a moment but seemed to accept my answer. "Okay."

"Good." I felt like it was settled.

"You should tell him, though."

"He'll be gone by tomorrow." And my troubles would be over—at least temporarily.

Katie seemed to consider. "I suppose avoidance is another approach."

"It's worked for me so far." I tuned into Joe speaking about the potential road access. He was eloquent, empathetic and enthusiastic.

"He's got a nice voice," Katie noted in an undertone.

It was true. The audience was riveted to his words, nodding and smiling, bursting into applause after he finished speaking even though he hadn't promised any action.

The MC then asked him about the arts and culture complex.

He gave almost the same answer, and, again, no one seemed much bothered by its vagueness. They listened carefully, nodded to each other, laughed when he made little jokes and applauded at the end as if he'd said something astounding.

"How does he do that?" I asked Katie beneath the cover of the applause. "I mean, okay, he's got the gift of gab, but they're eating right out of his hand. He could recite a plumbing manual and they'd clap."

Katie chuckled at my joke. "That's obviously how he got himself elected. He's giving them what they want."

"But what does he stand for?"

"Happy voters."

"That's what's so frustrating."

"About Joe Breckenridge?"

"About politics. I hate all the wishy-washy. Take a stand already."

Joe was now listening politely to William's outline of the arts complex project status. He nodded in spots then led the applause at the end, saying what looked like congratulatory words to William.

If I had to guess, I'd say the crowd was equally split between those excited about the arts and culture complex and those excited about the road extension. The national park improvements were a smaller project, the next phase of ongoing longer-term upgrading, so it didn't garner the same level of interest.

For me, it was satisfying to see so many in the community were supportive of the arts and culture project. I couldn't wait to get started on the community engagement.

Katie and I made a clean getaway from the town hall meeting, and Joe left Windward the next morning. I knew that because they covered his departure on the local news. Katie then offered to fly back to Sacramento and orchestrate my apartment move so I could start the job right away.

She was still determined to live with me in Alaska for a couple of months until her teaching job started, seeing it as an adventure vacation for herself. I was more than happy to have her company. The Captain Pettigrew house was plenty big enough for both of us.

A rabbit warren of small rooms and twisting corridors, the

old house featured gleaming hardwood floors and walls, ornate period furniture, a massive dining table, and a china hutch full of wonderful pieces of Wedgwood in a turquoise-and-russet pattern. The living room held a pair of massive French Provincial armchairs, taupe with a golden luster on the wood accents. They had cloud-soft cushions and deeply tufted backs. They sat across from a satin burgundy sofa accented with gold stitching and tiny fleurs-de-lis.

The side tables, the stained glass lamps and a grandfather clock were meticulously reproduced and restored. Luxurious emerald drapes framed the paned windows, held back by thick ropes that added to the opulence.

The house had four bedrooms in all, one on the main floor set up as an office. I took the master that was also on the main floor, thinking it would be most convenient for the long term. Katie picked one of the sloped-ceiling second-floor bedrooms with a queen-size bed, a little reading nook and three dormer windows. Thankfully, the bathrooms had been remodeled recently. And the kitchen was a perfect combination of period look and modern convenience, with white-painted cabinets, long butcher-block countertops and a faux woodstove that ran on propane gas.

Four days in, with a hundred nooks and crannies left to explore, I still couldn't believe I had the chance to live here.

I didn't have a car yet. I'd decided against moving my five-year-old compact from California. It would be easier to buy something here in town. Plus, I'd need four-wheel drive once winter arrived and the roads turned snowy and slippery. While maneuverability was important in Sacramento, with crowded traffic and tight parking stalls, stability counted around here. In Alaska, roads were wide, parking was generous and pickup trucks were the most popular mode of transportation.

My house was less than a mile from the Chamber of Commerce offices, so I'd taken to walking to and from work. My temporary office cubicle was a hived-off space at the top of the staircase beside the Chamber of Commerce. William told me I was also welcome to work from home until the temporary field office was set up with construction trailers out on the building site. But that would be several weeks down the road.

For now, although I loved the little office in Pettigrew House, I also liked working around the people in the Chamber of Commerce building.

"Morning, Adeline," receptionist Stella Atwater called out as I entered the main floor. Thirty-three, dark haired, dark eyed, stout and very fit, she was the backbone of the Chamber, knowing everyone and everything that happened around Windward.

"Morning," I replied as her little beagle, Snuffy, peeked out from under her desk then trotted over to meet me, tail wagging. "And good morning to you, Snuffy." I bent to give him a scratch on the head.

"William is looking for you," Stella said.

"Did he try to call?" I reached into my bag for my phone, thinking I must have missed the ring, maybe while I was passing the Starfish Restaurant renovation site a few blocks back. They'd been jackhammering the patio concrete.

Stella shrugged. "He just asked me to send you up to his office. It didn't sound urgent or anything. He's not upset."

I'd have been surprised if he was upset. William was easy to get along with, focused on his work but incredibly even-keeled. I was guessing it would take a lot to upset him.

I headed straight up the stairs, dropping my bag in my cubicle and tucking my phone into the back pocket of my gray slacks, then pushing up the sleeves of my speckled gray-and-white pullover.

William's office was down a short hallway, past the little unisex bathroom and around a corner to the back of the building.

I knocked on his partly open door.

"Yes?" came the reply.

I opened the door.

He waved me in with a smile, his phone at his ear. "Certainly. She's here right now."

I slipped into the guest chair across his desk to wait.

"And we appreciate the opportunity," he said. "The Forberg." He made a note on a scratch pad, hung up the phone and gazed at me for a moment.

"Morning," I said into the silence, attempting to gauge his expression.

Stella was right. He didn't seem upset. He seemed…curious.

"Good morning," he said back.

I didn't want to be nosy, so I didn't ask about the call, waiting to see if he'd share.

Instead, he stood up and rounded to the back of his chair, leaning the heels of his palms against it. "That was Congressman Breckenridge's office."

I stilled, going on alert.

"The congressman wants to discuss additional funding options for the project."

"That's a good thing," I ventured, thinking funding was always a good thing.

"With you."

Well, that part wasn't good. "Why me? Wait, how does he know I'm on the project?"

William drew back. "I don't know. Why wouldn't he know you were on the project?"

"We didn't announce it. And then he left town."

"I don't think he left the planet. It's been mentioned on a few news websites now, and it's been in the paper, of course."

I realized my reaction had sounded inane. "Sure. No problem. Just the three of us?" I assumed William would be on the call.

"Just the two of you."

It took a second for William's words to sink in. "You know more about the project than I do. He's interested in getting to know our team."

"You're the head of the team."

"He already knows me," William said.

I almost spoke up to say the Congressman knew me too… almost.

"Before he goes to bat for us, he wants to assure himself we can execute the project."

"We can," I said, annoyed with Joe for inferring that I

couldn't manage a commercial construction project. What did he think I'd been learning all these years? Both my master's and my PhD studies had included practicums and internships. I knew what I was doing.

"This is an opportunity, Adeline. We're not fully funded yet, and we need a significant federal commitment before we break ground."

I steadied my emotions. I was a professional, and this was part of the job. "Of course. I understand completely. Did his office set a time for the call?"

"No need."

I blew out a breath of relief. If they hadn't set up the call yet, other priorities might come up, and there was a chance it wouldn't happen.

"He's on his way back to Alaska."

"No."

William looked baffled by my reaction. "What do you mean, no?"

"I mean… I'm surprised. He just left. I thought he went back to DC." I hesitated. "That's what was reported."

"Well, I suppose his schedule changed." William peeled off a yellow note from on top of his desk and held it out to me. "The Forberg Club, five thirty."

"Tonight?" I didn't even get a day or two to get used to the idea?

"Tonight. He'll have booked a meeting room. So just check with the front desk. Have you been there before?"

"No."

"Really? Kodiak Communications has a membership."

"I don't work for Kodiak."

"Right. It's on Peel Road, just off Evergreen toward the water. There's a private elevator from the lobby to the third floor."

I came to my feet and took the little slip of paper. "I'll find it."

A few choice words echoed through my brain as I walked back to my desk.

"Game," I said out loud as I put my phone down on the

desk and plunked into my chair. "Set and match. Well played, Congressman." I closed my eyes for a brief second and gave my head a shake.

Then I squared my shoulders and powered up my workstation. This was a professional meeting, not a personal one. I would have every available fact, figure and talking point committed to memory before I got anywhere near the Forberg Club.

Joe wanted to talk arts and culture complex? Fine. We'd talk arts and culture center and absolutely nothing else.

The Forberg Club was the closest Windward came to a five-star establishment. Since I'd packed mostly Alaska casual, I dressed up the single dress I'd brought as much as I could. It was basic black, with a snug, sleeveless bodice and a lightweight A-line skirt that fell to midthigh. I topped it with a cropped, lightweight burgundy sweater for color. I'd brought a pair of heeled black ankle boots that were workable. Then I added a platinum starfish necklace that twinkled with little diamond chips along with my favorite diamond stud earrings my brother Mason had given me for my twenty-first birthday.

Since the jig was up anyway, I wore my contacts and moussed the waves out of my newly blond hair so it flowed smoothly across my forehead, hanging partway down my cheek on the right side. The style and color took a bit of getting used to, but I'd decided it was at least fresh and fun.

I'd expected to be shown to a meeting room at the Forberg, but the hostess took me on a circuitous route through the well-spaced, polished wood tables and round-back leather chairs of the dining room.

Joe rose from a corner table in a crisp white shirt, a silver tie and a perfectly cut suit.

"Adeline." He smiled, coming around to pull out my chair as the hostess took her cue and left us alone.

I gave him a disapproving look. "This isn't a date."

"I know. It's a meeting." He gestured to my chair.

"We're in a restaurant."

"We're in a business club."

I deepened my frown.

"I'm starving," he said. "I had a tight connection in Anchorage."

"They didn't serve a meal in first class?"

"Somewhere over Montana, but that was hours ago. Sit down."

I hesitated a second longer, though I wondered why I was being so obstinate. It was probably better that we were meeting in public anyway. "You know I'm expected to ask you for money."

"We don't have to talk about that right now. Sit down, relax." His low tone was right in my ear.

"That's asking a lot." But I sat down.

"You won't be sorry," he said as he returned to his own seat. "They serve great steaks, seafood—whatever you're in the mood for."

"Our first community engagement event will be next week." I started right in on my rehearsed spiel. "And we're framing up other engagement tools such as a feedback form and a survey for the website. The website launch will coincide with—"

"Would you care for a drink?" he asked.

Out of the corner of my eye, I saw the waiter coming up on our table. I stopped talking.

"A glass of wine?" Joe asked me. "A martini? Old Fashioned?"

"Wine is fine," I said. The last thing I cared about was what I had to drink. "Whatever you're having."

My answer seemed to surprise him. But he quickly rolled with it. "Do you have a bottle of Château Cinq Rivières 2003?"

"I expect we do," the waiter answered. "If not, is the 2005 acceptable?"

"Yes. That would be fine."

"I'll be right back." The waiter left the table.

"As I was saying, the website launch will coincide—"

"Adeline."

"—with the first public meeting, so that the marketing efforts for—"

"Are you going to do this all night?"

"Talk about the arts and culture complex? Yes, I am."

He fought a grin.

"Don't you dare act like I'm delightful. I'm not being delightful."

"You are delightful."

I stifled an exclamation. "You *see* why you make me so frazzled?"

"No, I don't. I don't see how I can possibly make you frazzled. You barely even know me."

"I know enough."

The waiter came back with a bottle of red wine, cradled in a white linen napkin so Joe could read the label. "Cabernet sauvignon Château Cinq Rivières 2003."

"Perfect," Joe said.

The waiter produced a corkscrew and extracted the cork, carefully pouring a measure into Joe's glass.

Joe swirled it around for a minute to aerate it before taking a sip.

"That's fine," he said to the waiter, who then poured my glass before topping up Joe's.

"As I was saying," Joe continued as the waiter walked away. "You don't know me at all."

"I've known you for years."

"You practically run out of the room every time I show my face."

"I sat next to you at dinner last August."

I escaped his wry smile by taking a sip of the wine. The wine was fantastic—off-the-charts fantastic. Okay, so maybe there was an upside to this meeting, after all.

"One hundred points?" I asked, setting down my glass.

"Don't change the subject."

"This is a fantastic wine."

"That's why I ordered it. You barely spoke to me last August."

"There were eight of us at the table."

"And you talked to the other six."

"Mostly to Sophie. She was new to the family then." My long-lost cousin, Sophie, had met us for the first time only weeks before that dinner. I'd felt obligated to ensure she felt welcomed into the family.

"Why are you deflecting?" His blunt question gave me pause.

I looked straight into his eyes for the first time since I'd arrived. I was thinking maybe Katie was right and it was time to be honest. "Reflex, I think."

"Now, *that* was honest." He lifted his glass.

I followed suit and took another sip. "Do you blame me for rebelling?"

"Against your father and Braxton? No. Against me? Yes."

"I don't see how I do one without the other. I feel like a bride from some noble family in the Middle Ages, bartered for a suitable match, an advantageous alliance, a dowry, the whole bit."

"Have I ever once proposed?" His question was delivered so seriously but was so ludicrous that I had to stifle a laugh.

"And for the record," he continued in the same vein, "nobody ever offered me a dowry."

I shook my head, fighting off the grin.

He smiled serenely. "But you are a valuable little treasure. A few hundred years ago, your family could have done well," he teased.

I all but growled at that.

He ignored me. "Spirited. Beautiful. At least you were before you cut off all your hair."

I self-consciously touched the short wisps of hair beside my ear.

"I'm joking," he said. Then he lowered his voice and leaned slightly forward. "I'm sorry. That was rude. You're still beautiful, though I did love the color it was before. Why did you change it?"

I had no intention of telling him the truth on that count. I adopted a breezy tone, lifting my wineglass as I spoke. "Something fresh for the summer. A celebration of graduation."

"Congratulations on that, by the way… Dr. Cambridge."

"I don't plan on using the title." I took another sip.

"Up to you, of course. Although I'd enjoy seeing you make your brothers use it when they address you."

I couldn't stop a smile at the thought of my brothers' reaction to that.

I quickly smoothed out my expression. I didn't want to have fun tonight. "Say, did you ever meet the Chicago guy?" I jumped on my first idea to change the subject.

"What Chicago guy?"

"My predecessor on this project."

A blank look on his face, Joe shook his head.

The answer confirmed my suspicions about the purpose of this dinner. "We're not here to talk about arts center funding."

"We can talk about arts center funding."

My expression called him out for lying. "But that's not why we're here."

He swirled the wine in his glass again and took another drink. "Let's get that out of the way. What do you need?"

William had given me very specific instructions for a deliverable. The federal government had announced the Rural Expansion Fund, a special pot of money for lower-population states to improve their infrastructure. Competition was going to be tough, but Windward had a good chance of getting approval for one project—either the arts and culture complex or the road expansion.

"We need your pledge to support the arts and culture complex on the official state application to the federal Rural Expansion Fund."

"Done. It's a worthwhile project that the whole community can benefit from, and I'm sure you'll do a powerhouse job executing the build. Tell William you had to work really hard to talk me into it." He lifted the bottle and topped up each of our glasses. "Now can we relax and enjoy dinner?"

I decided to take yes for an answer, and we settled into king crab salads and fresh halibut with wild mushroom risotto.

Joe dropped the subject of my family and the two of us while I let the funding and project discussion end. Instead, we compared thoughts on a just-released feature film that had been set in Juneau, moving on to other movies, then books, disagreeing on some but finding common ground on others.

We both liked biographies and classic spy thrillers, especially Hitchcock and Orson Welles.

Near the end of the meal, I caught sight of Nigel Long two tables over. I might not have noticed him except that he was looking quite intently our way.

I smiled to be polite, and he smiled back, but his features didn't line up. His lips curved, but his eyes stayed sober, leaving me with the now-familiar unsettled feeling.

"What is it?" Joe asked as I turned my attention to the dessert menu in the middle of our table.

"Nigel Long," I said.

"I saw him come in."

"I get the feeling he doesn't like me."

Joe glanced over. "It's me he doesn't like."

"Why not?"

"Governor Harland is not my biggest fan."

"Why?" I opened the slim dessert menu, more as a distraction from Nigel's gaze than because I was still hungry.

"The governor wants the access road, not the arts and culture center. I wouldn't commit to backing him."

"Nigel told me the governor was supportive of the arts complex."

Joe gave a grim smile. "He would."

"Sneaky. I haven't really warmed up to the guy."

"He's always polite to me. But he's the kind of guy who interacts solely with power, money and titles."

Coming from a family with means, I understood what Joe meant. "You must get that all the time."

Joe nodded. "It's frustrating, never knowing if people actually like you or think you're smart or funny."

"You're smart and funny." I was honest before I thought to censor myself. I decided it must be the wine.

"People nod at my wisdom and laugh at my jokes even when they're secretly thinking I'm wrongheaded and boring."

"Because you control the purse strings."

"I influence them."

I felt a little guilty then. "You do know that's why I'm here."

"I know exactly why you're here, Adeline."

"Do you hate me for it?"

"I admire you for it."

I was confused by the answer, since I was one of the people using him for money. "Why?"

"Because you manned up, or womanned up, and put your responsibilities ahead of everything else and came on out here for the good of your project, even though it was the last thing you wanted to do. Let's treat ourselves to some dessert."

I expected him to open his menu, but he rose from the table instead and straightened his jacket.

"What are you doing?"

"No need to hang around the Nigel Longs of the world," Joe said with a sidelong glance at the man. "I know a better place."

Three

We made our way down the shore to a bustling restaurant called the Pirate Pies. It was a funky little open-air place over-looking a rocky beach with waves and salt spray billowing up nearby. The breeze was brisk, but high plastic barriers sheltered the diners. The Plexiglas was scuffed and scratched, slightly obscuring the view of the late-night setting sun.

Joe shucked his jacket, and we climbed onto side-by-side bar-height chairs at the end of a long, narrow table where three other parties were already seated spaced along its length.

"This doesn't seem like you," I said as I got settled on the worn paint of the wooden chair. Mine was blue, or used to be blue, where Joe's used to be yellow.

He glanced around. "In what way? The delicious pies or the fantastic view?"

"You know what I mean. It's not stuffy."

"Who says I'm stuffy?"

"You've always been stuffy around me."

"Not when I'm on the ranch."

"Been on the ranch much lately?" I asked with an arch of my brow.

"I rode at your dad's place in August."

It was true. Joe usually rode horses with one or both of my brothers when he visited our family. The Cambridge horse stable was a sideline left over from my great-grandfather. Our home was on rare Alaskan agricultural land, and we still ran horses on the lush grasses, leasing the horses out to an eco-tourism outfit in the summer season.

"Hey, Joe," a man called from down the table.

"Evening, Ben," Joe responded with a nod.

"Have you met my wife, Petra?" The man motioned to the woman at his side. "We liked what you had to say about the park at the town meeting."

"Glad to hear it," Joe answered. "Nice to see you, Petra."

I could see a few other people glancing Joe's way.

"Are the wheelchair-accessibility trail upgrades going through this year?" another woman asked.

"Definitely," Joe told her. "They'll be fully accessible all the way to hot springs."

"That's good." The woman nodded. "My mom hasn't been up there in years, and she'd love to go back."

"Is your mom Jane Mitchell?"

"That's her."

"Tell her I say hi, and I'll keep her posted on the progress."

"Thanks, Joe," the woman said, looking pleased.

"Joe this, Joe that?" I whispered to him, surprised by his laid-back manner. "Not Congressman Breckenridge?"

"They're good people," he said back in an undertone. "They've had my back, and now I've got theirs." Louder, he said to me, "I'd try the key lime if I was you."

Someone else chimed in, "The pecan's to die for."

"I'm having bumbleberry," a new voice added.

"If you get the apple, definitely go with *both* the cheese and the ice cream."

I gave appreciative smiles and nods to all of those making suggestions before turning to Joe. "And what are you having?"

"Key lime," he said, looking surprised by my question. "Would I steer you wrong?"

We both had key lime, and it was as to die for as any pie I'd ever tasted. Afterward, Joe walked me home, insisting on it even though it was only a few blocks more, and it was barely twilight. This close to the summer solstice, the sky stayed blue all night long.

"William must really want you to stay," Joe observed as we walked up the scuffed concrete sidewalk to the Pettigrew house porch.

"I'd have stayed without the house," I said as we passed through the row of white pillars on the porch.

I was feeling unusually relaxed around Joe—maybe it was his manner with the people at the Pirate Pies, or maybe it was the reminder of his ranching roots. But, in the moment, taking Katie's advice seemed like the most practical path forward.

I turned to face him at the door, deciding to be up front and honest about where I was going in life and his role in it. "This project is a fantastic opportunity for my career."

"I'm glad to hear that."

"I really want it to work out. I want it to go smoothly and simply."

"Seems like it probably will."

"I have plans for my future," I continued. "I hope you can understand that. I don't want pressure from my dad and Braxton to interfere."

"I understand," he said with a nod.

"That includes you." I wanted to be crystal clear.

He gave a ghost of a smile. "I know what you're saying."

I turned and inserted the key and turned the cut-glass doorknob. "Thank you."

"But I have a proposal."

I paused, looking back at him as the door swung partway open. My defenses came instantly up. "Please don't ruin the evening by asking me to marry you."

His grin was slow; clearly, I'd amused him. "It's not that kind of a proposal."

"That's a relief."

He eased in a little closer, planting his hand, straight-armed against the doorjamb, lowering his voice to a deeper timbre. "Let me kiss you good night."

The shake of my head was instantaneous.

"Hear me out," he said.

I squinted at his earnest expression, bracing myself.

"You insist there's nothing between us, no hope for a relationship."

"Because there's not."

"Then prove it. Let me kiss you good night and prove your point to both of us once and for all."

I wasn't buying it. It couldn't be that simple. "Are you promising to drop the idea?"

"I haven't exactly been promoting it up to now."

That was fair. He hadn't.

I admitted it. "You've been...persistent...patient."

"Patient is a bad thing?"

"You're always just—"

"Waiting." His voice was a rumble as he bent his elbow and eased closer still. "I'm waiting for you to give me a chance."

"There is no chance, Joe. My family can't simply *will* us into being a thing. Life doesn't work that way."

"Okay. But back to my proposal." He waited. His dark eyes once again seemed to be searching my soul.

"Okay. I'll do it. But only if you promise, if you *promise* to stop hovering on the periphery of my life."

"Yeah?" He looked happy.

"You heard the whole thing, right?"

"I heard."

"Well, then..." I took a bracing breath, tipped my chin and tilted my lips.

"Don't look like you're going to the gallows."

He almost made me smile with that. I did feel a little like a condemned woman. "At least you gave me a last meal."

His palm came up to frame my cheek. "Plus dessert." He bent his head, moving in closer. His breath puffed softly against my face.

I steeled myself.

"Adeline."

"What?"

It was a beat before he answered. "Never mind." His free arm gently circled my waist while his fingers sifted into my hair, cupping the base of my neck as his lips brushed mine.

The first touch was light but somehow electric. Little pulses of energy sent a warmth through my chest and left me shocked to stillness.

He kissed me again, more firmly this time, his lips engulfing mine with such surprising tenderness that I kissed him back. It caught me off-guard.

I felt like I couldn't trust myself. His forearm tightened across the base of my spine, and I molded against him, feeling his body heat teasing me from my shoulders to my knees.

He deepened the kiss, and I opened to him, feeling a surge of emotions propel me further. My arms wound around his neck, and I clung there, tipping my head back, accepting kiss after kiss.

I was vaguely aware of him pushing open the door and kicking it shut, then backing me into the front hall. I was more aware of his hands moving down my backside, along my thighs, coming to the hem of the little black dress.

I gasped for air, filling my lungs, giving myself more energy to kiss him harder, explore the contours of his shoulders, push the frustrating barrier of his suit jacket out of the way, not caring that it crumpled to the floor. His cotton shirt was thin, and I could feel the ripple of his taut muscles, their smooth roll to his biceps that felt strong and sexy. Powerful.

I leaned into his chest and kissed him through the white cotton, dampening the fabric.

He gave a low moan, and his hand swooped up the inside of my bare thigh, under the filmy skirt to the silky panties that were no barrier at all.

His lips were back on my mouth, his tongue tangling with mine. His hand cupped my breast, and my nipple tightened, sending shards of arousal to my very core.

It was my turn to moan.

His shirt was a barrier now, and I pulled the buttons free, running my hands over his smooth chest, kissing his skin, tasting the salt.

He shucked his shirt and then pushed down the strap of my dress, kissing my bare shoulder. He kissed his way across my chest, between my breasts, baring more cleavage as he went.

I tipped my head back, offering my neck, my lips and everything else.

He scooped me into his arms, kissing my mouth as he crossed the room.

In seconds we were in my bedroom.

He lowered me to the bed and stripped off my panties, tossing them away. It had only been seconds since his mouth had been on mine, but I missed his lips already.

Then he joined me there, kissing me over and over. I tugged

at my dress, and he pushed it out of the way before getting rid of his pants.

I wrapped my legs around his glorious nakedness. He tried to speak, but I was beyond listening. I kissed him hard and deep, arching against him, pulling him into me, telling him yes and whispering his name on harsh gulps of air.

He held me tight, increased his rhythm, kissed my lips, my face, my neck and my breasts. Desire spiraled in a hot, tight core, blocking out the room, the house, the world as pleasure pulsed faster and faster between us until it sang like a starburst, engulfing me in glorious relief.

The first thing that came back was Joe's breath in my ear, then his heartbeat against my chest, then his slick skin and his slightly trembling fingertips feathering along the curve of my hip.

I knew what I'd done. And I knew why I'd done it. I hoped he understood.

"I think *that* proves my point," I said in a choppy, breathless voice.

"Sure," he answered, his chest rising as he inhaled. "No attraction there, nothing to build on."

I was glad we were on the same page. "Exactly."

He eased his weight from me, moving to his side. "It's too bad, though."

"Why?" I didn't think it was too bad at all. Now we could both get on with our lives.

"Because that was some mind-blowing sex we just had."

"*Sex* being the operative word."

"Okay." He sounded half confused, half amused.

I turned my head his way, pulling back just enough to focus and reinforce my point. "If this was romantic, you'd have bought me flowers, read me poetry—"

"Poetry?"

"—discovered my likes and dislikes and eased your way into gentle, respectful lovemaking."

"Poetry?"

"This was a hormone-fueled, chemistry-laden, instinctive scratch-an-itch kind of thing. It had nothing to do with romance or genuine attraction." I paused for a breath, because I was still pretty winded. "I don't know about you, but it's been a while for me."

"You're saying this was nothing but pent-up sexual energy?"

I gave him a smile and an approving pat on the shoulder. Once I touched him, I wanted to keep my hand right there, but I forced myself to pull it away.

"That's one way to look at it." He turned so he was staring at the ceiling.

"So." I made my tone brisk and no-nonsense. "I assume you're heading back to DC now and I can carry on here?"

"That was my plan."

"Good. You'll still support our financial aspirations?" I wanted to be able to report back to William tomorrow that the meeting had been successful.

The back of Joe's hand still touched mine, and he lifted them together. "I'll support you, Adeline."

I gazed at our joined hands for a moment, marveling at the differences. His was large and rugged, the fingers long, his skin thicker and slightly callused.

"Can we keep this all quiet?" I asked. "I mean, my family—"

"I won't say anything to your family." He sounded affronted.

"Thanks, Joe."

He unexpectedly kissed my hand. "You're welcome, Adeline. This is not how I expected our meeting to end."

"Me, neither. But I'm relieved we got everything settled."

William was beyond pleased that Joe had given us his support. Alaska's Senator Rachel Scanlon was a wild card; nobody knew which of the two projects she'd support. Governor Aaron Harland claimed to be neutral, but we now knew he wanted the access road.

I was more than relieved to have my family's matchmaking nonsense put to rest between me and Joe. I felt like a huge weight had been lifted from my shoulders. Joe had also promised to keep quiet about me being in Alaska, so I wouldn't have to worry about my father and uncle interfering, either.

The arts and culture center's first two community engagement meetings attracted a range of arts and community groups, along with many other Windward citizens. The meetings went well, and with Joe's support on the financial front, the on-site office was being set up for the initial planning work so we could apply for the rest of the funding.

I was busy putting the broad strokes of the community recommendations into a coherent report and helping William set up contracts with architectural, engineering and construction companies. The mayor had even sent us an encouraging email, asking to be involved and offering assistance from the city of Windward.

Since I didn't need any furniture for the Pettigrew house, Katie had put most of my things in storage, arriving with boxes full of our personal items. I was most excited to get my full computer station up and running, but I was also thrilled to be able to expand my wardrobe.

In the home office, she and I pushed a two-cushion sofa off to one side, parking it in front of a built-in bookcase. Then we decided one of the lamps had to go to give me enough room for a proper workstation. Luckily, the antique desk was huge, and a side table could be pulled around to set up my biggest monitor.

It became obvious that the house was built in an era when few electrical outlets were needed. But a power strip solved that problem, and we held our breath as we got ready to power everything up at once. We hoped the load wouldn't trip the breaker—like it had in the kitchen when we ran the microwave, the blender and the coffee maker all at the same time.

"You don't dare bring a coffee maker in here," Katie said, unplugging two of the lamps on the far side of the room to lessen the load.

I'd decided I could make do with the overhead light. "And... contact." I pressed the button for the last of my three monitors.

We both looked around the room.

"Hold real still," Katie said.

"I think it's going to work," I said.

"We have achieved electricity!"

I clicked an icon with my mouse and watched the architectural software package fill the screens. "Better than that. We've achieved technology." I could now put my notes and drawings into the proper tool.

"This calls for a celebration."

It was Friday afternoon. So, in just a couple of hours, I'd be officially off duty until the next public meeting on Sunday afternoon.

"We need cake," Katie said.

"We could walk down to the grocery store," I suggested. "The bakery's almost two miles away." I didn't mind the walk, but that was a long way to carry a cake home, especially in the warm sunshine.

"I meant make our own. I've been dying to take that oven out for a test drive. Besides, now that we've unpacked, I feel like nesting."

"You want to bake a cake?"

I was definitely not the most domesticated person in the world. I'd grown up with chefs doing the cooking at our house in Anchorage, and there were great takeout restaurants in Sacramento. There'd been little need for me to cook for myself, never mind bake. The closest I came was toasting my own bagel and spreading it with cream cheese.

"Baking is fun," Katie said. "You've got some ripe bananas in the kitchen. It'll be almost healthy."

"Banana cake?"

"With cream cheese frosting."

I wasn't about to say no. "You'll have to tell me what to do."

"Easy-peasy." She started for the kitchen. "We'll need a mixing bowl and a couple of pans."

We had fun hunting through the kitchen cupboards, finding everything from cheese graters and corkscrews to the baking pans and ceramic mixing bowls we needed for our cake.

Katie found instructions for the oven and got it heating. Then she set me up mashing the bananas while she mixed butter and sugar.

"I took your advice," I said. I'd been waiting to talk to her in person about Joe.

"You're mashing them really smooth?"

"Mashing?"

"The bananas."

"Oh, sure, that, too."

"What else?" She'd found an electric mixer for the butter and sugar, and the whirr of the motor filled the air.

I waited until she was done and scraping down the sides before I spoke. "With Joe."

She stopped what she was doing and turned to look at me. "What Joe?"

"He came back again."

"Here? To Windward?"

"Yes."

"When?"

"A few days after you left. Turns out the funding push gets complicated." I continued my banana-mashing efforts. "There's competition between the arts and culture complex and the road extension."

Katie was still staring at me. "And the Joe part?"

"William wanted Joe's support to push the project in DC, and Joe said he wanted to get to know the team to decide if we could execute the project."

"Team? What team?"

"Exactly," I said, glad Katie caught on right away. "*I'm* the team. So, we met at the Forberg Club."

"What's that?"

"Very high-end, very snooty, private mover-and-shaker kind of place down on Peel Road near the water."

"You, Joe and William?"

"Me and Joe."

"Just the two of you?" Katie looked intrigued now.

"Yes. It was the perfect opportunity. So, I did what you said."

Katie smiled with obvious satisfaction as she crossed to the fridge and pulled out the egg carton.

"I threw it all out there," I continued. "I told him in no uncertain terms that I wasn't going to succumb to my family's machinations. There was no romantic future for us, and I just wanted to be left in peace to take on the job I was doing here." Even thinking back now, I was proud of my direct, straightforward delivery.

"And it worked?" She cracked the eggs into the bowl and gave them a stir into the mixture.

"It worked," I said. "He seemed to respect me for my upfront honesty. And then we had sex."

"I'm so glad—" Katie's expression fell. "Wait. *What?*"

"It was nothing—you know, not romantic in any way, just chemistry."

Her complexion flushed a little. "You had *sex* with *Joe?*"

"Yes."

"While explaining to him there was no chance of a romance between you two?"

I could see how she might misunderstand. "You kinda had to be there to—"

"Adeline."

"He dared me to kiss him." I realized how that sounded. "The point being it would prove we weren't attracted to each other."

She stared at me in condemning silence.

I explained some more. "It was a chemical thing. No hearts, no flowers, no romantic, candlelit lead-up or anything." I cast my memory back. "Well, there were candles on the table at dinner, but not like that."

"Why would you *do* that?"

"We got a little carried away." I supposed you could call it a lot carried away.

"No kidding."

"These are all mashed."

She hit the trigger on the mixer and finished blending in the eggs. Then she set the mixer aside and held out her hand for the bananas. "And what did he say?"

I moved to hand them over. "About what?"

"About the Dodgers. About *the sex.*" She emptied the mashed bananas into the bowl.

"Oh, he understood." We'd been surprisingly in sync afterward.

"Are you sure? Bring over the flour."

I went for the big white bowl where we'd mixed flour, salt and baking powder. "I'm positive."

"You have to blend the wet with the dry quickly. Don't overmix," she said, demonstrating. "Grab the pans and give them a spray."

I doused the pans with nonstick spray and set them next to the mixing bowl.

"Now, what *exactly* did he say?" she asked.

"I don't remember exactly. He said it was great sex."

Katie's expression broke out in a grin. "Was it?"

"Yes." I searched my memory a bit more. "He also said it was nothing but pent-up sexual energy and he'd still support our financial ask for the project."

"Well, then." She looked amused as she spooned the batter into the pans.

"What's so funny?"

"In a million years, I never would have thought to use great sex to chase a man away. Open the oven."

I crossed the kitchen and opened the big-windowed door. "Neither would I."

Katie set the pans side by side on the top rack.

"But sometimes things just work out." I closed the door while she set the timer. "Wine while we wait?" I asked.

"You bet." She rinsed out the dishcloth and wiped the counters while I opened a bottle of merlot and poured.

We settled at the tiny kitchen table in an alcove overlooking the compact backyard.

She lifted her glass. "To great sex and men who support your financial asks."

I chuckled and clinked glasses. But when I brought the wine to my lips, a sour aroma suddenly invaded my nostrils. "Hold it. I think this has turned." I took an experimental sniff.

Katie took a sip. "Tastes fine to me."

I wrinkled my nose. "Are you sure? This is off."

She drank again. Then she reached out. "Maybe it's your glass. Hand it over."

I did.

She took a sniff. "I don't know what you're talking about." She sipped. "This is perfectly fine wine."

I wondered if my palate had been permanently ruined by the bottle Joe and I had shared at the Forberg Club. That would be tragic. I didn't want to have to buy expensive wine for the rest of my life.

Katie was giving me an odd look.

"What?" I asked.

"When exactly did you and Joe have sex?"

"After the meeting. We came back here."

"What day?"

"I don't know, beginning of last week."

"Ten days? Twelve?"

I suddenly got where she was going, and my stomach lurched in horror.

"Adeline, are you pregnant?"

"No." I did some frantic math. "It's not—" I scrambled for my phone and brought up a calendar, running my fingertip along the weeks. "There. See. I'm—" I looked back up at Katie. "Five days late."

She groaned and did a forehead plant into her palm.

Three hours and one pregnancy test later, Katie and I were in the living room staring at each other in silence for long stretches. She'd finished both our glasses of wine while I'd gone with a cup of lemon tea. It tasted better anyway.

"I shouldn't have been ovulating," I said. "Like…no way."

"Sometimes it happens," she said.

I closed my eyes, trying to calm myself down.

After a minute, Katie spoke into the silence. "You okay?"

My mind was spinning. But reality was reality. I managed a small smile. "Maybe it will help if I say it out loud?"

"Say it out loud."

"I am having a baby."

Katie gave an understanding nod. "Okay. Right. We should ice the cake. It'll be cool by now."

"You've had two big glasses of wine," I pointed out.

"It's not illegal to ice a cake when you're over the limit."

I managed a wider smile.

"That a girl." She rose to her feet. "Keep your sense of humor."

I followed suit. "I can't exactly sit around and fret for the next nine months."

"I hope the cake at least tastes good to you," Katie said as we returned to the kitchen.

"I've finished my education." I was talking more to myself than her, telling myself to look on the bright side. "I can do a lot of my work from home. Daycares exist. Nannies exist." Being a single mother hadn't been part of my life plan yesterday, but it looked like it was now.

She poked experimentally at the butter and cream cheese that were softening in the mixing bowl. "I could stay in Alaska, help out."

"You have a good teaching job that you've spent eight years working for."

"I know. But I can't leave you here all alone."

"I won't be alone in about eight months." I was frankly surprised at my ability to make a baby joke this soon. I felt a little bit proud of that.

Katie returned my smile. "It's softened. And it's dairy—good for you."

"Probably the bananas are, too."

"Potassium." She opened a bag of confectioners' sugar. "What are you going to tell Joe?"

"Just the facts." I tried to imagine Joe's reaction, but I had no frame of reference for him receiving unexpected news. I realized I'd only ever seen him in social situations. What if he had an unexpectedly bad temper?

"You going to call him in DC?"

"Maybe I'll just send a text."

"You *can't*." She looked at my expression and saw I was joking.

My phone rang just then, vibrating against the table where I'd left it earlier. For a split second, I was afraid it might be Joe. But it was my cousin.

"It's Sophie," I said to Katie, picking up and putting cheerful into my voice. "Hi, you."

"You're in Alaska?" Sophie sounded excited.

"You heard." I pretended it was no big deal, even as my heart sank. If Sophie knew, then the whole family knew.

"Yes! Joe told Mason he talked to you in Windward, that you've got some big-deal construction project going on over there."

"That's where I am," I said, silently cursing Joe. So much for him keeping my secret. I didn't know why I'd thought I could trust him.

"So, when are you coming here? Want me to send Stone to pick you up?"

Nathaniel Stone was Sophie's new husband, a vice president at Kodiak Communications. Like my brothers, he had a pilot's license and used corporate planes to fly all over Alaska.

"Not yet," I said, planning to stall for as much time as possible. "My stuff was only just delivered today. The project is going full speed, and I've got all this unpacking."

"I understand," she said. "But I can't *wait* to see you."

"Me, too." Sophie was the person I'd most look forward to seeing in Anchorage.

Katie had paused on the other side of the kitchen and was pointing to the mixer.

I nodded and ducked around a corner in the hallway so she could make noise. "How's everyone there?" I asked Sophie.

"Braxton's behaving himself," she said on a laugh.

"What does that mean?"

"He's not bugging me for grandchildren this week."

My hand went subconsciously to my stomach, thinking that against all odds, I was going to be the first one to have a baby. It was no secret that both my father and his brother, Braxton, hoped for numerous grandchildren to perpetuate the family dynasty.

Braxton had lost hope of ever having any grandchildren

until Sophie showed up last year, believing she had a long-lost cousin in Anchorage. No one was more stunned than her to discover she was Braxton's biological daughter. Now he could hardly wait for grandchildren, and Braxton wasn't one to be patient.

"Glad to hear it," I answered her.

"How'd it go with Joe?" she asked, trying hard to sound casual.

She knew about the family's matchmaking aspirations. Out of everyone, Sophie had the most sympathy for me. On the other hand, she really liked Joe and had suggested on more than one occasion that I give him a fair shot. Still, she was great, and I was lucky to have her as a cousin.

I wanted to tell her the truth. But I couldn't ask her to keep anything from Stone, so there was no way I was sharing. "He told me he'll help us get federal money. For the construction project, I mean. There's a program, but we need his support."

"Any catch?"

"No catch." Except for the fact that he'd outed me to my family. That was a catch I hadn't seen coming.

"Nothing?" She sounded skeptical about that.

"We did have dinner."

"And...?"

"It wasn't as bad as I expected." I was being honest, even if I was leaving some gaping holes in the information. Dinner had gone better than I'd expected. "He didn't propose marriage or anything."

He'd specifically not proposed marriage, for which I was grateful.

"You're paranoid, Adeline. He just wants to get to know you."

"Is that what Stone told you?"

"That's what Joe told me."

"Wait, you've been talking to Joe about me?"

Her tone turned airy. "People come to me for advice, Adeline. I can't help it if they trust me."

I was worried now that they'd co-opted Sophie to the cause. "What did you tell him?"

"To give you space."

I blew out a sigh of relief. "Thanks."

"Don't thank me. It's my true opinion. I honestly think that gives him the best shot with you."

I thought back to how Joe had behaved at dinner, very low-key and unassuming. It hadn't worked—at least, not completely. But I had let my guard down toward the end of the evening.

I could see now he'd been following Sophie's advice. Which could mean he hadn't given up yet—only given me the distance I craved as part of a strategy. Now, *that* was an unsettling thought.

"When do you think you'll have time to visit?" she asked.

"I'll have to play it by ear for a bit."

"Okay. I won't say I'm not disappointed. Make it soon, okay?"

"Soon as I can," I promised. "Say hi to everyone."

"Will do. Glad you're back."

I wasn't exactly glad, and I wasn't exactly back. "I'm excited about the project."

"Good. Talk later." Sophie signed off.

When I returned to the kitchen, Katie was smearing fluffy cream cheese icing on top of the two-layer cake. It looked delicious, and I couldn't wait to dig into a big slice.

"She knows you're here?" Katie asked, briefly glancing up.

"Joe told Mason, and Mason told Stone, and I'm sure the two of them will have told everybody. It's exciting news, me being back in the zone."

"I supposed it was inevitable." She finished with a flourish. "Cake?"

"Absolutely. But he said he wouldn't tell them." I was still grappling with my disappointment over Joe's betrayal.

"Did he mention the sex?"

I shook my head. If Sophie had heard I'd slept with Joe, it would have been the first thing out of her mouth. At least that part was still a secret.

Katie set the bowl and utensils in the sink.

I took two plates from the cupboard while she located a long, sharp knife.

"When are you going to tell him?" she asked as she cut generous slabs and set them on the plates.

I got us a couple of forks. "Seems like something I should do in person."

My number-one priority was to convey the information, but it was probably a good idea to see his expression when he reacted. I realized I had absolutely no earthly idea what to expect.

We carried our cake to the kitchen table.

"Is he coming back soon?" Katie asked.

"That seems unlikely." I took a bite of the cake. The moist sweetness exploded deliciously in my mouth. "Wow. That's fantastic. Where'd you learn how to cook like this?"

"My nana. She has a hundred recipes stored up inside her head. One day soon I'm going to write them all down."

"I want this one." As I said that, I realized how very unlikely it was that I'd have time to bake, especially now, especially with my life about to turn itself upside down. "A baby," I said, then I took another bite.

"It's hard to wrap your head around it."

"Impossible." I couldn't even picture my belly swelling up. I knew it would be weeks before that happened. But I also knew time had a way of slipping by.

It seemed like only yesterday that we'd graduated. And now we both had jobs. Katie had gone to California. Now she was back. We'd finished moving, and Joe had been here—twice.

"I have to go there to tell him." That much was certain.

She nodded. "I agree."

I made a concrete decision. "Next weekend, quick turnaround to DC. I'll charter a jet."

Katie stared at me in silence for a beat. "I forget, you know."

"Forget what?"

"You act really normal all the time, and I forget you're so rich."

The money rarely mattered to me. "I don't often pull out the trust fund platinum card. But I think I will this time."

"Do you literally have a trust fund?"

"It's just shares of the company from my grandfather. But they pay dividends, and those tend to add up."

Katie coughed out a laugh. "*Tend to add up*. I know you're talking about significant money if you're flying private at the drop of a hat."

I shrugged. "The money just sits there."

"Until you need a jet."

"You want to come along?" I knew I would appreciate the company.

"Are we talking those huge white leather lounge seats and flutes of champagne?"

"I don't know if the seats will be white. But I'm looking for speed so, yes, that'll come with luxury."

"I'm in." She immediately sobered. "Sorry. I shouldn't be talking like this will be fun."

I didn't blame her. It might not be fun, but it was absolutely surreal. "At this point, it is what it is."

My hand went to my stomach again. I didn't know whether to laugh or cry or wail in frustration. I did know none of those things would change reality.

Four

I expected Joe to meet me in the reception area of his congressional office, since security had called up for permission to let me in the building.

But he wasn't there. The compact space was impressively opulent, with a small walnut desk, two tufted pale green guest chairs and a low table all arranged beneath tasteful oil paintings of Alaskan wilderness scenes. The receptionist sat against the wall with a closed door beside her.

"You must be Dr. Cambridge," the thirtysomething woman said as I paused inside the doorway. She wore a burgundy wraparound coatdress with a slim skirt, a wide fabric belt and oversize buttons decorating the collared vee neckline.

Along with being nervous, I now felt underdressed in my cropped black pants and fall leaf–patterned blouse. Since it was a half mile walk from the hotel, I'd stuck with low-heeled sandals with gray leather cross-ties. I'd thought the look was neutral, but now it struck me as halfway between smart casual and pool deck.

I hadn't calmed down any on the walk over, so half of me was dying to turn and run. "Adeline," I said. "Please call me Adeline."

"The congressman is finishing up a meeting."

"I don't mind waiting." It felt like a reprieve. Maybe I'd be able to get myself together before his meeting ended.

The door beside her suddenly opened, and Joe appeared. "Adeline." He sounded half surprised and half worried.

"I'm sorry to bother you," I said.

"No. Not at all." He looked to the receptionist. "Bree, can you cancel my ten thirty?" Then he gestured me inside. "Come on in."

"I can be quick," I said as I started his way.

"Did you come all this way to lobby for the project?"

"Not exactly."

"Do you need something? Can I help?"

"I have some news," I said but then decided that didn't sound right. "I have an update."

"Great." He sounded happy now, even eager.

I was sure about to change all that. I walked through the door to his inner sanctum.

His desk was gleaming cherrywood with two matching guest chairs covered in padded dark green leather. His art echoed the paintings in the reception area, while a small meeting table took up one corner. It was surrounded by four wooden chairs. The only other furniture were two compact armchairs sitting together under the window. Joe went there and gestured for me to sit down.

As I sat, my stomach did rapid flip-flops. I wished I'd had a few more minutes out in the reception area to compose my speech. Everything I'd thought of last night sounded terrible inside my head right now.

"What's up?" he asked, leaning forward.

I resisted an urge to draw back like a coward. Instead, I squared my shoulders. Then I swallowed.

He cocked his head. "Has something gone wrong?"

I managed a tight little nod, ordering myself to say something—anything.

His brow furrowed. "Adeline?"

"I'm pregnant," I blurted out. Then I clamped my jaw, not quite believing I'd said it so bluntly.

Joe didn't react, and I wondered if the shout had been inside my head.

Then his brow lifted, and his eyes got round.

"I didn't mean for it to come out like that," I said.

It took him another second to speak. "I'm not sure leading up slowly would have helped."

"I wanted to tell you in person."

He opened his mouth again but then closed it without speaking.

I knew I had to be patient. I'd had a week to get used to this, where he'd had a full thirty seconds.

"I can leave you alone," I offered, half rising.

His hand shot out to stop me, touching my thigh. "No. Don't leave. Don't—"

I sat back down.

We both sat in silence for a few minutes.

"I just wanted to let you know," I said.

"You came all this way?"

"Nothing needs to change. Definitely not right away. We can carry on as normal." I had months left before the pregnancy would even be obvious.

"Normal?"

"I get there'll be long-term decisions, but right now—"

"Who else knows?"

"Just my friend Katie."

"Is she trustworthy? Will she tell anyone?"

"She won't tell anyone." I wanted to make a snide remark about him not turning out to be so trustworthy, about him telling my family I was in Alaska after he'd promised he wouldn't.

"What about your family?"

"Why would she tell my family?" Katie hadn't ever met my family.

"We need to tell your family."

I stood then. "Oh, no, no, no. I already heard from Sophie."

He rose with me, looking baffled. "You just said they didn't know."

"About my being in Alaska," I clarified.

"What about it?"

"You told Mason."

"So?"

"I *asked* you not to." I didn't know why I was diverging from the main topic, but I was still annoyed that Joe had almost immediately betrayed my confidence.

His voice rose a little. "You meant about being in Alaska? I thought you meant about having sex."

"Both."

"Well, you didn't make that clear. You thought they wouldn't notice you were in Alaska?"

"They noticed really fast when you *ran to them* with the gossip."

"It wasn't gossip. It was a casual conversation, a topic of mutual interest. I really thought you meant the sex."

"Fine," I said, deciding to believe him on that point.

"We have to tell them about the baby."

I took a step backward, waggling my finger at him, coming up against the chair. "Oh, no, we don't. Not yet."

"As soon as possible."

"I've got plenty of time." I wanted a plan, an outline for my life, for what it was going to look like as a single mother before I let my well-meaning but interfering father and the rest of them in on the discussion.

"I'm not keeping something like this from Xavier and Braxton."

"*You* wouldn't be keeping it from them."

But Joe was nodding. "That's my baby—" His gaze dropped to my stomach, and his entire demeanor changed. Reality seemed to have hit him in a wave. His voice dropped lower. "This is my responsibility."

I might have gown angry or laughed at the thoroughly dated concept, but it was easy to see he was wrapping his head around the magnitude of our situation.

"Don't panic," I said.

He met my gaze. "Panic? This isn't panic. This is recognition that my relationship with your family is very important to me."

That wasn't exactly news. "Don't worry. They'll still support you."

He flinched. "That's not what I—"

"I don't hold your priorities against you. Hey, I had dinner with you to finance a public project. That was hardly a noble move on my part."

He looked annoyed now. "I don't care about me. I care about them. I respect them both. I'm not going to lie about something this important, and I'm not willing to spring it on them at the last minute."

"They're going to be happy, Joe. No matter how it happened,

this is a grandchild, the next generation. There will be champagne corks popping all over the Cambridge mansion when they get word of this."

"So, there's no downside," he said, a subtle but calculating expression on his face. "To telling them now?"

"Now? *Now?* What do you mean, now?"

"When are you going back to Alaska?"

I hadn't decided exactly. The private jet company only needed three hours' notice. "Soon."

"Good. I'm coming with you."

"There he is," Katie said while we waited on board the jet at ExBlue Executive Airport.

Joe's sleek black car had stopped outside on the tarmac. He rose from the back seat and retrieved his suitcase from the open trunk.

I watched his lithe movements as he closed it and headed for the plane.

"If your baby has to have a father…" Katie said, craning her neck in the rear-facing seat to see through the rounded window.

"You mean genetically speaking?" I wasn't about to argue against that.

"He's definitely got the looks and athleticism," Katie said.

"It's the arranged-marriage vibe that stops me cold."

Katie grinned and sat back in her seat, facing me. "I hear you. I can only imagine who my parents would pick for me— an accountant or maybe a dentist."

"You have something against accountants and dentists?"

"Too precise, too rules oriented, no imagination."

"You're a physicist."

"Astrophysicist. That means I can deal with unknowns, hypotheses and speculation."

I held up my palms in surrender. "Don't worry. I'm not trying to pick your husband."

She waved as Joe stepped onto the plane. He handed off his suitcase to the male attendant, then leaned into the cockpit.

Katie leaned toward me. "I want someone exciting."

"Maybe you shouldn't work at a university. Lots of tweed and uptight in the faculty there."

She seemed to consider that fact.

Joe turned my way then, a bright smile on his face. He'd obviously had a satisfying conversation with the pilots. Maybe they were based in Alaska. If so, they might be voters. He could have taken the opportunity to chat them up.

"Morning," he said, ducking slightly under the low ceiling as he walked, then swung into the seat across the aisle from me.

There was a seat facing Joe's, plus two more and a sofa behind us. Behind that was a restroom.

"Joe, you remember my friend Katie," I said.

Joe quickly offered his hand. "Nice to see you again, Katie."

"Likewise," she said as he sat back and settled in.

The attendant came down the aisle to stand between us. "Would anyone care for a drink after takeoff?" he asked.

Joe looked to me.

"Orange juice if you've got it," I said.

"Of course, ma'am." He looked to Katie next.

"Mimosa?"

"Certainly."

"Coffee for me, please," Joe said. "Black is fine."

"Coming up shortly," the man said. "We're about to begin our taxi. Can I ask you to please buckle up?"

We all reached for our seat belts while the jet engines' pitch went higher and louder outside our windows. The sound subsided a bit as we started forward, trundling toward the runway.

We lifted off and climbed fast. The jet had a lavish interior, but it was predominantly built for speed and would get us to Alaska in under five hours. As it leveled out, the attendant made his way back, a silver tray balanced on one hand.

"Mimosa," the man said to Katie, setting a crystal flute on a small napkin in front of her, making me just a little bit jealous.

"Orange juice," he said next.

The juice was in a tall, frosty glass with plenty of ice. It looked freshly squeezed and delicious. I felt a bit better about it.

"Coffee for you, sir." The man put a tall black mug on the table in front of Joe. "I'll be making French crepes for breakfast, if that's acceptable. Standard bacon, eggs and toast are also available. I'll give you a few minutes to decide."

We were headed for Anchorage, where we'd pick up a rental car and drive straight to the family's mansion. We didn't have any time to waste since I had to be at work Monday morning.

Overnight, I'd come around to Joe's way of thinking. The more time my family had to get used to the idea of a baby, the better it was for everyone. It would be selfish to keep it to myself just because I was nervous.

I wasn't that nervous. Single moms weren't a big thing anymore. Sure, some pregnancies were accidental, but many single women simply decided it was time to have a family. Who was to say I wasn't one of those?

Not that I'd tell my family this was planned. I'd be straight with them. No matter the circumstances, I was certain the baby would be treated as extremely happy news.

"You should take an extra day," Joe said, as if he'd guessed where my thoughts had gone.

I shook my head. "I'm not asking for a personal day this early in my tenure."

"Why not?"

"Because it would be unprofessional."

"Do you *want* to stay over in Anchorage?"

I thought about Sophie and how nice it would be to have a visit with her. "Sure. But I'm not going to ask."

"I could ask."

"Oh, no, you don't."

"Why not? It's a big deal."

"You can't pull rank on William."

"I won't lie," Joe said. "I'll just tell him we'll be meeting there."

It felt wrong, but I was tempted. I looked to Katie for a second opinion, and she shrugged.

"William?" I heard Joe ask.

I whirled my head his way and saw he was already on the phone. *"You're not,"* I hissed.

He gave me a wink. A *wink*, like we were conspiring together to ditch gym class or something. "Joe Breckenridge here. How are things with you?"

I looked back at Katie, who seemed amused by the turn of events.

"I'm very well, thank you," Joe said. "Listen, could you possibly spare Adeline on Monday? I'm going to be in Anchorage, and I was hoping to meet with her. She can visit her family while she's there."

I was more than nervous now and shook my head at Joe, making a slashing motion across my throat.

"I am," Joe said easily. "I will. Thanks, William, appreciate that." Joe ended the call.

"You—" I didn't even know what to say.

"William is thrilled. He sees it as another chance for you to co-opt me. Which it is."

"I don't have to co-opt you. You're already on board. And I already told him that."

"In politics, there's always room for more schmoozing. Look at it this way, you might be in Anchorage, but you're still working for the good of the project."

My phone rang then. I checked the screen and saw it was William.

I put a finger to my lips for quiet and took the call. "Hello, William."

"Adeline," he opened heartily. "Good that I caught you."

"I know, I'm here with—"

"There's been a development." William sounded rushed.

I hoped he wasn't annoyed. "Yes, the congressman—"

"The governor's flat-out defecting, and it looks like the senator's in play." William had seemed unflappable up to now. But he was clearly agitated. "Congressman Breckenridge's support is more vital than ever. If he wants you in Anchorage, then *I* want you in Anchorage."

"What changed?" I asked, earning me curious looks from both Joe and Katie.

"I'm trying to figure it all out. There's been a budget cut in the fund and Governor Harland pledged his support for the road extension. He's leaning heavily on the senator to support him. It seems like Nigel's in thick with the senator's staff, so you need to talk to the congressman. You know what to do?"

My gaze went to Joe, who was watching me with open curiosity. "I think so."

"Don't lose him, Adeline. He's our last hope."

"He's already—"

"We need *more* than just Breckenridge on our side. We need Breckenridge to keep Senator Scanlon on our side, or we can pack it all up and try again in two years."

It had been months since I'd been home.

My brother Mason was in the great room when we walked through the front door, and his smile beamed as soon as he saw me. A split second later, he frowned. "What did you do to your hair?" But he came straight over and pulled me into a warm hug, just like he always did. After a second, he pulled back, apparently to confirm it was really me under the short blond locks. "Did you lose a bet?"

"I'm fine. Don't you like it? I was in the neighborhood."

He grinned again and then glanced past me—doing a double take at Katie, I presumed, given the goofy expression that came over his face.

I turned to her. "This is my friend Katie Tambour from Sacramento—well, my housemate right now. Katie, this is my brother Mason."

Mason moved her way, offering his hand. "Welcome to Alaska, Katie."

The melodic tone of interest in his voice was embarrassing. But Katie was gorgeous, so I wasn't surprised.

"Nice to meet you, Mason," she said, and I could hear the note of humor. My brother wasn't the first guy to turn sappy on her.

"Joe?" Mason sounded surprised now. "What…? Where…?" He looked around the circle at the three of us. "Something up?"

"We landed at the same time," I said without elaborating.

"I'm enjoying Alaska very much so far," Katie said, pulling Mason's attention away from Joe.

I knew it was deliberate, and I silently thanked her for being my wingperson again.

"The air," she continued. "You should advertise the clean air in your tourism ads. You all must have the best lungs in the world."

Mason drew in a breath—seeming to test her hypothesis.

"Adeline?" It was my brother Kyle now, slightly younger but almost a copy of Mason. He also pulled me into a warm hug. "I like it," he said, ruffling my short hair. "Way to go bold."

After the hug I watched him take in Katie.

"Who's this?" But his attention quickly switched again. "Hey, Joe. I didn't know you were coming."

"Last-minute decision," Joe said, shaking Kyle's hand.

"Kyle, this is my friend Katie Tambour from California." I made the introduction a second time. "Katie, this is my other brother, Kyle."

"Hello, Katie from California." He glanced around at the small group. "Are we having a party or something?"

"Adeline!" It was Sophie calling out this time. "I *love* it!" She dashed in for a hug while Stone sauntered in behind her.

"Nice color," she said. "Nice cut." She bent sideways to look around me.

"What's all the commotion?" My uncle Braxton's voice shifted the atmosphere a little bit. "Adeline? Well, it's about time you dropped in. Does your dad know you're here?" He didn't say a word about my hair.

"We just got here," I said. I went to Braxton and gave him a more perfunctory hug.

"You brought Joe?" There was curiosity in his tone.

"Joe brought himself," I said.

Joe strode over. "Nice to see you again, Braxton. I'm on the periphery of Adeline's project down in Windward."

"That arts thing?" Braxton asked. His gaze switched back and forth between the two of us. It was quite annoying the way he tried to read minds—even more annoying that he was so good at it.

"It'll be a big complex—national money, significant impact on the economy of the region," Joe said.

Braxton looked satisfied by that answer, and I silently thanked Joe for distracting my uncle.

"I brought a friend along," I said to Braxton.

Braxton gave Katie a polite nod. "Kyle, let Sebastian and Marie know we have guests."

"Happy to," Kyle said and headed for the kitchen.

"How long will you be staying?" Braxton asked me.

"Just a couple—"

"Adeline?" It was my father, Xavier.

I turned to face him. "Hi, Dad."

He was frowning instead of smiling, and I wondered if he was about to question my new haircut. "What's wrong?"

I touched the back of my hair. "Nothing."

"You sure?" He took in Joe and Katie.

"I convinced her it was time to visit," Joe said.

"Joe's funding Adeline's little project in Windward," Braxton said.

"It's more than a *little* project," I said, annoyed at the characterization even though I was glad to switch topics. I also wasn't thrilled by their presumption of Joe's benevolence.

My dad's hug was slightly warmer than Uncle Braxton's, but still more reserved than most.

"We always appreciated the congressman's help," my dad said, the hug over quickly. "Nice to see you again, Joe."

"Happy to be here," Joe said.

"Let's get Katie settled," Sophie put in, for which I was grateful.

"Good idea," I quickly agreed, moving with Sophie toward the grand staircase and motioning for Katie to come along.

She sidled up to me and whispered in my ear. "You actually *live* here?"

I saw Sophie smile.

"I used to," I said as we walked.

Katie took in the high ceilings, the multiple cream-colored leather furniture groupings in the great room, the stone fireplace and the wall of glass that showed off the backyard.

"It's like a hotel," she said in awe.

"I felt the same way the first time I saw it," Sophie said, mounting the wide staircase. "You'll love the guest room."

"So, you didn't grow up here?" Katie asked Sophie.

"Not even close. An apartment in Seattle."

"But she got rich all on her own," I put in.

"Not this kind of rich," Sophie said with a laugh.

"No wonder you're chartering jets," Katie said.

Sophie gave me a look. "Jets?"

Katie flashed me a silent apology.

"We were in a hurry. Turns out the governor's supporting a competing project." I rattled on with unnecessary information, hoping to distract Sophie. "And the governor's trying to co-opt the senator, and my boss wants me to get Joe to hit up the senator to support us instead."

We came to the top of the stairs.

"Well, you can get Joe to do anything you want," Sophie said. "We can all see how he feels about you."

This time Katie shot me an amused grin.

"Here's the guest room," I said to her, opening the door with a flourish.

Katie took two steps inside and stopped.

I tried to see it through her eyes—the high ceilings and exposed beams, the banks of windows along two walls. The floor was natural wood, highlighted by a plush, forest green area rug. It wasn't all that much different than my room, since the same decorator had designed them both.

Out of practicality, the room had a king-size four-poster bed. The windowed corner held a conversation area with a sofa, two plush, overstuffed armchairs and a couple of glass-topped tables, while a marble-framed gas fireplace took up most of one wall and a dressing and closet area led into a bathroom with a soaker tub, a separate shower and dual sinks.

Sophie slipped past Katie to watch her expression.

"Been there," Sophie said with a laugh.

Katie moved forward and spun around. "This is…mind-blowing."

"Pro tip," Sophie said. "When Marie insists on doing your laundry, just say yes. Life is simpler that way."

"We won't be here that long," Katie said.

Sophie looked at me, her brow arched in a question.

"I have to be at work on Tuesday," I said. "In fact, this is work. My big objective for tomorrow is to secure Joe's support on the senatorial front."

Sophie looked confused. "You're joking, right? How long does it take to crook your little finger?"

Katie stifled a laugh.

"Things have gotten weird," I said. I didn't want to tell Sophie the pregnancy news before anyone else, but I didn't want to stand here and pretend everything was status quo, either.

"Weirder than usual?" she asked. "I mean, you're here, Joe's here, your dad and Braxton are here. The three of them together always make you jumpy."

"True," I agreed. "I've seen more than I expected of Joe over the past few weeks."

Sophie looked happy to hear it. "Are you warming up to him?"

I hesitated, trying to frame up something that was true but not too revealing.

"I told her to be straight with him," Katie put in. "All this tippy-toeing around wasn't doing anyone any good."

"What did you say?" Sophie asked, looking disappointed.

"It's obvious he's co-opted you now," I said back.

"I like him, too," Katie said.

I gave her a look that said she was a traitor.

She gave me her favorite shrug. "You said it yourself—everyone likes him."

"Because he's a good guy," Sophie said. "You have reverse Romeo and Juliet syndrome."

I tried to glean her meaning. "Reverse—"

Katie jumped in. "Your parents push you together, and you throw yourselves apart."

"I don't think that's a thing," I said.

"It sounds plausible to me," Katie said.

"Whose side are you on?"

"Yours." She moved to rub my shoulder. "Completely yours."

Our gazes met, and I knew we needed to get the big reveal over with.

"We should go downstairs," I said.

"Okay, but we're having girl talk after dinner," Sophie said emphatically.

"Guaranteed," I said, knowing that much was true.

I hadn't purposely waited until dinner, but there were a lot of different conversations going on around the house, and I couldn't seem to corral everyone together until then.

I let Sebastian pour me a glass of red wine, intercepting a shocked look from Joe. I gave an imperceptible shake of my head to tell him I wasn't planning to drink it. But if I'd said no to wine, I would have drawn attention to myself. I didn't want that just yet.

Then Sophie turned down wine in favor of ice water, and I realized I could have gotten away with it.

"A toast," Braxton said from one end of the table. "Welcome home, Adeline. Nice to meet you, Katie. And welcome back, Joe."

We all raised our glasses, and I pretended to drink.

"I need to tell you something," I said before the separate conversations could start up again.

Joe was seated across the table, and I suddenly wished he was beside me for moral support. I knew it was silly. Having him closer wasn't going to change a thing.

"Yes?" my dad prompted. He was at the opposite end of the table from Braxton, cornerwise to me.

"I'm…" I looked at Joe.

He seemed calm.

I took a breath. "Pregnant."

There was a moment of surprised silence. I'd expected that.

"No way," Sophie called out, sounding totally delighted. She hopped up from her chair between Stone and Joe and rushed around the table to give me a rocking hug.

"A grandchild?" my dad said, sounding proud.

"Wait," Mason said. "Didn't we miss a few steps here?"

I knew it was a natural question, and I knew I had to answer, but I wanted to bask in Sophie's unbridled joy for a moment or two longer.

"The baby is mine," Joe said.

Most froze in surprise.

Braxton beamed. "Congratulations, son!"

My father reached for my hand and gave it a squeeze. "This is *wonderful* news."

"Why didn't you spill earlier?" Sophie demanded on a laugh, still hugging me.

I met Joe's gaze as we both realized our mistake.

Sebastian had apparently overheard the excitement, because he walked into the dining room carrying two bottles of champagne on a silver tray. His efficiency was unsettling.

"Dad, no," I quickly said in a firm voice. "It's not what you think. We're not—" I waggled my finger back and forth between me and Joe. "We're *just* having a baby together. *That's all*."

Everyone stopped talking and stared at me, clearly looking for an explanation.

My dad's eyes narrowed as he turned his head to Joe. "What does she mean, just a baby?"

Joe stepped up. "Adeline and I had a date, one date."

"You're not getting married?" Kyle asked.

"You're not engaged?" Mason looked at my hand.

"What do you mean, you're not getting married?" Braxton demanded thunderously.

Sebastian stepped lithely back out of the room.

Sophie's arm loosened a little around my shoulder.

"You'd better be diamond ring shopping," my dad said to Joe on a growl.

"It's not Joe's fault." I didn't want them turning on him. I could feel Katie's astonished stare at my left side. I was thinking twice about making her sit through this.

"You're having his baby," my dad said.

"We didn't want to spring it on you—"

"This feels pretty springy," Mason said.

"—at the last minute," I finished. "We just found out. We don't know what it means for the future."

"Well, *I* know what it had better mean for the future," Braxton said.

"Braxton," Joe said. Then he looked at my dad. "Xavier. I will do whatever Adeline wants, up to and including marrying her."

I glared at him, angered by his bait and switch. He was saving himself and throwing me to the wolves.

"But for now," he told them firmly, "*back off.* This is Adeline's decision, and hers alone. You are *not* going to push her into something she doesn't want to do." His hard gaze included Mason and Kyle. "Hear me? All of you?"

There was muttering and nodding among the group.

"I'm still thrilled," Sophie whispered in my ear.

I gave her arm a squeeze. Now that it was out in the open, I felt a bit of a thrill myself. It felt more real, like there really was a baby in my future—a *baby.*

Katie reached out to me then, touching my shoulder.

My gaze met Joe's, and I gave him a tentative smile. He'd had my back against my family. I didn't remember anyone ever doing that before.

"Hey," Sophie whispered even more softly in my ear. "Nobody knows, but I'm pregnant, too."

I turned to stare at her in open astonishment.

A glint in her eyes, she backed away a couple of steps and returned to her seat beside Stone, who squeezed her hand and gave her a kiss on the hairline. Love shone from his eyes.

The cooking staff began quietly and unobtrusively serving a summer greens salad.

I caught Sophie's gaze again and gave her a little nod. I wanted her to share her good news. She cocked her head in a question to confirm what I was saying, and I nodded again.

She leaned over and whispered to Stone, who looked at me as well.

I smiled at him with pure happiness.

Holding Sophie's hand, he spoke up. "Not to be outdone, but Sophie and I have news, too."

Everyone's attention went to him, and the servers discreetly pulled back.

"We are also expecting a baby." He raised Sophie's hand to his lips and gave her a kiss.

Braxton jumped to his feet and went to Sophie as congratulations erupted all over again. This time there was no bad news trailing it to cause a scene.

Braxton hugged his daughter, and I thought I saw a glimmer of tears in his eyes. I was reminded that only a year ago he'd believed he'd never have grandchildren. My heart squeezed with joy.

Sebastian reappeared with the champagne while another cook set flutes of ginger ale in front of Sophie and me.

Katie leaned over to whisper to me. "You okay?"

"I'm good. Sophie gave me a heads-up. This'll distract everyone."

"I hope so," Katie said, accepting a glass of the champagne. "They seem as single-minded as you told me."

"I know. But Joe helped." I looked his way again and found his gaze on me.

He sent me a *you okay?* chin dip, raising his brow.

I nodded. Sophie and Stone's happiness wasn't a negative for me, not in any way.

Braxton rose, lifting his flute of champagne. "To our expanding family."

People roundly echoed his words with cheers.

Five

"Girl talk is much more fun with wine," Sophie complained, staring at her glass of ginger ale.

"Sorry," Katie said, sounding guilty.

The three of us had settled on padded Adirondack chairs on the shared balcony between my bedroom and Sophie's old room overlooking the backyard and the horse paddock. Katie was the only one with a glass of wine.

"So, what is your plan?" Sophie asked me. "Short term, I mean. Next few months."

"Get the community on board with the preliminary plans, push for federal funding, figure out how to neutralize Nigel Long. He's in tight with the senator's staff."

"So, your instincts were right," Katie said.

"Who's Nigel Long?" Sophie asked.

"He works for the governor. He pretended they were in favor of the arts and culture center, but they double-crossed us when the funding ran short."

"What are you going to do about it?"

"We've scheduled sector meetings and public meetings. The arts pitch is an easy one—who doesn't want more artistic undertakings in their community? But now we have to fight on the economic front. We'll have to frame up the tourism opportunities, artisan exports, improved quality of life in Windward that would attract entrepreneurs, tech and otherwise."

"So, nothing babyish, then?" Sophie said.

My hand went to my stomach as I once again thought of the life growing there. "I don't expect there will be much to do for a while."

"I've already been shopping for maternity clothes," Sophie said.

"How many weeks are you?" Katie asked.

"Nine."

"You're ahead of me. I think I'm five, based on how the charts say to count it, anyway. I have an appointment with my doctor next week."

"That is early." Sophie looked concerned. "You told us really early."

"Joe was worried. He didn't want to keep it from Braxton and Xavier."

Sophie looked thoughtful. "They're not going to give up now, you know, wanting you two to be together."

I gave a dry chuckle at the understatement. "I've known those two men my entire life. They're regrouping."

"Joe was good at dinner, though," Sophie said.

I agreed with a nod.

"Do you think it was a ruse?" she asked.

"I don't think so," Katie put in. "I mean, I've only just met Joe, but he doesn't strike me as underhanded."

Neither Sophie nor I responded to the statement.

"You think he *is*?" Katie asked in obvious astonishment.

"There's a lot at stake," I said. "For Kodiak Communications and for Joe."

"It's a mutually beneficial arrangement," Sophie said.

"For Adeline to *marry* Joe?" Katie frowned.

"For Braxton and Xavier to be in tight with the congressman."

"And for him to be in tight with them," I said.

"You've made yourself perfectly clear," Katie said. "You'll do what you want to do, regardless of what they'd like."

"I know. They know that, too."

"But they will try to push you two together," Sophie said.

I wished I could keep a step or two ahead of them. But I'd never been able to do that.

The door to Sophie's old room opened and closed, and I leaned back to see who it was.

Kyle sauntered out onto the balcony.

"You do know this is girl talk," I said to my brother.

"I'd rather visit with this generation than the old, stodgy one," Kyle said, sitting down in an empty chair.

"We're talking about babies," Sophie warned.

"I like babies," Kyle said. He had a glass of wine in his hand, and he took a drink. "I can't wait to be an uncle."

I suspected he wanted to chat Katie up.

The door opened again, bringing Mason inside.

"I knew the party would be up here," he said, sitting himself down on the last empty chair. "What are we talking about?"

"Babies," Sophie said. "You two sure you want in on this? It might get icky."

"You think I wouldn't change a diaper?" Kyle asked.

"He wouldn't change a diaper," Mason said.

"Sure would."

"The topic was cute maternity tops," Sophie said in a sing-song voice. "With polka dots and flowers—"

"And kittens," Katie added in a lilting tone. "Don't forget the kittens."

"Kittens," Sophie affirmed.

I couldn't help but smile as the wind came out of my brothers' sails.

Mason rallied first. "So, you're not pregnant, Katie?"

"I am not," she said and took a pointed sip of her wine.

"What is it you do down in California?"

"Teach," she said, "Soon, anyway. At Cal State."

"See, this is interesting," Mason said to Sophie. "And what is it you're going to teach at Cal State?"

"Astronomy." I raised my glass in a toast to her.

Mason looked surprised. "You can take that at Cal State?"

"Indeed."

"Isn't it a tier-one school?"

"So?"

He shrugged. "Okay." He paused for a second. "Well, I'm a Taurus."

Katie didn't miss a beat. "So, bullheaded."

He smiled. "That's cute. What else can you tell me?"

"You mean, like your future?"

I knew this wasn't the first time someone had gone off on an astrology tangent with Katie. Clearly, she was going to roll with it.

She set down her wineglass. "I'll have to see your palm." She motioned him over.

"Really?"

"Yes."

"Never heard of that before." But Mason rose and held his right hand out to her.

"Hmm," she said, running her finger along the creases of his hand. "Oh, my." She looked up at him. "Have you ever had this done before?"

"No."

"Did you read your horoscope this morning?"

"No."

I looked at Sophie and saw her pinch her lips tight together. She was obviously fighting off laughter.

Kyle didn't look amused. If anything, he looked a little jealous.

"Anything go wrong today?" Katie asked Mason, a faux-concerned expression on her face.

He shifted, perching himself on the wide armrest of the chair. "No, why?"

"Oh, well." Katie looked at her watch. "I guess there's still time."

"*Here* you all are." Stone walked onto the balcony, beelining for Sophie.

He took her hand, helping her to her feet, then sat down and pulled her onto his lap.

Joe came in next and took the chair Mason had abandoned.

"Can we stave it off?" Mason asked Katie, staring at his hand, his expression worried. "Maybe sing a song or chant something?"

Joe looked to me and nodded their way. "What's she doing?"

"Telling his fortune, I think," I answered.

"She does that?" Joe looked lost.

"She's an astrologer," Mason said without turning.

"I'm an astronomer," Katie corrected.

"That's an astrophysicist," Stone told Mason.

"Well, that's a relief," Mason said. "I thought you were a legit fortune teller—that I was in real trouble."

I couldn't tell for sure if Mason had been genuinely confused or just playing along the whole time. Then his eyes lit up with amusement, and Katie tossed his hand back to him.

He turned to see he'd lost his seat to Joe.

"Mind if I share?" he asked Katie, squatting on the arm of her chair.

The look she gave him was incredulous. "I barely know you."

He held up his palm. "I already let you take a look at my secrets. I swear, I'm harmless."

Katie looked at me for confirmation.

"I'll vouch for my brother. I have indeed always thought of him as fairly harmless." I made a face at Mason, and he returned it.

Everyone laughed, and Katie settled back in her chair.

"How long are you staying?" Kyle asked me.

"It depends. Could be as long as two years."

"Here?" He pointed down at the deck, seeming surprised.

"In Alaska," I corrected. "If Joe works hard and we get all the funding we need."

"It's a huge project," Joe said. "Naturally, there are detractors."

"Can Kodiak Communications help?" Mason asked.

"Sponsorships," I immediately said. "There'll be some community fund-raising events in the fall. We'll have to get the bulk of the funding from Washington. And the state will kick in some. At least I hope they'll kick in some." Now that the governor had come out against us, that might be more of a challenge. "Raising community funds will demonstrate the level of public support."

"Congress doesn't mind investing public money," Joe added. He pulled a face then, making it obvious he was joking. "But we like to know it'll eventually translate into votes."

The group chuckled easily.

"So, we can expect to see more of you?" Mason asked me.

"Depends," I said.

"On Dad and Braxton?"

"On *all* of you."

"Feisty," Kyle said with a grin.

"Are you mocking me?" I asked him.

"Are you mocking her?" Joe asked from where he was seated next to Kyle.

"Wouldn't dream of it," Kyle said.

"Yes, I'll be home more often," I admitted. Now that they all knew I was here, and now that I'd made my position on Joe abundantly clear, it would be nice to visit more often.

"I have to go back for the fall," Katie said. "I'm a little bit sorry about that."

"Do you ski?" Mason asked her.

"I surf."

"Well, having good balance is half the battle. You can come back in the winter and try skiing."

"You say that like it's a hop, skip and a jump instead of cramming in a middle seat and transferring through LAX and SeaTac."

"There must be an easier way than that," Kyle said.

"Not if you want a discount fare."

"She lives in the real world," Sophie said. "I remember the real world."

"We're not going to let her fly coach," Mason said, sounding offended.

Katie turned to look at him, bracing her hand on the empty armrest. "*Let* me?"

"Allow me to rephrase," Mason said.

"Oh, do rephrase."

Joe looked amused, and I shared a smile with him. Mason might not have been seriously flirting, but he was doing something.

"As our *guest*, we would expect to happily cover the cost of your transportation," Mason explained.

"You do that for all your guests?" Katie challenged.

"Hello?" Joe shook his head. "And here I've been buying my own tickets all these years?"

Mason shot him a narrow-eyed glare. "Not helping, Breckenridge."

"She'll come to visit me," I said, sounding purposely smug and self-satisfied.

"Her, I'll come to visit," Katie said, backing me up.

"But not me?" Mason asked, pretending to be offended.

"So far all you've done is steal the arm of my chair and mistake my profession."

"She's got you there," Stone said. "Anybody need another drink?" He took orders and left.

When he came back, he surprised Sophie and I with thick chocolate milkshakes.

"Oh, this is dangerous," I said, stirring the straw through a dollop of whipped cream. "I hope you thanked Sebastian for us."

"I did."

The conversation had broken into a few groups while Stone was gone. Katie and Mason had found something more agreeable to talk about, and she'd focused solely on him. Sophie had shared her plans with me for everything from prenatal vitamins to nursery decor. Joe and Kyle were talking about a new undersea backbone data cable that would connect Alaska overseas.

As I finished my milkshake, Joe moved my way. He crouched down beside my chair. "We should talk."

"We're heading in now," Stone announced, standing with Sophie.

Kyle came to his feet and stretched. "Me, too. Night, guys."

They all cut through Katie's guest room, and Joe pointed that we should go to mine.

"Got everything you need for tonight?" I asked Katie as I rose.

"I'm good." She started to move, but Mason's hand touched her hip, and she paused.

"See you in the morning," I said, leaving them to their conversation.

It was quiet in my bedroom. It felt intimate after the family dinner and the boisterous balcony conversation. My room was generously sized, with high ceilings, thick carpets, opaque blinds over the wide window, a gas fireplace and a bigger bed than I needed, plus a comfy sitting area.

"How are you doing?" Joe asked, his tone gentle as he moved in front of me.

I half expected him to take my hands in his, but he didn't.

"Fine," I answered. I was fine. I felt a little disoriented, but also like the worst was over.

"You know Braxton and Xavier won't stop pushing us together," he said.

"Did they say something?" I sure didn't want to have to fight the battle all over again tonight.

"Not to me."

"They need to accept reality. I was clear. *You* were clear. Thanks for that, by the way."

"You're welcome."

"I'm not used to someone standing up for me."

"That's because you've always been so independent."

"It's because the group of them, you included, have always wanted the same thing."

He seemed to contemplate my answer. "How old were you when your mom passed away?"

I was jolted by the sudden change in topic. "Twelve, why?"

"I was thinking you've been surviving in the world of men for a long time."

I didn't disagree with that. I remembered my sense of relief when Sophie showed up. I was so excited to have a female cousin, thrilled when she got together with Stone, because I knew that meant she was staying in our lives, my life, for the long term.

"Thank goodness for Sophie," I said.

"Thank goodness."

"Now that I've seen her, I wish I was staying a little longer."

"I can—"

"No, you can't." I put my hands on my hips and took a stance. "You can't use your power to corner my boss."

He looked amused. "I don't see why not."

"Because I'm an independent woman who can take care of herself, remember?"

"Okay."

"Don't you dare touch that phone."

"I won't."

"But speaking of my boss—"

"Hold that thought."

"You don't know what my thought is."

"I can guess. Before we go there…" He looked hesitant.

"What?"

"Can I—" He cast his gaze down to where the back of his hand hovered over my stomach. "Just for a second."

"Yes. Of course." I was touched that he wanted to.

He turned his hand, placing his palm against my abdomen. His palm was warm and tender, and we both stared silently.

"Nothing to feel yet," I finally said, my voice hushed.

"I know it's there. She's there? He's there?"

"We won't know that for quite a while." But the thought of a gender overwhelmed my emotions. I felt staggered and disoriented, and I reached for Joe's arm to steady myself.

"It's sinking in," he said, his hand still cradling my stomach.

"For me it's in waves. I'll get distracted and forget, and then I'll remember and panic." I gave a little laugh. "And then I'll feel happy, which will turn to scared, which will turn to excited. I'm all over the map."

He pulled me into a hug, and it felt wonderful. And then I felt flustered because it felt wonderful.

"You're not alone," he said.

I gently but firmly eased back from his embrace, worried I was letting my emotions cloud my judgment.

"This doesn't change anything," I cautioned him. I didn't want him to get the wrong idea. I didn't want him to think he could use this baby to pull me into a romantic relationship I was certain I didn't want.

"Adeline, it changes everything."

"I mean between you and me."

"So do I."

"Joe."

"Can I say something?"

"No." I could see in his expression and in his posture and

hear it in his tone that he was going to take another run at a potential relationship between us.

"I'm going to say it anyway."

"Then why ask?"

"I don't know."

I braced myself. "Go ahead, but know up front that the answer is no."

"It could be temporary."

I shook my head.

"We could pretend, just for now, let the world know there's a you and me. That way, when the baby comes along, nobody is stunned, nobody is surprised, public opinion doesn't get rattled by something that seems like a secret or an accident or something unsavory."

My hackles rose, and my hand went protectively to my stomach. "This baby is *not* unsavory."

"I know that."

"Then why did you say it?"

"Have you *met* the general public? Because I've met them. They look for unsavory. They feast on unsavory. The more stability you give this baby, the more secure you make his or her future."

I could see what he was doing here. He was worried about his political career. And maybe he was right to be worried about his political career, since some people still judged men who didn't step up and marry the mother of their children. But I wasn't responsible for his political career, and our baby was not going to be some kind of good or bad publicity for his next election.

"We won't tell them," I said staunchly.

"Well, that'll make it worse. Because they will figure it out. They always figure it out eventually. And then you'll come under scrutiny along with me." He was a good orator, a great debater.

I knew I had to step back and regroup. "I'm not giving you a yes."

He smiled a little at that, and I could see the satisfaction in his eyes. "That's not a no."

"You feel like you won this round, don't you?"

He held his arms out as if surrendering. "There are no rounds, Adeline. There's just you and me, and we're both on the same side."

"Go," I said, because I could feel myself wavering.

Somewhere deep down inside I wanted to believe that, wanted to be on the same team as Joe. But I wasn't ready for that yet.

"Okay," he agreed with a nod, but instead of going straight for the door, he paused. "Sleep well." He touched my cheek, then he gently brushed his thumb across my lower lip, leaving a warm tingle in its wake.

And then, he was gone, the bedroom door closing behind him.

Breakfast was always a contrast in our house. My dad and Braxton were served formally in the windowed breakfast room off the back of the kitchen while the rest of us grabbed coffee and whatever yummy baked goods Sebastian and his team had on hand. We downed them in the kitchen—on our feet half the time—before rushing off to school or work. My brothers and I had started the habit as teenagers, and it carried forward to this day.

This morning there were cranberry scones and vanilla-glazed cinnamon buns in baskets on the counter. The scones were still warm, and I split mine open to spread it with butter.

"I'm not saying no to these," Katie said, setting a cinnamon bun on a little plate in front of her.

"Hop up," I told her, pointing to the six high swivel chairs around the central breakfast bar.

"Coffee?" Sophie asked us from where she stood in front of the built-in coffee maker. "Mocha, espresso, latte or, I suppose, coffee?"

"Mocha for me," Katie said.

"Latte," I answered, thinking it was never too early to move into better pregnancy eating habits. Between the dairy in my coffee and the vitamin C in the cranberries, I hoped I was off to a decent start. I took the seat next to Katie.

Stone wandered in and helped himself to a scone.

"Coffee?" Sophie asked him.

"Go sit down," he said. "I've got it."

"Morning," Joe said from behind me.

I felt a warm shiver run up my spine. "Morning."

Sophie slid the mocha across the countertop to Katie.

"Anybody mind if I come and live here?" Katie asked as she popped a morsel of the cinnamon bun into her mouth.

"Plenty of room for everyone," Mason said as he walked in. "Where am I in the coffee lineup?"

"I'm making Adeline a latte," Stone said. "What'll you have?"

"Regular coffee." Mason slid on the seat on the other side of Katie. "I take it you liked the bed?"

"To die for," she said before popping another gooey bite in her mouth.

"Isn't it?" Sophie asked. "That was my room for a while. I don't know where they got that bed, but it's a dream."

"You want a new bed?" Stone asked Sophie.

"No."

"You like the guest bed better?"

"I like our bed just fine," Sophie said, rolling her eyes behind Stone's back.

"Because we can go shopping."

"Adeline?" My dad appeared in the entrance to the breakfast room. "Do you mind joining us for a minute?"

I could tell by the tone of his voice that they were about to pressure me again, and I reflexively looked to Joe. He might be more on their side than mine, but he was the closest thing I had to an ally.

"I'm coming, too," he said, steadying my elbow as I got down off the chair.

"Take this," Stone said, handing me my latte.

"You're a good man," I told him, joking in spite of the nervous flutter in my stomach.

As Katie had pointed out, I could always say no to whatever my dad and uncle asked. But they had a knack for making me feel guilty about it.

"Don't worry," Joe said in an undertone as we walked.

"I'm not worried," I lied. I'd known they wouldn't simply give up after last night, but this was pretty early in the morning for a second round of debate.

"Just give me a signal if you want me to pull you out." His tone made me smile.

"Like touch my nose and tuck my hair behind my ear?"

"That'll work." There was a thread of laughter in his voice, which I appreciated.

I sat down at the round breakfast table for eight with its white tablecloth, bone china and fresh flower arrangement. I took a spot partway around from my dad and Braxton. Then I took a sip of my latte.

"No pressure on her," Joe warned them as he sat down.

Braxton looked affronted. "This isn't about pressure."

"It's about logic and reason," my dad said.

"I have a job," I told them both, deciding to claim power by taking the lead. "It's a good job, and I'm excited about it. It's going to be my focus for the next couple of years."

My dad looked amused. "You don't think a baby's going to divert your focus?"

"I didn't mean that. I meant—" I canted my head toward Joe "—a relationship is not my priority right now."

"How do you know that?" Braxton asked reasonably. "A relationship can be a strength."

"Sure," I agreed. "When it's a real relationship."

My dad continued with the tag-team approach. "There are all kinds of relationships."

"Did you two rehearse this?" I asked.

"Don't deflect," my dad said.

"That's not an answer."

Braxton jumped back in. "We're only wondering if you've thought through the advantages, the numerous advantages of being with Joe."

"Stability," my dad said. "For you—"

"I'm already stable."

He gave me a warning with his narrowed eyes. "—for the baby, for the family."

There it was. "Please tell me you're not embarrassed about having a single mother in the family."

My dad looked genuinely affronted. "Of course not."

"Nobody cares about that," Braxton said.

"You seem to care."

They both shook their heads.

I was more convinced than ever that they'd rehearsed their arguments.

"You know why we've always supported a match between you and Joe," my dad said.

"Supported?" I raised my brows. "Is that what you call it? Don't you meant pushed? Planned? Orchestrated? Demanded?"

"Demanded?" Braxton asked and looked to Xavier. "That's a little strong, I think."

"You can't *will* me into Joe's arms." Everyone went quiet for a second, and I knew what they were all thinking—that I'd leaped eagerly into Joe's arms. "You know what I mean."

"We supported a match," Braxton said, "because of the strength it would bring both families."

My age-old resentment flared to life. "I'm not—"

"Let me finish, Adeline. For example, you said yesterday the senator isn't yet on board with your construction project. You said the governor had pulled his support. Unfortunately for you, the senator is going to support the governor. That's just how it has to work."

They were telling me my project was dead in the water. I hated to hear that, because they were likely right. They were always right about politics. They were crafty and smart, and they had their fingers on the pulse of the state. There was a reason Kodiak Communications had grown so big under their management.

"Adeline," my dad said. "If we were to announce your engagement to Joe—"

I started to object, but my dad kept talking.

"*If* we were to make that announcement and plan ourselves a big, splashy wedding, Senator Scanlon would step back and look at the chessboard."

I decided to bite. "What would the chessboard tell her?"

Joe sat forward. "That I was making a play to run for governor."

Both my dad and Braxton nodded.

"Are you in on this?" I demanded of Joe.

"No. I gave you my best reasons last night."

"She'd just *jump* to that conclusion, would she?" I asked all of them.

"Oh, she would," Braxton said. "We wouldn't have to say another word."

"And you do see her next logical move," my dad said.

Even I could see it. "Senator Scanlon rethinks her position on the arts and culture complex because Governor Harland has a real challenger in the next election."

"She's got it," Braxton said to my dad.

"That's—" I tried to think of the right word.

"Life in the major leagues," Braxton said.

"My reasons all still hold," Joe said to me.

"Marriage doesn't have to be forever," Braxton said.

"But it would sure smooth the way in the short term," my dad added.

"So, an actual wedding. As in, we'd really, truly get married." I couldn't believe I was considering it.

Losing the arts and cultural center would be a blow—both for me and for the citizens of Windward. It wasn't enough on its own to sway me. But Joe had made more sense than I'd been ready to admit last night. We needed to keep our baby, our child, out of the public fray.

"I live in DC most of the time," Joe said to me. "You'll be in Windward. We could easily stay out of each other's way."

I took in my father and uncle, barely accepting what my own sense of logic was telling me. "I can't believe this," I said out loud.

Confusion crossed both of their faces.

"You won," I told them in a quiet voice. "It all makes sense. I should marry Joe."

"Marry Joe?" Katie said with a frown.

"Marry *Joe*?" Sophie said with a wide grin.

"Marry Joe," I repeated, shaking my head.

We were at the horse paddock, and I leaned my elbows on the top rail. I'd needed some air and to get away from the house for a little while. Watching the horses had always been soothing.

"Okay, I *really* missed something," Katie said, the bright sun behind her, shadowing her expression.

"Joe's a great guy," Sophie told her, tucking her own golden-brown hair behind her ears in the light breeze. "I've seen quite a lot of him over the past year, and I really like him." She glanced at me. "Sorry."

"You don't have to take sides," I said. "I like him, too."

"Hello?" Katie glanced back and forth between us. "You cut your *hair* so he wouldn't find you."

Sophie was clearly baffled by the statement. "What does her hair have to do with Joe?"

"It's her disguise," Katie said, gesturing to me as if it was patently obvious.

I looped my fingers around a fence rail and leaned back. Since it hadn't worked, the disguise effort seemed amateurish now. "I was hoping to stay under the radar," I said. "You know, come back to Alaska without people noticing I was here. I figured new hair might help."

Sophie scoffed out a laugh. Then she sobered. "Wait, you're serious. Did it actually work on Joe?"

"Not for five seconds."

"Well, he's been thinking about you for most of the past decade. It'd take major cosmetic surgery or something to throw him off."

"I wore my glasses."

"I still like it, though," Sophie said, reaching out to brush my hair across my forehead. "I'm glad you did something dramatic."

"Back to the marriage?" Katie prompted as a pair of eagles soared past over the treetops. "Last I heard it was *a thousand times no.*"

A horse whinnied in the pasture, and the rest lifted their heads to look.

I tried to explain. "With the baby coming—"

"Have we time-warped here? You don't need to get married just because you're pregnant," Katie said.

"No, I see what she means," Sophie said. "Joe's in the public eye."

"What, deadbeat dad isn't a good look for the campaign?" Katie asked.

"It's not about Joe's political career," Sophie said with conviction. "Is it, Adeline?"

"More *because* of Joe's political career," I admitted.

"I'm not liking him so much anymore," Katie said with a frown.

"A baby's not noteworthy if the parents are together. If they're not, well, somebody's going to make it into a story."

"That is *not* a reason to get married."

"It doesn't have to be forever," I said, watching Splendor, a champagne horse and one of my favorites, walk toward us.

"Don't write Joe off like that," Sophie said.

"I'm going into this with my eyes wide-open," I said. Splendor shook her white mane. "And I get something out of it, too."

"Husbands aren't the prize they used to be," Katie said.

"My dad and Braxton said it'll make the senator think twice about pulling support for the arts and culture complex."

Sophie and Katie were both silent for a moment. A couple other horses followed Splendor.

"You've lost me," Katie said.

"Me, too," Sophie said to me. "Something we agree on here," she said to Katie.

Katie gave a smile.

"The two masters of machination think Senator Scanlon will read the engagement announcement, conclude Joe is going to make a run for governor and think about hedging her bets."

"You *believed* that?" Katie asked incredulously.

"No, it makes sense," Sophie said.

"It does." I was convinced they were right.

The horses grew closer. I wished I had some apples or carrots to share.

"Alaska's a lot like a small town," Sophie told Katie. "Everyone knows everyone. With the Cambridge brothers backing him, Joe would have a real shot at becoming governor."

"And *that's* what this has always been about," I said. "It's just never been in my interest to go along with it."

"So, you'd get the project funding," Katie said.

"If everything goes according to plan."

"Well, I guess I can buy into that as a reason."

"You're a mercenary," Sophie said to her.

"I'm pragmatic." Katie shrugged. "Same thing, I suppose."

Katie had her back to the fence, and I gently moved her forward before Splendor could nudge her shoulder and startle her.

"What?" Katie asked, and I pointed.

She turned and her eyes went round. "Where'd those come from?"

"Can I be a bridesmaid?" Sophie asked, petting Galahad's nose—a friendly chestnut gelding.

"Absolutely," I said. I scratched behind Splendor's ears.

Katie raised her hand and wiggled her fingers in the air. "Oh, me, too."

"Better do it soon." Sophie indicated her stomach. "If you want me to fit into the dress."

"Will the wedding be big and splashy?" Katie asked, looking like she was seriously warming up to the idea.

"I'd prefer the courthouse," I said honestly.

"Oh, no, you don't," Sophie said.

"Did you have a big wedding?" Katie asked, hesitantly moving a little closer to the horses. Benjy and Boomer were eyeing her through the fence, looking for some attention.

"It wasn't big, but it sure wasn't a courthouse thing. It was wonderful, intimate, just what we wanted. But this, *this* calls for something opulent and extravagant." Sophie patted Galahad firmly on the neck. "You're making a statement and sending a message."

Sophie and Stone's moving ceremony on the waterfront had been a joy to attend. But their situation was completely different than mine and Joe's. It occurred to me that opulent and extravagant might cover up the lack of depth in our feelings.

"I agree," I said to Sophie. "Opulent and extravagant is the way to go."

"So, we can help you plan," Katie said, sounding even more enthusiastic.

"You're a sap as well as being a pragmatist?" I asked her.

Sophie gave Katie a conspiratorial look. "Joe's not going to care what we do so long as it hits the Alaskan news."

"Budget?" Katie asked Sophie, her brow rising.

Sophie gave a chopped laugh at that. "Xavier and Braxton will spring for a space shuttle flyby if we ask them."

"I know a couple of people at NASA," Katie said.

"No space shuttle," I insisted, knowing it was a joke but genuinely worried about how big these two might go.

Six

Sophie and Katie had gone big.

I hadn't paid much attention to the wedding planning, because my engagement to Joe had worked exactly as my dad and Braxton predicted. With the senator's support, the next round of funding for the arts and culture complex was approved, contracts were awarded and my on-site office was up and running.

The response from the community was gratifying. We'd hired a second architectural firm, plus engineers and construction companies. Volunteers were eager to stay involved, and we had several advisory committees set up from the arts community, the economic and tourism sectors, and from the city beautification board.

The plans included a performance theater, gallery and exhibition space, a convertible ballroom, classrooms, public spaces, and a top-floor restaurant overlooking the water. The exterior was designed in curves and angles, using natural materials and a color scheme that would blend with the mountains and the ocean.

Multilevel parking would be tucked away at the side of the building, screened by a narrow green space, while the prime outdoor area would be staged and landscaped for performances and festivals. My excitement built by the day, especially now that construction companies were on-site and we were getting ready to pour the foundation.

Sophie and Katie had taken the wedding planning completely off my shoulders. Katie had seen more of my family than me these past weeks. It freed up my time to focus on work and meant I didn't have to dwell on the fact I was marrying Joe. Other than wearing my engagement ring—a beautiful solitaire with a twisted band and diamond chips inset—not much had changed.

But that was going to end this weekend in Anchorage.

Thursday was the final dress fitting. Since Sophie and I were the same size, she'd been the model for the dress, sending me pictures along the way. It was, in a word, spectacular—bright white with drop cap sleeves, a sweetheart neckline, a tight bodice with shimmering beaded lace flowing softly to layers of chiffon in the billowing ball gown skirt, then finished with matching beaded lace along the hem.

Then Friday was the rehearsal dinner, Saturday the ceremony, and I'd been told I was going on a honeymoon to Joe's family ranch on the Kenai Peninsula. They had a beautiful guesthouse on the shore of a small lake where we'd have privacy. I loved the Kenai Peninsula, so I looked forward to the mini vacation, even if I did feel like I was an actor participating in someone else's wedding.

Though I'd tried to slow them down, the days and the events flew by, and in what felt like moments, I was standing in front of the full-length mirror in the bathroom off my bedroom in the mansion, dressed in the gorgeous creation with Sophie's stylist Kari-Anne offering me the choice of a crystal hair comb, a spray of tiny white flowers or a veil.

"I'm not wild about the veil or the flowers," I told her. "Would the comb hold okay with my hair so short? I was thinking at the back."

Kari-Anne looked doubtful. "I can give it a try."

"Ask me now if I miss my hair," I said to Katie. I'd had the auburn roots lightened to match the new color. It had grown out some, but it was still very short.

"Your new hair is really pretty," Sophie said with a tone and enthusiasm obviously intended to placate an anxious bride.

"I was only joking," I assured her.

I wasn't a typical stressed-out bride, worried about having a perfect day. Quite the opposite. In an hour or so, I'd walk down the aisle in this very stately princess dress, with something bride-like on my head, say some temporary vows to Joe, spend a couple of days in woodsy luxury to make the package complete, then get back to my regular life.

"What do you suggest?" I asked Kari-Anne.

"How about this?" She pulled at the wires that held the

crystals, straightening them and shaping the comb into a long, thin line. She anchored it a few inches back from my hairline.

It was a tiara look, which I would never have considered, but it was delicate and subtle against the light blond hair color.

"Oh, yeah," Sophie said as Kari-Anne stood back.

"That's awesome," Katie said.

Their bridesmaid dresses were twilight-blue chiffon with sweetheart necklines, off-the-shoulder straps and flowing skirts. Their bodices were snug, pleated with a front knot. We'd all gone with diamond earrings and pendant necklaces. They both looked terrific. You couldn't even tell Sophie was pregnant.

I smiled at the sight of us all in the mirror.

"We're gorgeous," Katie said.

"You two have done an amazing job," I said.

Sophie rubbed my arm. "You'll do great."

"I suppose you ordered me a big ol' bouquet."

They laughed and exchanged glances, telling me the flowers were going to be as extravagant as the dress.

"Wait till you see it," Sophie said and ducked out of the room.

Kari-Anne followed her.

As soon as they left, Katie's expression sobered. "You're sure about this, right?"

"Not in the least." My answer was flippant.

Who could be sure about something like this? But I was going for it anyway. All day long I'd kept a smile on my face and pushed reality out of my mind, knowing the wheels of fate were churning and I couldn't stop them if I tried.

Katie seemed to see past the facade. "Seriously, Adeline. You're *getting married.*"

"I know. I can tell by the outfit."

"Quit joking around."

"I can't." At this point I was afraid to stop joking.

"It's not too late to back out."

"No," I said firmly. "Well…maybe." Then I shook off the wayward thought. "I made this decision when I was calm and rational. I'm not changing it while I'm panicking."

"Panicking is not a good sign in a bride."

"All brides panic." At least, I thought they must panic, because every wedding was a very big deal. For better or worse, you were hitching your life to someone else's.

My heart began to thump against my chest.

"Sophie?" Katie's tone sounded worried as Sophie came back into the bathroom, the big bouquet in her hand.

She took in our expressions. "What happened? What's going on?"

"You were a bride," Katie said to her. "Did you panic right before the ceremony?"

"No." Sophie looked confused.

Katie nodded her head at me. "Adeline's panicking."

"I'm fine," I said. I just needed to catch my breath.

"Adeline?" Sophie asked with concern, moving closer.

"Let me see the bouquet," I said in a hearty voice, holding out my hand while the room seemed to grow hot. My stomach knotted, and a funny buzzing sound came up in my ears.

"She's white as a ghost," Katie said.

I felt her hand on my arm.

"I'm getting Joe," Sophie announced.

"No!" I managed. I didn't want Joe to see me like this. I just needed a minute to gather my thoughts.

But Sophie left anyway.

"Sit down." Katie steered me to the little bench in front of my vanity counter. "Breathe."

I did. I focused on breathing, telling myself to buck up already, that this was just another step in the grand plan. I was playing a role, dressed in a costume. Joe would play his part. We'd smile, gaze at each other, pretend we were happy, and it would all be over before I knew it.

"Adeline?"

I lifted my gaze to see Joe walk in and Katie slip out of the bathroom.

He was dressed in a crisp, very formal black tux, a white shirt and a silver tie. His hair was finely trimmed, and his face was perfectly shaven.

He crouched beside me. "What's going on?"

"Isn't this bad luck?" I managed.

"The bride passing out before the ceremony is bad luck."

"I'm not passing out."

"Sophie said you turned gray."

"I didn't turn gray."

He took my hand. Then he took my other hand, too. "You're freezing."

"We are in Alaska."

"It's July."

"I'm nervous," I admitted. "Aren't you nervous? There are… Do you know how many people are coming to the wedding?"

"I don't know. Maybe five hundred."

"That's a lot of people." I swallowed. "For us to lie to."

He lifted my hands to his lips and gave them a gentle kiss. "We're not lying to them."

"Misleading, misdirecting." A person could call it whatever they wanted.

"We really are getting married, Adeline."

"Does your family know the truth?" I wondered if we'd have to keep up the facade around his parents and his two sisters.

"They know you're pregnant. They know we weren't dating before it happened. They don't know the whole backstory like yours does, but they know this isn't exactly a normal marriage."

I searched his expression. "Are you having second thoughts?"

"Not a one."

"Why? How can you walk blithely into a sham marriage?"

"Is there a reason we didn't have this conversation before now?"

"No." The answer didn't sound right to my own ears. "I wasn't really thinking about it before." I looked down at myself. "This dress, the hair, the flowers."

"You look very beautiful."

"I look like bad luck."

He gave a half smile. "You know you're sounding a little emotional."

"I think maybe I am a little emotional." I was trying to think straight, but fear and uncertainty were clouding my mind.

He gently touched my chin with his index finger. His finger-tip was warm. His gaze was warm. "We're going to be fine."

"You don't know that."

"I'm going to do everything in my power to make sure we're fine."

I believed him. "Do you generally succeed at things like that?"

"Mostly, yes."

"Well, I mostly fail." Today was the culmination of a cascading series of my failures in life.

"You don't have to change your life for this, Adeline." His gaze lowered to my still-flat stomach. "Well, you know. There is the baby."

He coaxed a smile from me.

"We'll take it one step at a time," he said. "I promise."

"Okay," I said with a little nod. "Okay."

He stood and held out his hand to me.

The knot in my stomach loosened a bit as I reached up to take his sturdy, warm hand. I then rose to my feet.

"You really do look amazing. I hope they take lots of pictures."

"Sophie hired three photographers."

"We can always count on Sophie." He searched my face. "You good?"

"I'm good." I was. At least I was better. The room temperature felt normal again, and the buzzing was gone from inside my ears. I took those as good signs.

I looked down at the oversize, elegant bouquet of cream and blush roses, cradled by succulent greenery and white jasmine, that was resting on the countertop. "You have to wonder what they're going to spring on us for a cake."

"None of that matters." Joe took my hand again and rubbed his thumb over my engagement ring.

"What matters to you?" I wanted to remind myself of why we were doing this.

"Our baby."

"Not your political career?"

"Sure. Your career matters to you, too."

I couldn't deny that. I removed my hand from his. "It does."

"Beauty of this marriage," he said, "is it helps everything."

"That's the beauty of it." I felt like my mind was clear again.

"See you in the church?" he asked.

"See you in the church."

I was relieved to have the vows over and done with. I'd stared at the middle of Joe's forehead the whole time I spoke. His kiss to seal the deal had been quick, and I was prepared for the tingle it left on my lips. I didn't feel married yet, but I expected that would take a little time.

We were through the well-wishes at the church, and the photos in the park were finished as well as the more formal ones taken in the glass room at the Cannery House Pavilion, where the reception was being held. Afterward, I was tired of smiling and putting a blissful light on in my eyes.

Sebastian had presided over a seven-course, sit-down dinner for five hundred people. On top of that, Sophie and Katie had outdone themselves with the cake. It was iced and decorated in pure white with hints of gold and a cluster of fresh Alaskan wildflowers curving partway around the base. It was accompanied by dozens and dozens of gold-dusted lemon buttercream cupcakes set out on multitiered china platters. A great idea, I thought, since cutting five hundred slices of cake would have taken forever.

Hands together on a gold-plated knife, Joe and I made the ceremonial cut.

A waiter was on standby to transfer the first slice to a plate for us.

"You ready?" Joe whispered, putting a small nibble on a fork for me.

I appreciated that he wasn't making a big messy production out of it.

I took the bite and raised the fork, then did the same for him.

He grinned in faux delight, clearly as aware as I was of being the center of attention. He gave me another quick kiss on the lips. This one tingled, too. I wondered if that sensation would ever go away. I also wondered if we'd even do any more kissing. After tonight our obligations would be over and there'd be no more reason for public displays of affection.

Conversation started up, humming through the room as the guests relaxed after dinner and a small army of waiters began distributing cake and cupcakes. Champagne was being offered table to table, and the bar was seeing a fair amount of traffic. People looked like they were having fun, and that made me happy.

Stone had moved along the head table to chat with Sophie, while Mason, Kyle and Katie stood in a conversational group with Joe's sister Elaine.

"Joe." A beautifully dressed young woman pulled up the chair next to Joe. She looked to be about thirty-five, with long black hair and lovely fine features. She was wearing a deep burgundy halter dress in a filmy fabric with an A-line asymmetrical hemline.

"Hi, Charmaine," Joe said. "Adeline, have you met Charmaine Tan? She's my media assistant."

"Nice to meet you, Charmaine." Since I hadn't read the guest list, I had no idea who'd been invited on Joe's side. It made sense he'd invite his political staff.

Charmaine grinned at both of us. "You're trending."

"Trending what?" Joe asked.

"Trending, trending." She held up her phone and waved it back and forth. "They love Adeline. I mean, *love* her."

Joe's hand wrapped around mine. "What's not to love?"

"You should read some of this," she said, holding out her phone with eager enthusiasm.

"Charmaine." Joe glanced meaningfully around. "You do realize we're in the middle of a wedding."

She gave a little chuckle. "Don't I know it. It's demographic gold—eighteen-to thirty-five-year-old women, who are romantics, followed closely by eighteen-to thirty-five-year-old men. Let's face it, Adeline, you're hot."

"Excuse me?" Joe said.

"Don't be naive," Charmaine admonished. She gestured up and down my dress. "I mean, come on."

"It's our wedding," Joe repeated. "Put your phone down and have some cake."

"Not on your life. Numbers like these don't come along every day."

"Are you live-posting our wedding?" I asked.

"Of course," she said, thumb scrolling along her screen. "You walking down the aisle—great bouquet, by the way, and the dress is to die for. The kiss, in the park, entering the reception."

Joe took the phone from her and gaped. "Did we plan this live social media event?"

"What do you mean?" she asked.

"I mean, did the office put together a formal media strategy for my wedding?"

"Not exactly. I'm an opportunist."

Joe didn't look happy. "You should have given Adeline a heads-up."

Charmaine seemed taken aback by the criticism. She looked at me. "You didn't expect people would post pictures? I'm not the only one doing it."

"You're not?" I shouldn't have been shocked, but I was certainly surprised.

"It's not just the official feed that's blowing up. You have a hashtag. Hashtag JoeAdelineBliss, all one word."

I looked blankly at Joe.

Neither of us seemed to know what to say.

"This is fantastic," Charmaine said, excitement and encouragement in her voice. "So, where are you going on your honeymoon?"

"Don't tell them," I quickly said. I didn't think anyone would go to the trouble of following us down the Kenai, but I never imagined my wedding would be livestreamed, either.

Charmaine looked affronted at that. "I won't disclose the information. I want to book a ticket and come along."

"On our *honeymoon*?" Joe asked incredulously.

My feelings echoed his, though not for the usual reasons. I

was bringing along my laptop. I couldn't exactly correspond with the project team while I was on my honeymoon, but I had plenty of detail design work I could move forward on alone. I didn't want to have to pretend it was a regular honeymoon for the benefit of Charmaine or the internet public.

"We need to keep this going," Charmaine said. "It's not like I'm going to cramp your style. Just a few shots at dinner, or in a hot tub, or on a walk along a beach."

"No," Joe said, his voice firm.

I breathed a sigh of relief.

"Did you see this?" Katie arrived beside my shoulder, her phone in her hand. "You two are famous."

"I heard we have a hashtag," I answered.

"More than one."

"The public loves them," Charmaine said to Katie.

"I'm Katie." Katie reached across me to shake Charmaine's hand.

"Charmaine, Joe's media assistant."

"You must be loving this."

"I can't stop calculating the ad value."

Katie grinned at that. "Millions, I bet."

"Millions indeed."

"You're a mercenary," I said to Katie, craning my neck to more easily talk with her. "And Charmaine wants to come on our honeymoon."

"That's a great idea," Katie said.

I gave her a glare.

"What? Isn't positive publicity one of the—" She cut off the question and gave me a meaningful look.

She was right. We were trying to boost Joe's congressional soft power in Alaska.

"I like her," Charmaine said of Katie, her thumbs moving fast over her phone.

Mason came up behind Katie. "We're heading out to the patio bar," he told her. "You thirsty?"

She gave him a bright smile. "Sure. I'll come along. You good?" she asked me.

"You don't think I'll take care of her?" Joe asked.

"You better." She squeezed my shoulder goodbye.

"What do you think about Charmaine's suggestion?" Joe asked me. "About the honeymoon?"

"It wasn't what I planned." I wasn't keen on having an audience while we were meant to be having pretend stolen moments. It wasn't that I expected anything sexy to happen. More that I didn't want us to be forced to spend too much time together looking blissful. I was sure Joe would bring along some work as well.

"She can stay up in the main ranch house."

I knew that would keep her a couple of miles away from us. We'd still have plenty of privacy.

"Sure," I said, giving in for the greater good. Who was I to say no to this golden publicity opportunity?

"Should I check for cameras?" I asked Joe as the bellman left the honeymoon suite at the Blue Bowhead Hotel. We were overnighting in Anchorage, then Stone was flying us down the Kenai Peninsula to the ranch.

"Even Charmaine's not that tenacious," Joe said on a chuckle as the door swung shut behind the man.

"She seemed pretty tenacious to me." I'd changed from my wedding gown to a mottled gold sheath of a cocktail dress, and Charmaine had taken several shots of our formal departure in a limousine. Now, I was anxious to get out of my shoes and put my feet up on something soft.

The hotel suite was the finest in Anchorage—a sprawling living room of sofas and armchairs around a stone-decorated gas fireplace, a round glass dining table with upholstered chairs, a huge whirlpool tub in its own cedar-planked, plant-festooned room with a skylight and about a hundred candles. Through a double doorway, I could see the bedroom was massive, with a four-poster bed, a love seat and tall corner windows.

I took one of the sofas, kicked off my high-heeled shoes and stretched my legs across the opposite cushion. Then I leaned back and closed my eyes.

"You okay?" Joe asked.

"I'm glad it's over," I answered honestly. "My feet are killing me, and I think my smile is going to crack."

"You thirsty?"

I was. I started to rise.

"I'll get it," he said quickly, removing his tux jacket and draping it over a chair. "What do you want?"

"A big ol' lime margarita with a salted rim."

"So, fruit juice," he said, making his way around the breakfast bar to the kitchenette.

"Whatever they've got," I said. "So long as it's liquid."

He brought me back an orange juice and a bottle of water for himself.

"You don't have to go nonalcoholic for me," I said as I opened the little wide-mouthed glass bottle.

"I'm not." He sat down on the opposite sofa.

We both gazed at each other for a minute.

"So…" he said.

"So…" I said back.

"We seem to be married."

I gave a mock toast with my juice. "Mission accomplished." I paused. "I didn't expect the rest of the world to get quite so excited about it."

"Me neither."

"Did we do the right thing?"

"Yes," he answered without hesitation.

Then he rose and ambled over, stripping off his silver tie along the way, unbuttoning the collar of his shirt and flipping the switch that turned on the gas fireplace. He reached down and lifted my feet, sitting then setting them to rest on his lap. "Tell me what you're thinking."

I tried to put my feelings into words, buying time by taking another sip of juice. "I'm wondering what happened along the way."

"Along what way?"

"Growing up. I was always so sure, so confident I knew exactly what I wanted, or at least what I should try to accomplish and what I should avoid. Now this…*this*."

"Not part of your plan, I know."

"I always wanted independence. I didn't like being a Cambridge, didn't want expectations put on me, didn't want my life's path charted before I could even figure out what life was."

"If you know what life is, you're way ahead of everyone else."

"I felt like I was off to the right start in California, down there in school." I took another drink, pondering the shakeup of my girlhood vision and about to launch into another list of complaints. But then I realized I was becoming self-absorbed. "What about you?" I asked instead. "Did you grow up wanting to be in Congress?"

His features relaxed as he set his bottle of water on the side table. The light from the fireplace flames flickered against the planes of his face, and he wrapped a hand around one of my feet. "Can I?"

I startled a little from the unexpected touch. But he began massaging the arch, and I wanted to groan in pleasure.

"Sure," I said. What woman in the world would say no?

"This seems like a married kind of thing to do," he said with a quirky little smile as his fingers dug into my foot in an incredibly gratifying way. He massaged in silence for a moment. "I wanted to make a difference. No, that sounds too altruistic. I wanted to fix things. When I was in eleventh grade, we did a civics project on politics and decision making. It was the first time I thought about who made the rules of society and how those rules change people's lives, hopefully for the better, sometimes for the worse."

"Wanting to change people's lives still sounds very altruistic."

"I wanted things to work logically and reasonably."

"That doesn't sound much like politics to me."

"Turns out it's not." He switched to my other foot.

I had to stifle a groan again and started thinking maybe this married thing wasn't such a bad idea.

"There are intentions and agendas and backroom deals. And everybody needs to reapply for their job every two or four or six years, and they reapply to a very fickle group of voters. So that becomes the focus, unfortunately."

"You think you can do more as governor?"

"In some ways, yes. But I've got plenty of things I still want to do as a congress member."

"I assume Charmaine knows about the governor's run."

He nodded. "Charmaine has done this for a few years now. She's experienced enough to know how a public profile, especially a positive public profile, translates into leverage. She's doing her job."

"On *our* honeymoon." I wasn't sure why I said that. It wasn't like it was a real honeymoon. "I brought my laptop," I added. "I'm assuming you brought some work to do?"

"I know you can't ride horses, but I thought we'd go salmon fishing or whale watching. The charters off the island are world-class."

"You think we should fish?"

"Or we could go hiking if your feet aren't too sore."

I'd barely noticed, but his massage had moved to the back of my calf.

"You want us to spend our honeymoon together?" I asked, trying hard not to focus on the way his strong fingertips loosened my tight muscles.

"You didn't read the instruction manual for this, did you?"

"I guess with Charmaine coming along and everything, we will have to put on a show."

"Adeline." His hand stilled.

I fought my disappointment.

"I like you," he said.

I looked over and met his warm, coffee-dark gaze.

His eyes held mine captive as he switched to my other leg, moving this thumb into a knot just below my knee. "I just plain like you."

I held back a moan of pleasure. "So, you want to hang out."

"Yes. I want to hang out."

My mouth had gone dry, so I sipped some more juice.

His strokes became longer, touching the back of my knee,

warming my skin with friction, sending shimmers of arousal along my thighs and higher still.

I felt myself slouching down, subconsciously easing closer to him, my silky dress riding up, giving him easy access to my bare thighs.

He feathered his fingertips across my goose-bumped skin.

I bit down on my bottom lip, my eyelids dropping closed. I let the desire pass through me, heating my belly, prickling my skin.

"Adeline?" His voice was husky deep.

"Yes?" Mine was breathless.

His hand smoothed higher still, caressing the inside of my thigh.

I sucked in a gasp of anticipation, my body tightening around itself.

But he stoked back down again, to my knee, my calf, my ankle.

I regretted it instantly. "Adeline?" he asked again.

"Yes?"

His hand made its way up.

I squirmed, and he stilled.

I grasped his hand, pulling it higher.

He tugged me his way, sliding my backside over the sofa, sending my skirt to my waist, baring the lacy white panties that had gone with my wedding dress.

He touched their high-cut border.

I watched as he ran his fingertip along the lace, dipping below it, following the curve of my hip, downward, downward.

"Adeline?" His voice rumbled through me.

"Yes?" I didn't expect an answer, but this time he gave me one.

"You maybe want to go have a wedding night?"

I lazily opened my eyes. I didn't want to move an inch. I wanted him to keep doing exactly what he was doing.

There was a dare in his expression—a tease and a dare—and he moved his fingertip another inch.

I stifled a gasp of pleasure. "You mean with sex and everything?"

He leaned down and put a row of featherlight kisses along my thigh. "With sex and everything."

"Oh, yes," I said, and he scooped me into his arms.

I lay back, stretching naked on the cool, smooth sheets of the luxurious bed, and Joe followed me down, smoothing my hair away from my face.

"You are the most beautiful vision I have ever seen," he whispered.

"Don't tell Sophie and Katie."

He gave me a puzzled smile. "Why not?"

"They had me in a fifty-thousand-dollar dress earlier."

"This is better." He stroked a hand lazily over my shoulder, dipping between my breasts.

"Plus a tiara," I said, my breathing speeding up.

His palm moved lower, settling on my stomach, stopping there, cradling me below my navel.

I cast my gaze down. "There's nothing to feel yet." I'd been checking every day, but my stomach hadn't changed a bit.

"The waiting only makes it sweeter," he said, then removed his hand and leaned down to kiss me there.

My heart fluttered and my chest tightened with wayward emotion.

He kissed me again and again, moving across my navel, higher and higher, spreading hot kisses that left cool, damp traces behind.

Desire coiled inside me. I reached out to him, smoothing my hands over his bare shoulders, reveling in his naked, solid strength.

He slowly shifted above me, over me, settling in the vee between my legs. His gaze fixed on mine as he lowered his lips, capturing my mouth, kissing me deeply, enfolding me in his arms.

The power of his kisses flowed through me. I inhaled the fresh scent of his hair, molding myself against him, wrapping my body around him, savoring every touch, every taste, every scent, anticipating the glorious moment we'd become one.

My hips reflexively arched, but I could feel his hesitation. "I don't want to hurt—"

"You won't," I said, pulling him to me.

"Tell me if—"

"You won't," I repeated.

I kissed him deeply, and his moan vibrated against my lips.

As he pressed inside, his hands began to roam. Desire overtook my senses. Our rhythm increased, sweat slickening our bodies, and passion lifted us higher and higher.

I cried out his name as the crescendo engulfed me.

He groaned and shuddered, his weight coming down to press me into the soft bed.

"Adeline," he whispered in my ear, his fingers tangling in my hairline. He kissed my swollen lips. Then he kissed them again.

He slowly rolled to his back, bringing me on top of him.

I lifted my head to focus.

His chest moving up and down, he tucked my hair behind my ears. "Do you still think we're scratching an itch?" He parroted my earlier words.

"I feel pretty scratched."

His expression faltered.

"In a good way," I quickly added, resting my head on his shoulder. "In a very good way."

He was silent for a while, our breathing gradually slowing in the silent room.

His hands were light on my bare back. His heart beat against mine as I rose and fell with his breaths.

"Did you eat at the wedding?" he asked in a soft voice.

"Not much," I said. I glanced at the bedside clock. It was well after midnight.

"I'm starving," he said. "How about you?"

"Hungry." I was hungrier than usual these days, that was for sure.

"Pizza and milkshakes?"

"I'm in. Can we get Hawaiian?"

"Anything you want." He gave me a kiss on the hairline. "But you have to move so I can call down."

While Joe made the call, I wrapped myself in a hotel robe and wandered back into the living room. I looked at my phone and saw my messages were stacking up. Friends and acquaintances, some people I'd barely met in college and high school, plus a huge number of students from classes where I'd been a teaching assistant, were all writing to congratulate me on getting married.

Curling up in an armchair, I scrolled through, skimming most of the messages as more arrived. I switched to email and found the same thing. I would have bet that I didn't even know this many people. And I didn't. But for some reason they all felt like they knew me.

"Something wrong?" Joe asked as he joined me, wrapped like I was in a fluffy white robe.

"There are hundreds of them," I said, reading as I scrolled: congratulations, best wishes, I'd love to call you, I'd love to hear from you and I'd love to make you a job offer. "This is wild."

He came around beside me.

"Emails, texts." I held up my phone so he could see. "It's not just social media chatter. I'm getting job offers."

"Anything good?" he asked with a little smile. He didn't seem to think it unusual.

"Nothing specific. Do you get this sort of thing all the time?"

"Not that many messages, not all at once." He moved to the twin chair next to mine and sat down.

"Check yours," I said.

He reached for his phone and brought up a screen.

"What are people saying to you?" I asked him.

"That I'm a lucky man."

I rolled my eyes in his direction. "No, seriously."

"Lots of congratulations, compliments to you, your dress—"

"It was a great dress."

"Asking for media interviews." He scrolled a little farther. "Uh, no."

"Uh, no what?"

"No, I'm not doing an interview on my honeymoon."

"Not even with Charmaine."

"Charmaine won't ask questions. She'll just take pictures. Here's one from her."

"Charmaine is writing to you at one thirty in the morning?" And I thought I had a dedicated team.

"She sent it earlier." He kept reading.

"Is it important?" It must be important. Charmaine would know what was important and what wasn't. I liked her from the start.

"There's a thing," he said.

"A bad thing?" I asked.

"A work thing." He seemed to hesitate. "There's a retreat near Charleston, South Carolina, the Select Committee on Regulatory Reform."

"That sounds fun." The sarcasm in my tone was pretty clear.

A knock on the suite door interrupted my joke.

"You'd be surprised," Joe said as he went to answer.

A waiter wheeled in a large, silver-covered platter and two tall vanilla milkshakes decorated with whipped cream.

The aroma was enticing, and my stomach gently rumbled in appreciation as Joe tipped the man and sent him on his way.

Not standing on ceremony, I rose and removed the silver cover and helped myself to one of the milkshakes. The aromas of ham, pineapple, cheese and the tender-looking crust were enticing.

Joe separated the plates from the cloth napkins and silverware. "You'd be surprised."

"About?" As far as I could see, we had exactly what we'd ordered. Using a serving knife, I transferred a slice of pizza to my plate.

"The Committee on Regulatory Reform."

"I don't think it would surprise me."

"It is exciting. At least I think it's exciting. Or maybe *satisfying* is the right word. Their work will change how all the other committees are managed going forward. We have the power to streamline everything from the passage of bills to the allocation of money to emergency response."

I sat back down in the armchair with my pizza. "I'm not really feeling the excitement."

He set his pizza and milkshake down on the coffee table, freeing his hands, clearly intending to use them to further illustrate his points. "How about this?"

I took a bite and settled in.

"It's a social occasion as well. Meetings during the day, but a pool, a beach, cocktails, a little sightseeing and dinner."

"That helps, I guess." I didn't know why he cared what I thought. I wasn't going to any great lengths to convince him that moving the theater ten degrees east was a stronger choice for the building silhouette for the arts and culture center.

"Charmaine thinks you should come."

I swallowed. "What?"

"I've received congratulations from every member of the committee. They all want to meet you. Charleston would be the perfect opportunity. It's not for two weeks."

My heart sank just a little. "I have work."

Joe nodded. "I know."

"I can't just up and leave the team for beachside cocktails in Charleston." I would have hoped he'd already understand that.

"It's only a couple of days."

"Plus travel time, that's four days. That's the better part of a week." I resented having to justify it.

He picked up his pizza and nodded, but I could see the disappointment in his expression.

"Joe."

"It's fine," he said.

"It can't be like this."

He looked my way. "Like what?"

"Like we're a traditional married couple—like I'm a political spouse who drops everything to attend functions with you."

It took him a minute to answer. "Nobody suggested you were that."

But he just had.

Seven

The honeymoon went off without a hitch. Charmaine respected our privacy but got several great publicity shots—the two of us enjoying a romantic balcony dinner, dancing under the midnight sun, and Joe on horseback, looking like a sexy rugged cowboy, with me perched on the corral fence watching. He'd gone out on a ride with his father then, giving me some time alone to dive into my work.

We tiptoed around each other for the most part. He didn't press me on coming to DC, and we didn't make love again. I was glad about both those things. After the unexpected wedding night, I felt like the honeymoon had set the right tone for our marriage.

Afterward, Joe stayed busy in Congress, while I pushed forward on the arts and cultural complex. We'd agreed to announce my pregnancy at three months. The calendar had clicked over, and I was beginning to wonder when the baby would start showing. I'd shared my curiosity with my doctor, and she'd told me I'd be growing out of my clothes soon enough and not to wish my trim waist away.

I was in the trailer office at the job site today, dressed in blue jeans and a navy cotton shirt over a pink tank top with a pair of steel-toed boots. My hair was getting back to its normal color and long enough now to be pulled back in a ponytail. I had a high-vis vest and an orange hard hat hanging on the wall in case I was needed out on the job site.

With the construction plans finished and finally approved, we'd doubled up on the crew size to get the foundation poured and the framing done before winter closed in on us. Concrete trucks came and went along the access road outside. Generators hummed, and clanking echoed from the two cranes setting up on the far side of the site. The days were still plenty long, so we had two full shifts, making the job roll out even faster.

My phone rang—a DC number, but not Joe or anyone in my contact list. I felt a brief shot of concern and quickly picked up. "Hello?"

"Adeline?" It was a woman's voice, one I vaguely recognized.

"It's me," I answered.

"It's Charmaine from Congressman Breckenridge's—I mean, Joe's office. Sorry, habit. I hope I haven't caught you at a bad time."

"No, it's fine. Is everything okay?"

"Good. Yes, all good here. I'm about to shoot you our official announcement on the baby. Congratulations, by the way. Joe wanted me to run it past you before we posted it. The photo is from the honeymoon, that late shot on the wharf in front of the lake. I really like the silhouettes and orange clouds in the background. Do you mind taking a look?"

"Sure. No problem." It was hard not to appreciate Joe's consideration in asking for my final approval.

"Great. Sent. You should get it any second." She paused. "While I've got you on the line…"

I could hear the hesitation in her voice. "Yes?"

"I know you weren't available for the Charleston event, and I understand. Joe's told us all how busy you are on the construction project. But I wondered if next Saturday might be even a remote possibility for you? It's the regulatory reform committee again. They're hosting a who's who mix-and-mingle event. Joe probably mentioned it already—the rumblings of offering him the chair?"

"Yes. Of course." I was bluffing. I had no idea what she meant.

"I probably don't have to tell you that he'd be the first Alaskan, the first Westerner and the youngest member to actually chair that committee. It's a pretty huge deal."

Joe hadn't said anything to me about becoming chair of anything. Then again, he didn't talk much about his job. We didn't talk all that much about anything, really, except to confirm all was well with the pregnancy.

"I know he ignores gossip," Charmaine continued. "And you probably do, too."

"Gossip?" I asked.

"Oh, nothing new. Just…you know…the stuff about you being in Alaska all the time and him being here. The baby announcement will—"

"Who's gossiping?" I couldn't help but ask.

"Nobody important."

Gerard, the head engineer, opened the office door, letting in the construction noise.

I gave him a five-minute hand signal, so he nodded and left.

"What's that?" Charmaine asked, obviously hearing the noise.

"Mostly diesel engines. I'm at the job site."

"Oh, I *am* disturbing you."

"What's the gist of it?" I asked. "The gossip, I mean. The latest," I added so she wouldn't guess that I didn't have the slightest knowledge of any news.

"Same old, same old—what does it mean that they spend so little time together. I *know* you're both busy, and that's our stock answer, but—" She stopped abruptly, seeming to think better of continuing.

"Go ahead," I said. "Please."

"You know what people are like, especially in this town, always looking to stir up trouble, especially the congressman's enemies."

"Joe has enemies?"

"*Everyone* in DC has enemies. Mostly people who are jealous. Every little notch of success and you pick up hundreds more. It's the way it works, the way it's always worked."

Listening, I couldn't help but feel guilty. I didn't intend to be a prop in Joe's political life, but I didn't want to cause him harm, either. The marriage had worked out well for my career so far, bringing the senator on board as my dad and uncle had predicted and catapulting our fund-raising efforts beyond our wildest hopes. It seemed like Joe deserved to get something out of it, too.

"Would it help if I came to the event on Saturday?" I was guessing that was why she'd asked.

I assumed attending the event would involve hanging on his arm, gazing adoringly into his eyes and laughing at every one of his jokes. Not that I ever had trouble laughing at Joe's jokes. He had a great sense of humor.

"Enormously. Could you do it?"

"I can try." I wasn't certain I could get away. It would be a stretch.

"Joe will be thrilled," she said.

"Can you hold off on telling him?"

My words were met with silence.

"Let's wait to see if I can get the time off. I don't want to make him a promise I can't keep."

At the very last minute, I'd managed to get away. There wasn't time to book a private jet, so I'd rushed to catch a red-eye out of Anchorage, thinking I'd call Joe in the air. But we were delayed taking off, then the in-flight Wi-Fi was malfunctioning.

Although my seat fully reclined, anticipation of seeing Joe had kept me awake. A dozen scenarios ran through my mind—him surprised, happy, annoyed, aloof. I didn't sleep at all on the plane.

When we finally landed at Ronald Reagan, my luggage was missing. And by the time I'd filled out all the forms in the wee hours of the morning, I was a zombie. I grabbed myself a hotel room near the airport and crashed for the next eight hours. Then I awoke to a dead phone battery with the charger packed away in my lost luggage.

The dead address book was down the list of my immediate worries. Time was running out, and without my suitcase, I needed to buy myself a new dress, pick up something in the way of formal jewelry, plus find a good cosmetologist who could work fast, since my makeup bag was missing along with everything else. On the upside, I'd ended up in a very service-oriented hotel, and the staff stepped up to help me with everything, including a rack of lovely dresses from the shop for me to choose from.

A stylist at the hotel's salon took one look at my part-blond, part-auburn hair and declared it a disaster area. When he found out I was attending a congressional event, he called over two assistants and they worked a miracle, matching the auburn tone and adding volume to create a pretty updo.

With my makeup professionally applied and me running only fifteen minutes late, with a still-dead phone in my new evening bag, the limo stopped in front of the event ballroom. The driver insisted on escorting me to the door.

"Your name, please, ma'am?" the doorman asked, tablet in his hand.

"Adeline Cambridge," I answered, trying unsuccessfully to peer at his list. "But I might not be on your—"

"Do you have an invitation, ma'am?"

"I'm a plus-one." I guessed that was the simplest way to put it.

"I'm afraid guests are also required to be preregistered. It's for security reasons."

I was impressed that the limo driver stood by waiting while I tried to talk my way in.

"Is there someone I can speak to?" I asked. "Maybe a manager who could vouch for—"

"We're not able to make exceptions, I'm afraid."

Another security guard moved to stand beside the first, likely because he was curious about the line forming behind me.

"Can I help with something?" the second man asked.

"Sir, I'm afraid Ms. Cambridge is not on the list."

The new, apparently higher-ranking security guard looked me over.

I couldn't imagine there was anything to make him suspicious. I knew I looked good all dressed up, exactly like the kind of guest they would expect at the high-end event. Still, his brow furrowed, like he thought my dress might be a knock-off or something.

"Is it possible to call Charmaine Tan?" I asked, thinking

there had to be a straightforward way to clear this up. "She works for Congressman Breckenridge."

"All guests are required to have prior security clearance," he repeated.

I didn't want to do it, but I could see I had no choice. "What about Congressman Breckenridge? Could he clear me to come in?"

The man's lips thinned now. Clearly, he wasn't about to bother a congressman over a woman he thought was trying to crash the party.

I leaned in closer, and both men tensed, obviously ready for anything.

But all I wanted to do was lower my voice. "I'm *Mrs.* Congressman Breckenridge."

The first man paused at that. They looked at each other, obviously gauging my honesty.

"It has to be pretty easy to prove one way or the other," I offered.

"Wait right here, ma'am," the higher-ranking one said.

"Can you step to one side?" the original guard asked me, though his tone was more polite now. He obviously thought there was at least an outside chance I was who I said I was.

"Of course." I didn't want to hold anyone else up.

The driver moved with me.

"Thanks for waiting," I told him.

"Not a problem. I'm guessing you really are her."

"I am."

"You mind if I tell this story back at the garage?"

"Sure." I gave him a grin. I couldn't see the harm. Everyone had only been doing their jobs, and quite professionally.

A few minutes later, Joe appeared, walking at a brisk pace. He spotted me and practically elbowed his way past the security guard.

"Adeline?" He was clearly shocked to see me there.

I was surprised Charmaine had kept quiet all the way to now, not that I'd confirmed I was coming. Up to the last minute, I'd thought I wouldn't make it.

"Happy ending," the driver muttered to me in an undertone.

"Thanks for your help," I told him.

"Enjoy your evening." He stepped back.

Joe pulled me into a hug, and a few cameras flashed in my peripheral vision. I realized I was going to have to get used to that.

Aware of the people around us, I gave him a brilliant smile. "Sorry I'm late, darling. There was a flight delay out of Anchorage." I expected that sounded reasonable for anyone overhearing.

"No problem," he said, also smiling for the cameras as he put an arm around my waist and guided me toward the entrance.

Nobody stopped us this time, and in minutes we were in a calm entry hall outside the main ballroom.

"Why didn't you *call* me?" he asked.

"Some things went wrong. Lots of things went wrong."

"How did you know to come here?"

"Charmaine. I didn't think I could make it, so we didn't say anything to you. And then the flight was late, and I was desperate to sleep, but my phone died, and they lost my luggage, so I couldn't recharge the thing. And, wow, making up for lost luggage takes a lot of time."

"Charmaine *knew*?" There was frustration in his tone as we passed a few curious-looking people.

"Look happy," I warned him, looking happy myself.

His brow furrowed, and he gave a little shake of his head.

"The gossip. Look happy. We're blissfully newlywed, remember?"

My words seemed to penetrate, because he quickly smoothed out his expression and put on a smile.

An older couple spotted him and diverted across the lobby to approach us. "Congratulations on the baby, Breckenridge." The gray-haired man heartily shook Joe's hand.

"Thank you, Mr. Renfrew."

"Call me Seth. Call me Seth."

"Thank you, Seth. This is my wife, Adeline."

Mrs. Renfrew stepped closer to me. "I recognize you from

your pictures. Congratulations, dear." The older woman was neatly coiffed and beautifully dressed in flowing black silk.

"Thank you, ma'am."

"Please, call me Maisie. I've been wanting to meet you since the wedding."

"The Renfrews are major patrons of the Bernadette Theater Organization," Joe said.

"That's a very worthy cause," I said, knowing a little bit about the work the organization did with youth performers.

"We have six children of our own," she said.

My eyes went wide. "Six?"

"And seven grandchildren," Seth added.

"We got a little carried away," Maisie said to me. Her tone turned conspiratorial, and she leaned in close. "Optimally, I'd recommend two, maybe three."

"I think I'll take your advice," I said back.

"It was great to see you both," Joe said to them, shaking Seth's hand one more time. "Please, enjoy the evening."

I could see out of the corner of my eye another couple waiting to talk to Joe. They were younger and expressed the same congratulations on the baby, and Joe told me they were involved in grizzly bear habitat remediation. The woman was excited to learn I'd once encountered a grizzly in the wild.

They were followed by a group of five, then another couple, then a young man on his own. I started to lose track as we slowly inched our way toward the ballroom.

"Is it always like this?" I asked Joe when we finally made it through a set of double doors. My jaw was already sore from smiling and talking.

"That was more attention than usual," he said, drawing back to take in my outfit. It was a full-length champagne satin dress, strapless with a straight neckline and a beaded bodice, dangling crystal earrings, and a matching necklace, and new, twinkling, barely there heeled sandals that I'd decided I loved.

"Your hair looks fantastic," he said.

"They added some volume." I gingerly touched the back of my neck. I couldn't take credit for growing out that much in only a few weeks.

I looked around the elaborately decorated ballroom festooned with white linen tablecloths and chair coverings, fine crystal, tall fresh flower centerpieces, and a beautifully draped stage. I saw gazes begin stopping on us. For a moment I felt like a bride again, the center of attention. Then I felt like a gazelle on the Serengeti as a few people eased their way closer, casually, like they didn't want to spook us.

I moved closer to Joe and took his hand. "They're all staring," I mumbled.

"They're looking at you."

"That's what makes me nervous."

He tipped his head close to talk privately. "Nervous? Are you kidding? I just heard you stared down a grizzly."

"My brothers were with me. Mason had a twelve-gauge."

He gave my hand a little squeeze. "Well, now you have me."

"Are you armed?"

"Only with my wit and charm. Hello, Judge Palomino."

The chitchat and introductions started all over again until we finally made it to our assigned table with three other congress members, one man and two women, along with their spouses.

"You made it," Charmaine whispered in my ear from behind, her hand coming down on my shoulder.

Joe turned and gave her a look that said he was displeased.

Charmaine caught the look, and her expression faltered before she turned her attention back to me. "I've been calling and calling."

"I'm sorry," I told her. "My phone died last night, and the charger is lost somewhere in the bowels of the airline's luggage storage. Or maybe it's on its way to London by now. I didn't have your number, and I had to buy a new dress and—"

"It's *not* a problem," Charmaine quickly said.

"And I was the last to know because…?" Joe asked, his voice low as well.

"That was my fault," I said.

Joe looked back and forth between us. "So that's how it's going to be?"

"It's not going to be anything," I said. "I asked her not to tell you because I didn't think I'd make it. Simple as that."

"You're blowing up the internet again," Charmaine said, clearly not seriously bothered by Joe's criticism. She held out her phone for us to look.

"Can you charge Adeline's phone?" Joe asked Charmaine.

"Right away."

"Can you do that here?" I asked her.

"The hotel will have charging stations in their business center. I'll take care of it. I'm hearing from the Sunday shows," she said to Joe as I gratefully got out my phone.

"Local?" he asked.

"Yes, but also New York."

"The big ones?"

"Simone Sackett wants you on live. Nothing hard-hitting, just a human angle."

I handed Charmaine my phone. "That's a good thing, right?" I knew the Simone Sackett show. It was highly popular, carried nationally on Sunday mornings and often excerpted later by the networks.

"What do you think?" Joe asked me.

"Whatever you want." I didn't see that it had much to do with me.

"So, you'll *do* it?" Charmaine asked me.

I took in their surprised expressions. "What, *me*?"

"Both of you," she said. "Oh, wow, she'll be my best friend all month."

"Wait," I said sharply, then realized I'd attracted attention from the others at the table. I lowered my voice. "I thought you meant Joe."

"Nobody wants to book me on a Sunday show," he said.

"You're the draw," Charmaine told me. "It'll be easy, straightforward everyday things, like *when's the baby due?*" She took in my stricken expression. "If you want to be vague about it, you say something along the lines of *late spring*, or *early summer*, and then you pivot by saying, *and we're really excited to decorate the nursery.* I guarantee you the next question will be about the nursery."

"I—" The idea of live television was beyond daunting.

"If you get really stuck, you can always change the subject entirely by saying something like, *the important thing to remember is thousands of children benefit across the nation from the new preschool program.*"

I couldn't see myself doing that.

Joe took my hands in his. "How about this? If you get stuck on anything, anything at all, just touch your nose and tuck your hair behind your ear."

I couldn't help but smile, remembering it had been my signal at breakfast with Braxton and my father.

"That'll be his signal," Charmaine said.

"I'll start talking and you won't have to say a word." Joe's words were reassuring.

"Do you want this?" I asked him. I was still feeling like I'd benefited more than him from our partnership.

"*Yes,*" Charmaine said eagerly.

"Only if you're comfortable," Joe said.

"Okay," I said, taking a bracing breath. I could be the good wife for another day.

Charmaine had somehow magically sent three different outfits to Joe's condo, all in my size. But it was near midnight when we arrived, so I decided I'd figure out what to wear in the morning.

"This is really nice," I said, taking in his long living and dining room, the view through the kitchen doorway and the stairway the went up from the entryway to the second floor.

He paused next to a big corner sofa and two matching armchairs that faced a brick fireplace. "You can't be all that impressed. I've seen your house."

"That's not my house. It's my family's house."

"Yours as much as theirs." An odd expression crossed his face. "You think maybe we should have written a prenup?"

It was the first I'd thought of it, but I had a hard time taking the idea seriously. "Why? Are you after my house?"

"So, *now* it's your house?"

"A court might see it as partly mine. You know, for the purposes of your settlement." I strode a little way into the room and ran my fingertips across a marble sculpture. "You've got some pretty nice stuff here yourself, Congressman Breckenridge."

"Shopping?" he asked.

"Maybe."

"Your family's worth quite a bit more than mine."

I gave a shrug. "Maybe. But I could use a few Black Angus cattle."

He smiled at that. "Why didn't you ask for a prenup?"

"Why didn't you? Seriously, Joe, if things didn't end well, you don't think Xavier and Braxton would take you down?"

Joe chuckled. "They would." He let the subject drop and glanced at the stairs. "I've got a guest room up there. It's my office, but if I move a few things, I can pull out the sofa bed for myself."

That sounded complicated and time-consuming, especially considering we had a morning flight to Manhattan. "What time do we have to get up?"

"Five should do it."

"Let's just crash in your bed." It wasn't like we'd never shared one before.

"You okay with that?"

"We are married."

He gave a roguish grin. "We are."

"I meant for sleeping," I said. *"Sleeping."*

"Upstairs." He pointed. "First door at the top. En suite's all yours. I can use the bathroom at the end of the hall."

Talking about bed made me realize I was really tired. I started for the stairs, and he followed me up.

"Do you have some pajamas I can borrow?" I asked as we entered his spacious bedroom. "Just the top would work."

He paused. "I was, uh, going to go with boxers."

"You don't own pajamas?"

He shook his head. "Shirt? T-shirt, dress shirt? Help yourself to whatever you want." He gestured to a wide walnut dresser and a walk-in closet door.

He left me to it, and I hesitated, feeling like I was invading his privacy, but curious all the same. Like the rest of the condo, his bedroom was nicely laid out, with a king-size bed and two small armchairs set out in a bay window. It was done in grays and blues with a pale wood parquet flooring and a large, framed oil painting of his ranch house above the bed.

I'd really liked it on the Breckenridge ranch, and I wondered if I'd ever get a chance to go back. I hadn't wanted to ride a horse while I was newly pregnant, but I liked riding, and the Kenai Peninsula was one of the most ruggedly beautiful places on earth. I could picture the two of us on a cliff-side trail overlooking the waves of the ocean.

It would be three of us by then, I realized. I put my hand on my flat stomach and tried to imagine it growing round. It felt a little harder than usual, but otherwise, there was no change. I told myself to take my doctor's advice and stop feeling impatient.

I hesitated over opening Joe's dresser drawers. I didn't know what I expected to find, but I couldn't bring myself to rummage around in them.

I went to the closet instead, finding a row of pressed shirts, mostly white. I helped myself to one then headed for the en suite bathroom, closing the door behind me. Alongside his shaving kit I found liquid soap and a stack of fresh washcloths. Towels were stacked beneath the counter, with two big bath sheets hanging next to a walk-in shower.

After washing my face and removing my contacts, I went to work on my hair, pulling out the fasteners and combing it free. It felt very good to shake it loose. It also felt good to step out of my shoes. They were beautiful but hard on the feet by the end of the evening. I stripped down and buttoned myself into Joe's shirt. It smelled faintly of his earthy soap brand, and I held the fabric to my nose for a moment. Then I rolled up the sleeves, put my glasses on, folded my clothes into a stack and carried them back into the bedroom.

Joe was sitting up in the bed, chest bare, covers at his waist, his tablet on his lap. The shadow of his beard looked sexy across his square chin in the soft lamplight. He watched me walk to the opposite side of the bed. "You sure don't make this easy, Mrs. Breckenridge."

"Mrs. Breckenridge?" I asked on a laugh as I lifted the corner of the covers.

His tone was husky. "The very sexy Mrs. Breckenridge."

"Oh, no, you don't," I said, tempting though it was to slide into his arms—unnervingly tempting. "We have about five hours before your alarm goes off. You did set an alarm, right?"

"All set," he said as I swung my legs under the covers. "They might call you Mrs. Breckenridge tomorrow. Will it bother you?"

"I'll be more bothered by invasive questions about my personal life." I got settled on the comfortable bed and smoothed the covers. Deciding two pillows were too many, I tossed one onto an armchair.

"Do you think we should get our stories straight?" he asked.

"I was planning to stick to the truth. Well, except for the pregnancy timing. That's nobody else's business."

"How did we meet?" he asked.

I turned my head to look at him, gauging if he was joking. It didn't look like he was joking.

"The Kodiak Communications family picnic," I said.

He looked puzzled. "We did?"

"I was eleven, and you were heading off to Harvard. You won the obstacle course *and* the one-mile run. Mason was ticked off. He said it wasn't fair that you were so smart and so athletic."

"You were just a kid."

"I remember thinking you were funny. You did a backflip at the end of the obstacle course and still had the fastest time."

"Sounds like I was a show-off and you were in braces. We have to come up with a better story than that."

I smiled, because I *had* worn braces back then. "When do you remember us first meeting?"

"In your backyard, the first Saturday evening in June after your first year at Cal State, somewhere around eight o'clock. I was senior adviser to Governor Walmsley and trying to get your uncle's support for his reelection. You were tanned, wearing faded cutoffs, a cropped white T-shirt and a pair of white canvas sneakers, and I was thinking your dad should have had me arrested for where my mind was going."

I gave a little laugh, thinking it had to be a joke. He couldn't possibly remember what I'd been wearing one summer eight years ago.

"I was drinking twenty-one-year-old McIsaac when Braxton called you over and introduced you."

"I don't remember." I'd met a lot of people in suits during those years, many coming by the house to talk business with my dad and Braxton.

"That's okay. I wasn't trying to make an impression. I was trying to keep my hormones under control. You were gorgeous then...still are." His gaze took in my makeshift nightgown and heated in a way that I recognized. "And you look way too good in my shirt."

I swallowed, dampening down my own hormones. "Are we going with that, then?"

"That I lusted after you when you were nineteen? I don't think so."

"How about you were a longtime friend of the family, and neither of us remembers the exact moment we met, but it was likely at a business event in Anchorage?"

"Boring," he said.

"You want to come up with an interesting lie? I think we're better off sticking as close as we can to the truth. You know, within reason. Vague, like Charmaine suggested."

"Let's say we met at a Kodiak Communications corporate function and pretend we remember which one."

"Are you sure we should be winging this?" Now I was worried we hadn't planned enough in advance.

A live television interview seemed overwhelming at the moment. I stifled a yawn. Then again, the pregnancy had me more tired than usual. Maybe I only needed some sleep.

He smiled sympathetically. "We'll be fine. Just remember—" He tucked my hair behind my ear. "The secret signal."

"I will." That much I could do. I took off my glasses and snuggled down under the covers, determined to get some sleep.

I'd do a whole lot better tomorrow if my brain wasn't sleep-deprived.

What felt like ten seconds later, Joe's alarm was chiming, waking me out of a toasty, warm sleep.

I shifted and instantly realized his arms were wrapped around me. My back was pressed snugly against him, his face burrowed in the crook of my neck, trapping my hair.

He inhaled. "Morning."

"Uh…" I wasn't exactly embarrassed—well, embarrassed to like it so much, and embarrassed to want to turn in his arms and to kiss him and see where that led.

But he pulled away before I could do anything. "You want breakfast? Coffee before we head to the airport?"

"A shower," I said, pulling myself together. If I was going to be on live television, my priority was a wake-up shower and a hair wash.

Simone Sacket's questions started off easily enough, where we'd each grown up and thoughts about Alaska.

Then, sure enough, she asked how we'd met.

Joe took the question, smoothly answering what we'd discussed about a corporate function.

But then she turned to me.

"How did that work later?" Simone asked. "You spent a lot of time in California, and Joe was in DC. How did you get together?"

"Well…" I stumbled a little and gave a chuckle. "Alaska is a very big state, geographically. But in many ways it's also very small. You get to know the people here." I took a breath, wondering where to go with this line of talking.

I almost gave in and did the nose touch and tuck my hair behind my ear signal. But then I met the warmth of Joe's gaze, and my mind flew back to our dinner and dessert and that first night we spent together.

I relaxed and couldn't help a small smile.

He smiled back.

"We hadn't seen each other for a while." I stuck to the truth. "And when we did, something clicked." I took another breath.

"It just clicked, and we knew it was more than a friendship. What we were feeling went way beyond our family's relationship."

Joe's gaze warmed further and his eyes softened on me, and it felt like the rest of the world disappeared.

Simone cleared her throat. "Well... I guess we can all appreciate a story like that. Thanks to you both for coming in today."

Joe finally broke our gaze, looking to Simone. "We were delighted to be here. Thank you for having us."

As the sound tech unclipped our microphones, and we slid from our high stools, Joe took my hand.

Charmaine, who had watched from the wings of the studio, was like a puppy full of energy and eagerness, telling us that social media was blowing up again. She swore they couldn't get enough of us, that we were an Alaskan royal couple—fresh young faces taking the lower forty-eight by storm.

I took her enthusiasm with a grain of salt. I knew she was paid to ramp up the excitement around Joe. But then Joe's phone rang, and he checked the screen.

"It's Bellamy," he said as we headed down a back hallway of the studio building toward the exit.

Charmaine's eyes got very round, and even I knew Joe had to be referring to House Leader Jerome Bellamy.

"Nice to hear from you, sir," Joe said as we all paused.

I looked up and down the hallway, wondering if this was a crisis and wondering if it was supposed to be confidential. There was no one in the hallway but us.

I pointed and whispered to Charmaine. "Should we get out of his way?"

She looked surprised by the question and shook her head. Clearly, she was intent on listening in.

"I appreciate that," Joe said into the phone. "Yes, we did." He didn't look shocked or concerned, so I concluded it wasn't a disaster or an emergency. "Absolutely," he said.

Charmaine and I looked at each other. It was clear neither of us had the slightest idea of what the conversation was about.

"Thank you," Joe said. "See you then."

Charmaine broke a grin and nudged me on the arm. By

BARBARA DUNLOP   135

the sparkle in her eyes, I gathered *see you then* was a sign of something good.

"You're meeting with him?" she asked as Joe pocketed his phone.

"Dinner," Joe said, and Charmaine squealed.

"He's not going to do that unless—"

"Let's not get ahead of ourselves," Joe said.

"Unless what?" I asked, curious.

Charmaine grasped my shoulder. "Joe's in the running for committee chair. He's *really* in the running now."

Joe slid a guilty look my way. "I told him we'd come."

A cool wave of concern washed over me. "We?"

"I'm calling Hilda," Charmaine said, thumbing her screen. "When?" she asked Joe.

"Tonight," Joe said to me.

"We?" I repeated, knowing what he had to mean but affronted that he'd try to commit me like that. I'd flown all the way down here for the party, then I'd agreed to the interview and he was *still* pressing his luck.

"You don't say no to the leader," Joe said.

Charmaine shook her head in agreement. "You never say no to the leader."

"I do," I said. "He's not my leader."

Charmaine's expression fell. "Hang on," she said into her phone, then looked helplessly at Joe.

I could see I was causing a minor catastrophe.

"He wants to meet you," Joe said. "He saw the segment and liked it."

"I don't even remember everything I said." That wasn't my argument for going home today, but it was true.

"I don't want to push you," Joe said.

"But you just accepted an invitation on my behalf."

"I know you're not political," Joe said. "And this is my thing, not yours. And you didn't sign up for all of this. But I'm a junior congressman—I don't tell the leader I'll have to call him back with an answer to his invitation."

"I have to go home," I said. "I have work to do. My work. To me, it's just as important as your work."

"I'll charter you a jet," Joe said.

Charmaine looked even more shocked by that.

"At personal expense," Joe said to Charmaine.

"No, I'm still here," Charmaine said into the phone.

"As soon as dinner's over, I'll drive you to the airport. On a private jet, you'll have a proper bed to sleep in for the trip back, and you can go to work in the morning like you planned."

When he put it that way, I felt churlish saying no. It was obviously important to Joe, to both of them. I wasn't heartless.

"Fine," I said.

"The congressman and his wife are having dinner with the House leader," Charmaine said breathlessly into the phone.

"But we have to talk first," I said to Joe in a no-nonsense tone.

"Sure." He answered seriously, but his eyes held a happy glow.

"I can't just sit there touching my nose and tucking my hair behind my ear through the whole dinner. Jerome Bellamy will think I'm unfriendly or rude."

"We've got hours."

"You've got that thing," Charmaine interrupted. "Lunch with the youth reps. And we better hurry and catch the flight back."

"After that," Joe said and started to walk for the exit again. "Just you and me. We'll sit down somewhere and—"

"The botanists are at three thirty. There's a photo op in the park garden," Charmaine said. She was scrolling through her phone now, having disconnected from Joe's executive assistant, Hilda Newsome.

"Well, do I have five minutes somewhere to spend with *my wife*?"

"Sure, yes, of course." Charmaine scrolled. "I'll push the staff meeting so you'll have time to get ready for dinner."

"Just do what you have to do," I said to Joe, accepting that he was a ludicrously busy man. We'd exited to the sidewalk, and Joe's car pulled up to the curb.

"Push the staff meeting," he said to Charmaine.

The driver hopped out to open the back door, but Joe beat him to it, so the driver opened the front door for Charmaine.

"I need to find something to wear, anyway," I said. Plus, I'd need a few other necessities if I was going out for another evening.

"Cocktail dress? Separates? A black suit?" Charmaine spoke to me even while she kept reading things on her phone.

"I am capable of shopping," I told her, getting set to climb into the car.

She looked up. "Oh, sorry, habit."

Eight

My suitcase arrived in Windward five days after I got home. The airline called to say it would be delivered to my house in the evening. I could have lived with losing the nightgown, underwear and makeup, but I was happy to get back my go-to black dress and a favorite set of earrings.

I was reviewing preliminary theater sketches from six interior design firms. We wanted to get the decorating contract in place before the end of September. My front doorbell rang, and I went to answer, wondering if I should tip the driver or if the airline took care of that.

I retrieved a ten-dollar bill from my purse on the way, deciding better to be safe. So, the guy got a double tip. He was working an evening shift and could probably use a little extra. Then, on second thought, I switched to a twenty.

The driver knocked again just as I opened the door.

Sophie was standing on the porch. "Surprise!"

"What?" I looked behind her, still thinking I'd see the driver before realizing that was silly. Then I looked for Stone.

"I came for a visit." She was carrying a small suitcase.

My gaze went to her belly, which was slightly rounded under her sweater. "You look pregnant."

She laughed. "Are you going to let me in?"

"Yes. Yes, of course." I stepped back. "Where's Stone?"

"Back in Anchorage."

"You came by yourself?"

She set her bag down in the foyer. "Of course."

"Right. Of course. I don't know why I asked that." I shut the door behind her, embarrassed that I was buying into the fragile-pregnant-woman myth. I was pregnant, and I wasn't the least bit fragile.

"I came for some girl talk," she said.

"Is something wrong?"

"No." She studied my face for a second. "Is something wrong with you?"

"No. Did you hear something was wrong with me?" I gestured her toward the living room. "Leave the bag. We can take it upstairs later."

"I heard you went to DC," Sophie said, choosing to sit down in an armchair before kicking off her flats.

"That was quite the trip," I said, folding myself onto the end of the sofa. I was wearing a loose pair of low-waisted, softly worn jeans, an oversize T-shirt and a pair of thick knit socks to keep my feet warm.

"Stone talked to Joe yesterday."

I tried to imagine what Joe might have told Stone that would bring Sophie to Windward for a sudden visit. He and I had parted on perfectly amiable terms, even if it had been in a rush after the dinner with the House leader.

"Please tell me that's not why you're here," I said.

"I've been meaning to come for a while." She stretched her neck to look around. "I like this place, by the way. Funky."

"I keep finding little nooks and crannies everywhere. They've obviously tried to keep the antique authenticity of the house. But I think most people only stay for the weekend or a couple of weeks. It's not a place you could move into with all your stuff."

"Where's your stuff?"

"Back in Sacramento. Katie put it in storage for me."

"Are you going back there?"

I shrugged. "Probably not."

"You want to move it to the house in Anchorage? There's loads of room there."

That was always an option. The family house had a dozen bedrooms, a huge garage, a full basement and numerous outbuildings.

"Maybe," I said. "It's not a priority. I've been too busy to think about it."

"I guess, with the job, the baby and Joe all on your plate."

"Speaking of babies, you look *terrific*, Sophie." I pulled

my T-shirt tight against my stomach. "I'm only just getting a little bit of a bulge."

Sophie grinned. "Oh, the growing will go fast now. Next you'll be getting kicked."

"Are you feeling movement?" I sometimes lay perfectly still at night and tried to feel something. So far, I hadn't felt a thing.

She nodded. "It's still faint. Stone said he could feel the kicking once, but I think he was imagining it."

For a moment, I felt jealous of Sophie's relationship with Stone. It would be nice to have the baby's father by your side experiencing all the stages. But I shook off the melancholy. My situation was what it was. Joe wasn't here with me, and here wasn't where he was supposed to be.

"Joe told Stone you were a big hit in DC."

I gave a chuckle remembering the surreal experience. "Charmaine, Joe's media assistant, was beyond thrilled with the coverage. Did he tell you we did an interview?"

"I saw it on the network's website."

"They posted it?" I don't know why I'd expected it to be a one-shot deal. It was slightly unnerving to know people could continue to watch me. I struggled again to remember what I'd said.

"You were great. Very poised, very articulate, very pretty."

"I can barely remember anything I said."

"Do you want to watch it again?"

"No!" I couldn't imagine anything more unnerving than watching my hesitations and missteps on a screen. "I'll just take your word for it that I pulled it off."

"Are you going back?" There was something off in Sophie's question. It sounded too casual, too smooth.

My suspicions were triggered. "Why?"

She shrugged. "It sounds like it was good for Joe to have you there."

"Did Joe send you?"

She looked insulted. "Would I come here as a spy? As Joe's spy?"

"No, but you might come here as Stone and Braxton's spy."

Sophie's husband was intensely loyal to my uncle Braxton,

since Braxton had adopted him from the foster care system as a teenager and raised him as if he was his own. There wasn't much Stone wouldn't do for Braxton and Kodiak Communications, I knew that. And if Joe's success fostered Kodiak's success, and if Braxton had asked a favor of Stone, Stone might have enlisted Sophie in the effort.

"Never," she said emphatically. "I want what's best for you."

"I appreciate that." My mind was back on the DC trip now. "I guess Stone told you about the dinner with Jerome Bellamy."

"He mentioned it."

"According to Charmaine, it was epic."

Charmaine had followed up by phone earlier today, pushing me for more engagements. She was a tenacious, single-minded woman, and she didn't know Joe and I were anything but a simple married couple. It was frustrating to have to dance around the reasons for my reluctance to go back and see Joe.

"She says it's all part of the vetting process. For putting Joe's name forward as committee chair. She said it's a thing, him being so young and from Alaska. I know the committee work is important to him—they cover the kinds of things that got him into politics in the first place."

"So, that's good," Sophie said, clearly puzzled by my tone.

"They want me back. That's what's not good. The chair will be appointed at the end of next week, and they're saying I could help with a final push."

"Joe asked you to come back to DC?"

"Charmaine did. More like she hinted very strongly." I guessed by the way she danced around it that she was under Joe's orders not to outright ask.

"But that's not happening," Sophie said.

It wasn't a question, but I answered anyway. "No. I took a really big risk coming back to Alaska, because this job is so good for my career. I'm not compromising it by zooming off to DC every time Joe needs his plus-one."

Sophie's tone was dismissive, almost amused. "He does *not* call you his plus-one."

That was true.

"Has your boss complained?" she asked.

"No. He's a big fan of Joe's, especially now that the senator's on board with the arts and culture center funding."

"Okay." There was something critical in the tone of that word.

"What okay?"

"Nothing."

"What are you getting at?"

"It sounds like you wouldn't compromise your job if you helped Joe out, that's all."

"That's not what I said."

"It kinda is."

"You *are* a spy."

"No, no, no." She was shaking her head.

"Then why do you want me to become Joe's political help-mate?"

"Did I say that?"

"You're about to."

Sophie hesitated just long enough for me to know I was right. She was framing her answer. I'd seen her do that with Braxton. It was a tell that meant her answer was nuanced and meant to be persuasive.

"See?" I said, having proven my point.

"This thing with you and Joe—"

I couldn't help being flippant. "You mean the marriage thing?"

She cracked a smile at that. "It was supposed to benefit you both. It boosts Joe's political career and funds your construction project."

"Plus, the baby," I said, although she was mainly right.

"Yes, of course." Her tone softened. "The baby. The baby will be born in about six months. Your arts and culture complex will be well on its way to success by then. Don't you want Joe to get a boost, too? You know, before your deal comes to an end and you go your separate ways."

"I gave him a boost last week." I'd stepped up, and Joe had already been noticed by people in high places. They were considering him. I couldn't make him a better fit just by showing up.

"It sounds like the committee chair seat would be a real launching pad for him."

"Is that what he told Stone?" I asked.

"He did."

"See, I *knew*—"

"Stone didn't ask me to talk to you. Come on, Adeline, he'd never do that. But here's the thing. I'm thinking of you."

"Of me." My skepticism was clear.

"Yes. Once Joe is on a solid trajectory toward the governorship, you'll have more options. The higher his positive profile, the less impact your parting will have on his career."

I wanted to argue back. But what she said made a certain kind of sense. I knew this was how she'd always brought Braxton around to her way to thinking—by making sense.

"I know you, Adeline. You might rail against your family and their calculated plans, but you can't bring yourself to harm them. The more they need you, the more tempted you are to help." Her tone was heartfelt. "It's the same with Joe. The more he needs you…"

I opened my mouth, but then I shut it again. Sophie truly was on my side. It might be counterintuitive, but she was right. The better grip Joe had on the governor nomination, the less he needed me, and the freer I'd be to pursue my own dreams.

After Sophie left for Anchorage, I sat down with William to see if it was possible to take a few days off next week. Our team was expanding by the day, and between the architecture and engineering firms, construction companies, interior decorators, and the multitude of subcontractors, the day-to-day work was quite well in hand.

It helped that the community consultations were finished. So, when William and I put our minds to it, we realized I could work remotely for a few days without impacting progress on the project.

I waited until I got home that night to call Joe.

"Hello?" He sounded half-asleep, and I immediately felt guilty about the time zone difference.

"Did I wake you?" I asked.

"Adeline? Everything okay? The baby?"

"Everything's good. I'm fine. I'm sorry. I thought you'd still be up."

"I am up." He sounded more alert now. "I was reading a financial report on the sofa. I guess it got a little boring."

"Financial reports will do that to you." I could hear him moving around.

"How are things in Alaska?"

"Good, everything's good. We're even slightly ahead of schedule, which is useful, since we've only got a few weeks left until the snow falls." I didn't know why I was procrastinating. It wasn't like I had bad news.

"You'll want to be weathertight before November."

"Yes. Right. Joe—"

"Something *is* wrong."

"No. I'd tell you if it was. I've been talking with William and, well, I can manage a few days off next week if it helps. You know, for you. If it helps for me to fly down—"

"To *DC*?" He sounded stunned—not happy, just astonished.

"Yes. Maybe. That is, if you want me to." I wasn't getting the reaction I'd expected. Restless, I stood up and walked from my office into the living room.

"That's great!"

Okay. That was more along the lines I'd been thinking. "Yeah?"

"Come as soon as you can. Charmaine's going to jump for joy."

I swallowed and was suddenly thirsty, so I turned for the kitchen. "Oh, good. Not the Charmaine jumping for joy part. I don't think that's necessary. I mean the part where it's helpful."

His tone turned lower. "You know it's helpful."

"I thought it might be. I mean, last time we scored a good dinner invitation."

Joe was silent for a moment. "This means a lot to me, Adeline."

"I'm…" I chose my words. "Happy to help out. I want to help out."

"Next week would be perfect timing," he said.

"Tuesday work for you?" I poured myself a glass of ice water.

"Yes. I'll book a jet."

"You're not booking a jet."

"Oh, yes, I am."

"Joe."

"My pregnant wife is flying over three thousand miles to support my career. She's not taking the milk run through Anchorage and Dallas."

"It's more direct if you take the red-eye."

"You're not schlepping your way through three different airports again."

I had to admit, I did love the idea of skipping security, boarding in Windward then getting off at ExBlue airport. "Fine," I said, sounding more reluctant than I was feeling. "I mean, thanks. Thanks, Joe."

"Anytime. Literally, anytime."

I heard the background clink of an ice cube on his end. "What are you drinking?" I took my water back to the living room and picked out a comfy chair to sit down.

"Bourbon and water."

"I miss bourbon. Well, I miss wine more. But I'd take a bourbon right now. I've only got the water part."

He chuckled. "Want me to switch to plain water? Keep you company?"

"No." There seemed little point in that. "I want you to enjoy the bourbon for both of us."

We were quiet for a moment.

"How's the baby?" he asked.

"I felt a kick."

"You *did*?"

"Just a little one. More of a flutter, really." Emotion hitched in my chest then, and I felt the need to change the subject. "Sophie came to Windward for a couple of days."

"Stone said she was going to visit."

"He reported that to you?"

"It was random conversation. Stone's a great guy. I talk to him. He talks to Sophie."

"Well, aren't you three thick as thieves."

"You are definitely not writing my next campaign slogan." There was a thread of humor in his voice.

"Charmaine said they're naming the committee chair at the end of next week."

"You've been talking to Charmaine? Who's thick as thieves now?"

"She didn't ask me to come down." I paused, wondering if I wanted to press the subject. "You know, I feel like we've got go-betweens in our relationship."

"Does that surprise you?"

It didn't. But I didn't like it. We might not have a real marriage, but we were both intelligent adults. We should be able to figure out how to communicate with each other.

"Adeline?" he prompted.

"Can we work on that?" I asked. "Eliminate the go- betweens? Just tell each other what we need."

This time it was Joe who paused. "Sure."

"You don't sound sure."

"We can work on that while you're down here."

"Between meetings and social events?" I asked, trying to lighten the mood but sounding sarcastic.

"What's really wrong?"

"Nothing. Just that. I guess I'm tired of trying to figure this thing out."

"You want to talk it through now?"

"No." It would be better in person. "Tell me what to expect when I get there. What are the events?"

"There'll be a formal thing Friday night after they announce— I mean, if you can stay that long."

"Sure." I decided if I was going to do this thing, I might as well go all the way.

I started to mentally compose my wardrobe and consider my schedule. My repatriated black dress, for sure, and something professional for any business functions. I had a pair of steel-gray slacks that were loose enough to still wear. I'd add

my teal silk blouse and a classic black blazer. I felt a little thrill
for a moment thinking about cute shoes. Practical footwear was
standard in Alaska, and steel toes were required on the job site.

"There'll be various brunches, lunches or dinners," Joe said.
"I think there's a presentation to a youth club Thursday afternoon. The kids are always great at those things. I don't know
the whole itinerary, but does that help? Is that enough?"

"Yes."

We both went silent again.

Joe was first to break it. "I'm looking forward to seeing
you."

"Me, too." Now that it was settled, I pictured myself in his
DC condo…in his bedroom…in his white shirt…in his bed.
My skin heated, and my breath hitched in my throat.

I was in DC by noon, and Joe picked me up at the airport.
I was surprised by that. I'd expected him to make some arrangement, maybe a driver or even Charmaine. But I didn't
expect him to break up what had to be a busy day and drive
through traffic.

He hugged me, and I hugged him back, feeling the contours
of his suit against my lightweight dress as the flight attendant
loaded my bags into the trunk of his black sedan.

"No driver this time?" I asked as he opened the passenger
door for me. It looked like the kind of car that should have a
driver—sleek and black, polished to a high shine.

"I'm fully licensed in DC."

"I thought having a driver was a perk of the job." My dress
fluttered against my legs.

"It's definitely a perk. Especially where parking's tight, or if
I'm planning to have a drink or two, or if I'm getting dropped
off at the airport and the car needs to go back without me."

I sat down on the comfortable leather passenger seat, and
he rested his hand on the top corner of the door.

I couldn't resist teasing. "But if you sometimes have to
drive yourself, you're clearly not as important as I thought."

"So sorry to disappoint you."

"Doing your own parking? Mingling with the common folk?" I asked on a doubtful expression.

"I'm more than happy to mingle."

"You're such a man of the people."

"The people are pretty great." He grinned as he shut the door and walked to the driver's side.

"So, they mostly love you?" I asked as I fastened my seat belt and he settled in.

He shook his head and drove forward. "I wouldn't go that far. But I'm not powerful enough to make them angry."

"Yet," I said.

"Yet," he agreed as we passed through the security gate.

"Something to look forward to, then."

He glanced sideways. "You don't have to worry, you know. People like you even better than they like me."

I fought an amused smile and gave him a mock salute. "Noted. Where are we going first?"

"The condo. I thought you'd want to drop off your bags, maybe freshen up."

"Sounds good. But you don't need to babysit me if you've got things to do this afternoon."

"I'm going to show you off," he said and smiled my way as we turned off the airport road and into traffic.

"In that case, I'm definitely freshening up."

Traffic grew heavier as we made our way down Massachusetts Avenue. The streets hummed with choreographed city life—the sounds, the traffic and the surge of pedestrians were all intriguing to me after the quiet of Windward.

We pulled up in front of Joe's brick building. He retrieved my suitcase and let us in the front door. Neither of us said anything about sleeping arrangements, and when he started up the stairs, I allowed myself to think about a night in his arms.

I followed, and he turned into his room.

"There's plenty of room in the closet," he said, setting down the bag. "And there are some empty drawers in the en suite. Do you need space in the dresser?"

"The closet's fine," I said, struggling to come to terms with the intimacy of the situation. I decided to put first things first and dropped my purse on an armchair. "What should I wear today? And how much time do I have to change?"

He moved a little closer. "I thought we'd swing by the office first. Everybody wants to meet you. Charmaine keeps singing your praises."

"I hope I don't disappoint them." Experience told me Charmaine tended to be generous in her enthusiasm.

"How would you do that?" He shifted closer still, an amused little smile on his face. "Just do the usual thing. You know, be outgoing, erudite and witty. You are up-to-date on the trade negotiations with the EU relative to the aerospace industry, right?"

"Erudite?" I squared my shoulders and tipped up my chin. "I come from Alaska by way of California. We're laid-back and down-to-earth."

"Then you may have ended up in the wrong town."

"Ha-ha."

"Nobody's going to quiz you. Not that you wouldn't pass."

"I don't know a single thing about the EU aerospace industry."

"Neither does anyone else. Well, except for the negotiators. But they're way too serious to attend parties."

I wanted to kiss him. He had a unique magnetism up close like this, and I very desperately wanted to kiss him.

"What are you thinking?" His voice was husky, and it seemed like he could read my mind.

"Nothing," I lied.

"We were going to be up front with each other, remember?"

"Yes," I admitted. It had been my idea.

He took my hand gently in his. "So, then tell me what you're thinking."

I didn't want to do that. "It's really not..."

He shook his head, his features softening, a cute smile growing on his face. "Uh-uh. Put up or shut up, Mrs. Breckenridge."

"You go first," I countered. "What are you thinking?"

To my surprise, he didn't hesitate. "That I'm very glad to see you."

"Because I'll help with the committee chair appointment?"

"No." He playfully brushed his fingertip across the tip of my nose. "Because you're fun and adorable. Your turn."

My chest tightened and my breath hitched. I went with a partial truth. "That you're a very handsome congressman."

"That's a good start," he said, his tone lower still.

I felt myself sway toward him.

"Were you going to get changed?" he asked.

"I was."

"You should."

"I know."

We both stayed still, gazes locked.

He cupped my cheek in his palm, a glow coming up behind his eyes.

I tried not to lean into his touch, but the temptation was too much. I tipped my head to one side, drinking in the warmth of his broad palm.

He stepped forward and closed the gap. "Sex has always been the easy part for us."

He was right about that, and I was both relieved and gratified that he'd just thrown it out there. We were communicating. It was a start.

"We don't have time." My voice came out husky and breathless.

He wrapped an arm around my waist and eased me up against him. "Have a little faith."

I knew he was joking, but he kissed my neck while he slid my dress upward.

"Joe, we should—" I only got out the few words before desire flared to life inside me.

His kissed my lips then, and I instinctively kissed him back.

"I'm only helping," he said.

"Helping?" I tried not to laugh.

"You have to take it off to change." He eased the dress a little farther up my thighs.

"Are you telling me chivalry is not dead?"

"No, ma'am." His gaze was burning now, filled with hunger and passion.

My skin pebbled, arousal spearing deep within my core. I lifted my arms, and he peeled the dress upward, lifting it over my head and tossing it onto an armchair. I was wearing lilac lace with pink accents, little bikinis and a plunging bra.

He stepped back to look, then he feathered his fingertips over the small rounding of my stomach.

I looked down at the contrast between my smooth, pale stomach and his tanned, rough hand.

"You are *so* sexy," he rasped.

I was losing the battle to keep a hold of what little logic I had left. "Are we going to be late?"

"Yes." He came forward and swept me into his arms.

Our kisses were indulgent, then playful, then bordered on frantic as they deepened, and his hands splayed over my back. I was ready to fall onto the waiting bed. Ready to tear off his suit and fall naked into each other's arms all over again.

But Joe suddenly froze. He was breathing fast and his eyes were dazed with passion. "We're going to be *very* late if we keep this up."

My mind stuttered for a second.

He'd actually meant for me to change my clothes? It wasn't a ruse to get me naked?

I shook myself back to reality. "Yes. Sure. I'll…" I waved in the general direction of my suitcase. "You know."

"Hey." He put his hand on my shoulder to stop me.

I willed my heart rate to slow and my hormones to settle.

"Later?" he asked.

I gave a nod.

He nodded back and took another look at my lacy underwear. "I'll be thinking about what's hiding under your dress all afternoon."

Since we were going straight from the office to a cocktail party on the top floor of the Vista Green Club, I'd put on a black three-quarter-sleeve blazer over a sleeveless royal blue dress with a lace neckline. The blazer covered my bare shoulders and the more elegant details of the dress, leaving the smooth skirt and scalloped above-the-knee hem showing beneath. I converted the look for evening by leaving the blazer in Joe's car.

Joe had introduced me to dozens of people; I was struggling hard to keep the names straight. I left him to continue schmoozing while I visited the ladies' room and picked up a glass of ginger ale. Watching him now, he cut an impressive figure in his tailored suit, taller than most of the other men, his broad shoulders and strong chin distinguishing him.

"We meet again," came a smooth masculine voice.

I turned my head to see Nigel beside me, an ironic smirk on his face and a highball in his hand—something with a swizzle stick, a cherry and an orange slice.

"Hello, Nigel." I wasn't friendly, but I wasn't rude, either.

"You're here with Joe?" His gaze followed mine across the ballroom.

"Of course." There was obviously no other reason for me to be in DC, never mind at this particular gathering.

"Governor Harland is meeting with the vice president."

"Uh, that's nice." I guessed from his tone that I was supposed to be impressed.

Joe was approached by another group of people, all smiling and shaking his hand.

"I thought I'd check out what was going on here," Nigel said, taking a sip of his drink.

I sipped my ginger ale. It was cool against my dry throat.

"You know we're on to you, right?" Nigel asked, his tone going darker, the fingers of his free hand drumming the rim of his glass.

"On to what?" I asked, a hum of anxiety creeping over my skin.

"Don't play coy. This little charade you've got going with Breckenridge. The voters don't like being conned, Adeline."

"You don't think we're married?" I decided to go on offense in the hopes of covering the kernel of truth in his accusations.

He scoffed and gave me an eye roll.

"We had five hundred witnesses," I pointed out.

"How long do you think you can keep this up?" His gaze went to my stomach.

Surely he didn't think I was faking a pregnancy. "What is it you want, Nigel?" There were dozens if not hundreds of interesting people at this party. I didn't need to stand here listening to Nigel's accusations.

"Me? Nothing. But you should know the governor has connections, spies, if you will, and it's a long time until the next governor's election."

"Enjoy the party, Nigel," I said and took a step away.

He shot forward, his face only inches from mine. "Be warned—"

"Back away from my wife," Joe growled, coming into my view.

Nigel looked up, and his expression fell.

Joe had a good four inches on Nigel and wore the most serious expression I'd ever seen.

Nigel retreated instantly. "I was just saying hello."

Joe stepped to my side. "You okay?"

"I'm fine." I nodded. I was more annoyed than anything else.

Nigel shifted awkwardly. "I'll just be—"

"Leaving the party?" Joe asked, his intonation making it clear that it wasn't really a question.

"Yes," Nigel said. "I'm meeting up with the governor. Good night."

We watched him walk away, quickly disappearing into the crowd.

"The governor is in town to meet with the vice president," I told Joe.

"You sure you're okay?"

"He didn't even touch me." I was okay. Really.

"What did he say?"

"That he was on to us. He wants to know how long we think we can keep up the facade."

Joe looked puzzled. "What facade?"

"You know what facade." Sure, we were really married, but Nigel had obviously heard or guessed that it wasn't a romantic, honest, until-death-do-us-part marriage.

The conversation ebbed and flowed around us, drink glasses

clinking, people laughing, plenty of hearty smiles and crisp handshakes.

"There's no way he knows anything," Joe said.

"He told me they had spies."

"He's bluffing."

I wasn't so sure.

"Who would spy?" Joe asked. "Sophie? Stone? Your brothers? Katie?"

"None of them," I said. And it sure wouldn't be my dad or Braxton.

"There are a limited number of people who know the finer points of our situation."

"Still…" I couldn't help worrying a little bit.

"He name-checked the vice president?" There was a thread of amusement in Joe's tone now.

"I got the distinct impression this was the B-list event."

"Then he's a B-lister, too, since he wasn't the one rubbing shoulders with the VP."

"I should have called him on that."

Joe's arm went around me for a moment. "Let's forget about him."

I remembered something else. "He said the voters don't like being conned. It sounded like a threat, like he was going to reveal something."

"He was fishing. Our relationship happened fast. That's all he has to go on. Let's find Charmaine."

I was confused by the change of subject. "Does she need something?"

"A strong offense is the best defense." He took my hand.

I did a hop-step as he started walking.

It took us thirty minutes and four conversations to make our way across the ballroom to Charmaine. She spotted us coming and met us.

"Congressman," she greeted Joe. She was dressed impeccably, a shimmering, off-the-shoulder green cocktail sheath that flowed to just below her knees.

"You want to do a little social media?" he asked.

Her eyes lit up. "Absolutely. What do you have in mind?"

"How about some video footage?"

"I'll get us a camera operator."

"No, no. I want it to look casual, clandestine. Can you post it from somewhere nonofficial?"

"I'm liking your style, boss."

I viewed Joe with curiosity, surprised he'd gone all covert operative.

"We need a quiet corner," he said, looking around.

"Over there," Charmaine said. "Between the plant display and the dais."

"That'll work," Joe said, looping his arm around my waist.

"What are we doing?" I asked as we started walking.

The room was full, and a few people tried to get his attention as we made our way through the crowd, but Joe gave them a smile and a wave and kept on walking.

"Shouldn't you be chatting them up?" I asked.

"They'll still be there when we're done."

"Done what?" I was still in the dark about his plan.

Charmaine didn't have much information, either, but she didn't seem remotely concerned. She'd tucked herself in behind Joe, letting us clear her a path while she did something on her phone.

"This'll do," he said and came to a halt.

"What—"

He put his hands on my shoulders and turned me slightly sideways, then he mussed my hair a little in the front.

I couldn't help but smile. "Why are you messing me up?"

"I'm making you look casual. Pinch your cheeks."

"Are you serious?"

"Flushed is good," Charmaine said, looking me over. She reached forward and straightened my necklace, then pulled the right shoulder of my dress slightly askew.

I pinched my cheeks. "Exactly *what* are we doing here?"

She grinned happily. "How far away do you want me?"

"I don't want any sound," Joe said. "Just make the framing nice."

"Got it." She looked over her shoulder and took several steps back.

"Look happy," he whispered.

I couldn't do anything but look happy, since this felt so silly.

"Gaze into my eyes," he said.

I did.

"Now think about the baby."

I could feel my expression soften.

He leaned in and put his mouth close to my ear. "I'm going to touch your stomach," he whispered. "Give me a really slow smile." He pressed his warm palm against my stomach, cradling the small bulge. "I can't wait to feel the first kick," he said.

I tried to give him the slow smile, but emotion was so thick and tight in my chest that I had to blink.

"You're the best," he whispered and drew me into an enveloping hug in slow motion.

I wrapped my arms around his neck, all but soaked in the emotion.

"That," Charmaine said, walking back to us, "was *sensational*. Adeline, you deserve an Academy Award." She held up the phone and played the clip for us. "I swear, she had a tear in her eye."

Joe grinned. "Take that, Governor Harland."

I quickly shook my equilibrium back into place.

"The governor's here?" Charmaine asked, looking around.

"No, but his staff's been trash-talking our marriage."

Her fingers worked fast on her screen. "You two are a little bit scary."

"It's not me," I protested.

"That's why I love working for you," she said to Joe. She touched the screen with a flourish. "This is going to be fun to watch."

Nine

Joe was appointed to the committee chair position, and Nigel went quiet. In Windward, construction crews all made their deadlines, so the arts and culture center was ready for the harsher weather when the snow started to fly. As it piled up, I made a few more trips to DC, attending events with Joe so Charmaine could keep up our social media posts and make us look like happy newlyweds. Funny thing was, I *was* a happy newlywed.

I looked forward more than I should have to sleeping in Joe's arms. But I pushed away the niggling worry. Joe was a good conversationalist and a great dancer, and he knew a lot of interesting people. And it seemed to me that Sophie's plan was working, since Joe seemed to be in constant demand by the movers and shakers of his political world.

Things were running smoothly enough on the construction project that we dropped to a skeleton crew over the holidays, and I decided to spend them in Anchorage with Joe and my family. Charmaine enlisted Sophie as her temporary photographer, and Sophie posted shots of happy pregnant me and solicitous husband Joe in front of the twenty-foot family Christmas tree, then outside walking in the snow.

We got a sunny, relatively warm day and hitched a sled up to a team of horses. Then we took some very romantic shots outside in the snow. Sophie and I went for a sleigh ride while Joe and Stone went riding with my brothers. He was sexy dressed up as a cowboy, and, after the ride, we cuddled around a bonfire sipping hot chocolate under the bright stars.

Katie came up to spend New Year's. On our last day, Sophie, Katie and I settled in the cozy den in front of the gas fireplace for some girl chat, even if Katie did roll her eyes at some of the pregnancy talk. Snow was falling outside the windows, and there was a panoramic view of the fat flakes outside the windows. I was going back to Windward soon, Joe going back to DC. I was sorry to see the holidays end.

When Stone got home and our chat broke up, I went in search of Joe, wanting to catch the final hours of our last day together in what felt like a happy paradise.

I heard Braxton's voice and guessed Joe was with him. They were beyond the stone fireplace in the great room, just out of my view.

"Right behind our backs," Braxton said with disgust.

"Harland could be lying," my dad put in.

"He knows too much for it to be a bluff," Joe said.

"And he got it from somewhere," Braxton agreed.

"They'll throw everything they've got at us. They won't pull their punches." Joe's voice got louder as I drew closer.

"But a spy?" my dad asked, incredulously.

"Can you come up with another explanation?" Braxton asked—demanded, really.

"Here?" Joe asked. "In your house?" He looked up and saw me. "Adeline," he said, toning himself down. It was framed as a greeting, but I knew he was alerting my father and my uncle to my presence.

Their backs to me, both older men turned.

"What's going on?" I asked them all.

"Just a little chitchat," Braxton said.

"You're going with *that*?" I counted incredulously. Then I looked at Joe, challenging him to lie to me, too.

"What did you hear?" Joe asked.

"Oh, no, no, no." I waved his question off. "That's not how this is going to work. What's Governor Harland doing?"

The three men all looked at each other.

I crossed my arms, tempted to tap my foot. "You can't come up with a plan while I'm standing right here," I told them.

Joe rose and came to me. "I don't want you to worry."

"I'm not some delicate little flower."

"You're six months pregnant."

"And it hasn't affected my brain."

"We think there's a spy in the house," Braxton whispered. Joe and my dad glared at him.

"She wants the truth," Braxton said.

"In the house? This house?" I couldn't help lowering my voice, too, and glancing over my shoulder.

"The governor's office knows way too much about the family's personal business," Joe explained. "Someone's been feeding them information."

"I thought Nigel was bluffing," I said.

"Nigel?" Braxton asked.

"Back in September," Joe said. "Nigel Long was bragging that they were onto us."

"It sounds like they were."

"Who here would cooperate with Nigel?" I asked.

It wasn't a family member, that was for sure. And I couldn't imagine it was Sebastian or Marie or someone who'd been with us for years. Maybe someone temporary had overheard a conversation or two.

"*That's* what we're about to figure out," my dad said.

"How?" I asked, thinking Joe and I should have taken it more seriously back then, feeling partially responsible.

"It's not an insurmountable problem," Joe said, looking into my eyes.

"I want to help," I told him.

"You can help just by acting as you normally would."

"You mean fake normal, pretend-marriage normal."

"Assume people could be listening."

"This is creeping me out," I admitted. I hated the thought that I couldn't let my guard down even inside the house.

"That's what I wanted to avoid," Joe said.

"Coddling me was a bad plan. We should tell everybody." My brothers, Sophie, Katie—any one of them could give something away in front of a staff member or acquaintance.

"We will," Braxton said. "Carefully."

I nodded, agreeing with that. Then I glanced around again, wondering if there were microphones hidden in the lamps.

"We'll sweep for electronics," my dad stated.

It seemed overly dramatic, but I realized it was way too easy these days to hide a listening device anywhere.

Another thought occurred to me. "Maybe they hacked

our phones, turned them into hot mics. I read where you can do that."

"It's harder than you think," Joe said. "But we'll check that, too."

"What is wrong with people?" I asked rhetorically.

"All you have to do is go back to what you were doing," Joe said. "What were you doing just now?"

"Thinking I could use a snack."

"You want me to get you something?"

"No. I can do it. That would be what I'd normally be doing."

"Then carry on." Joe touched my arm and leaned in, giving me a kiss on the hairline.

I took a breath and gave myself a bracing mental shake, settling the new information into my brain as I headed for the kitchen.

I couldn't help padding quietly over the carpet, glancing around, wondering if someone was peeping around a corner at me, watching what I was doing.

"I do not want to keep sneaking around," Katie said as I approached the entryway.

The words stopped me cold. No way did she mean what it sounded like she meant.

"Nobody cares." It was Mason's voice, and when I eased forward, I saw he was leaning, hip braced against the breakfast island.

Everybody cared. I couldn't see Katie, but my brain reeled with the notion that my brother and dear friend could be plotting against us. It simply wasn't possible.

"I care," Katie said, sounding impatient.

"Then what do you want to do?" he asked, straightening and moving.

I eased farther forward to see him go to her, standing at the coffee maker.

"I don't know," she said, sounding distraught.

Stunned to my toes, I was about to march in and demand answers when Mason reached to smooth her hair.

His voice went lower, smoother, deeper. "Ignore it?"

"Maybe."

"No." There was a chuckle in his voice. "Not an option." He kissed her.

He kissed her, and she kissed him back, and reality hit me with a wave of relief.

They weren't spying on Joe and me. They were falling for each other.

I started to step back, but Mason saw the movement.

He jolted from Katie and stared straight at me. Regret flashed in his eyes. "Sorry."

I was relieved and surprised and happy for them all at the same time. "For liking Katie?"

Hearing my voice, she whirled around, looking guilty.

I continued talking to my brother. "I like Katie. I like her a lot."

Her face was flushed as she stared at me. "We—"

"You don't have to explain," I said. "I get it. And I respect your privacy and my brother's."

"We don't know what it is," she said.

"It's very...new," Mason finished.

"You both seemed into each other the first night you met," I pointed out, thinking I should have guessed back then. They'd started off sparring but then were the last ones to leave the balcony.

They glanced self-consciously at each other, and I realized I was intruding on a highly intimate conversation. I raised my palms and took a step back. "Forget I was here."

But Katie stepped forward. "Adeline—"

"Don't worry. It's not like Joe and I don't have a complicated romance."

Mason's attention shifted to something behind me.

Joe's hands closed gently over my shoulders. He leaned down, humor threading his tone. "*This* is you doing fake normal?"

It was anticlimactic to discover the culprit was a temporary cook's assistant gossiping to someone with a girlfriend in the governor's office. It wasn't a sophisticated spy network, and there were no hidden microphones in the house. There was also no malware in our phones, so we were able to go back to our usual behavior.

Katie liked Mason, and Mason liked Katie, but with so many miles between them, it was hard for their relationship to go further than that.

I was working long hours with the decorating team as they installed the millwork, finished the walls and finalized the flooring and furniture choices. Theater seats were on their way from Europe, while the lighting was back-ordered, and we were struggling to find an installation specialist for the sound system.

Sophie and Stone's baby was due in less than a week, so we were all on alert, and I was making sure I had my phone with me every minute.

William and I stood on the concrete floor of the main complex. Though we wore steel-toed boots, hard hats and vests, we stayed back from the scaffolding where workers were installing the drop ceiling.

"The planters will curve around the staircase," Maddy, the head interior designer, was telling us. "I want to bring them out three feet at the apex to give us room for larger trees. With the clear stories above, we could have a real conservatory space with benches, tables and a cobblestone walkway."

My phone pinged, and I immediately thought of Sophie going into labor. My stomach contracted in what I assumed was a sympathy pain, and I smiled to myself as I discreetly pulled the phone from my pocket to check the screen.

It was a business text, not about Sophie.

I sighed my disappointment and tuned back into Maddy.

"I don't see a problem with the traffic flow," she said, walking partway across the room to show how much space would be left as a result of her suggestions. She raised her voice. "It wouldn't interfere with event lineups to the main desk. And it would give such a nice interior space for winter. Imagine, real greenery and a parklike atmosphere in January."

Since it was February now and bitterly cold, I had to agree with her on that.

I felt another twinge in my stomach and shifted my stance.

I wondered if cousins could be psychically connected during childbirth. Maybe I'd hear from Sophie any minute now. Maybe she and Stone were already on their way to the hospital in Anchorage.

"As a reflection of the main space," Maddy said. "Let me show you what I was thinking for the retail area." She started to walk that way.

I looked at William to gauge his thoughts, wondering if he'd be open to a change at this stage of construction. There was time to do it, although we did need to watch our budget. A change here, an upgrade there, and we were moving into our contingency funds.

I fell into step with him several feet behind Maddy. "What's your—" A sharper pain crossed my stomach, and I gasped, stopping to cover it with my hand.

That had *hurt*.

"Adeline?" William asked, concern in his tone.

"Something's weird," I said, still thinking of Sophie.

"Do you need to sit down? Some water?"

"Maybe." Sitting down sounded like a good idea.

He pointed to a card table and two folding chairs near the bottom of the staircase.

Maddy had stopped and was looking back at us.

When she saw where we were headed, she came our way. "Everything all right?"

"Fine," I answered even though a low-grade soreness had settled into my stomach.

I sat down, and she crouched in front of me.

"Is it the baby?" she asked.

"I don't think so. It's way too soon. My cousin Sophie is—" The sudden sharp pain gripped me again, and I groaned.

"Call an ambulance," Maddy blurted to William.

"That's overkill," I said, but thinking maybe I would call my doctor.

"It might be," Maddy agreed. "But let's not take any chances."

I slipped my phone out of my pocket again and pulled up my doctor's office contact. "Dr. Reed," I said to both of them.

"Good idea," Maddy said, but she made a phone sign to William at the same time, and I knew they were calling for an ambulance.

I was slightly embarrassed, especially now that we'd caught the attention of some of the construction workers.

"Reed Clinic," Jill the receptionist answered.

"Jill, it's Adeline."

"Oh, hey, Adeline." Jill's voice was cheerful. "How are you doing?"

"Okay," I answered. "Well, a little funny."

Her tone immediately changed. "Funny how?"

"A few pains in my stomach."

"Sharp or dull?"

"A little of both." A sharp one hit me again, and I clenched my teeth.

"Adeline?"

"I'm here." My tone was tight, and I could feel sweat breaking out on my skin.

"Can you come in this afternoon?"

Maddy held out her hand for my phone.

It seemed easier just to hand it over.

"This is Maddy Schmidt. I'm with Adeline now, and we've called for an ambulance." Maddy stopped to listen. "I agree." She paused again. "Sounds good. We'll meet her there." She ended the call and handed back my phone.

"No more messing around," she told me sternly.

I could already hear the ambulance siren. The sound was gathering even more attention from the workers.

"I can walk," I said and started to get up.

Maddy put her hand on my shoulder. "Sit."

"That's an order," William added as he strode for the front door to meet the paramedics.

"Well, this is embarrassing," I said to Maddy.

"You're doing what's best for the baby."

I decided to think of it that way and nodded, even as a man and a woman dressed in navy blue uniforms wheeled a stretcher my way.

They helped me on board and immediately took my blood pressure.

The woman cupped my stomach with her hands. "Contractions?"

"I don't think so."

She kept still for a couple of minutes, then another pain hit, and I tensed up.

"I felt a tightening," she told me gently.

"That was me," I said.

"How old are you?" she asked.

"Twenty-eight."

"How many weeks pregnant?"

"Thirty-six."

She keyed her radio. "I have a twenty-eight-year-old female patient, thirty-six weeks pregnant, showing signs of premature labor."

"I'm not." I shook my head and reached for her arm to stop her. I didn't want people getting ahead of themselves on this.

"Her doctor's en route to the hospital," Maddy told the paramedics.

"I don't think I'm in labor," I told the paramedic. Technically, I knew it was possible. But these pains weren't all that bad. I'd had worse with the flu.

"Try to relax," she told me. "We're going to take good care of you."

The stretcher started to move, and I closed my eyes to keep from getting dizzy.

They loaded me into the ambulance, and in minutes we were pulling up to the back entrance of the hospital.

To my surprise, Dr. Reed got into the ambulance. My first thought was they'd realized there was no point in taking me inside. It was a relief. I had a lot of work left on my desk. In fact, my purse was still in my office. I needed to go back for it.

I started to sit up, but Dr. Reed stopped me.

"You're just fine right where you are," she said.

"I need to get my purse."

"Someone can pick it up for you." She put her hands on my stomach.

"So, I don't need to go inside?" The pains had subsided.

She didn't answer, just smiled and checked a tablet that the paramedic handed her. "Have you felt anything like this before?" she asked me.

"They're gone now," I said.

"Was this the first time?"

I nodded, then the pain came back, and I gritted my teeth.

The doctor nodded to the paramedic. "Let's call an H-flight."

The name registered in my mind—the Alaska Air Ambulance service.

"What?" I asked in confusion.

"You're in labor," Dr. Reed said in a steady reassuring voice. "Protocol is the Anchorage hospital before thirty-six weeks."

"I am thirty-six weeks."

"You're not quite over the wire yet. The good news is, this is early labor, so you've got plenty of time."

"I'm having the baby?" I was struggling to wrap my head around that.

"I'll have Jill call Joe to let him know."

"Joe's in DC." I knew Joe was going to flip out over this. He'd planned to come to Alaska two weeks early to make sure he didn't miss the birth.

Things got blurry for me after the air ambulance landed in Anchorage. I remembered a ride to the hospital and moving from the stretcher to a bed. For some reason Sophie showed up. She held my hand and talked me through the intensifying pains, telling me Joe was coming and would arrive soon.

Then Stone showed up and took Sophie away, and I was annoyed, since she'd been helping me breathe. I went into what felt like self-hypnosis for a while. A new nurse came in and checked me out.

Then I was hit with the urge to push. The nurse was kind, so was the doctor. But I wanted Joe and I wanted Sophie, my dad, too. And I wanted the pain to stop already. But I pushed hard, and when they put the tiny baby girl in my arms, my heart nearly burst from my chest with joy.

Joe rushed into the delivery room, a mask on his face, a cap on his head and a green gown flapping around him.

He came to a screeching halt when he saw us.

"You made it," I said, feeling a tear squeak out of the corner of my eye.

"Almost," he said, his gaze going to Matilda.

In my head, I'd already named her. I didn't know why. We hadn't even talked about names.

"Close enough," I rasped around a dry throat. "I only just met her this minute."

He put a hand on her little head, and his voice shook. "She's beautiful. You're beautiful." He leaned down to kiss my forehead. Then he kissed Matilda's.

The nurse gently took her from my arms. "I promise I'll bring her right back."

I watched them go, feeling euphoric now that the labor pains had stopped. "She was early," I said.

"Are you doing okay? Need anything?"

"Water," I said.

He looked around and found a pitcher and a glass, giving me a sip through a straw.

"It was something." I winced, remembering the waves of pain that had blocked out the world. "Sophie was here. But then she left."

"She's in labor."

"Now?"

Joe nodded.

"Poor thing." I felt a wave of sympathy. I sure wouldn't want to go back to those labor pains.

The nurse returned with Matilda wrapped in a pink blanket with a little pink cap on her head. Her face was so sweet—blue eyes, a tiny nose, a little bow of a mouth that moved. She didn't cry, just blinked like she was absorbing everything around her.

"Dad?" the nurse asked in a singsong voice, holding her out.

"You sure?" Joe asked me, looking scared.

I nodded and gave him a smile, my heart filling again as he took the tiny bundle in his big hands.

"She weighs nothing," he said in awe.

"Six pounds, three ounces," the nurse told him.

While Joe stared at the baby and whispered silly words, the nurse helped me into a fresh gown and changed the bedding around me, tucking me in with heated blankets before she left. The warmth felt heavenly.

"Hello, baby girl," Joe was saying. "Hello."

"I think she's Matilda," I said.

He looked at me in surprise.

"Is that okay?" I asked. "I took one look at her, and that's what the name was."

"It's absolutely okay," he said. "Matilda, would you like to go see your mommy now?" He gently put her into my arms.

I held her warm little body against my heart, checking out her face, her hands, counting her fingers. I leaned my head back against the upright mattress, sighing in pure bliss.

With the warmth all around me, my eyelids grew heavy, and I felt Joe's hand slip beneath Matilda.

"Maybe I should take her," he said softly.

I managed a nod as I drifted off.

I heard my dad's voice in the distance, followed by Joe's and Mason's.

Then I must have slept for a while, because a baby's cry woke me and a nurse was telling me Matilda was hungry.

I successfully fed her and felt relief. They'd moved a bassinet into the room, and I tucked her in, sitting down in the armchair beside it to drink some juice and then a big glass of water. I was incredibly thirsty again.

The door opened, and I looked up, expecting Joe to be back. But it was Stone.

He had a huge grin on his face and a little blue bundle in his arms.

I laughed out loud. "You have a baby!"

Matilda stirred but didn't wake up.

"How's Sophie?" I asked.

"She's great. Two doors down. Sleeping right now."

"Let me see," I said, starting to rise.

"Stay put," Stone said, coming my way and crouching down. "This is Lucas Nathaniel."

I didn't know if it was my maternal hormones kicking in, but Lucas Nathaniel was just about the most handsome baby boy I'd ever seen. "We don't have a middle name yet."

"That's because sweet Matilda was in such a hurry to get here. Love that name, by the way."

"You talked to Joe." I guessed a lot had happened in the three hours I'd slept, including Lucas.

"He went for a coffee with Braxton and Xavier. They're over-the-moon giddy about being grandfathers on exactly the same day."

"My dad, giddy? And *Braxton*, giddy? I'm having a hard time picturing that."

"You'll see it for yourself soon enough."

I reached out and touched Lucas's hand. "Congratulations, Stone."

"Congratulations to you, too." He checked out Matilda. "She's beautiful. You did good, Adeline."

The door opened again, and this time it was Joe.

"The party's in here," he said softly.

"Have you seen Lucas?" I asked him.

"I have."

Stone straightened. "I better go back to Sophie."

"Can I visit her?" I asked. I felt perfectly strong enough to walk down the hall.

"I'll let you know when she wakes up," Stone said, then nuzzled Lucas's cheek before heading out the door.

Joe rested his hand on Matilda's back. "Do you want to lie back down?" he asked me.

"I'm happy sitting. I wouldn't mind some more water."

"You bet." He went to the bedside table for the jug sitting there. The ice cubes clinked together as he poured some into my glass.

We gazed at each other in silence for a long time.

"So, now what?" I asked. I felt like we'd skipped over a month of planning.

"Now—well, tomorrow morning, the nurse said—the three of us go back to the house. Xavier and Braxton have a surprise for you."

"A crib, I hope." So far, Matilda didn't even have a place to sleep.

"A crib, yes. And a nursery. Well, a new bedroom for you with a nursery attached. They were already renovating for Sophie and Stone, so they doubled up."

I was happy about the crib. I wasn't one hundred percent sure on switching my bedroom for a nursery suite. It seemed abrupt, somehow. It was silly, given the circumstances, but a shimmer of déjà vu ran through me at the thought of my dad and Braxton planning my maternity leave.

"Adeline?" Joe asked, worry in his tone.

"I'm good." I pushed away the negative reaction and gave him a smile. "I'm great."

Ten

Matilda and Lucas grew fast. Just over three months old, they were smiling, shaking rattles and starting to roll over. Both had doubled their birth weights, and they interacted more and more with their grandfathers, laughing and cooing. They were utterly fascinated with each other.

Joe had offered to sleep in my old bedroom, leaving the new two-room nursery suite to me and Matilda. But he'd ended up in my room every night for the first few weeks, holding and rocking a fussy Matilda. Soon he was crawling into bed with me, holding me close like we'd done in DC. And once we started making tender love in the quiet wee hours of the morning, it was hard to stop.

He had to work in DC but logged a whole lot of miles traveling back and forth as much as he could.

Matilda fussed at night, but she took long naps during the day, giving me time to check on emails or make calls to the project supervisors in Windward. I was technically on maternity leave, so I stuck to an advisory capacity, but I loved getting progress reports and new pictures as the facility came together.

The snow melted away, and the sun was warm these days, bringing green shoots up on the lawn and out in the horse paddock. The babies were napping, with Marie watching them, and Sophie had suggested a horseback ride. We liked getting outside in the sunshine, and she was loving learning to ride.

I put Sophie on Splendor, since she was such a sweetheart, and I took Galahad for myself. The two horses were best friends and loved being together.

Barney, the stable manager, kindly tacked the horses up for us, since our time was limited before the babies woke up hungry. But we headed out the gate down to the river trail. My thigh muscles protested a bit. I hadn't done this much riding in years.

"It's so nice to get out," Sophie said as we walked the horses side by side. She inhaled deeply.

"You're good for me," I said with a smile.

At first, I'd been reluctant to leave Matilda alone for more than five minutes, worrying she'd get upset and want her mommy, but Sophie had encouraged me to push it a little. And Marie assured me she knew how to soothe a fussy baby. Now I appreciated our little escapes.

"How am I doing?" she asked.

I checked her posture. "Straighten your back a little."

She did.

"Not too stiff," I warned her.

"It's hard to be straight without being stiff."

I smiled, understanding her complaint. "Splendor will feel your tension. Elbows a little closer in."

She moved them.

"That looks good," I said. "You want to trot?"

"Sure," she said, bracing herself.

"You're stiff again," I warned.

"I'm about to bounce up and down."

"Would you rather just walk?" There was no rush. The horses were always here, and Sophie had plenty of other teachers between Stone and my brothers.

"I want to learn faster," she said.

"That's not the way it works. It's better not to rush."

"So, we can walk, and I'll still be learning."

"Absolutely. Look, the robins are back."

"That's a good sign?"

"A good sign of spring." The sun was warm on my back, and the sky was a beautiful blue. Tiny leaf buds were coming out on the trees. With the longer days, the forest would be bright green in a couple of weeks.

The winters might be long in Alaska, but you couldn't beat the summers.

We did the river loop, coming back up at the far end of the paddock, crossing the field to the stable.

"Blue flag up," Sophie said, and we broke into a trot.

We'd worked out a signal system with Marie. A blue flag

on the balcony meant Lucas needed his mommy. A pink flag meant Matilda needed me.

We slowed and stopped the horses in front of the stable. Sophie dismounted and handed me Splendor's reins.

"See you up there," she said, heading through the soft dirt to the gate.

I moved to dismount and led both horses forward, hoping to meet Barney and hand them off. There might not be a pink flag flying, but I felt an urgency to get back to Matilda.

I came to the open stable door and heard voices.

"Whatever it takes to keep her happy," my dad said.

I was still thinking about Matilda, and I agreed with her grandpa.

"You know I'm already doing that." It was Joe who answered.

I agreed on that front too. He was a wonderful daddy.

"This next phase is the crux of it all," Braxton said.

The next *phase*? My brain stumbled over the phrase.

"We still have six months left, Joe said."

"The real clock started back in January."

"It's not like we've been slacking," Joe said dryly. "The perfect Alaska family is a huge lift for the effort."

"No complaints there," my dad said in a hearty, placating tone.

Unease gripped my chest.

Galahad shook himself, jangling the tack.

"We should sit down with your team soon and map it out," Braxton said.

I heard the creak of leather and realized at least one of them was mounting up.

"I like that Charmaine," Braxton added. "She's got her eye on the prize."

There was a warning in Joe's tone. "I'm not rushing Adeline out on the campaign trail."

"Who's talking about rushing?" my father said. "But talk to William about timing. Because the longer she stays in Anchorage, the better for us. We can run things from here, set up some early events."

"Family friendly," Braxton put in, and I could hear the satisfied smile in his voice.

My dad gave a chuckle. "Whoever my daughter doesn't charm, my granddaughter sure will. Although when you get seriously out on the trail, you might want to think about a nanny."

"Does she even have to go back to Windward?" Braxton asked. "It sounds like they're doing just fine there without her."

"It's not like the funding's going to disappear," my dad added.

"True," Joe said. "Nigel is laser-focused on the governor's race right now. He won't mess with the project funding."

Shocked, I took a step back, not wanting to hear any more plans the trio of traitors had for my life. Splendor nuzzled my shoulder, pushing my Stetson askew.

"Great," my dad said heartily.

"We're in agreement," Braxton said back.

Joe started to speak, but Barney arrived.

"All done?" he asked me.

"I'm done," I said, feeling shell-shocked, with a driving urge to get back to Matilda and run.

I made it back to the house and into the bedroom, pushing the door closed and leaning back against it. Matilda was still sleeping, so I showered, scrubbing hard, trying to forget what I'd heard and what it meant.

As I dressed and dried my hair, the old feelings of manipulation and betrayal came over me. The worst part was it was my own fault. I'd blithely and happily gone along with their plans.

I'd stuck around for three months, three long months. I'd all but made my marriage to Joe real. We were essentially living as husband and wife. We were sleeping together, raising Matilda together, making glorious love whenever we could.

We hadn't talked about the future, but my plans hadn't changed. I was finishing the Windward project. Then I was moving on to my next urban planning job. I didn't know where it would be, but I wanted to be able to pursue it, with Matilda, whatever it was.

Annoyed with myself, I went to my computer. I brought

up my CV and started on an update. The Windward project wouldn't end for several months, but I felt better, more in control, planning for the long term.

I decided to pick a company name, set myself up properly as a business. Maybe I'd use my initials, AEC Planners, something straightforward like Urban Planners, or maybe something northern, a nod to Alaska, since that experience had already proved valuable. Plus, it would be unique. Then again, it was too niche.

Matilda woke up, and I changed her.

In my newfound zeal, I'd discovered I could calm a baby while typing. So, I updated my CV, registered AEC Urban Planners as a business, designed a basic logo, ordered a thousand business cards and composed an email to William telling him I'd be returning to Windward ASAP.

The bedroom door opened, and Joe sauntered in wearing blue jeans and a plaid button-down shirt. "There you are." He lowered his voice when he saw Matilda sleeping in the middle of the king-size bed. "We just got back from the lookout trail. Barney said you and Sophie went riding earlier."

"We're back now," I said, keeping my attention on my keyboard.

"What's going on?" he asked pleasantly, moving my way.

"I'm writing to William."

"Oh."

"I need to get back to work. I've been thinking about hiring a nanny."

Joe stilled, going silent.

"I think that might be easiest," I breezed on. "My hours aren't exactly regular, and I like the idea of Matilda getting used to one person."

"What?" Joe finally sputtered.

"For childcare," I said, proud of my matter-of-fact delivery as I looked up from the screen. This was harder than I'd imagined. "It would provide continuity. I mean, I don't have to be full-time right away. The Pettigrew House is close enough to the construction site that I can pop back and forth as much as I need. It's a great setup, really."

"We should talk about this," he said.

"What's to talk about? It's been the plan all along."

"I thought you were settled here."

"Why would you think that?"

"Because you seemed…"

"Happy?" I asked. I had been happy, and I could see now that was my big mistake.

"Yes."

"Well, I'm going to be happy in Windward now."

"Adeline, this is a decision for both of us."

"Wrong. It's my life."

His gaze flicked to Matilda. "She's my daughter, too."

I swallowed and hardened my heart. "You know the way to Windward."

"You're saying I should *visit*."

"Yes."

He drew back, and I hated the look of betrayal on his face. I wasn't betraying him. I was living up to our original bargain.

"I made these," I said, turning the screen toward him, hoping to shift the conversation. I'd felt empowered while I designed the business cards, like I was staking out my own turf. But now I had to force a hearty tone into my voice. "Professional or what? Graphic design software is amazing these days."

He looked at the card design. "What is happening?"

"What do you mean?" My chest felt hollow. Whatever his culpability in plotting with my family, I knew I was blindsiding him with this.

"Did William ask you to come back?" Joe pulled out his phone.

"Don't you dare call William."

Joe looked up, clearly bewildered by my tone.

"This is my job, Joe. My life, my career, and I'm going back to it. Like we planned all along."

Matilda squirmed on the bed, vocalizing as she woke up.

Joe was quick on the draw and lifted her into his arms. He kissed the top of her head and settled her, still sleepy, against his shoulder. "You can't leave me, Adeline."

My heart hurt. For a moment, it actually hurt.

I cleared my thickening throat. "I'm not leaving you, Joe. I'm simply moving on to the next phase."

He did a double take at my choice of words, and for a split second I was afraid he knew I'd overheard.

"That was our deal," I quickly added.

"I don't like our deal. I want a new deal."

"You mean you want me to come around and do things your way? Their way?"

"I don't want—"

I waited, but he didn't finish the sentence. No surprise there, since me coming around was exactly what he wanted.

"I was never going to be Mrs. Governor Breckenridge. That was my dad's dream, Uncle Braxton's dream, your dream. My dream was to be independent and—"

"And free," he finished, sounding defeated.

"And free," I agreed, reminding myself how important self-determination was to me.

There was a hollow ring to his voice as he nodded at the computer screen. "It looks like you're halfway out the door."

"You mean halfway to living my own life."

His jaw clenched and his eyes hardened. "Then don't let me stop you." He turned for the door, Matilda still in his arms.

"Joe!" I called out, irrationally terrified that he was taking her away from me.

He turned back.

I realized my fear was way off base. They were only going downstairs. I shook my head. "Nothing."

Comprehension seemed to dawn on him. He looked down at Matilda. "Can you imagine?" he asked softly, accusingly. "Can you even imagine not being with her?"

I couldn't. The door closed behind them, and I collapsed on the bed, my head whirling and my heart aching.

"Adeline?" Sophie knocked a few minutes later. After a moment, she opened the door.

I wanted to tell her to go away, that I wanted to be alone. But my throat was so tight, I couldn't make a sound.

She came to my side, sitting down, putting her hand on my

shoulder. "I saw Joe downstairs. He looked—" A confused look slipped across her face. "What happened?"

"I can't do it," I said, my voice raw.

"What can't you do?"

"Stay."

She stilled.

"They never stopped plotting. They want me to be the good full-time political wife, by Joe's side through the election, and then move into the governor's mansion."

"That's a surprise?" Sophie squeezed my shoulder.

I pulled myself into a sitting position. "It shouldn't be, should it? How did I forget? Are they that good? Am I that gullible?"

"You're not gullible." She paused. "But they are that good. You've seemed so happy."

"I know." I nodded. "I am. I was. I obviously let my guard down."

"You're a new mom—sleep-deprived." Sophie gave a little laugh. "Survival is the best you can hope for those first few weeks. I know I'm still exhausted."

"You have Stone."

"And you have Joe."

I shook my head. "Not really. We're just pretending." I suddenly felt teary.

"Don't," Sophie said softly.

"It's hormones."

"You'll make me cry, too."

"I can't believe how hard it was to tell him." I vividly remembered the expression on his face. It was seared into my soul.

"What did you tell him?"

"That I was leaving."

"Oh." She sounded sad.

It was sinking into me now that I was truly leaving—Sophie, Joe, the mansion, everybody. And I was miserable about it. "How did my feelings get away from me like that?"

She took my hand in both of hers. "Adeline."

I closed my eyes, wishing I could go back to this morning—with the sun streaming in through my window, Matilda cooing in her crib, Joe's arms around me—when all seemed right with the world.

"You fell in love," Sophie whispered.

It took a moment for her soft words to register.

"With Joe," she added and tipped her shoulder against mine. "It hurts this much to leave him because you love him."

I shook my head in denial. I wouldn't have been that foolish.

They might have convinced me to marry him, but they couldn't convince me to love him. That one was up to me. It was all up to me. It was *only* up to me. And it wasn't what I wanted. Then or now.

My voice was a hoarse whisper. "I would never—" My throat closed and I couldn't finish. I couldn't voice the denial, because it was true.

Sophie cocked her head.

"Do you think he knows?" I asked with growing dread. If Joe knew I'd fallen for him, then he knew he held all the cards.

"He doesn't know."

"Don't tell him," I insisted.

"You have to tell him," she countered.

I pulled away, my voice a high-pitched squeak. "*Why* would I do *that*?"

"Adeline."

"Why?"

She shook her head. "In case he loves you back."

But Joe didn't love me back.

"I'm a political tool for him. That's not love."

"A political tool? You can't really believe that."

"You should have heard them, Sophie. Him and Xavier and Braxton. It was so…cold and calculated."

"He can love you and still want to be governor."

"It's way too convenient."

"Love isn't logical."

I couldn't bring myself to buy into her theory. "I'm his means to an end."

Sophie gazed at me a little longer. "Are you sure about that? You better be sure about that."

I nodded. I was sure, as sure as I could be, since the perfect Alaskan family was what Joe had planned all along.

Conversation felt stilted at dinner. I was uncomfortable, wondering who knew what, wondering if Joe had told my dad and uncle I was leaving, or if Sophie had told Stone I'd fallen for Joe. Kyle was away, and Mason left the table early to take a call.

Although Sophie did her best to keep up the chatter, I escaped right after Mason and pretended to check on the babies, who were with Marie during dinner.

"Adeline?" My dad followed me out of the dining room.

I stopped halfway through the great room, giving in to the inevitable, swearing to myself I'd hold my ground. I'd done it before, and I could do it again. The eighteen-year-old who'd insisted on turning my back on my home state and the family business and going to college in California was still inside me. And she was tough.

"Joe tells me you're going back to Windward."

I turned. "Of course he did." I'd bet the three of them shared all the gory details about me disrupting their plans. They'd already plotted their next move.

"Are you sure it's not too soon?" My dad's expression of concern might have moved me if I didn't know his real motive.

"The timing is perfect."

"Matilda is so young."

I didn't see any point in pretending any longer. "I've held up my end of the deal, and now I have a life to live."

"Don't do something impetuous."

"This is not impetuous. We did the engagement. We did the wedding. Joe got the chair appointment. And now we've had the baby. I'm tapping out, Dad."

"But there's so much more to—"

"You'll have to do it without me."

I saw Joe walk up before my dad did.

"Xavier," Joe said in a cautionary tone.

I was glad for the interruption, but I wished it wasn't Joe. I wished it was anybody but Joe.

"Adeline, if you'll just—"

"Leave it," Joe interrupted.

My dad turned on him. "You think you'll have better luck?"

"Got a minute?" Joe ignored my dad and spoke to me, nodding toward the patio doors.

"You won't have better luck," I told him with certainty, but I moved toward the door anyway. If the conversation had to be had, I was all for getting it over with.

We stepped into the sunny evening breeze. The days were longer and the sun was stronger as summer approached. I moved to the rail, watching the horses in the distance, focusing as they munched on the new green shoots, wishing my life was that simple.

Joe paused beside me. "You want to walk?" He gestured to the staircase that led down to the yard.

"Yes." I preferred to be out of my dad's and Braxton's view.

We took the long staircase to the backyard, then followed the concrete pathway that led to the edge of the woods, to the trailhead that went to the waterfall.

When I couldn't stand the silence anymore, I spoke up. "You told them."

"Not much."

Something rustled the bush beside us, and I took a reflexive step toward Joe as a rabbit hopped out of the underbrush and crossed the path in front of us.

He put an arm around my shoulders. "I'll keep you safe."

"I wasn't scared." I shrugged out of the embrace.

"Okay."

We walked a little farther on the packed dirt.

Joe broke the silence next. "So, this is what will make you happy?"

"You mean following my life's dream?" I asked, trying for sarcasm but not quite pulling it off.

He paused. "That's not a real answer."

"It is my life's dream." I was excited to go after it. At least I had been excited to go after it. Before my lovely Matilda came along, before my feelings for Joe got so complicated that I could barely work my way through them.

The sound of the waterfall came up in front of us, and we made our way out on the platform. A fine mist floated around us, cool and refreshing.

I braced my hands on the rail and stared at the rushing water.

Joe came up beside me, imitating my posture. "I want you to be happy, Adeline."

"Then we both want the same thing."

"But I don't want to lose you."

The mist dampened my face and my bare arms. "You'll know where I am. And I won't—" My heart hitched. "I won't keep Matilda from you. Not ever. I want you to see her as much as you want."

"I want to see her every day."

"You'll be in DC. You have your dream, too." Oddly, I wanted Joe to live his dream as much as I wanted to live mine. I wanted him to run for governor, and I wanted him to win.

"What if that won't work?" he asked. "What if me not being with Matilda, not being with you—with *you*—messes with my dream?"

"I can't," I said, and my voice cracked.

"No." He sounded contrite, and he shook his head. Then he turned to me, looking contrite. He touched my shoulder, then he pulled me into his arms. "That's not what I mean."

I sniffed. I hated that I was tearing up. But I couldn't seem to stop.

"I don't mean for you to change," he continued. "I don't mean for you to give up everything. I mean for us…for me… for…" He drew a shuddering breath, and I felt the heat and the power and essence of him all the way through to my core.

"I love you, Adeline." His deep words seemed huge in the forest around us. His arms tightened their embrace. "I love you. I love you. I love you."

"Joe, I—"

He drew back, his palms framing my face. "Don't walk away. Give me a chance. Let me think of something. Let me find a way that we don't have to be apart."

"I love you," I said, gazing into the depths of his dark eyes.

A slow smile grew on his face. "Okay." He gave a nod. "Okay. So, there's that."

"There's that," I said, smiling back at him.

"It's a start." He wiped the mist from my cheeks, leaned in and kissed me gently on the lips. "Oh, Adeline."

"I love you." I said it again just because I wanted to.

He kissed me more deeply.

It was long minutes before he drew back for breath.

"I'll come with you," he said.

I shook my head. "Your campaign."

"You should work anywhere you want. Take on any project you want. I'll figure out how—"

"I can find something here in Anchorage." I suddenly, urgently wanted to meet him in the middle. "Or in Juneau." Urban planning happened everywhere.

"You don't need to—"

I put my finger across his lips. "I can juggle both." I was sure of it. "We'll take campy selfies and do media interviews."

"You'll help with campaigning?" He looked like he could hardly believe it.

"We both deserve our dreams." I knew we could do it. With a little bit of ingenuity, I knew we could have it all.

A broad grin grew on his face.

"You're thinking about Charmaine jumping for joy, aren't you?"

"I'm thinking about you." He framed my face with his palms. "How amazing you are. And how you are going to knock their socks off."

I felt myself mold against him. It was going to be the easiest thing ever to play Joe's adoring wife. My entire being sighed in joy and relief as he bent to me for another kiss.

Epilogue

The landscaping wasn't yet finished, and a few snowflakes swirled in the crisp fall air, but the arts and cultural center was complete, and the community had come out in force to cheer the ribbon cutting.

The mayor's speech was over and the festivities had begun. We were inside now, out of the cold and enjoying the celebration. A local band was playing in the mezzanine, refreshments were being served in the big entrance hall and friends and neighbors were wandering through the complex, with tour guides stationed all around.

Little Matilda was behaving in Joe's arms, gazing around, drinking the world in like she always did. Next to a smiling Sophie, Lucas was squirming to get down, and Stone put his son's feet on the floor, holding his hands so he could pretend to walk. Lucas grinned from ear to ear with pride over his accomplishment.

Katie had flown up for the celebration, staying with us in the mansion. She'd spent her summer in Alaska—some of the time in Windward with me, but more of it with Mason, who'd taken to flying down to Windward in his Cessna at the drop of a hat to pick her up. I couldn't tell where their relationship was going long term, but they seemed very happy for the moment.

I caught sight of Nigel Long through the foliage of the conservatory. I knew the governor was here, but this was the first I'd seen of Nigel.

"Can you ignore him?" Joe asked me in an undertone.

"I'll try." I hated that Nigel had worked underhandedly against us, encouraged people to spy on us in our own home.

"Let them play their little games," Joe said, his tone completely unconcerned. "We'll beat them at the ballot box."

"We will," I said with determination.

Joe's run for governor was going well. With two months

until the election, the polls showed him in the lead, and he'd already picked up some notable endorsements. Governor Harland had been forced to play catch-up.

I saw Senator Scanlon arrive through the main door, her appearance causing a little flurry of attention.

"I didn't know the senator was coming," I said.

"Neither did I," Joe answered.

"Want me to—" I reached for Matilda to free Joe up to get to work. I'd learned from Charmaine and others that you didn't skip any opportunity for networking.

"She's fine," Joe said, keeping hold of Matilda.

Nigel tapped the governor's shoulder and pointed to Senator Scanlon. Governor Harland straightened his suit jacket and immediately hustled her way.

I watched the byplay as Harland beamed a smile, putting out his hand to shake and glancing around, obviously hoping the press would get a shot of the two of them together. Nigel took a photo with his phone.

"Coming up on social media," I whispered to Joe.

He grinned at me while Matilda smacked her little palms against his head, mussing his hair.

"Are you sure you don't want me to take her?" I asked again.

"Our vibe isn't DC uptight," Joe answered.

"It's messy father?"

"It's perfect Alaskan family."

To my surprise, Senator Scanlon only exchanged quick pleasantries with Harland and then moved on, her staff member—a young woman in her twenties—keeping up with her brisk pace.

The senator spotted Joe and angled toward us.

"Incoming," I whispered to him, at the ready to take Matilda.

"I see," he answered.

"Congressman Breckenridge," she said in a hearty voice as she approached, attracting the attention of the people close by.

Out of the corner of my eye, I saw my father spot her, assess the situation and head in our direction. You could always count on my dad to gravitate to power. Braxton was sure to be close on his heels.

"So nice to see you again, Senator," Joe said, shifting Matilda to one arm to shake hands.

"Hello, Adeline," the senator said to me.

"Hello, Senator Scanlon."

"Please, call me Rachel." She looked around the airy, bustling space. "I understand you're the driving force behind today's success."

"I was part of a team," I said.

"Don't let her be modest," Joe said, taking my hand. "She was at the helm the whole way through."

I saw Katie move in to take a couple of quick photos: Joe, me, Matilda and the senator. Charmaine had said Katie had a good eye for publicity shots, and I couldn't help but think Joe's trusty aide would be happy with these.

"Senator Scanlon." Xavier joined us.

"Xavier Cambridge. Hello, sir."

"I see you've met my granddaughter." Pride was clear in my dad's tone.

Rachel's smile went warmer still, and she reached for Matilda's hand, touching it lightly. "And aren't you the most adorable little girl."

Matilda grinned, then laid her head against Joe's chest.

"How's the campaign going?" Rachel asked Joe.

"Quite well—at least according to the polls."

"Brilliantly, according to the polls," my dad put in.

Rachel nodded to that. "I saw some of them. Debate prep?"

"Well underway," Joe answered.

"Good." She paused. "I'm looking at announcing an endorsement next week."

Joe's brow went up.

I didn't bother to ask this time. I reached out to gently lift Matilda from his arms.

Rachel winked at him. "I think you'll want to tune in for that."

"Thank you, Senator," Joe said, his tone sincere. "That means a lot to me, to us."

Rachel's gaze shifted to me and Matilda, then to Braxton, who'd just arrived. She smiled back at Joe. "You're truly the whole package."

I overheard Braxton whisper to my dad. "What?"

"Shhh," my dad whispered back.

Sophie and Stone moved our way.

Joe slipped an arm around me. "If by 'package' you mean the two best things that have ever happened to me. Then yes."

"You can tell that a mile away," she said. "Good luck in the election, Congressman. I know you'll be an asset for all of Alaska."

As she walked away, Joe squeezed me tight.

"That was—" I said.

"It was," he answered.

"Her endorsement?" Braxton asked on a note of amazement.

"I got some great pictures," Katie said, coming in close and showing them on her screen.

"Charmaine will be thrilled with this," I said to Joe.

"Hey," he whispered in my ear, drawing me a step back from the little crowd.

"What?" I looked up.

Matilda reached out and patted his nose.

"It's us," he said, gazing deeply into my eyes. "You, me and Matilda, over and above everything else. I love you two so much."

"I know." The private moment in the middle of the noisy flurry of people filled my heart. "We love you right back. So very much."

* * * * *

EVER AFTER EXES

SUSANNAH ERWIN

For Alex B.

Hope I did Finley justice!

Thanks for being a smashing sister-in-law.

One

"I hate weddings," Finley Smythe grumbled to the groom, who happened to be her half brother and favorite person in the world. "But this one will be perfect." She pinned the boutonnière of white rose, red berries and silver eucalyptus leaves on the lapel of his black tuxedo and stepped back. "There. Impeccable. And the rest of the day will follow suit."

Grayson Monk nodded at his reflection in the mirror here in the room set aside at the Saint Isadore winery for the groom and his attendants, and then turned to face Finley. "Nelle and I can't thank you enough for taking on the wedding planning. Despite your newly announced aversion. Which I'm fascinated by. I know how much you like events featuring cake."

"I don't have a problem with the idea of marriage per se." Finley crossed the room to find her corsage, the black satin skirt of her formal gown rustling. "If people want to legally tie themselves to another person and check the 'married' box on their taxes, that should be their prerogative."

She picked up the flowers. The straight pin hidden in the wrapped stems pricked her right index finger and she shook her hand out of reflex. A tiny drop of blood landed on the cream lace bodice of her dress. She stared down at it. The spot was nearly imperceptible. But it was a flaw on a day Finley swore would be flawless. "This is not an omen," she said under her breath. "Everything will indeed be impeccable."

"So why do you hate weddings?" Grayson asked, having moved on to straightening his tie in the mirror.

She carefully pinned the flowers to her gown. "I object to the baroque language that sets unrealistic, illogical expectations. Phrases like *true love* and *until death do you part* and *soul mates* should be outlawed." Especially *soul mates*. Finley knew from experience the concept was a fraud.

She looked up to find Grayson regarding her, his brown gaze unreadable. "I don't find the phrases unrealistic. Nor illogical."

"Well, you wouldn't, would you? Few people getting married do. Or they wouldn't get married." Finley shrugged. "Where are your other groomsmen? Shouldn't they be back from seating guests by now?"

"I asked for time alone with my best man."

"Or best person, as the case may be." She indicated herself.

"You always have been, in my opinion." Grayson smiled, then his expression sobered. "I didn't say this enough growing up, but thank you for always being there for me."

"Well, someone had to raise you after Mom died." Finley smirked at him.

"Since you're only twenty months older, I'm pretty sure we raised each other. Which is why I know this past year has been tough—"

She waved a hand, attempting to dismiss the sentimentality threatening to swamp the atmosphere. "Tough? Why? Just because my boss was found guilty of violating campaign finance laws and is currently serving time in a federal correctional facility and I'm out of a job? Pfft. Walk in the park."

"I know you're trying to make a joke," Grayson said, apparently undeterred from having a serious conversation. "And Barrett wasn't just your boss, he was your stepfather."

"And your full father, so if anyone had a difficult time, it was you. Not to mention your bride, whose family was destroyed by Barrett. But we don't need to compete in the Pity Olympics on your wedding day." She glanced at the clock on the wall. "If Luke and Evan don't show up soon, we'll have to pay the musicians overtime."

Grayson took her hands in his. She went still. She and Grayson were close, but they weren't a family that engaged in much physical affection. "I'm trying to tell you how much you mean to me. And to Nelle. By taking on the wedding planning, you allowed her to spend time with her father before he passed, and she is forever grateful. I hope one day we'll be the ones making jokes at your wedding when you're attempting to have a heartfelt exchange."

Finley snatched her hands back. "Why do people about to be married always want to drag their unmarried acquaintances with them into the deep end?" A knock on the door heralded rescue. "Come in," she called. "Especially if your job is to get Grayson out of my hair and in front of the altar."

Luke Dallas and Evan Fletcher crowded into the room, handsome in tuxedos, their smiles bright as they approached Grayson and engaged in the ritual round of handshakes and back thumps that occurred among close male friends. Not that she expected much support from the newcomers when it came to dismissing weddings as archaic social rituals. Luke was hopelessly besotted with his wife, Danica, and their baby daughter. Evan had earlier told Finley he was thrilled Grayson and Nelle were holding their wedding at Saint Isadore, the Napa winery owned by his fiancée, Marguerite Delacroix, because it would serve as a test run for his and Marguerite's own nuptials in a few months.

Finley sighed. Sometimes it seemed like she was the only rational person in the room. She clapped her hands, interrupting the men. "Are the guests in their seats?" she asked Luke and Evan.

"Yes, ma'am," Evan said with a grin.

"Good." She patted Grayson on the arm. "Let's get you married."

Even Finley had to admit Saint Isadore was a spectacular venue for a wedding. Most Napa Valley wineries were legally prohibited from holding weddings to protect the fertile land, but Saint Isadore, built in the late nineteenth century to resemble a Loire Valley castle, was grandfathered in. The ceremony was taking place on the expansive flagstone terrace that divided the wing of the castle that held the owner's residence from the larger section that contained the winery offices and operations. At one end of the terrace, a freestanding rose-and-ivy-covered trellis surrounded by chairs for guests served as the altar, while the other end of the terrace was set up for the dinner re-

ception to follow. Later, the trellis would be replaced by
a stage for one of Nelle's favorite Bay Area bands to per-
form, while the chairs would be cleared to create a dance
floor. All was arrayed against a stunning backdrop of
gently rolling hills marked by neat rows of grapevines.
The vines were still bare, but a recent storm meant the
entire countryside was covered in lush green vegetation.

Finley took her place next to Grayson under the trellis,
making one last visual sweep to ensure nothing was out
of place, no detail had been overlooked. Not a single mote
of dust marred her vision. Even the weather cooperated,
the February afternoon a temperate sixty-seven degrees
without a cloud in the sky despite the forecast for additional rain later in the week.

The string quartet issued the first notes of "Here Comes
the Bride" and Finley turned in unison with the guests to
see Nelle at the top of the makeshift aisle. Her white lace
and tulle gown made her appear like the fairy-tale princess
the press had proclaimed her to be when she and Grayson
first met. Nelle's and Grayson's gazes locked, and Finley
knew the rest of the winery had ceased to exist for them.
They only saw each other.

She exhaled a deep breath and her shoulders relaxed.
While there were still several hurdles to get through before the night would be over, the main objective of the
event would be accomplished: joining Nelle and Grayson in matrimony. She allowed her gaze to idly wander
over the guests' faces before turning back to listen to the
minister as he started his invocation—

She froze, her breathing stopped, her heartbeat paused.

The man in the third row—it couldn't be him. Why
would he be here? He had no connection to Nelle or Grayson. He definitely wasn't on the guest list.

Her pulse returned, faster, sharper, and she closed her

eyes to run through a quick, calming breathing exercise. It was just her mind playing tricks. She blamed the earlier conversation about *true love* and *until death do you part* for causing her subconscious to dredge up long-forgotten—and good riddance to them, too—memories.

She opened her eyes and flicked her gaze sideways, just to check, to reassure herself she was imagining things. The man in the third row—fifth seat from the left on the bride's side—stared back at her, his expression still with shock. She swallowed, attempting to work moisture into her suddenly dry mouth.

It *was* him. She wasn't making it up. Will Taylor was at the wedding.

Will Taylor, who'd taught her the concept of soul mates was a farce. Will, who'd destroyed any pretensions she once held about true love and relationships that were meant to be.

Will, who'd walked away without a backward glance fifteen years ago, tearing her into tiny shards with his parting words.

Somehow, she pivoted and faced the minister. Somehow, enough of the ceremony penetrated the fog that had suddenly enveloped her so she could hand over the rings at the right time. She even produced a smile—not a big one, but then she was better known for her smirk—when Nelle and Grayson were pronounced wife and husband, and she was able to forget Will enough to genuinely laugh and clap when Grayson swept Nelle into his arms for an exaggerated backward dip followed by a very prolonged kiss.

Then it was time for the wedding party to follow the bride and groom back up the aisle. Finley straightened her spine and held her chin high in the air. She would not look at him. She would not look at him. She would not—

Will's chair was empty.

Two

Come to California, his sister Lauren had said a week ago. *We can spend time together, have a few laughs...*

The last thing Will Taylor felt like doing was laughing. Not with the gut punch he'd just received. He had been so stunned, he sat through most of the ceremony unable to move, unhearing, unseeing, before leaving his seat to find an unused corner of the winery terrace in which to process what happened. Or rather, who happened.

Finley Smythe.

As beautiful as ever. Not that it came as a surprise. He hadn't followed her career—he wasn't keen on inflicting pain on himself—but occasionally he'd catch a glimpse of her as he scrolled through cable news channels or glanced at the photos accompanying a magazine article, standing behind her stepfather the congressman. And despite living in Chicago, far from Barrett Monk's district in California, he'd heard about Monk's fall from grace—who with access to the internet hadn't? He just didn't put the groom's last name together with the ex-congressman and thus Finley.

Her straight dark hair was shorter, her figure under her cream-and-black gown leaner than in his memories. But she still possessed her regal poise. Still radiated a magnetic charisma that drew all eyes to her even with a magazine-ready bride walking down the aisle.

As unobtainable and out of his reach as ever, as her brief but scathing glance let him know.

Will grabbed the first full glass he saw on a passing serving tray. He downed it, not caring about the contents. How was this possible? Of all the weddings in all the world, how did Lauren manage to be invited to one featuring Finley Smythe as one of the groom's attendants?

"Hey, I finally found you." His sister appeared at his side as if he had summoned her with his thoughts. "You disappeared rather fast. Feeling okay?"

He wasn't sure what he felt, but *okay* was not near the top of the list of the words to describe the emotions coursing through him. Still, he nodded. "I'm fine."

Lauren raised her eyebrows, her lips pursed. "Not buying it. Do you want to go back to the hotel?"

"Honest, I'm good." He beckoned to a nearby waitstaff member and exchanged his empty glass for a full one, taking a second one to hand to Lauren. "I'm drinking wine at a winery. What could be wrong?"

Lauren's expression didn't change. "If you didn't want to be here, you should have said something when I asked. Then I could've found someone else to be my plus-one. Someone who would be happy to be at one of the Bay Area's most exclusive social events."

He gave himself a mental shake. No need to let the appearance of an old flame mar the day. Even if the churning in his stomach made it clear the fires weren't as banked as he thought they were. He smiled at his sister. "I'm happy to be with you. Been too long since we've been in the same place."

"And whose fault is that?" She laughed when they both answered, "Mine."

Then she sobered. "I do appreciate you escorting me to the wedding when Reid couldn't make it." She glanced down at the shiny platinum band on the fourth finger of her left hand, next to a ring set with a diamond so big, Will was pretty sure it could be seen from the International Space Station.

He nodded. "Reid knows the bride, right?"

"And the groom, but Nelle works for a children's nonprofit and he's their key sponsor, so they talk often. Nelle and I have become friends over the past year and I really like her, but I was aware I wouldn't know anyone else here." Lauren threw him a glance from under her eyelashes. "Which is why I thought you would be the perfect person to take to the wedding, because these are your people. Y'know, wheelers and dealers and chief executive officers. The crème de la crème of the tech industry."

"They are not my people." And once upon a time, Finley made it clear he was not, and never would be, her person.

"Really." Lauren folded her arms over her chest. "Last time I looked, you were a tech CEO."

"EverAftr is based in Chicago, not Silicon Valley."

"So? Screenweb is building a reality TV series around you."

"They're building it around EverAftr. The idea is to follow people from all over the country as they look for their romantic partners."

"But you're the star of the first season."

"EverAftr is the subject of the entire series."

Lauren huffed, but humor twinkled in her eyes. "Fine. Pretend you're not wholly responsible for EverAftr's success and the key reason why the company landed a TV deal."

Will's gaze zeroed in on Finley, despite the cheerful throng of guests crowding the winery's terrace between them. Most of the time, he thought his excellent recall was a gift. His memory wasn't eidetic—he couldn't amaze his friends by listing all the details of a meal he ate six years ago—but his mind was like an easily accessible filing cabinet stocked full of facts and figures as well as sounds, textures and sights. And right now, all he could remember was Finley.

The satin smoothness of her skin under his fingertips.

The dazzling light in her caramel-brown eyes when he made her laugh.

The soft gasp tickling his ear when he moved his mouth lower, to—

"Are you sure you're okay?" Lauren waved a hand in front of his face. "You haven't heard a word I've said. And your cheeks are flushed."

Will blinked and the memories disappeared, to be locked securely away this time. He hoped. "Just cold. The wind is picking up. I'm surprised the reception isn't being held indoors."

"You have to be kidding. It's a gorgeous day and there are patio heaters all over. If we stop hanging out in this corner and mingle with the other guests, you'll be toasty warm." Lauren indicated the trays of food being passed several feet away. "Besides, aren't you hungry? I heard the winery uses a three-star Michelin chef as their caterer."

His gaze sought Finley anew, a magnet he was power-less to resist. She was gathered with the rest of the wedding party, taking post-ceremony photos. The golden late afternoon sun created a halo around her, making her appear like the angel he knew she wasn't.

He glanced away. So what if Finley and he were at the same event? He wasn't the same heartsick youth she knew and, judging by the brittle way she held herself as the photographer posed the groom's attendants, she had changed, too. He could manage a few hours in her company. He was an adult. One with a full life that was about to become more complicated—and public.

In fact, the wedding might be doing him a favor. Once Screenweb announced the reality series based on EverAftr and his involvement in the first season, the media would dig into his romantic past. Finley might have resurfaced at a much more inopportune time and place. This way, he could rip the bandage off in relative privacy.

Assuming, that is, if he and Finley ever spoke. Judging by the way she glanced in every direction but his, it appeared she was as eager to reunite as he was. Made sense. She was the one who made it clear that summer was just a fling, and barely an entertaining one at that.

Damn his nearly perfect memory. Because now he recalled how her words landed, tearing fresh wounds with every precise syllable.

"So, what do you say? Food?" Lauren tugged at his hand.

He shook off the specters of the past and smiled at his sister. "Sure. Let's grab some crab puffs. Or whatever they're handing out."

He couldn't resist one last glimpse of Finley. She stood deep in conversation with another woman. If she felt his gaze on her, she didn't give any indication. He straightened his shoulders and pushed away from the corner, following Lauren as she wove her way through the merry throng of guests and toward the open bar.

Finley was ancient history. And she would stay that way.

But throughout the cocktail reception, the dinner and the dancing that followed, his memories would not remain submerged.

Finley thanked her dance partner—one of Grayson's colleagues from his venture capital firm—and left the bright lights and loud music of the dance floor. She passed various knots of guests deep in conversation, acknowledging those who nodded at her with a smile and a wave, and found an empty section of the terrace wreathed in shadows thanks to tall potted trees. She leaned on the stone balustrade and peered into the moonlit darkness of the vineyards below and the hills beyond, taking a moment to catch her breath.

And to still her pulse, which had raced all evening but not from dancing.

It took every ounce of self-control she had—and Finley had a deep, almost bottomless reserve of control, ask anyone—not to follow Will Taylor around with her gaze like the lovestruck girl she used to be. Not to leap on the stage and grab the microphone out of the lead singer's hand and demand an explanation from him. Not only, "Why are you here?" but "Why?" full stop. Why did he walk away, never to contact her again? Why did he let her go?

Why didn't he see past her words and realize she'd been forced to break up with him? If they were soul mates as he'd insisted, shouldn't he have seen the truth?

But then, soul mates weren't real. And the concept of true love was a marketing tool used to sell greeting cards and animated films.

She sighed. She never was one to cry over spilled milk and Will was a grocery warehouse full of knocked over dairy products. A fifteen-year-old spill, so that milk was truly spoiled and lost. She would not give him the satisfaction of acknowledging his presence, even though she physically ached from the fierce battle going on between her head and her heart.

Her head said to ignore him. This was Grayson and Nelle's day. She had plenty of details and duties that required her attention. Will Taylor was not one of them.

Her heart wanted…oh, so many things. Too many to sort through. And this was exhibit B in why she hated weddings: they made people want to be with a special person who was meant for them and them alone. To believe such a person might actually exist. But then the next morning would arrive, bringing with it the inevitable champagne hangover and a cold dose of reality.

An alarm chimed and she took her phone out of her skirt pocket. One hour until Grayson and Nelle would get into the vintage Rolls-Royce with "Just Married" scrawled on the windows. Then the wedding would be at an end and she, too, could depart. The winery staff had assured her they would take care of getting the remaining guests safely to their next destination and cleaning up, leaving her free.

But free for what? The only employer she'd ever had was behind bars in a federal penitentiary. And since she'd helped to put him there, it was probably safe to say she wouldn't receive a sterling reference from him. Planning the wedding had kept her thoughts busy and her feet moving for the last year or so, but that had obviously come to a conclusion.

The wind ruffled the ends of her hair, the chill air cutting through the lace and satin of her gown. With no patio heater nearby, she was reminded it was indeed February. She put the phone away, intending to return to the dance floor, when she overhead a woman mentioning Grayson's name.

Finley peered around the potted tree. A few feet away, a couple stood in close embrace, no doubt thinking they had this corner to themselves. Not wanting to disturb them—or face questions about why she was skulking alone—she remained still.

The man laughed. "Sure, Grayson is a great guy. Really happy for him, especially after what happened."

"I noticed the ex-congressman didn't make an appearance," the original female speaker said, an arch note in her tone.

"Might have been difficult for him, considering he's in prison." The man laughed. "Regardless, don't think much love is lost there," he continued. "Can you imagine if you were Grayson and your father was found guilty of misappropriating campaign funds? Good thing Grayson's reputation was already solid in the venture capital community or he'd never be trusted with investors' money again."

Finley clenched her fists but stayed silent. The situation with Barrett was scandalous and sordid, but also sad. Grayson grew up hero-worshipping his father only to discover Barrett's feet were not only clay, but hollow and full of rot.

She would never forgive Barrett for what he did to his son.

"Grayson will be fine, but I do have to question his judgment," the woman said. "I mean, really, including his sister in the wedding? When she worked arm-in-arm with their father and must have been up to her neck in the same corruption? Wonder what strings were pulled to keep her out of prison."

Something hurt. Finley glanced down and realized her nails were digging into her palms.

The man laughed. "There's one set of rules for people like the Monk family and another for the rest of us. I'm surprised the dad was caught in the first place. C'mon, let's go say goodbye and get back to the hotel."

Finley counted to thirty and then peered around the tree again. The couple was gone. She shivered, and the goose bumps on her skin had nothing to do with the night breeze.

It was one thing to intellectually understand her career was gone, and any avenues she'd wish to take to return to politics were closed. It was another to have random people confirm she would be viewed with suspicion wherever she went. Even at her brother's wedding.

But at least the couple's derision wasn't pity. She was tired—so tired!—of soft voices asking if she was okay. Tired of whispered conversations and solicitous gazes behind her back, when acquaintances thought she couldn't see or hear them.

She always saw and heard them.

She rolled her eyes. Maybe cloying, maudlin expressions of condolence made other people feel better, but as the object of their sympathy, they turned her stomach. She should find the unknown couple and thank them for their honesty.

But at the moment, her new sister-in-law was due to change out of her wedding gown and into clothes more comfortable for travel. Finley had volunteered to ensure Nelle's dress made it to the specialty cleaners while Grayson and Nelle were on their honeymoon. She might as well check in to see if Nelle needed anything else.

Stepping out of the safety of the shadows, Finley walked briskly toward the large oak door leading to the winery's gift shop and, beyond it, the private rooms set aside for the event. She kept her gaze locked on her phone. Hopefully, anyone who spotted her would assume she was attending to important wedding-related duties and would think twice before intercepting her. She had her right hand stretched out to pull the door open, her head still down—

The heavy door swung out, almost hitting her. She stumbled backward. The stiletto heel of her left shoe caught, slid on a loose pebble. The shoe went in one direction, her foot in another. Her ankle twisted as her balance escaped her.

Stars of pain exploded, filling her vision. Her arms flew out, flailing, her hands seeking something, anything to grasp. Her eyes slammed shut, anticipating the imminent rough landing on hard stone.

"I have you."

Solid, strong arms surrounded her. Her fingers clutched at fine wool covering firm biceps underneath as she scrambled to regain her footing. But when her left foot touched the ground, pain shot through her ankle, taking her breath away. She remained in the embrace of her Good Samaritan until the throbbing dulled enough for her other senses to register again, bringing her heartbeat and breathing back to something resembling normal. Warm hands continued to hold her, reassuring her she wouldn't fall.

After what felt like an eternity but was probably only a few seconds, Finley regained her balance enough to stand, keeping her weight on her good foot. The sting receded as she wriggled her bare toes. He ankle was just twisted, not sprained or broken. She exhaled and straightened up, and then turned to thank the person who came to her assist.

Her breath disappeared again.

Will.

Three

Will saw the accident happen as if in slow motion. The door began to swing out. The man pushing it open, his head turned, looking at his companion instead of checking to see if someone was on the other side. Finley, nose-deep in her phone as she headed for a direct collision. Her wide-eyed surprise as she narrowly avoided being hit by the solid oak doors. Her foot slipping, turning. Her scared gasp as she started to fall.

Will couldn't think. He refused to feel. He could only react. His pulse beat in his ears, a heavy percussion felt more than heard.

He caught her.

Finley's chest rose and fell in quick successive breaths and hyperventilation was added to his concerns until she got her breathing under control. He wrenched his gaze away, suddenly aware the lace of her gown did not fully conceal the swells of her breasts, teasing the shadowy valley between them.

"Are you okay?" he asked, his voice a rasp.

She nodded, her eyes remaining unfocused. Using his arm for leverage, she stood up straight. A wing of black hair fell across her face and she brushed it back with her free hand before turning to him. "Thank y—"

Her smile of gratitude froze. Shutters slammed down, rendering her gaze opaque. She dropped his arm as if she had just spotted a radioactive warning.

Over the last decade or so, he'd thought many times about what he would say if he bumped into her. Something smooth. Suave. Charming, but distant. A polite acknowledgment that would firmly indicate he had long since moved on and she was a nothing but a pleasant if fading memory.

"You should see a doctor about your ankle," he said, his voice raspy in his ears.

That was not one of the phrases he'd stored up all these years. His mind raced, seeking and discarding what to say next. Perhaps, "Hello, Finley, nice to see you?" But it wasn't nice. *Nice* was a word used to describe running into an old neighbor at the grocery store. *Nice* didn't cause throats to tighten and hands to sweat. *Nice* didn't bring images buried long ago to roaring life, sharper than ever.

She shook her head, tiny movements, but he saw them. Then she bent down and straightened the abandoned shoe on the terrace before slipping her left foot back into it. When she finally caught his eye, she smiled.

If smiles could freeze, he would be an ice sculpture. "Thank you for your advice," she said. "But what I need isn't your concern."

And never was, nor ever would be, her Arctic-chilled tone implied. "Of course I'm concerned. Anyone with common human decency would be. Maybe if you had some—" He bit the rest of his words back.

"If I had some...what? Decency?" If he thought the atmosphere was cold before, now it resembled an eternal winter. "You—" She snapped her crimson-dark lips closed as Lauren joined them.

"Hi." His sister gave Finley a friendly wave before tucking her left hand through his elbow and turning to him. "Sorry if I'm interrupting, but the band is playing my favorite song. You owe me a dance."

Finley's gaze zeroed in on Lauren's engagement and wedding rings, the solitaire diamond's size and brilliance evident even in the dim glow of the overhead string of lights. Her smile returned, wider and more brittle than before. "Excellent idea. You two go dance."

"Finley, this is Lauren. My—"

Finley held up her right hand, stopping his words. "Thank you for your assistance. Please, enjoy the rest of your evening." She nodded at Lauren and her smile faltered, only to appear again, smaller, but more genuine. "Both of you. Have fun. Now if you'll excuse me, I have bridal party duties that require my attention."

She turned, still a bit unsteady on her left foot, and yanked open the door to the winery's gift shop. "Get that ankle looked at," he called after her.

She gave no indication she heard him. The door slammed shut behind her.

Lauren crossed her arms over her chest. "What was that about?"

He shrugged, hoping his sister would interpret the movement as nonchalance and not because he was finding it difficult to form words, much less parse the emotions roiling through him. "She almost fell. I caught her."

Lauren's gaze narrowed. He cut her off before she could ask another pointed question. "You didn't tell me the groom was Barrett Monk's son."

Finley never talked about a brother. On the other hand, he was pretty sure he never mentioned Lauren or his other sister.

They'd had to sneak away from their respective duties to be together as it was. They hadn't spent a lot of their stolen time discussing family members.

"Why did I need to tell you?" Lauren looked at him as if he'd grown a third ear on his forehead. "The story was all over the national news. I've been to your place. You don't live under a rock."

Will shook his head. "Never mind." If he pursued this line of conversation, Lauren might ask him questions he wasn't in the mood to answer.

He never told his family about that summer. Lauren had been in high school and involved in her own teenage dramas at the time. And at first, he could hardly believe someone like Finley was his and so he didn't want to jinx it by telling too many people. Later, he realized that the relationship had been a mistake from the start and there was no reason to tell anyone the joke had been on him. "You said something about dancing?"

"Song's almost over now, but I'll accept another glass of wine."

"Deal. Lead on to the bar."

But as he followed Lauren through the crowd, the scent of pomegranate and spice—Finley's scent, warm and opulent and uniquely hers—remained with him, unlocking more memories he thought long lost. The sooner he left the wedding—the sooner he left California—the sooner he could put his past behind him and concentrate on his future.

It was going to be a long night.

Finley paused outside the room set aside for Nelle's use, taking a moment to smooth her hair, straighten her skirt and get her heartbeat under control. Her cheeks felt cool to the touch so hopefully her complexion was back to normal. There was nothing she could do about her vision, which still swam with the sight of the ginormous diamond ring and platinum wedding band on the hand of Will's companion.

She knocked on the door and waited for Nelle's cheerful "Come in!" before entering and taking the nearest chair, tucking her still-throbbing left ankle behind her right.

Nelle sat at the vanity table occupying the far wall. Her hair was no longer in the complicated updo she wore for the wedding and she was brushing out the last of the curls. She'd already changed into gray trousers and a soft navy sweater Finley had seen her wear many times before— probably because the top had been a gift from Grayson.

Nelle caught Finley's gaze in the mirror and smiled. "Hi. You're early."

Finley glanced at Nelle's wedding gown, carefully draped over the sofa next to the vanity. "Looks like I'm late. Did you have any trouble getting out of the dress?"

Nelle shook her head and then swiveled so she faced Finley. "Yoselin helped. You just missed her," she said, referring to her matron of honor. "And your timing is perfect. I wanted a few minutes alone with you."

Finley lifted her eyes toward the ceiling. "I expected sentimental drivel from Grayson. But you, Nelle? I'm crushed."

"Even fairy godmothers get to be thanked."

Finley laughed. "I'm hardly a fairy godmother. If I could wave a wand and make problems disappear, I'd start with my own."

And she knew exactly what she would zap first. That portion of her mind that stubbornly retained memories of Will, despite her best efforts to delete them.

Her fingers still carried Will's impression. The smooth, fine wool of his jacket. The unbelievably broad shoulders. The hard, bunched muscles of his arms as he held her. The–

Too late, she realized Nelle was speaking.

"—doubt anyone with a magic wand could have planned a more wonderful day for Grayson and me. Honestly, no matter what words I use to thank you, they're inadequate." Nelle's eyes shimmered, causing Finley to glance down.

One of the things she appreciated the most about her new sister-in-law was Nelle's ability to remain calm when situations became fraught—at least in Finley's presence. A Nelle capable of impersonating a watering can was new to Finley, and while she supposed allowances must be made for brides on their wedding day, she wasn't up to dealing with other people's emotions. Not after Will Taylor. Not when Finley struggled to keep such a tight control on her own emotions, she wanted to scream from the exertion.

Her gaze landed on the pinprick spot of blood on her cream lace bodice, now a brown fleck. Little did Nelle know how flawed the day had turned out to be, at least for Finley. She straightened in her chair and looked Nelle in the eye. "Don't you dare cry. I sent the makeup artist home, and you still have photos to take in the getaway car."

Nelle laughed, and sniffed, and carefully dabbed the area under her eyes. "I wouldn't dream of it."

"Good." Finley nodded. "Because I rented a classic Rolls-Royce, and mascara stains are hell to get out of vintage leather."

"Speaking of getaway…" Nelle rose from the vanity and came to stand in front of Finley. She had a white letter-size envelope in her hand. "This is for you."

Finley's stomach squeezed, and for once that day Will had nothing to do with it. "I don't—I was happy to plan the wedding. In fact you did me a favor by letting me do it. But I don't need Grayson's or your money—I'll be fine—"

"Never in doubt." Nelle dropped into the chair next to her. "You're Finley Smythe."

Her stomach still roiled. But she managed her trademark smirk. "Damn straight I am."

"But—" Nelle held up the envelope "—even you can use a getaway. And I'm not referring to a car with 'Just Married' written on the windows."

Finley eyed the envelope and moved to stand, the better to grab the wedding gown and make a fast exit, but she sat back down when her ankle protested. "My transportation is already taken care of for tonight, thanks." She took her phone out and looked at the screen. "And speaking of getaways, it's almost time for you and Grayson to make yours. Are you all set? Do you have everything?" She opened the text app and started a new message to the winery staff while she continued her conversation with Nelle. "Let me check in and make sure the chef packed a to-go box for you and Grayson. Neither of you had enough to eat—"

Nelle laid her hand on top of Finley's, stopping her movements. Finley gave Nelle her best imperious stare, but Nelle's hand did not move. "What?" Finley asked.

"The wedding, the—" Nelle waved her free hand "—

events of the last year. Despite everything, you constantly put Grayson and me first."

Finley narrowed her gaze and opened her mouth to protest.

Nelle cut her off with a firm shake of her head. "I've learned there is indeed a human being underneath that shark suit of yours, so don't give me your barracuda stare of death."

"Barracudas are fish, not sharks. And obviously my stare is not working, or you wouldn't have my hand still trapped."

"Sorry." Nelle sounded anything but apologetic. However, she released Finley's fingers. "You're always looking for ways to take care of us. And we appreciate it, more than we can express. But who takes care of you?"

Nelle's soft words reverberated in the silence that followed. Finley sat back in her chair, pinned by the force of her sister-in-law's gaze. Damn her ankle. Otherwise, she would already be far away. Away from Nelle's questions, away from ghosts of the past who materialized all too solidly, away from reminders that her carefully chosen life stratagems resulted in ruin. "I don't need anyone to take care of me. Obviously."

Nelle shook her head. "I didn't say anything about need. Of course you are more than capable of taking care of yourself. Let me try a different question—what are you going to do now that the wedding is over?"

"Go to the hotel, draw a hot bath and enjoy a fine bottle of wine." She checked her phone again. The basket of food for the newlyweds was already in the car. Another item she could check off her list. "And as soon as you and Grayson take off, I can put my plan in motion. Ready to go?"

Nelle remained seated. "And after the bath water is cold and the wine is gone? What are you doing next week?

Next month? Next year? What are your goals, now that your past career has been cut off?"

Ouch. Finley regarded her sister-in-law. "I see I've taught you well since we met. Going for the jugular. Nice."

Nelle grinned at her. "I learned from the best." She waved the envelope. "I meant what I said earlier. Words cannot express how grateful we are to you. But maybe this gift will."

Finley finally took it from her. "I swear, if this is money—" She ripped the envelope open.

It didn't contain cash or a check. Instead, she pulled out sheets of paper. What looked like a map and printouts of instructions and security codes and directions to…

She caught Nelle's gaze. Her sister-in-law was beaming.

Finley raised her eyebrows. "You're giving me your honeymoon? I mean, I love my brother—and you—but don't you think three's a crowd?"

"One of our honeymoons," corrected Nelle. "Grayson surprised me a few days ago with his wedding gift. We're going to Masaai Mara in Kenya. Which leaves this—" she picked up a sheet of paper that had fallen from Finley's lap and returned it to her "—open and available. And we both thought you should take our place."

The words blurred on the pages. "But—"

"No *buts*. It's all arranged. Two weeks of luxurious pampering with no one else around and nothing to do but enjoy yourself. And you can invite a friend to join you."

Finley ignored the last part. The only people she would consider bringing with her on a lavish vacation were going on their honeymoon in Africa. Not that she was vacationing in the first place. "This is very kind of you both, but I can't—"

"Can't what?" Nelle stared down Finley. "Can't miss work? Turns out that isn't a problem."

"I taught you too well," Finley muttered. "Harsh, but true."

"I'm sorry." This time the apology was sincere. "But Fin, please, we want to do something for you. And we thought you might appreciate an opportunity to decompress and reassess. The media attention and public scrutiny have been overwhelming for Grayson and me at times. We can only imagine how much harder this past year has been for you."

Because everyone thinks you were party to Barrett's corruption as his campaign manager and chief of staff.

Nelle didn't have to say the words. Finley heard them loud and clear. Derision from strangers she could handle. Pity from acquaintances was uncomfortable and distasteful, but she could brush it off. Nelle and Grayson feeling sorry for her... That was overwhelming. And not in a good way.

"I can't accept this." Finley stood, putting all her weight on her uninjured foot. "I appreciate the thought. But I don't need to decompress." She handed the papers back to Nelle.

Nelle rose and placed the printouts on her abandoned chair. "Even sharks need rest."

"That's what the hot bath and bottle of wine are for." Finley managed to make it to the sofa and picked up the wedding gown without too much of a limp. "I'm going to put the dress somewhere safe, and then I'll meet you at the car."

"If you change your mind—"

"I won't."

"If you do," Nelle continued, unfazed, "all the information should also be in your email inbox."

"See you in fifteen minutes." Finley exited the room, the gown in her possession. The need to protect the delicate fabric that overfilled her arms provided a convenient excuse for walking gingerly.

Finley lived by three rules: Never let others see her at anything but her best. Never react when someone scored a direct hit on one of her weaker spots. Never look back, only forward.

She'd broken all of them in the last five hours.

She *hated* weddings.

Four

Finley did not get her hot bath or her bottle of wine. Last-minute questions from the staff kept her at the winery long after the guests had left. By the time she reached her suite at the nearby hotel, she had just enough energy to put ice on her ankle—hours too late, but still—and fall into bed.

Sunlight streaming through the windows she forgot to cover woke her before she could get her much-needed eight hours of sleep. She blinked and sat up, at first too bleary to remember where she was. Then the memories of the night before flooded back, and she fell against the pillows.

Not every memory was bad. She'd never seen her brother look so happy. Joyous didn't even begin to describe his expression when he looked at Nelle. And Nelle's gaze overflowed with love and delight. The two of them were almost enough to make Finley reconsider her stance on whether *happily-ever-after* existed outside of nonsensical fairy tales.

Almost.

Because along with her memories of Grayson and Nelle driving away in wedded bliss came the feel of Will's arms around her: warm, sturdy, solid as steel. His unforgettable scent, woodsy and multilayered. The scorn in his voice when he assured her his offer of assistance was only out of common human decency, implying she lacked the same.

Will's companion, her proprietary left hand on his arm bearing an unmissable set of wedding rings.

Finley flung the covers off. She needed to get up and start her day. Start her life, for that matter. Nelle was right about one thing last night. Finley had thrown herself into planning the ceremony and the reception that followed. And while she excelled at the task, she recognized she also used it as a distraction. As long as she was neck-deep in seating charts and catering negotiations and band contracts, she could ignore thinking long term.

Until this morning.

She picked up the phone from the bedside table and ordered room service for breakfast. Then she grabbed her toiletries and headed to the bathroom to take a bracing shower while waiting for her food to arrive. Since people liked to compare her to a shark, she might as well act like one and swim forward, never backward.

The morning sun blazed bright, although rain was forecast for the West Coast later that afternoon. Television meteorologists were making worried noises about "the storm of the century." But Finley had grown up in California and she was well aware most weather events were given hyperbolic names simply because anything that deviated from the sunny norm was unusual—and the grandiose titles made for good TV ratings. She dressed to spite the predicted precipitation in a long, diaphanous skirt and a thin silk sweater with a low V-neck. And when room service knocked on her door, she directed the server to wheel the cart to the terrace, the better to enjoy the warm rays.

The eggs were done to perfection, the orange juice was fresh-squeezed and the bacon had just enough crunch. Her mood lifted with every bite. So what if Barrett was in a federal penitentiary and her name was mud? Mud was merely soil and water. It could be wiped clean. She was good at her job and had invaluable experience navigating the halls of power in Washington, DC. Besides, Barrett's scandal had long faded from the evening news and the late night comedy shows, his story replaced by others' misdeeds and follies. She started to make a list of people to call to arrange coffee or drinks—

Her phone rang. She frowned. Grayson and Nelle should be enjoying first class in the sky, on their way to London for a few days before making the connection to Nairobi, and she couldn't think of who else would need to get a hold of her so early in the day. A glance at the screen revealed her caller was Sadiya Khan, and Finley's frown deepened. She answered. "Please tell me you're calling to gossip about the wedding."

"Did you know Barrett was involved with Senator O'Donnell's wife? Or rather, soon-to-be former wife?" Finley's lawyer asked without preamble.

"What? No." Suddenly, breakfast did not sit well in her stomach. Senator O'Donnell was embroiled in an insider trading scandal that made Barrett's campaign finance fraud look like a five-year-old raiding his piggy bank by comparison. "Why do I get the feeling there's a second part to your question?"

Sadiya sighed. "Erica O'Donnell wrote a book."

"People do that," Finley responded. "What does—"

"She's trying to create a bidding war among publishers. We got a heads-up tip that you're featured in the manuscript."

Finley sat back in her chair. "Why would I be in Erica O'Donnell's book? I think we've spoken maybe…twice?… in the last ten years."

"She claims you're the one who originally put together the insider trading ring and then you leaked her husband's involvement to the press."

"What?" Finley took the phone away from her ear, stared at it in disbelief, then returned it. "What the—that's utterly preposterous—why would I do that?"

Sadiya sighed. "According to her, you were angry Senator O'Donnell was the frontrunner for the presidential nomination and wanted to wreck his political career."

A cold, hard ball settled in Finley's stomach. She wasn't sure if it was born of rage or frustration or a combination of both. "This is ridiculous. Why would I care if O'Donnell got the nomination or not—"

"You wanted Barrett to be the nominee, so you could pull the strings behind the scenes. But Barrett refused to challenge Senator O'Donnell because he didn't want Erica to be hurt if their affair was exposed. So he instead announced his early retirement from Congress—"

"Wait, what?" Finley blinked several times, hoping the movement would help her process what she was hearing. "Barrett stepped down because of his health."

"Not according to Erica. He was chivalrously protecting her reputation. In retaliation, you went on a scorched earth campaign and blew the whistle on Barrett's fraud, while setting up the O'Donnells for insider trading. She goes into explicit detail—"

The ball in Finley's stomach was definitely rage. The world turned hazy white with edges tinged with red. "That's the most awful, outrageous, scurrilous—"

"We're going to fix this." Sadiya's calm tone cut through the fog enveloping Finley. "She's making even more extreme claims about other people."

"More extreme?" Something vibrated against Finley's ear and she realized it was her phone, due to her trembling hand. "Hard to believe that's possible."

"She's flinging dirt in all directions to see what will stick."

"And she knows it will stick to me, thanks to Barrett's scandal." Finley's nose burned and there was a suspicious prickling in the corner of her eyes. She swallowed and forced the tears back. She would not give Erica O'Donnell the satisfaction of making her cry, even if out of rage, even if no one saw her do so.

"What Erica knows is she's up to her neck in the same schemes as her husband and also facing indictment and serious jail time. She's creating diversions, hoping to send the investigators and the press off on wild-goose chases."

"You know how the media works," Finley said through numb lips. "Write headlines first, retract only if forced to later."

"Not all. But some outlets, yes," Sadiya agreed.

Normally, Finley appreciated Sadiya's no-nonsense, cut-through-the-bullshit approach. But at times, like now, she'd appreciate a little fudging of the truth, just for re-assurance. A large, albeit invisible, weight pressed down on her shoulders. "Am I to assume a tsunami of reporters is headed my way? Again?"

Sadiya was silent for a moment. "I'm speaking to the best defamation lawyers in the country. We'll get you cleared. But for now..."

Finley screwed her eyes shut. She definitely regretted the orange juice. The citric acid burned holes in her stomach. "But for now, brace for impact."

"That's my advice."

"Okay." Finley took a deep breath, thankful Grayson and Nelle were headed overseas and would be difficult to reach for the next month. They should enjoy their honeymoon without having to wade through yet more scandal thrown at their family.

As for her, she would get through this. She got through the press circus when Grayson abruptly dropped out of his run for Congress. She survived the round of constant media badgering when Barrett was indicted for fraud, and the second, even more ferocious round when he went on trial. This was merely Erica O'Donnell trying to drum up interest in what was no doubt a sensational piece of fiction, hastily written to make money before she, too, went to federal prison.

"We'll put the brakes on as fast as we can," Sadiya said. "In the meantime—"

"Don't knock over any banks and draw even more attention. Got it." She opened her eyes and glanced across the lush garden courtyard that separated her cottage suite from the others. The morning continued to be gorgeous. More people were taking advantage of the momentary sunshine and temperate breezes to also have their breakfast on their private terraces. Lucky people, who probably had no concern deeper than getting in a round of golf or touring nearby wineries. People like—

Will.

She froze. No, she did not conjure up his image. That was Will on the terrace directly opposite hers, separated only by a strip of emerald green lawn lined with profusely flowering rosebushes.

If she thought Will looked more attractive than any human had a right to in his suit the night before, that was nothing to seeing Will in a T-shirt that clung to his broad shoulders and skimmed over what appeared to be an impressive set of pecs. Those were new, her brain couldn't help noticing. Well-worn jeans draped just so over narrow hips and powerful thighs. He was carrying two cups of coffee and thankfully wasn't looking in her direction—because he was talking to his female companion from the night before, who laughed and affectionately punched his shoulder before taking one of the cups from him.

"Finley? Did I lose you?"

"I'm here." Finley almost knocked over her chair in her haste to get inside her suite and draw the curtains across the windows before Will could spot her staring at him with her mouth half-open like a drooling teenager at her first pop idol concert.

Not that she cared if Will saw her, obviously all alone and frowning into her phone. Not at all.

No, she only went inside because she'd learned it was better not to give the press anything when they were on the hunt. And for all she knew, journalists were already descending upon the hotel. Grayson and Nelle's wedding hadn't exactly been a secret—anyone with a gift for research on the internet would be able to find the details—and if they weren't already prowling the grounds, they would be soon.

"Sorry," she continued, locking the French doors behind her. She tucked the phone between her right shoulder and ear and then opened her suitcase on the luggage rack, not caring to fold her clothes before throwing them in. "I decided to multitask and pack while we talked."

"Good idea. I don't know who else was tipped off about the book. And regardless, it will become public knowledge sooner than later." Finley heard her slight intake of breath, which she knew meant Sadiya was considering her words. "Do you want me to call our security contractors? I can have guards at your place in a few hours."

Finley stopped taking clothes off hangers and sank onto the bed. "You think I need a security detail? Seriously?"

"Senator O'Donnell is popular with a certain segment that likes to make threats on dark corners of social media. It's only a precaution," Sadiya hastened to add. "You haven't received any that I know of. Just thinking ahead."

"Hold on a minute." No, she did not want guards. The last thing she wanted was to become a virtual prisoner in her place of residence, mostly because she was currently residing in the guest cottage on Barrett's estate, a three-hour drive southeast from the Bay Area. Barrett had been in ill health even before his indictment, and Finley had moved in to oversee his medical care. She'd sublet her Washington, DC, apartment, and she never had looked for a new home of her own.

Too many memories. Too many people angry at her. Finley knew she'd done the right thing by alerting the authorities to Barrett's fraud, but others saw her as disloyal. A turncoat. A traitor to the man who married her mother and took her in when she was a three-month old baby, and to the Monk family name, which had been prominent in California politics for generations. According to them, she was the viper in the family's breast who brought down a dynasty and destroyed not only her stepfather, but her brother's promising political career. It didn't matter to them that Grayson chose of his own free will to drop out of his race for Congress.

She took the phone away from her ear and opened her email app. She started scrolling—yes. Nelle had made good on her promise and Finley had all the information she needed. Nelle even promised appropriate clothes would be waiting for her since, as Nelle phrased it, "your usual wardrobe might not be appropriate."

Finley put the phone back up to her ear. "I have a better idea."

Will watched Finley stalk into her suite and close the door behind her, most of her breakfast left untouched on the table. He hoped he wasn't the reason why she felt the need to abandon her food, then mentally shook his head at his own ego. He didn't mean a thing to Finley Smythe, except perhaps as a lingering bad odor from somewhere vaguely in her past.

At least she appeared steady on her ankle, not that he paid much attention to that part of her anatomy. When he blinked, the image of Finley's curved hips and long legs, revealed by the morning sunlight streaming through her thin skirt, was seared on the inside of his eyelids.

"Ground control to Major Will." Lauren waved her hand in his face. "Can you hear me?"

"Sorry." He'd spent enough time dwelling on Finley. Still, his gaze would not leave the spot where he last saw her. "You were saying?"

"I've been thinking about the television series. Are you *sure* you want to do it?"

That got his attention. "Why?"

"It's just…" Lauren chewed on the inside of her cheek, a nervous habit she'd had since childhood. "A TV show… It seems so…public."

"Of course it's public. It's marketing."

"Yeah, but the show is about *you*."

"Not just me."

"So you could drop out of appearing and production would still go forward?"

Will sipped his coffee, considering his words. "Screenweb bought the series based on my participation in the first season. Without me, they said it was just another reality dating series and they weren't interested. If I don't appear on camera, then no, they won't move forward. But the goal is to hook viewers and run for many years," he added.

"Which the series won't do if *you* don't successfully find someone," Lauren pointed out. "The whole world will be focused on you. If you don't end up marrying whoever the app matches you with, it's bad news not only for the series but for EverAftr as a company. Tell me you've thought this through."

He'd spent most of the sleepless night before doing nothing but thinking it through. "Our algorithm matches people based not only on their likes and dislikes, but also on intangible strengths and weaknesses as well as communication styles. It's why our customers have had such success. There's no reason why people won't be successful on camera as well." He smiled. "Are you doubting my work?"

Lauren rolled her eyes. "Of course not." She held up her left hand, her rings sparkling in the morning light. "Reid and I are proof your work is brilliant. But this isn't meeting someone privately via the app. It's a risk."

"You know the questionnaires and tests are extensive and highly vetted. I've made my preferences very clear." He'd double-checked them after seeing Finley again. He'd emphasized constancy, steadiness and dependability in his answers—all things that Finley had proved not to possess.

"If you say so." Lauren did not sound convinced.

He smiled. "It seems you don't believe the answers we've prepared for the press. Here's one more reason. Ji-Hoon is one of the producers."

Lauren's mouth formed an O. A former neighbor of their parents, Ji-Hoon Park had been one of Will's earliest cheerleaders. He helped Will get his first job in tech, and later introduced Will to people who became his future business partners. When Will started exploring the idea that turned into EverAftr, Ji-Hoon gave him the seed capital. "How's he doing? I haven't spoken to him lately. I need to call him."

"The last round of chemotherapy was tough, but he's hanging in. And he's thrilled to return to the industry, as he calls it." Ji-Hoon had tried to break into film and television acting as a young man, but roles for Asian men had been few and hard to come by. He returned to Illinois and eventually became a successful commercial real estate broker, but never lost his dream of making a splash in show business. Now Will had the opportunity to return all the favors Ji-Hoon did him by bringing Ji-Hoon on board as a producer on the series.

"And," Will continued, "we put a condition on the sale of the series to Screenweb. They'll team up with shelters and nonprofits working to prevent partner abuse and run an awareness campaign before every episode. EverAftr is earmarking fifteen percent of our revenue for those organizations."

"You could have led with that." Lauren flopped into the nearest chair and took out her phone, indicating she was through arguing with him.

"Now you know." He saluted Lauren with his mug, and then put it down on the low table next to her. "I have a long drive to Los Angeles. I should return to my room to pack. Thanks for the coffee."

She looked up. "Take the inland route. It's not as pretty as the coast, but faster."

"I live in Chicago where February equals dark and cold. I'm not going to miss my chance to catch ocean views."

"Forecasters are predicting a major storm," Lauren

warned. "I'm glad my flight is leaving before the rain is supposed to hit."

"You forget I worked in Santa Monica for a few years. I laugh at California's attempts at weather."

She shook her head. "Just drive safely."

He kissed the top of her head. "I should be back in time to say goodbye before you leave for the airport. But if by some chance I miss you, have fun in Tokyo. Say hi to Reid."

He chuckled as he left. Chicago's rain was freezing in February. And if wasn't rain, it was sleet. And if it wasn't sleet, it was a snowstorm. A little California precipitation? Child's play.

Hours later, his knuckles white on his car's steering wheel as he tried to peer out the windshield, the wipers moving at high speed helpless against the torrential rain, he was no longer laughing.

Five

Finley attempted to push her hair out of her eyes, but the wet strands stayed plastered to her skin. Of all the days for weather forecasters to be right, they had to pick this one. She shivered. The skirt and sweater she'd thrown on that morning were little protection against the chilled wind and stinging rain.

At least she found Running Coyote Ranch. And not a moment too soon. What should have been a relatively easy six-hour drive south from Napa to Santa Barbara had stretched into nine hours thanks to the weather. She'd wanted to arrive before sunset but now the sky was completely dark, the moon and stars extinguished by thick clouds. Almost blinded by the heavy rain, she'd inched her way up the narrow canyon road with only her car's headlights to guide her. After what felt like a decade since she exited the highway, she reached the top of the hill and pulled into a wide circular drive—and upon leaving the car, stepped into a puddle she'd swear was big enough to go kayaking in, ensuring her sandal-encased feet were as wet as the rest of her.

This was what she got for not packing an umbrella, not that it would have been any help. The wind would have blown it inside out within a matter of minutes. She pulled up Nelle's email on her phone and found the entry code to punch into the keypad next to the immense carved doors. "Please work, please work, please work," she chanted under her breath. She was in no mood to get back into the car and search for alternate accommodations in the small community at the bottom of the long, twisty road she just crawled up.

The keypad made a clicking noise. Finley tugged on the doorknob. The door pulled open with ease. She crossed the threshold—

Oh. Wow. Yes.

Yes, this would do nicely as a place to stay for a few weeks, until Sadiya and her colleagues could get a better handle on the response to Erica O'Donnell's explosive claims.

According to Nelle's email, Running Coyote Ranch was built in 1928 by a now-forgotten silent film star, who spared no expense to create a haven where she and her fellow celluloid legends could relax and play in private. Designed in the Spanish Colonial Revival style, a popular architectural choice in Southern California at the time, the ranch was a stunning example of what money could buy—especially when there was access to Hollywood craftsman, many of whom had made the two-hour journey north from the film studios in Los Angeles to construct the ranch's main house and outbuildings.

Finley left her suitcase to drip on the thick square terra-cotta tiles in the expansive entryway. She ventured into large living area just beyond, marveling at the colorful smaller tiles that outlined the stucco arched doorways and the intricately painted wood beams that held up the coffered ceiling. One wall was mostly fireplace, built out of roughhewn stone, tall enough for Grayson—who was well over six feet—to stand in. Chestnut brown leather sofas, wide and long enough to comfortably hold a spooning couple for a nap, faced each other in front of the wrought iron fire screen. Additional chairs, some draped with blankets that looked so soft they must be pure cashmere, were arranged to create areas for conversations. Bookcases lined the other three walls, filled with colorful book spines interspersed with displays of pottery and artistic photographs of Southern Californian landscapes, while deeply piled sheepskin rugs were scattered across the floor, adding additional notes of warmth and coziness. Beyond the arched doorway, she caught a glimpse of additional rooms, also decorated in the height of luxurious rustic chic.

She couldn't wait to explore. But—she took a step and her wet skirt wrapped around her legs, chilling her anew— first, she needed to change her clothes. And maybe get a good night's sleep.

She returned to the entryway to recover her bag and discovered a binder on the long, low bench set against the wall. An envelope with her name on it rested on top. She flipped through the binder first, noting it held a map of the ranch, a plan of the main house with her room's location marked on it, plus any instructions she would need for the house's appliances during her stay. Inside the envelope was a card from Grayson and Nelle.

Dearest Finley,
We knew you wouldn't be able to resist. Welcome to
Running Coyote! Since this was originally meant to
be our honeymoon, the staff already had instruc-

tions not to disturb guests until asked for. Mariam Stern, the chief of staff, will be expecting your phone call when you want housekeeping services. We planned to do our own cooking and the kitchen should be fully stocked, but the ranch has a chef on standby. If you'd like your meals prepared, you can arrange that with Mariam.

Finley nodded. That would be among her immediate priorities in the morning. Food should only exist already arranged on a plate or in a take-out container as far as she was concerned.

Mariam's husband, Tim, is the ranch manager. We told him you're an excellent equestrienne and he has horses ready for you if you want to go riding. The Sterns live in the compound at the bottom of the hill and cell phone service can be spotty in the mountains, so there's a CB radio in the kitchen in case of emergency.

Running Coyote has a heated Olympic-size swimming pool and spa, a fully equipped gym, and the hiking trails are spectacular. Oh, and help yourself to anything in the bar as well. Have a wonderful time! And we hope you brought someone special with you...

Nelle and Grayson.

She rolled at her eyes at the last sentence. Like she'd had any time over the last decade or so to nurture a relationship. Besides, she'd probably combust of frustrated irritation if she were stuck on the ranch for days on end with anyone but maybe Grayson or Nelle. And even then, it would be a close race as to which one of them would grow sick of the other's company the fastest. She resolutely put the image of Will, laughing at something his companion said, out of her mind. His companion, who wore a spectacular set of wedding rings.

Finley folded the card and placed it back in the envelope, then tucked it and the binder under her arm as she followed the directions to the guest suite. Her own company was perfectly sufficient. Even if the ranch screamed "romantic getaway" around every corner and she was essentially on a honeymoon of one.

She opened the door to the suite and instantly congratulated herself on accepting Nelle's offer. The three connected rooms—a sitting room that led to a bedroom and an adjoining bathroom—were the epitome of hospitable luxury.

She couldn't wait to take a long, hot bath in the deep tub, big enough to comfortably stretch out in. And then there was the bed—in this case, a king-size four-poster with the fluffiest white duvet she'd ever seen, a rust-and-brown cashmere blanket at the foot, and so many pillows even Finley, a notorious bedding hog who loved to tuck herself in with a mountain of goose down around her, was satisfied. The closet was open, allowing her to catch a glimpse of enough long-sleeved plaid shirts, denim jackets, jeans and cowboy boots to clothe the entire cast of a revival of *Oklahoma!* And if Finley's first action was to grab the bottle of white wine sitting on the table tucked into the picture-perfect reading alcove, well, she was officially unemployed and on vacation.

She didn't bother with the wineglasses placed next to the bottle.

Will regretted not taking his sister's advice to take the inland route between Napa and Los Angeles instead of the coastal highway. If he had, maybe he'd already be at his destination instead of just creeping by Santa Barbara, which was still one hundred miles north of LA.

The rain was relentless. He slowed his speed even farther and tried to keep a decent following distance between himself and the vehicle in front of him, but the poor visibility, especially now that night had fallen, did not help. He blinked, his eyes scratchy and dry from focusing so hard—and red taillights suddenly lit up in front of him, far too close for comfort.

He slammed on his brakes. The rear end of his rented Porsche Cayman fishtailed. He steered into the slide and brought the car under control, just in time to keep the Cayman's front bumper from sliding into the pickup truck directly in his path. By some miracle, the car following Will managed to avoid a collision as well.

Adrenaline still pumping hard through his veins, he peered through the windshield. The deluge let up just enough for him to see that the highway had been turned into a parking lot. Cars that had once been steadily, if slowly, flowing down the road were motionless.

He sighed and dug down deep to find his well of patience. He'd need it.

Forty minutes later, Will had progressed only two miles. Worse, the rhythmic sweep of the wipers and the syncopated patter of rain on the car's roof were inducing drowsiness. He tried loud music to stay awake. He tried blasting the air conditioner. But he finally gave in to an inescapable fact: he had to get off the road or he would fall asleep at the wheel. The car's navigation system indicated the next available exit was Lobos Canyon, but it lacked symbols for hotels or even a fast-food restaurant...

Wait. Lobos Canyon. He knew Lobos Canyon. Of course. He left a quick phone message for Lauren and then took the off-ramp as soon as he got to it. The directions came back easily to him, even in the dark and rain, and before long he turned onto the steep road that wound up into the hills. He was so intent on not missing a curve and accidentally plunging off the side of the canyon that he missed the first driveway that led to his destination. The road was too narrow to turn around safely in the dark, and he didn't trust the Porsche's tires—designed to sail down smoothly paved freeways—on the muddy, stone-filled terrain. That left him the second driveway, meant for delivery vehicles, horse trailers and tractors. When he arrived at the end of the gravel road, he realized he was closer to the stable than he was to the main house. Fine, he would just have to walk the rest of the way. Across a field. A wet, sludge-filled field.

By the time Will reached the residence and punched the access code to unlock the rear service door, the parts of his clothes that weren't covered in a thick layer of mud were soaked through. Water dripped down the nape of his neck and off his nose while his sneakers squelched with every step, leaving dirty puddles in his wake. Not wanting to traipse dirt through the main living quarters, he located the nearby laundry facilities. He kicked off his shoes and left them to air out on the utilitarian tile. Then he stripped off his shirt, wrung it out as much as he could and put it on an adjacent rack to dry.

His jeans were molded to his skin. He would deal with getting out of them later. Preferably just before jumping into a hot shower.

His laptop remained in the Porsche, but his sodden suitcase presented another problem. Rather than risk trailing muddy water through the residence, he grabbed a change of clothes—luckily, the inside of his bag was still dry—and his dopp kit, leaving the rest of his things with his shoes and shirt. Then he set off to find accommodations for the night.

Reid and Lauren had told him on his last visit that they always kept the guest wing ready in case of unexpected drop-ins. And if anyone fit that description, it was him. The house was dark, but his gift for remembering even small details came to his rescue. He easily found the stairs that led to the private suite. The door noiselessly swung open, revealing the sitting room with two closed doors, one leading to the spacious bedroom and the other to a bathroom that would be at home in a five-star luxury hotel.

He could almost feel the warm spray of the shower on his skin now. He dropped his things on a nearby chair and opened the door to the bathroom, unbuttoning his jeans as he walked into the space—

And froze.

Several items hit his brain's processing center, all at once.

One, the bathroom was not dark, as he expected it to be, but lit by flickering candles perched on the shelves that lined the wall between the oversize claw-foot bathtub and the walk-in shower.

Two, the air was heavy with steam and smelled of roses.

Three, the bathtub was filled with foamy bubbles. And floating in the midst of the bubbles, her head leaned against the wall of the tub and her eyes closed, was a nude Finley.

Six

The bath water was steaming hot, the wine went down deliciously smooth and Finley was finally, for what felt like the first time in over a year, utterly at peace. Oh, sure, her life was still stuck in the same place and the specter of Erica O'Donnell's egregious claims hung over her, but at the moment? Pure bliss.

If this bathroom was any indication of the care and attention paid to every detail by the ranch's owners and staff, she was very much going to enjoy her stay. She had her pick of bubble baths and foaming bath powders. Candles came thoughtfully paired with a lighter, making it easy to set them ablaze and appreciate their flickering ambiance. There was a tray to place across the tub should she feel like reading while reveling in a soak—she'd noticed the sitting room attached to the bedroom came with fully loaded bookcases. And there were cleverly hidden speakers if she wanted to listen to music.

She chose a bubble bath with roses on the label, the scent transporting her to a time when all she had to care about during long summer days and the too-short nights was finding the most secluded spot in the garden in which to meet her love. But she was too tired to concentrate on words on a page and couldn't be bothered to find tunes to match her mood. The slight lapping of water at the tub's edges as she shifted was music enough to her ears.

All was calm, all was dimly lit and warm. She found herself drifting in and out of consciousness, never falling truly asleep but lulled into a waking dream.

A dream starring Will. A Will who broke into a wide smile whenever he spotted her. Who never hesitated to hug her, to caress her, to even pick her up and spin her around as if it were the most natural thing in the world. As if she were the type of person who should be touched once her consent was given, frequently and with care. As if she should be held.

Such ideas had been foreign to her before she met Will. Her mother must have picked her up as an infant, surely? But by the time Finley could start storing memories, Grayson had arrived. She became the "big girl," who shouldn't want or need to be carried like her baby brother.

Then her mother had fallen ill, and neither Finley nor Grayson were held much. Finley's recollections of her mother weren't numerous, and mostly revolved around a dim, quiet room when their mother was intermittently home from chasing miracle cures interspersed with hospital stays. Finley and Grayson would be ushered in to kiss their mother good-night, but recollections of other activities weren't forthcoming.

She couldn't remember any gestures of affection from Barrett. But Grayson's warm, open heart must have come from somewhere. Or maybe he was born with it.

For all that Barrett wasn't her biological father, she was the one who most resembled him when it came to personality. She used to pride herself on being as cutthroat as he was.

Until that summer. With Will. A summer that opened up new possibilities. New avenues. A whole new way of being. A new person for her to become.

What would have happened if she had refused to believe Barrett, told him firmly to stay out of her life? Chose Will and a vastly uncertain future? Who would she be now?

She opened her eyes.

Will stood before her, his eyes wide, his mouth moving but no sound coming out.

She closed her eyes again. Of course she saw Will. It was only natural her mind would conjure him, after running into him at the wedding. She was warm and relaxed and the wine burned low in her stomach. Who else would she think about but—

A shirtless Will, whose shoulders and chest had not been that broad and developed when she knew him. And he definitely hadn't had six-pack abs. Or worn well-made jeans that clung to his narrow hips and powerful legs and…wait.

Her eyes flew open again. "What in the everlasting holy f—"

"Sorry—I had no idea you were here—" Will slapped his left hand over his eyes as his feet backpedaled, his other hand outstretched to fumble for the door. "This isn't—I just wanted to get off the freeway—"

"What the—why in the—how are you here?" Bubbles. The bubbles, which had once heaped high, were almost gone. She was barely covered. Will could see, well, everything.

Not that she was ashamed. Nudity was a natural human condition, and she had no issues disrobing in front of other adults at, say, the changing room at the gym. But he was *Will*. And she swore Will would never see her naked again.

Never.

And she would be damned if she acted like a demure virgin in front of him, using her hands and arms to cover the pertinent bits while wearing nothing but a blush. Been there, done that with him, and that ship had long sailed, anyway. She splashed around, her thoughts as frantic as her movements, until she finally remembered the plush towel on the low bench next to the tub. She reached for it. "How did you—did you break in? No, wait, how did you even know Running Coyote existed? Are you following me? What the *hell*, Will?"

She wrapped the towel around her while still sitting in the bathtub. The towel soaked up water and became heavy and sodden, but at least she could keep her vow to never be nude in front of him again.

Will continued to back up, his hip encountering the edge of the Carrara marble counter. He muttered but kept his hand in front of his face. "Sorry," he continued to repeat as he edged his way toward the doorway. "I'll give you your privacy—" He hit a sharp corner and grunted in pain. "Damn it."

Finley huffed. "Oh, for crying out loud, turn around and use your eyes before the bath turns ice cold and I die of hypothermia."

His outreached hand finally found the doorknob. "I'm leaving—"

"Now," she ordered.

"Be careful. The floor can be slipper—"

"I can exit a bathtub just fine, thank you very much."

"You hurt your ankle the other day. The stone tile is a hazard—"

She resisted the urge to throw the loofah at him. "Get. Out."

Will closed the door behind him. Finley exhaled, trying to get her breath under control. She was trembling, and she was pretty sure it had nothing to do with wearing a soaking wet towel while sitting in a tub of cooling water.

What is Will Taylor doing at Running Coyote?

Will leaned against the closed door to the bathroom. His mind, so good at running several computational problems simultaneously, was stuck in a loop and had no indication of escaping it.

Finley Smythe was here. At his brother-in-law's ranch getaway.

A nude Finley, luscious and glowing in the candlelight. Her sharply angled face relaxed, appearing younger than when they first met. Her breasts, perfectly sized for his hands, almost but not quite hidden, their deep-rose peaks breaking through the foam. The dark triangle between her legs, just visible beneath the water.

Only his shock kept him from making a bigger fool of himself in front of her. Because if he thought he was immune to Finley Smythe, the heavy fullness in his cock as he relived his first sight of her told a different story. Sometimes he couldn't decide if having a near photographic memory was a blessing or a curse.

But what was she doing here? He knew Reid and Lauren and the newly married Monks were friends—after all, that was why Will was able to attend the small, highly exclusive wedding. Apparently that friendship extended to Finley. Although, at the reception, Finley and Lauren didn't seem to be well acquainted.

He shook his head, hoping it would jog his thoughts free. It didn't matter who, when or why. The pertinent facts were easy enough to parse. Finley was here. So was he. The weather was awful. Neither of them should be out in the storm.

The ranch had far more than one bathroom and bedrooms were plentiful. If he stayed the night, the house was big enough that he didn't have to set eyes on her again before he left in the morning.

So why was he still lingering outside this particular bathroom door? Damned if he knew. He grabbed his things from where he had flung them on the chair and strode to exit the guest suite.

A crash from the bathroom stopped him in his tracks. He turned back and was knocking on the door within seconds. "Finley?"

"Go. Away." The words were gritted, as if uttered from between her teeth. As if she were in pain.

"What happened? Do you need a doctor?"

"What is it with you and your rescuer complex? I'm fine. I knocked over a candle, that's—ow!"

Visions of flames surrounding Finley dashed through his head. "I'm coming in."

"I don't need your hel—" Her voice trailed into a loud yelp.

That did it. Will opened the door and flipped on the light switch. Finley sat on the wooden bench built into the wall next to the tub, wrapped in a soaking-wet towel. The remains of a large glass candleholder littered the floor. But it was the blood, on the tile and smeared over Finley's feet, that caused his stomach to flip. "What happened?"

"I stepped on broken glass and cut my foot," she grumbled. "And who said you could come in?"

"You did," he said. "By yelling in pain."

"I did no such thing."

"Someone did. And since the staff don't live in and I know this place isn't haunted, you're the only suspect." He grabbed a washcloth from the basket next to the sink and wet it under the tap, then stood in front of her. "Show me the injury."

She hesitated, her lips pressing together in a firm line.

He handed her the cloth and turned to leave. "Fine. Have it your way. Good luck spotting any glass that might still be embedded on your own."

"Wait." When he turned around, she huffed and stuck out her left foot. "Here."

Finley projected an impregnable suit of armor around her that made her imposing. Larger than life. Even when they had been together, Finley always seemed to have descended from a higher, more exalted plane than where he and other mere mortals dwelled. But when he took the wet cloth back from her and knelt before her, he realized with an electric shock that he had forgotten some things about her after all. Like how without the sharply tailored suits and shoes with heels so tall and thin they could double as weapons, she was rather petite in build. The contrast between the untouchable Finley he'd built up in his mind over the years versus the all-too-vulnerable woman before him made him dizzy.

But only for a second.

He ran the cloth over the cut. Finley inhaled a sharp hiss, her foot trembling in his grasp. The glass had sliced deep, but the wound was clean and free of additional shards. He threw a quick glance up at her. She was stone-faced, her gaze landing anywhere but on him. "You'll live," he said, his voice rough.

"Thank you once more for your keenly observed medical assessment." She kept her face turned away.

"There are bandages under the sink." He rose, then pointed at her. "Don't move."

She indicated the soaking-wet towel wrapped around her with a sweep of her hand. "And to think I was just about to make my debut on the red carpet."

"Don't try to stand." He found the first aid kit at the back of the sink cabinet. She remained exactly where he had left her, frozen in place. Her knuckles were white from clenching the rolled edge of the tub, their color matching her complexion.

He returned to his kneeling position. "Still don't like the sight of blood, I see."

Her gaze snapped to meet his. It was the first time they made eye contact since he entered the bathroom. "I don't know what you're talking about."

Her words were full of bravado, but she focused on the ceiling as he examined her injured sole, her foot shaking in his grasp. It was yet another reminder that a vulnerable human being existed underneath Finley's highly polished surface. A reminder he didn't need, damn it. He was perfectly fine thinking of Finley as a glossy two-dimensional image designed to dazzle and seduce but lacking anything resembling real depth.

"No, of course you don't. There's another reason why you're holding on to the tub as if you are about to faint. Or as if it were a wooden door floating in the ocean and the *Titanic* just sank." He threw her a brief grin. Finley used to tease him about his lack of film knowledge. He mentally thanked his sisters for forcing him to watch that movie with them on a rainy Sunday afternoon.

"You're the one who told me not to move."

"When have you ever done what people tell you? Least of all me." He finished bandaging her foot and sat back on his heels. "Done. It's safe to look now. Or to go back in the water, as the case may be."

"That's *Jaws*. You're mixing up your pop culture history references. Some things never change." But her hands relaxed, her shoulders visibly falling to settle in their usual position. Her foot stopped trembling and pink bloomed on what had been ashen cheeks.

Yes, Finley was all too human. And an attractive one at that. One who had a power like no other to make his blood boil—but not in anger. No, his last argument with Finley left him cold and desolate. But passion... She was the only person he'd met so far who could instinctively find his ignition switch, rendering him hot and hard and lacking in conscious thought in seconds flat. Just one sideways flick of her glance and—

He made the mistake of looking up. Her dark eyes glittered in the dim light. Her full lips parted as she inhaled. And he was suddenly, intimately aware they were alone in the ranch house.

The steam in the air wrapped around them, narrowing the world to Finley and him. He still cradled her foot in his hands. It would be all too easy to slide those hands up to her calves. And then higher. The towel barely reached the tops of her thighs. She wore nothing underneath. In a different time, a different place, her legs would fall open for him. He would just have to lean forward and his mouth would be perfectly positioned to...

He swallowed. Then he stood, both to regain his equilibrium and to remove the glistening, tempting skin from his gaze.

"Not everyone had the leisure time as kids to watch old movies around the clock." He fell back into their old argument as if they had last discussed his abysmal knowledge of pop culture and film history fifteen minutes ago instead of fifteen years, and some of the swirling tension dissipated.

Some.

"It's adorable you continue to think that's how I grew up." She wriggled her toes on her hurt foot. "Everything works."

"Did you expect otherwise?"

She threw him a look from under her eyelashes. Now that her foot was bandaged, he could see her armor clinking back into place. Walling her away from his grasp, as before. "You always did like playing the good Boy Scout, so no. I didn't expect you to rub salt in the wound. Literally, that is. Metaphorically, that's a different story."

Metaphorically, Finley's expression promised to rub salt mixed with lemon juice into any emotional wound of his she could find. Not that they were hidden. Finley brought all the old hurts to the surface.

"No. That's more your style. No pain, no gain, especially when it comes to other people, right?" He turned to leave. "You're welcome, by the way," he threw at her over his shoulder.

"I was the one enjoying a nice, leisurely, *solo*—" she stressed the last word "—bath when you barged in and everything went to hell as a result. I could've bandaged my own injury."

"Of course. Once you woke up after fainting at the sight of blood. Hitting your head on the stone tile in the process." He reached for the door handle.

She huffed loudly behind his back. "What are you doing here, Will? This was supposed to be Grayson and Nelle's honeymoon. You were not invited along."

That paused him in his tracks. Now that Finley mentioned it, he did recall Lauren mentioning the ranch house would be occupied by guests. He'd been so eager to get out of the rain and get some rest, he didn't question his decision to exit the freeway. He turned to face Finley. "Running Coyote belongs to Reid Begaye."

"I'm aware of that fact," she said tartly, appearing fully recovered from her earlier bout of light-headedness. She perched on the wide edge of the tub as if it were the throne of her own personal country. "Reid is good friends with Nelle. He offered the ranch to Grayson and her as a honeymoon location. When they decided to go elsewhere, they transferred his offer to me."

"Reid may be friends with Nelle, but he is my brother-in-law. He recently married my sister Lauren. I was at your brother's wedding because Reid couldn't make it and Lauren didn't want to go alone. You met her, briefly."

Finley's eyes widened. "Oh. I thought maybe she was…"

"My wife or girlfriend?" He shook his head. "Don't have, either." Then he mentally kicked himself. Why did he tell her that? He hastened to add, "I was driving from Napa to Los Angeles. The weather caused backups on the freeway. When I saw the exit for the ranch, I decided to get out of traffic and the rain. I had no idea you were here. Honest."

Finley's unreadable gaze searched his, but then her shoulders relaxed. Just a fraction of an inch.

She opened her mouth to speak, but he cut her off before she could form words. "Don't worry, I'll leave. Give me a few minutes and I'll be back on the road."

She shifted, and then checked to make sure her towel remained in place. "Is it still raining?"

They were both silent for a minute. The sound of water pelting the roof with rapid force filled the room.

"Sounds like we should start building an ark." She sighed. "Reid will cut off his generous support of Nelle's nonprofit if you leave and hydroplane into a ten-car pileup. You need to stay."

"Not if it will make you uncomfortable." It was one thing to know Finley and he happened to be at the same wedding, surrounded by crowds of merrymakers. It was another to be aware they were the only two people in residence at the ranch, late at night.

She rolled her eyes. "You already did your good deed for the day and rescued the fair maiden—twice if we include Napa—so quit the noble martyr act. This place is large enough to be a boutique hotel. I doubt we'll even see each other."

He wasn't thrilled with the idea of getting back on the dark, slick roads himself. He'd just have to take some of the emergency sleeping aids he had on hand for travel so thoughts of Finley and rehashing how that summer had gone so terribly wrong wouldn't keep him awake. "If you're sure." He hesitated, knowing he was about to pry, but decided to do it, anyway. "I hope no one will mind I stayed here alone with you."

"If you're trying to ask if you need to worry about a jealous partner somewhere out there in the rain, the answer is no, I don't have one. And I'm all out of engraved invitations, so you'll just have to settle for my word that I'm okay with the situation."

Finley was right. Running Coyote had more than enough space for two people. There were plenty of other bedrooms. The guest suite had the most amenities, as Reid and Lauren kept it stocked for spur-of-the-moment company, but the other rooms were luxurious by any standard. The offer certainly beat spending the night fighting the rain and the other cars on the freeway. "Fine. I have to leave first thing to make my meeting in LA as it is."

"I'll be sleeping in." She rose from her seat on the side

of the tub. Her posture was straight, her head held high, but he noticed she did not put weight on her injured foot.

He also noticed the curve of her calves, the long length of her thighs. The juncture between her legs, just hidden from view by the towel. He shifted. His jeans remained tight in the crotch, and not because they were still soaked from the rain.

Finley cleared her throat. "Now that we've established whether you are staying or not, I would like to slip into something a bit more...dry."

Heat settled on his cheeks. "Of course. Sorry again for disturbing you. Good night."

"I doubt we'll run into each other in the morning. So—" Something bright flashed in her gaze. "Farewell, Will."

Her words struck a target he wasn't previously aware he possessed. No, he had no intention of seeing Finley again. He didn't want her phone number. He wasn't planning on friending her on social media, not that he used it much. His assistant ran all the accounts the production company set up for him to use during the filming and promotion of the TV series. The TV series, which would lead to finally finding his perfect life partner if all went to plan. A partner who would be the opposite of Finley in every way.

But the finality of her tone took him aback, to his displeased surprise. She was just as adamant as he was about returning to the state of radio silence between them, apparently. Her words shouldn't make his throat tight and his stomach twinge. But they did.

He focused on the last thing she said. Farewell. As in "fare well"—in other words, be well. Not goodbye, which had no implied wish for his future health.

Will liked numbers. Coding made sense to him. He could fix almost anything in coding by understanding the structure. Language wasn't as cut and dried as ones and zeros. But like numbers, words carried meaning.

"Fare well, Finley."

He shut the bathroom door behind him.

Seven

The noise woke Finley up. Loud and immediate and strong, the roar shook the walls as if a freight train had slammed into the ranch house. The windows rattled. The bed bumped the wall. Finley sat up, wide awake despite having just fallen into a fitful sleep.

The room was dark. So dark, she blinked a few times to make sure her eyes were open. At first, she had no idea where or even when she was. She'd been dreaming of that long-ago summer in Washington, DC, the details vivid and specific. Dreaming of her first meeting with Will.

They were both college interns on Capitol Hill, enrolled in a program that allowed them to earn credits for the spring semester of their senior year while working. She attended a private women's college in the Bay Area. He was finishing up at the University of Illinois Chicago. They met at a rowdy mixer at a bar in Georgetown. She was the ringleader of the party, dancing on tables, urging others to join her, enjoying her first month of being twenty-one. He was in the corner, absorbed in reading a policy paper.

At first, he annoyed her. How dare he ignore her and her friends? They were fun, something he emphatically wasn't. She decided to interrupt his intent perusal, draping herself across the back of his chair and criticizing his paper over his shoulder. They quickly got into a battle of wits over the pros and cons of the paper's subject. Their conversation lasted all night and into the early morning hours, Finley's friends leaving one by one with puzzled stares on their faces. When she discovered he hadn't seen that summer's blockbuster movie, she insisted he go with her to see it the next day.

She couldn't remember the name of the film. She could describe every inch of stubble on his cheeks, how his lips felt against hers. In her dream, he'd been leaning over her, his gray-blue eyes black in the cinema's darkness, staring at her like she was something precious and rare...

Another rattle and the windows vibrated. Her heart beat rapidly. Her throat was dry. She used every breathing exercise in her repertoire to bring her harsh panting under control so her ears could strain to listen for additional noises.

All was now quiet. But what had happened? An earthquake? She scanned the room, looking for the safest place under which to shelter if the ground shook again, and reached for her phone. She rolled her eyes at the low-battery indicator. Great. She'd plugged the phone into the charger, but she must not have plugged the charger into the wall. A half-hour encounter with Will Taylor and she was so flustered, she forgot the most basic routines of modern life.

The screen read five o'clock in the morning. She

quickly scrolled through news alerts and her social media accounts. No reports of earthquakes in the Santa Barbara area from official sources. That meant she didn't need to worry about aftershocks—or worry that an even bigger jolt was on its way. Her heart rate returned to something approaching normal.

The torrential storm, on the other hand, was receiving plenty of attention around the internet. The past summer had seen an increase in brush fires, leaving the landscape denuded and barren. People were speculating about the effect of so much rain on hillsides that no longer possessed the vegetation to anchor the topsoil and prevent landslides.

She swung her feet out of bed. Whatever had woken her up may not be an earthquake, but it made a very solid building shake. She needed to know what caused it, to assure herself she didn't need to evacuate to somewhere safer.

Besides, she should check on Will. Just to make sure he was okay, of course. Nelle would never speak to her again if she allowed Reid Begaye's brother-in-law to suffer. No matter how much Finley wanted him to—no.

She didn't want Will to suffer. On the contrary.

She shook her head. Now was not the time for messy thoughts. They'd have to wait. She felt around for her running shoes next to the bed and slipped them on. Then she flipped the bedside lamp's switch.

Her room remained dark.

Her pulse sped up again. And went into triple time when a knock sounded at her door. "Finley? You okay?"

She jerked the door open before he finished speaking. Will stood in the dark sitting room, an opaque outline blending into shadows. She could barely see him. But she felt his presence. "I'm fine. You?"

"Fine."

"What caused that noise? I thought the windows were going to come out of their frames."

"Earthquake?"

"No reports of tremors on social media."

"Power is out. Generator didn't kick in for some reason."

"I noticed."

Will didn't immediately respond but she heard his breathing, steady and low. The sound gave her a reassurance she didn't realize she needed, but was grateful for. "I'll take a look around the house, see if I can find what's wrong with the generator," he said.

"I'm coming with you." She closed the bedroom door behind her. "There has to be a phone landline in this place."

Will shook his head. "Reid got rid of the landline a while ago—said the nuisance calls disturbed his peace—but the CB radio in the kitchen should work. Runs on batteries."

"Good. We'll go to the kitchen."

"I'll go," he reiterated. "Stay here. You've already injured your ankle and foot. I'd hate to see what you hurt next."

"First, if I want to come with you, that's up to me, not you. Second, I put on sensible shoes. See?" She turned on her phone's flashlight app and shined it on her legs and feet.

Too late, she realized she was wearing a thin T-shirt that barely covered the tops of her thighs. Will's gaze dropped, and then lingered.

Her legs always were one of her best physical assets.

She refused to be embarrassed. Besides, the T-shirt concealed more than the towel had last night. And it wasn't as if Will hadn't explored every millimeter of her, with his touch as well as his sight. She might be rounder here, more angular there, but she never cared what the beauty media said was the socially acceptable standard for women's appearance and she wasn't going to start now. She certainly wasn't going to play coy in front of Will. And if seeing her reminded him he'd once had her, all of her, and chosen to walk away—so be it.

Still, she turned the light off, plunging them both back into the darkness. "My phone didn't charge. Need to conserve battery," she said, and then wondered why she was explaining. She cleared her throat and found her best businesslike voice, the one she used to communicate with interns and staff members and nosey journalists. "Want to use your phone?"

"Mine is completely dead. It didn't charge, either. Storm must have knocked the power out after we went to bed. But I can get us to the kitchen without light. Since you won't stay here."

"We don't know what caused the noise. And if this were a horror movie and you left me behind, I'd be the first one picked off by the serial killer and it would be your fault." Actually, the young adults who sneaked away to have sex would be the first ones murdered, but she didn't want to bring that up to Will for very good reasons.

"This is why I don't watch films. Fine." He grabbed her left hand.

"Hey!" She snatched her hand back. Her skin burned where it had briefly slid against his.

He sighed. "It's dark. There's no power. You can stay here where it's safe, no serial killers, until the sun comes up. Or we hold hands so I can make sure you don't trip and harm yourself."

"Of course there aren't any serial killers. I'm just saying if you watched movies like nearly every other human on this planet, you would recognize the situation." She steeled herself, then placed her hand in his.

His grip was warm, and strong, and infinitely comforting.

And arousing. She muttered a prayer of thanks under her breath for the darkness. Not only did she have a reason to hold on to Will, but her tightly pebbled nipples, pushing against the thin material of her shirt, were hidden from his view.

She never would have found the kitchen without using the map of the house Nelle had provided, but Will moved confidently through the corridors and connecting atriums, his guidance firm and unerring. It was even more of a turn-on. When did Will become so, well, sure of himself?

Or maybe… Maybe he always was, and she had been too preoccupied with her own issues to recognize that not all strength was loud and flashy, like Barrett's. Some strength was quiet. Thoughtful. Measured. Like Will's.

And she clung to that strength when she heard staticky voices in the distance. "What was that?"

"Still not serial killers. It's the CB radio. Someone is calling the house."

"Oh." But when she would drop his hand, his fingers tightened on hers.

When they entered the kitchen, the words became clearer, repeated every minute or so. "Running Coyote, this is base camp. Come in. Can you hear us? Over."

Will picked up the radio from its alcove. "This is Running Coyote. Tim, that you?"

There was silence on the other end. Then a burst of static. "This is Tim Stern. Who's this?"

"It's Will Taylor. Lauren's brother. Long story, but I'm here with Finley Smythe. What's going on?"

"Hey, Will. We didn't know you were coming. Is Ms. Smythe okay?"

Finley took the radio from Will and depressed the button to talk. "I'm good. Did you hear the noise? It shook the house. Everyone okay where you are?"

"We sure did hear it. We're all fine down here. But listen, it appears that noise was a good-sized portion of the hillside coming down. Mudslide."

Right. Her speculation about the effect of so much rain at one time on the parched earth had been spot-on. "How bad was it? I hope no one is hurt."

"That's the good news. No one was injured. And as far as we can tell, no buildings were affected, either."

Finley sank against the kitchen counter. Mudslides could be devastating. And fatal, if evacuation warnings didn't come in time or weren't heeded. "That's great."

"But…" Tim hesitated. "The road to the ranch? That's the bad news."

Will took the radio from Finley's suddenly nerveless grasp. "What are you saying? The road is gone?"

"Not gone," Tim said. "Still there. But buried."

"How buried?" Icicles dripped from Will's words.

"The boys are still out there, taking a look. But from what they've radioed me, I'd say you better plan on staying put for at least several days."

"I can't do that," Will stated.

Finley took the radio back from him and spoke to Tim. "There has to be another way to leave the ranch."

"Well, sure, if you like hiking and camping and you have a few days. There are some excellent trails nearby as we're surrounded by a national forest, but it will take you a while to arrive at anything resembling civilization. Might find coyotes, though. Cougars, too."

"Cougars. Awesome." She stared at Will. This wasn't

happening. She was not stuck at a ranch in the midst of nowhere with him.

"Don't forget coyotes," Will said under his breath.

"How could I forget? The ranch is named after them. Running ones, even." She pushed the talk button on the radio. "When can we expect you at the house, Tim?"

"Maybe on Friday, if all goes well. Depends on when we can get a cleanup crew out here and how fast they go."

Finley blinked. "Today is Monday. I was thinking lunchtime."

"Sorry, I didn't make myself clear. The landslide took out the road to the ranch between base camp—that's what we call the compound where Mariam and me and the boys who work on the ranch bunk—and the main house. Afraid you'll have to be on your own for a while. Hey, it's pretty provident Will showed up, isn't it? We were worried about you being all alone."

No, she did not consider it provident Will was there. At all.

Will took the radio back. "When did you say the road would be passable again? Friday?"

"I might be able to make it up there by Friday if we get enough of a path cleared, but I was thinking of walking or riding one of the horses. Cars, who knows? Depends on what other damage was caused by the storm, and who needs the cleanup crew the most."

Will nodded. Outwardly he appeared calm, as if he was merely discussing the weather. But the cords in his neck pulsed, a sign he was agitated. Funny, how details she once thought were lost forever to the past were now fresh and bright.

"Speaking of," Tim continued, "I'm doubly glad you're there, Will, because I need you to check on the horses in the upper barn. Most of the animals are down here with us at the main stables, but we left Trudy and Ranger near the house for Ms. Smythe to ride. You good with feeding them and making sure they're okay until I can get up there?"

The cords in Will's neck tightened. "Sure."

"Mariam says there is enough food stocked in the kitchen to last you for a good while. You two will be dandy."

Dandy was not the word Finley would use to describe the situation. Her stomach roiled.

"I hope she's not including the contents of the refrigerator. Electricity is out and the generator didn't come on," Will said.

Tim sighed. "I told Reid that generator system was useless. We have engineers scheduled to come out and look at it. Oh, and you might want to conserve water as the well pump house is on the same system. But there should be enough in the storage tank to last you until the power is back on."

Will stared at Finley. She stared back. "What are the chances of having the power restored soon?" Will asked.

His only answer was a burst of static. Then Tim's voice returned. "Sorry, folks, I got to run. The boys discovered some storm damage to the corrals, and I need to take a look. I'll get back to you soon." The radio went silent.

Great. No power, limited water, and no way to leave the ranch. With her only companion the man who'd demonstrated to her true love was a farce.

The sun had come up during their conversation with Tim, but the light was dull as a steady drizzle cast a misty filter over the landscape outside the windows. Heavy gray clouds pressed down on what Finley assumed would be an impressive vista under other circumstances. Obviously, escaping Will by spending the day basking by the pool was not a current option.

She picked up her phone. The battery symbol remained depressingly low. She checked her email, reading only the subject lines. Grayson and Nelle had landed in London: good. Her car was due for service: delete. Sadiya had an update on Erica O'Connell's book... Her finger hovered over the email, then clicked Open.

Sadiya's message wasn't long. Erica's memoir was still officially under wraps, but journalists were on the scent. Sadiya was fielding phone calls by the hour. She urged Finley to stay put wherever she was.

Finley sighed. That wouldn't be too hard. She returned to her email inbox, only for the screen to go black as the battery finally gave out.

The noise of pot lids falling to the terra-cotta-tiled floor caused her to glance up. Will was opening cupboards and drawers in the expansive kitchen. And the daylight showed her what she had been too stressed to notice earlier: he wore only beat-up sneakers and a pair of midnight blue boxers, low slung on narrow hips. His back muscles flexed as he rummaged through their contents and her gaze was caught, like a moth drunk on candlelight.

Finley believed she had filled her visual reference banks with images of a half-dressed Will the night before. But she'd been in pain—and damn it, he was right that the sight of blood was not high on her list of favorite things—and focused on appearing poised in front of him. Now she realized just how many details she had missed. Like the way his hair was just long enough to form perfect curls at the nape of his neck. The way his torso narrowed from broad shoulders to slim hips. The flawless globes of his ass as he bent down to look inside a cabinet...

He swung his head and looked at her from over his shoulder. A knowing smile spread over his face. *Busted.*

She cleared her throat. "So. I guess neither of us is leaving anytime soon."

"I'm not hearing you complaining." He smirked before standing up and opening another cabinet. Was it her imagination or did he flex his biceps more than was necessary?

His smug tone was not something she conjured up.

Face facts, Finley. If she had been in charge of the universe, she would never have encountered Will Taylor again. She would have been perfectly content going to her grave without knowing fifteen years of additional maturity only made him more attractive.

But she wasn't in charge. And fate, always a fickle devil who loved to laugh at people's best intentions, had other plans for her. Therefore, she had at least two choices. One, draw a line down the middle of the ranch house and declare the other side off-limits. Then lock herself into the guest suite and venture to the kitchen for food only when she was confident Will was occupied elsewhere. Ignore him, acting as if she was the only resident of the house.

Or two…acknowledge that she and Will were alone, together, and wipe the smirk off his face by beating him at the game of who could make the other sweat the most. And if history was anything to go on, they could make each other sweat quite a lot.

But this time, her heart would be locked away. This time, she would be firmly in control. Extravagant promises would not soften her into thinking he loved her. She would not be fooled again.

She would have her way with him—it went without saying he would have a good time as well—and then walk away. Match point to her.

She liked games. She especially liked winning them. And the bulge in his jeans the night before demonstrated he was not wholly indifferent, giving her an advantage.

She ignored inconvenient details, like his presence jump-starting her sorely neglected libido, roaring to sudden life.

Kicking off her running shoes, she hopped onto the stone slab counter next to him. "What are you looking for?" she purred.

"Taking stock of our supplies." He motioned at her. "Move to the left so I can get into that cupboard underneath you?"

"Of course." She elaborately wriggled her rear along the cool smooth surface. Her T-shirt rode up even farther, exposing more of her thighs.

Will's smirk disappeared. His expression remained impassive as he squatted down and opened one of the doors. She kept her right leg in his view. When it came to Will, she had two potent weapons in her arsenal, and she intended to use them.

She swung her uninjured right foot and her toes briefly grazed the tops of his thigh. "See anything interesting? Anything you'd like to have…later?"

The tips of his ears turned red, a sign she knew well. She smiled. Winning was going to be far easier than she'd hoped for. She brushed his thigh again, lingering a few seconds longer. "Or are you…hungry…now?"

He stood up, so fast she didn't have time to react and rearrange her legs so he wasn't directly between them. She scooted back, but quickly ran out of counter. He leaned forward. Her heart pounded as he braced his hands on either side of her.

His eyes were level with hers, so close the navy rim outlining his gray-blue pupils was discernible. His breath tickled her skin, raising teeny goose bumps. She could incline her head, just a hair, and she would know if he remembered exactly how she liked to be kissed.

Their gazes locked. The morning air was chilly, but she

was hot. Surface-of-the-sun hot. Her lips needed moisture and she licked them. Will's gaze dropped, tracing the path of her tongue. Then he leaned forward even farther. Their foreheads almost touched. Her nipples tightened as a rush of heat settled low in her belly. She closed her eyes, her mouth slightly open...

"You're still in the way." Will straightened up and moved to the section of the kitchen farthest from her.

She swallowed, attempting to regain control and flush the desire out of her system. Score one point for Will, but the game clock was far from running out. Plenty of opportunities to win this thing. "Sorry." She wasn't. Not at all. "What's convenient for breakfast?"

Will closed a drawer with more force than necessary. "Convenient? Nothing about this is convenient."

"Maybe not for you," she said, thinking of Sadiya's email. "You said something last night about a meeting. An important one?"

"Yes."

She raised her eyebrows in inquiry, but he apparently had finished speaking. "I see your conversational skills have atrophied."

She hopped off the counter and began to explore the butler's pantry adjacent to the kitchen, which Will hadn't looked in yet. She hated to admit it, but his Boy Scout instinct to assess their supplies was a damn good one. Especially since the kitchen's large, eight-burner professional-grade range was electric. As was the microwave, of course.

"I'm not your first choice of human beings with whom to be stranded and you're certainly not mine, but here we are," she called out, rummaging through a treasure trove of small appliances, all requiring a working power outlet. "We might as well make the most of it."

When several minutes passed without a response from her companion, she poked her head out of the pantry. "Will?"

The kitchen was empty.

She sagged against the pantry's floor-to-ceiling cabinets. Great. But wasn't this what she ultimately wanted? A life free of Will Taylor? Why was she upset if Will decided to keep as much space as possible between them until they were able to leave Running Coyote?

The sound of a throat being cleared got her attention. Will was just outside the pantry door. He'd thrown on well-worn jeans and a black sweatshirt. With his left hand, he held out a men's-sized long-sleeved flannel shirt. "It's freezing in here," he said. "Don't want you to catch a cold."

She blinked at him but slipped on the offered garment. The shirt was long enough on her to be worn as a dress and she sank into its enveloping warmth. It smelled like him, too. She fought the urge to deeply inhale.

So strange how, of all the senses, smell conjured the clearest, most detailed memories. She'd tripped down memory lane so often in the last few days, the path was well worn. But the shirt's scent, indescribable with words but immediately recognizable as him, caused vivid images to tumble in front of her eyes. Will, smiling at her as he handed her a drink at a congressional intern party. Will, stammering as he asked her out following their movie date. Will, slowly unbuttoning her shirt, kissing each inch of skin he exposed as if she were something precious and wondrous...

"Thank you," she finally remembered to say.

"We don't have access to a doctor or pharmacy. And with your recent track record of falls and cuts, better not risk illness." His tone was deadpan, but she saw the glimmer of humor deep in his gaze.

She folded her arms across her chest. "Does this usually work for you, rescuing women who have no need of your assistance?"

He threw a pointed glance at her injured foot and ankle.

Time to change the subject. "I'll take care of the horses. You can figure out breakfast."

He shook his head. "I told Tim I'd feed the horses. Why don't you go back to your room. Get some rest. You woke up pretty early."

She laughed. If he wanted to put space between them, he'd have to try harder than that. "Rest for what? My strenuous day of being trapped on this ranch? Besides, can you even identify one end of a horse from the other?"

"I'm assuming they eat with the end that has a mouth."

"Not an answer."

He walked to the closest kitchen counter and busied himself with opening a loaf of bread and taking a jar from a nearby shelf. "Peanut butter okay? Be warned now—you don't have many choices."

She watched him slather a bread slice with the thick spread. "Peanut butter sandwich. That takes me back. I haven't had one since the internsh—" She bit back the rest of her words. "Since forever."

Will handed her a completed sandwich along with a ripe banana taken from the fruit bowl on the counter. "Too bad. You used to devour them."

Their gazes met. Finley could only hold his for a second before she dropped hers to focus on her food. "I used to devour a lot of things, like ramen and microwave popcorn." *And Will.* "I'm guessing those are off the menu. Since we don't have a working microwave."

"Don't worry. You don't need to pretend you're one of the common people now. You're safe from supermarket specials." He bit into his own sandwich.

Her mouth went dry, but the crunchy peanut butter was not the culprit. "What do mean, pretend?"

His shoulders tensed and he put the rest of his sandwich down. "Forget I said anything. I'm going to feed the horses."

She followed him to the adjacent breakfast room and out the French doors that led to a sprawling flagstone terrace. Beyond, the lush green lawn sloped down to the Olympic-sized pool and the built-in cabanas surrounding it. At any other time, she would admire the view of the jagged hills wreathed in fog and dark clouds, but now all she saw was red. "Pretending would be continuing to act like passing acquaintances who share a history of polite nods and nothing more. If you have something to say to me, then say it."

"Stay in the house where it's dry, Finley."

"Stop giving me orders, Will."

He strode across the terrace until it ended and then took a path off to the left. "I wouldn't give you an order. You do what you want. You always do."

He muttered the last three words, but the wind carried them to her as clearly as if he had said them in her ear. She hurried after him. "And what is that supposed to mean?"

Will picked up his steps. She'd have to break into a trot to keep up. And while she would rather die than admit her pain to him, her injured foot and the ankle she had twisted were in less-than-optimal shape. The chilly mist-filled air raised goose bumps on her bare legs, also reminding her she wasn't dressed for a visit to a barn.

She stopped and turned around to reenter the house.

But not because Will told her to. And he was not off the hook. She was going to make Will explain himself. And remember he once couldn't get enough of her. But this time, she'd be the one walking away with her heart intact and he'd be the one left on his knees, gasping for oxygen.

She loved it when a plan came together.

Eight

Will heard Finley open the door to the barn—who else would it be?—but he stayed where he was, staring at the array of bales and containers in the stable's feed room. Not that he was surprised Finley wasn't sensible enough to stay inside the house where it was relatively warm. Finley never could resist having the last word. And once upon a time her last words made him laugh, so he was happy to let her have the final say.

But that was then.

Now? Will was no longer ensorcelled by Finley's allure. He was not going to fall under her spell again. Not after causing his heart a bruising case of whiplash when she turned cold and cutting without any advance warning. She could swing her impossibly long and luscious legs in his line of sight all she wanted.

Sure, his body reacted to her. He was only human. And Finley was everything he found desirable. He still had the same effect on her, too. Her eyes were normally the color of a glass of whiskey held up to the sunlight, a warm amber brown. But when Finley was aroused, her eyes became deep, dark pools. He could have drowned in her gaze when they were in the kitchen earlier.

He looked down and realized he had filled the horse's feed buckets with the wrong mixture. Cursing himself for letting Finley affect him, he threw out the contents and started all over.

This couldn't have happened at a worse time. The meeting in Los Angeles was happening in three hours. Obviously, showing up for it was in the realm of science fiction. He'd asked Tim via the CB radio to call the series producers and make Will's excuses, but he'd learned from experience the Screenweb executives were prickly, demanding and allergic to compromises. He only hoped when they heard a natural disaster was behind his absence from the crucial kick-off meeting, they would agree to continue with the original production timeline. Ji-Hoon deserved to have his dream come true, and they were in a battle against time.

His mentor was the only reason Will had said yes when the production company knocked on his door, seeking the next big reality dating series. He certainly didn't need the additional income. Even before the EverAftr app had become a hit, he held the patents on several innovative pieces of software that made streaming services and ISPs more secure, valued at millions apiece to the companies that purchased them. Savvy investing had caused his net worth to grow, to the point that if EverAftr were to disappear tomorrow, it would barely be a blip in his portfolio.

If he'd told his twenty-one-year-old self that he would be featured on *Silicon Valley Weekly*'s list of top tech execs to watch…maybe his younger self wouldn't have so readily accepted the label of "not good enough" and slunk out of Washington, DC, giving up his original goal of working for the Justice Department. Instead of law school, he'd gone back to his high school hobby of playing with software code and turned it into a career.

That choice hadn't worked out so bad, had it?

Focus on what matters now, he admonished himself. The company. The television series. At the kickoff meeting he was currently missing, they were supposed to discuss his potential matches for the first episode. He'd filled out his EverAftr questionnaires just before leaving for Napa, stressing his ideal qualities in partner, including constancy, steadiness and an even temper.

If only the perfect partner he'd described didn't appear boring and colorless now that he'd spent time with Finley again.

A horse snorted, breaking his reverie. He went to the doorway and saw Finley standing in front of a stall with "Trudy" written in erasable marker on its metal nameplate, stroking the nose of the buff-colored mare. She'd exchanged her running shoes for boots and changed into jeans that cupped her ass in ways that should be illegal.

Tucked into those jeans, she still wore his shirt.

"Aren't you a pretty girl," Finley cooed to Trudy. "I bet you're wondering why the nice man is standing in the room with your food instead of giving the food to you." She looked over at him. "Need a hand? I happen to know my way around a stable."

"I've got it, thanks." Of course she was familiar with horses. All his success, yet when he was with Finley he turned back into the kid who had never visited an art museum or seen professional live theater before meeting her. Uninformed. Unsophisticated. And in this case, unfamiliar with large hooved animals and their care and feeding.

She nodded. "Okay. Hay is in the greenish bales, by the way. The straw-colored bales are, well, straw."

"You're very helpful," he said dryly.

Her smile was dazzling. "Always."

After much comparison of labels with the instructions to ensure he had the right combination this time, he portioned the grains and roughage for each horse into their respective buckets and carried them out of the room. The dusty smell of cut alfalfa and the warm scent of horse surrounded him. He never thought stables could feel cozy—well, he never thought of stables at all—but although the weather outside was dark and foreboding, inside all appeared light and inviting.

Or maybe that was due to Finley. She'd entered Trudy's stall and was brushing the mare's coat with something resembling circles of jagged metal. "That looks more like a torture instrument," he said by way of greeting, opening the stall door to fill the feeder.

"Are you worried I'll use it on you later? Or are you hoping?" She wagged her eyebrows, making him laugh despite his best efforts not to. "This is a currycomb. Because your paddock is full of mud and you got it all over yourself, didn't you, beauty?" She stroked Trudy's nose, long, sweeping caresses the mare appeared to enjoy, judging by the way she nuzzled Finley.

It was ridiculous to be jealous of an animal. Will stomped over to the other occupied stall, this one marked "Ranger," and dumped the contents of the bucket in the appropriate place. The chestnut gelding ignored him in favor of his food. "You have the right idea, buddy. Take care of number one. Don't care about others."

But when he left Ranger's stall, Finley was nowhere to be found. He hadn't heard her leave, so she had to be around somewhere. "Finley?"

"In Trudy's paddock," came her distant voice.

He pushed Trudy's stall door open. On the other side of the enclosed space, there was a passage to a small dirt area covered by an overhang to protect it from the elements, and beyond that a fenced-in grassy expanse. Finley stood with Trudy where the grass began, nose to nose, as if they were communing. Then Finley took an apple out of her shirt's front pocket and, taking the first bite, she held out the rest to the horse on her flat palm. Trudy delicately ate the offering, and then sauntered to the far side of the paddock to supplement her breakfast, ignoring the humans in her space. Finley watched the mare go.

Will set out to meet her. As he drew closer, he realized he'd never seen Finley so…unguarded. Her shoulders were relaxed, her hands loose at her sides. The smirk that seemed to have taken up permanent residence on her lips was gone, replaced by a genuine smile.

Even in their most passionate encounters, he'd always known she was holding something back, giving him access to her body but not to the deepest corners of her soul. Now? He caught a glimpse of what she'd previously hidden from him.

She turned her head as he approached. Her sharp, teasing expression returned as her posture straightened and her arms folded over her chest. "Did you feed Ranger?" she called out.

The moment was over. The sting of disappointment caused his steps to falter, just for a beat.

"He's also a horse," she clarified when he reached her side. "Long nose, tail, four legs."

"I figured that out, thanks." He nodded at Trudy. "You two seem to be getting along well."

Her gaze softened as she watched the mare. "My mother loved horses. I grew up around them."

She did? "I didn't know that."

She glanced at him. "We didn't exactly spend our time in soul-baring conversations."

No. They'd used their time for other activities. "Still surprised you didn't say anything."

She laughed, if the harsh exhalation of air could be called that. "Oh, I'd given up my equestrian dreams by then. I won several jumping competitions as a child. But after my mom died and it became obvious I wasn't talented enough to compete at an elite level, Barrett decided horses were a waste of money and time and that was that." She shrugged. "I moved on."

When she broke up with Will, she'd dismissed their relationship with much the same words: "The internship program is over, so time to move on. We're done." He had been in too much shock—too much agony—to note anything other than her casual dismissal of what had been the most transcendent summer of his life.

He wondered—had deep grooves been etched around her lips then as they were now? Had the same opaque shutters slammed down over her gaze, rendering her true emotions unreadable? If he'd paid closer attention, maybe he would remember.

Then with a blink, her expression smoothed into her usual smirk. She closed the space between them, glancing up at him from under lowered lashes. "But I still enjoy riding." Her voice took on a husky timbre that put his nerve endings on alert. "Perhaps we would both enjoy getting back into the saddle."

"I don't ride."

She smiled. A wicked smile, full of heat and sin. "That's not what I remember. I recall you are quite the... passionate...rider. Endurance for hours, until we were both spent."

God help him, he was hard. Hard and aching, and just from a few whispered words—plus the images his memory supplied to accompany them.

Finley's gaze sparkled as her grin deepened. She knew what she was doing to him. She always knew.

With supreme effort, his brain wrested control from his cock. "I'm returning to the house."

He strode toward the gate that would give him the fastest exit from the paddock. Intent on putting as much space between him and Finley in the shortest amount of time possible, he didn't notice where the rain-soaked grass turned into a large patch of mud. Thick, viscous mud that grabbed his lightweight sneakers and didn't let go when he picked up his right foot.

He stumbled forward. His arms windmilled as he tried to maintain his balance. His other foot slid out from underneath him.

He landed on his hands and knees.

The mud made for a soft if messy landing. His equilibrium was the only thing that took a beating. Well, his equilibrium and his clothes, which would require an industrial-strength cleaning after this. He sat back on his heels, searching for the shoe remaining in the mud.

Finley came running up. Her boots stayed firmly on her feet. No wonder they were obligatory ranch wear. "Are you okay?"

"Nothing hurt but my dignity."

She laughed. "You look like the Abominable Mudman."

"I caught you when you almost fell at the winery. You don't return favors?" Rain dripped from his hair into his eyes. He pushed his hair back, then realized he'd only caked himself with more dirt.

She was laughing so hard, she was nearly doubled over. "Even if I'd been close enough to catch you, what makes you think I could have prevented your fall? We'd both be up to our ears in mud. Nuh-uh."

Her mirth was contagious, damn it. He chuckled. "You don't want to be muddy. But it's funny when other people are?"

"It wouldn't be funny if you were hurt. But since you aren't…" She hiccupped, and wiped tears from her eyes. "Here. To show I'm a good sport, I'll help you up."

She held out her hand. Will took it. She pulled with all her strength.

They both tumbled into mud, Finley landing on top on him. Legs to legs, chest to chest. Finley's soft, warm curves crashed against him. A whoosh of air left him, his breath knocked out in too many ways to count.

Shock made her still. Then after a second, she relaxed into him. His body recognized her instantly. She fit against him as she always did, as if her curves were expressly created to match the planes and dips of his musculature, despite the intervening years. His arms came up to embrace her before he knew what they were doing. He forced them back to his sides.

She lifted her head, her chuckle rumbling through both of them. "You did that on purpose," she stated. "But I agree. Dirty is far more fun when two are involved."

Was that a wriggle to go with her innuendo? Either way, he was aware that only a few layers of fabric separated them. His groin started to make demands his head wasn't sure it could override. "I didn't cause this. *You* didn't dig your feet in and lost your balance."

"Well, you—" She began to laugh again. "Will, you literally have mud in your eye. Or almost. Here, let me." She rolled off him and came to a kneeling position, tugging the shirt she wore free of her jeans. Then, using a clean portion of her shirttails, she leaned down and gently wiped his face. "There."

Their gazes caught. And held. His pulse, never sluggish when Finley was near, beat painfully in his ears. "Thanks."

Mischief danced deep in her eyes. The kind of mischief that once led to sneaking into public gardens after hours and ended with them naked and stifling their screams of pleasure so the security guards wouldn't hear them. "Of course. Who knows what's in this mud? Can't have you getting sick when we're without access to a doctor, remember?"

He remembered, all right. But the memories went much further back than this morning. And he was tired of fighting them off. Tired of acting as if every time Finley was near, his blood didn't turn to gasoline and her teasing smile wasn't an accelerant, lighting him on fire.

Turnabout was fair play, after all.

He rose to his feet, Finley following suit. She looked relatively pristine aside from splatters here and there, but then he'd taken the brunt of their fall. Mud was everywhere. It clung to his jeans, his shirt, his hair. "Right. Doctors. Is there anywhere else I should be concerned about? Like say, my hands?"

Finley appeared to ponder. "Maybe I should look. In case there's broken skin."

He held them out to her. Her own hands were none too clean, but they both knew his question was only a pretense. Her fingers slowly traced over his palms, his inner wrists, awakening nerve endings he wasn't aware existed. Tiny shock waves reverberated through his system.

She raised her dark gaze to his. "I think they're fine."

"What about my back? It's pretty muddy."

Her slow smile sent a lightning strike of heat to his groin. "I'm happy to examine your backside."

She took her time. And was very thorough. Her hands swept over his shoulders, down his spine, whispered over his buttocks. Her fingers lifted his sweatshirt, explored the area above his jeans waistband, coming close but never quite dipping below it. Who knew that area of skin was one of the body's most erogenous zones? By the time she reappeared in front of him, he was hard and heavy.

"I'm happy to report all appears in fine order." Beneath the mud streaks on her face, her cheeks were flushed crimson. He'd never seen her lovelier.

He nodded, trying to form words. Finally, he forced out, "What about my mouth? I'd hate to ingest something I shouldn't. Since we can't get to the doctor."

Her gaze dropped to the area in question, lingered. She shook her head slowly, then raised her eyes to his. The mischief was wiped away, replaced by dark flames leaping high. "You're good. But what about mine? Same reason, of course."

Her mouth was…perfect. A full lower lip, soft and pillowy, made to be nibbled on or tugged gently between his teeth. Her upper lip, a cupid's bow of peaks and valleys, wicked in shape and in action. His groin tightened farther at the memory of those lips taking him in, their pressure and pull… He managed to find his voice. "There never was any mud on you, Finley."

She stilled, her eyes losing their light. He frowned but had no time to ask what was wrong before she leaned forward, her hands making fists in his shirt at the shoulders. In her boots she was almost as tall as him, especially since he was still missing a shoe. She raised her head, and that perfect mouth hovered next to his. "Then do something to change that, Will."

He didn't need another invitation.

In Will's life, he'd had three supreme experiences. One, catching a foul ball in the seventh game of the 2016 World Series while cheering his beloved Chicago Cubs to victory. Two, receiving his first software patent. And then there was kissing Finley Smythe for the first time.

Now the list was blown up. Caput. Gone forever. Because nothing could ever, would never, rival kissing Finley in the middle of a horse paddock, covered in mud, the air chilled by mist and wind. Not that he was cold for very long. His blood, already heated, erupted into lava at the first touch of her lips against his.

His tongue played with the seam of her lips, demanding they open to him. Finley made a mewling sound and she crashed into him, her hands tangling in his hair, her tongue coming out to twine and rub against his. Her mouth was hot and wet and she tasted faintly like apple but mostly like Finley, a taste he realized he'd subconsciously missed all these years.

He grabbed her waist, pulling her harder against him. His wandering fingers got her the shirt untucked, so he had access to the warm woman underneath the flannel. His hands splayed against the satin skin of her back, exploring territory that once had been as familiar to him as his own image in a mirror. The knobs of her spine were more pronounced now, the curve of her belly a bit more rounded, but his mind soon stopped the comparison, too busy exploding with the knowledge he was kissing Finley, actually kissing her. Not a dream, not a fantasy.

He ached with want. Finley wrapped her legs around his, pressing her warmth against him. Her hands explored his shoulders, his chest, finding his nipples through his shirt and tweaking them just enough that a groan escaped him. She placed his hands on her breasts, moaning into his mouth and shuddering against him when his fingers and thumbs found the diamond-hard peaks.

She pulled back, just a hand's width. "Let's go back to the house."

He searched her gaze. Her eyes were dark and wild with passion, yes, but he read something else in her expression.

He read victory.

The fires, burning so high and fierce, swiftly banked.

He hadn't seen Finley in many years, but certain things were seared on his memory and Finley's expressions were among them. Once, she'd finagled an invitation to an exclusive White House gala for him, charming aides and assistants until she found someone willing to put him on the guest list. When he expressed admiration for her ability to cut through barriers thought impregnable, she'd waved a hand. "It's a game."

She had the same expression now.

He stepped back. He dropped his hands to his sides, clenching his fists so he wouldn't give in to the temptation to pull her close, lose himself in the heated flames again.

Confusion chased away the triumph he'd discerned. "Will? What's wrong?" Her smirk appeared. "Because I'm pretty sure we were both enjoying ourselves."

He shook his head. What was he doing? Hadn't he learned the first time? He couldn't be Finley Smythe's diversion when she wanted to amuse herself and nothing better was available to her.

He supposed he should thank her for reminding him why he'd agreed to personally participate in the streaming series based on EverAftr. Not only did he believe in EverAftr's algorithms and ability to match users with strong possibilities for lifetime partners—the company's successful matches were too numerous not to be proud of his work—he was growing tired of coming home to a silent town house. Both his sisters had recently married and while occasionally Lauren let slip something that raised his doubts about her relationship with Reid, his sister Claire was blissfully happy with her wife, Berit. He wanted what they had for himself.

He could've signed up anonymously for EverAftr, but his identity was bound to be leaked at one point or another. He didn't mind the bad press for himself should a disappointed date leak details to a gossip website, but the company didn't deserve any potential negative blowback. It wasn't EverAftr's fault his relationships rarely made it past the three-month mark, a fact for which he took full blame.

But on the series, his participation would be open knowledge. His dates would be filmed on camera, with the participants' full agreement, for the world to see for themselves. He welcomed the challenge of proving EverAftr's value in public, standing behind his company's promise.

Making his mentor's cherished dream come true was just the compelling cherry on top. Ji-Hoon believed in him when he needed the external validation the most.

But Finley? After that summer, she dismissed him. Threw away the offer of his heart and soul. She'd had bigger goals in her sights, and blithely dumped him to pursue dreams that didn't include him.

He couldn't fall under her spell again. Yes, he wanted her. Who wouldn't? She was smart and made him laugh and her intoxicating kisses were addicting. He shook with his craving for more.

But he wasn't an impoverished twenty-one-year-old student blinded by her glamour. He had a life. He ran a successful business. People depended on him.

He wanted her, but want wasn't enough. Not with so much else on the line.

"Will?" she repeated. She raised her chin, folding her arms across her chest.

"It's getting colder," he said. He wasn't just referring to the weather. "I'm going to the house to get rid of this mud. And then I need to work. You won't see me for the rest of the day."

"I don't—what the blazing hell, Will? That wasn't a flashlight in your pocket."

She was furious. And with Finley, anger didn't flare red hot. But it burned, in the way frozen metal seared unprotected skin.

"Be honest. For once." He stared her down. "Is this something you really want? Am *I* someone you want? Or are you just bored?"

She didn't say anything. She didn't need to. The forked lightning in her gaze answer enough.

He shook his head. "I find you desirable. I've always found you desirable. I'll find you desirable when we're a hundred and four. But I can't do this again. I'm not and never was your toy."

He opened the gate to the paddock. Closing it behind him, he marched toward the house.

It took every ounce of strength he possessed, even tapping his reserves, not to turn back, pick her up and carry her back with him.

Nine

Finley stared at Will's receding back. Her mouth moved but her brain could not come up with words. And she would be damned if she let Will have the final say. "You better not use up all the water!"

It was the only thing that came to mind. The rest was mixed up in a throbbing miasma of thwarted desire, anger and… Her belly fluttered, and not in the delicious, squeezing way it did when Will was near. This was more like the precursor to the kind of sour stomachache that kept her prone on the sofa.

She'd made an utter fool of herself. But there was one consolation: no one else knew.

Trudy snorted from her corner and looked up at Finley. Finley tended not to anthropomorphize animals, but Trudy's expression clearly read, *That was a fiasco.* Ranger peered over the fence that separated his paddock from

Trudy's and tossed his head as if to agree with his stable-mate. "Okay," Finley muttered. "You two know."

Nothing to do but wait until Will was safely inside the main house and doing whatever work he thought he could accomplish with a dead phone and no power, and then make her way to the guest suite. Alone. For the rest of however long she was trapped on this forsaken isolated ranch. It was back to her original plan: Operation Will Taylor Does Not Exist.

At least she wouldn't need to worry if the ranch's water heater required electricity to function. She would be taking a cold shower. An unfortunately short one.

The hours dripped by slowly for the rest of the day. Finley took her shower, the bracing water's effect nullified by thoughts of Will's biceps flexing under her grip, his mouth hot and demanding, his denim-clad thigh solid between hers, the rigid shape in his jeans proof he wanted her as much as she wanted him. She picked out a recent bestseller to read from the bookcase in the sitting room of the guest suite, but after reading the first page five times and still not comprehending a word, she decided the problem wasn't the book, it was her inability to concentrate.

She studied the binder outlining all the house amenities since she wasn't about to leave anytime soon, but that failed to eat up much time. Swimming was out of the question, thanks to the rain that decided to make a return visit that afternoon. Thunderstorms were rare in Southern California but not unheard of and with her luck, she couldn't rule out a direct lightning strike on the pool. Hiking was also off the agenda, not only because of the weather but because she wasn't keen on meeting the ranch's name-sakes while walking alone.

Next on her list was informing people of her current

situation. She ensured the kitchen was empty before entering it, then spoke to Tim via the CB radio, dictating emails for him to send to Sadiya as well as to Grayson and Nelle. Tim informed her the power company was working to restore the ranch's service, but the storm had caused several severe disruptions in the area so he didn't have a time estimate for her. Their conversation took care of another half hour, leaving her the rest of the day to relive what happened in the paddock.

By the time the clock read 11:00 p.m., Finley was all out of ideas to keep herself busy so she wouldn't wallow in thoughts of Will. The house was silent. Granted, the place was so big, Will could be throwing a party for thirty of his noisiest friends and she wouldn't hear them. But it was the type of silence that only came when all the residents were tucked in bed. No doubt Will was sleeping the sleep of angels after their early morning wake-up call, his conscience clear after rejecting her.

No such sleep was in her future. And her stomach, which had been too unsteady to accept much food during the day, loudly reminded her it remained mostly empty. A late night kitchen raid was in order.

Just as she suspected, not a creature was stirring, especially not her ridiculously attractive housemate. She opened and closed cabinets with as much stealth as possible, hoping to avoid yet another main course of peanut butter.

She struck pay dirt behind the sixth door. A bag of large, fluffy marshmallows. Chocolate bars from Italy, in a variety of shades from dark to milk to white. And was that…? Yes! Graham crackers. She gathered her bounty in her arms, intending to return to the guest suite, when she stopped to consider her options.

Standing in the dim, cavernous kitchen, goose bumps

had taken over every inch of her exposed skin. If she went back, she could wrap herself in bedding and she'd be warm enough, but wouldn't sitting by a fire be even better? Not to mention she could make real s'mores instead of eating the marshmallows and chocolate cold.

She located metal skewers and napkins, then added a bottle of pinot noir and a corkscrew to her finds before taking them into the living area. She'd noted the wide-tiled fireplace that dominated one wall of the room and the stack of logs piled high next to it when she arrived, along with a basket containing kindling and matches. Finley possessed few practical survival skills—given a choice of vacations, she'd pick a suite at a luxury hotel with hot and cold running room service over a remote campsite any day—but she prided herself on her ability to build a blazing fire. Dancing flames soon cast a gold glow over the room, making the large space feel cozier and warmer than it actually was.

She pulled nearby giant-sized floor cushions in front of the fire and settled cross-legged on top of them, draping herself with a cashmere blanket taken from the back of one of the leather sofas. She then pushed several marsh-mallows on a skewer and rotated them over the burning logs, ensuring an even outer brown layer.

A long exhale escaped her. She'd been in what felt like perpetual motion for so long—ever since that summer with Will, in fact. First, accepting Barrett's offer to work for him, climbing steadily from staff assistant to chief of staff thanks to toiling longer and harder than anyone else in his office. Then Barrett had had his first heart attack, prompting him to announce his early retirement from Congress. He'd asked her to prepare Grayson to run for Barrett's seat, ensuring the Monk family political dynasty would continue.

He didn't ask her if she wanted to run.

And she'd done what her stepfather expected of her. She became Grayson's campaign manager, helping him jump to an insurmountable lead in the polls. His election to Congress had been all but assured when he uncovered Barrett's misappropriation of campaign funds, leading Grayson to drop out of the race. After they jointly blew the whistle and Barrett was sentenced to a federal penitentiary, she'd thrown her entire self into planning Grayson's and Nelle's wedding.

It was oddly exhilarating to sit and worry about nothing except the gooeyness of her marshmallows, the melting point of the chocolate and the crunch of the graham crackers.

What did Nelle say when she made the offer to stay at Running Coyote? Staying here would give Finley space and time to figure out what she wanted to do next with her life? That turned out to be the understatement of the century.

If Finley were asked for a list, in order, of her favorite things to do, self-reflection wouldn't make the top ten thousand. She was a doer, not a philosopher. She made things happen.

Well, most things. Will didn't take the offer she made in the paddock. Her stomach panged, and she shoved another marshmallow in her mouth.

But Will was the exception that proved the rule. Normally, she had no trouble coaxing, cajoling and wheedling people into doing her bidding. Not that she exploited her powers for selfish reasons—well, again, except in the case of Will, and he'd had no problem resisting her. But in general, she used them on behalf of others. She pulled off a flawless wedding for Grayson and Nelle. As Barrett's chief of staff, she'd ensured her stepfather faced nothing but smooth sailing.

Of course, Barrett had kept many things from her, not the least of which was his ongoing embezzlement of campaign funds to pay for his lavish lifestyle. Finley had always assumed her stepfather came from inherited wealth—he was the latest in a long line of successful politicians and powerbrokers—but no, his money came from graft and corruption. Which made some of the claims Sadiya reported were in Erica O'Donnell's unpublished book believable. Finley no longer had any doubts that if there was an insider trading ring operating in certain Washington, DC circles, her stepfather would've been in the thick of it.

She sighed. Who was she if she wasn't Barrett's chief of staff? What did she want?

Will's voice asking her the latter question echoed in her head. She took a long swig from the wine bottle, but the burn of the alcohol only intensified the buzzing of his words. Not even the crack and pop of the logs as they broke apart, showers of sparks flying upward, could drown him out.

A shadow moved in the far corner of the room and she jumped. Pinot noir sloshed out of the bottle, dripping onto one of the pillows. "Damn it!"

The shadow grew closer and solidified into Will. He knelt beside her and held out one of her paper napkins. "Here."

She grabbed his offering and dabbed at the spill. The wine had landed on a heavily patterned area and didn't seem to be leaving a noticeable stain. "Heart attack much? You really need to work on announcing your presence."

"Sorry." He settled on the floor next to her. "At least you didn't cut yourself this time."

Whatever calm she had discovered fled at his nearness. Her stomach started to squeeze anew. Maybe s'mores had been a bad idea. "I was just going to bed. I'll leave you here."

But when she moved to stand, Will shook his head. "My room is freezing cold. I'm assuming yours is the same. You did what I was coming out to do—build a fire and sleep in here. Don't be a martyr on my account." He repeated her words back to her with a crooked grin.

"You're not worried I'm going to try to have my way with you?" His rejection still smarted.

He smiled. "Two participated in the kiss. Truce?" Then he nodded at the metal skewers and the bag of marshmallows. "S'mores. Inspired idea."

"Truce." She settled back on her cushion, but every nerve ending thrummed at having him so close. She busied herself by preparing another skewer of marshmallows, giving her hands something to do. "I was tired of peanut butter. And it's only day one."

"With luck, the road will be cleared soon."

"I'd settle for the power being back on." She glanced over at him. "Seriously, what kind of billionaire is your brother-in-law if he can't afford a working generator?"

She was teasing, but Will went still. She frowned.

"He's the kind that gives generously through his foundation. But who doesn't seem to have a lot of time for his new wife," Will eventually said, his gaze distant. Then he shrugged. "Or ranch maintenance. Apparently."

"I'm sorry to hear that. About your sister, I mean." She passed him the skewer and loaded one for herself. They sat, their gazes focused on the toasting marshmallows.

"So am I," said Will into the silence. "I feel responsible since I brought them together. But Lauren insists she's happy."

"Maybe she is." Finley pulled her skewer out of the fire even though the perfect brown had yet to be achieved. Talking about couples who promised each other forever only to discover forever had an expiration date was even further down her list of favorite things to do than self-reflection. "And just because you introduced them, doesn't mean you're responsible."

"Except I am. Reid's company invested in my app. He mentioned being a guinea pig for the initial alpha test, even though the app at the time was mostly populated with friends and family. I thought he was joking but I took him up on his offer anyway. Then he was matched with Lauren. The rest is history."

Finley paused, her s'more halfway to her mouth. "Wait. I'm confused. Your app is some sort of dating service?"

"EverAftr. Yes."

"EverAftr is *you*?" The room spun around Finley. She put her s'more down and grabbed the edges of her cushion, in a vain attempt to anchor herself.

Will ran the hottest matchmaking app in the country? EverAftr's success at generating long-lasting romantic partnerships had received so much publicity that even she, who stayed far away from online dating, had heard of the company.

Will, the man who proved to her that soul mates were mythical, made a fortune off creating pairings filled with hearts and flowers for others?

Yes, the s'mores were definitely a mistake.

"You weren't aware I ran EverAftr?" Will watched her closely. "I don't know if I should be insulted you didn't look me up on the internet. At least occasionally."

"Have you seen how many results are returned when you search 'Will Taylor' on Google?" She swallowed, but it turned into a choke. She started to cough.

"Do you need some water?"

She shook her head, grabbing the bottle of wine and taking a healthy swig instead. "I'm fine," she managed to get out.

"I hope your reaction doesn't mean you had a bad experience with EverAftr."

"No." She gathered her composure as best she could. "Never tried it. Never tried any dating app, for that matter."

"Right. I don't suppose you need help meeting people."

"More like I don't want to." She pressed the back of her hand to her lips. "Sorry. That sounds like I don't enjoy being social. I mean, I don't date."

"That's not the impression I got in the paddock." He took his own swig of pinot noir, but not before she saw his mouth twitch into a smile.

"I'm far from celibate. I just don't..." She shrugged. "Have relationships." She threw him a glance from under her eyelashes. "You missed out. Could have had your mind blown—among other things—with no-strings sex, but you turned me down. Your loss."

"I didn't turn you down, Lee. I said I'm not your toy." He finished off the wine, and then stood. "Want another red? Or should we move to white?"

"Red pairs better with chocolate. Or whiskey," she called after him. Her heart jumped into her throat, beating at least ten thousand times per second. He'd called her Lee. No one called her Lee, except him. And only when he told her he loved her, that long-ago summer.

Will returned with two bottles of red wine held by the neck in his left hand and a decanter of whiskey in his right. He placed them on the tiled hearth, then opened the bottle nearest him and offered it to her. "Want to share or have your own?"

A vision of his mouth on the wine bottle made her shift on her cushion. Sharing was infinitely preferable. "I can't finish a whole one. Surprised you didn't bring glasses, however."

"My hands can only hold so much. Didn't think you'd mind."

She knew exactly how much his hands could hold, and where. "Fine with me. Less to wash."

He chuckled. "Menial labor never was your style."

"I've washed plenty of dishes," she protested. "I clean my own apartment. This isn't the first time you've made a crack about me as if I'm a spoiled princess."

"You grew up among the one percent."

"Excuse me, Mr. EverAftr. Didn't your company just go public with a capitalization that puts companies like Medevco and HomeHotels to shame? You're one to talk."

"Didn't spend my childhood with a governor of California as a great-grandfather and a congressman for a father."

"Neither did I. Barrett is my stepfather."

"There's a difference?"

Hell, yes. She pressed her lips together tightly and stared into the fire.

Will held out the wine bottle. "Sorry. I'm guessing there was one."

She took it. "I don't mean to reinforce the evil stepparent narrative. Lots of people have caring stepparents who provide them with nothing but love and comfort. And my own father disappeared after I was born and didn't want to have anything to do with me, which makes Barrett parent of the year in comparison." She sighed.

"You never talked much about your family. I didn't know you were related to Barrett until halfway through the internship program."

"For a good reason." She stared into the fire. She told

very few people for fear of the rumors of nepotism. She wished she'd never told Will. "I suppose Barrett treated me like he would any daughter. Grayson was a son, and our genders made a difference to him. But Barrett probably shouldn't have been anyone's parent." She grabbed the wine from Will and drank deeply, and then handed it back to him. "Although I think I'm more like Barrett than Grayson ever will be."

"I don't see you going to prison for campaign finance fraud, if that's a consolation."

She laughed. It felt good. She hadn't laughed about Barrett in a very long time. "It is."

The alcohol settled in her stomach, its warm glow traveling along her veins and weighing down her limbs with relaxed languor. At the same time, admitting Barrett had been a less-than-ideal parent made her feel lighter. Younger. More carefree. She no longer had to keep up the pretense of a perfect family for the DC media. Or even for Grayson, who'd bought heavily into the image of his father as a crusading hero until he uncovered Barrett's fraud.

No wonder people said confession was good for the soul.

Of course, she still had to come clean about her own shortcomings. She inhaled, catching Will's gaze with her own, and then blew the breath out. "You weren't wrong, out in the paddock. I was playing a game. I apologize, sincerely. But I never thought of you as a toy. Not earlier today, and not then. You broke my heart, Will."

He blinked, followed by a bark of laughter. "Your heart? You broke mine by breaking up with me. Out of the blue."

"I didn't—"

"You did." All mirth was gone.

"You didn't let me finish. I was going to say I didn't

mean for us to break up." She reached for the bottle, but he kept his grip on it and wouldn't let go.

His gaze, dark and demanding, locked on hers. "Explain."

She gave up on the battle for the wine. She'd just have to get through her confession without an extra shot of liquid courage. "That summer...with the internship ending and graduation approaching, I applied for a position with the State Department."

"I remember. You wanted to travel."

"Yep." And she never did. Not as she intended. "But what I didn't tell you is Barrett called me into his office shortly before I had my interview. Said he received reports I was... I believe the word *gallivanting* was used... with another intern."

"Most college-aged people gallivant. In one form or another."

"Ah, but they weren't Barrett Monk's stepdaughter. A reflection on his distinguished family and storied name. And you have to admit, we gallivanted quite a lot. And weren't very discreet." She nodded at the bottle still held tightly in his hands. "Seriously, I could use some of that."

Will shook his head. "I want to know this is you talking and not the alcohol."

"Fine." She hugged her knees to her chest. "Barrett threatened to torpedo my application. Said I wasn't appropriately respectful of the opportunities he was providing. I needed to prove to him I was worthy of being a member of the Monk family. Which meant cutting out all extraneous activities. Like you."

Will's gaze burned into her. "Why didn't you say anything? I would have understood."

Hindsight being 20/20, of course she should've told Will everything. Been honest and up-front. Laid everything on the table. But she'd been twenty-one years old, an adult but not a worldly one, painfully young in so many ways. And above all, anxious for Barrett's approval.

She never knew her biological father, who'd left when she was an infant. Her mother had married Barrett shortly after, but after a long illness had passed away when Finley was thirteen. Barrett had become the only parent she had. And like most children, she'd wanted to make her parent proud—especially because Barrett rarely showed any form of affection, causing her to chase his approval even harder.

It had taken much mental health counseling over the past year to recognize the harmful patterns in her family relationships. But her realizations couldn't change the past. "I thought Barrett was right," she said finally. "He knew Washington. He understood politics. He had knowledge and experience on his side."

Will shook his head. "I get that. I don't get why you didn't tell me."

She saw the decanter out of the corner of her eye and grabbed it, removing the top to take a stiff drink. Whiskey fumes stung her nose as the liquid scorched her throat. She welcomed the momentary pain. "I stupidly thought if you and I were 'soul mates'—" she rolled her eyes "—as you insisted we were, then we'd stay together. Surely, nothing could separate us for good. Not even if I told you we should break up. You would just…dismiss…that hurdle."

She scoffed at her naivety, expecting Will to join in. But he stayed silent and still. So still, she was tempted to check if he continued to breathe. "You were very convincing," he finally said.

A log popped in the fireplace. The fire had dwindled to a few lone flames among the embers. She couldn't see his expression very well. But she was fairly certain the tightness in her throat was matched by his.

"Barrett persuaded me I needed to be. He said..." She reached again for the whiskey. "He said you were using me. For my connections and family name. For access to him." Will's left hand made a sudden movement. She hastened to add, "I assured him otherwise."

"I don't understand," Will repeated. "Why did you listen to him?"

Why? It was a question she'd asked herself more times than she cared to admit. "He was so adamant, so sure he was right. And—" She squeezed her eyes shut. "You have to admit using people to get ahead was an everyday occurrence in DC. I was scared. Maybe he was right. Maybe you didn't love me as much as I loved you. Maybe I was a stepping-stone to be discarded."

"How could you think that? No. Strike that. How could you think *I* thought that? I loved you. You knew that." His voice was a harsh whisper in the darkness.

"I thought I did." Her stomach flip-flopped at the past tense and she took another sip. The whiskey didn't wash away the acrid taste the memory left in her mouth. "You need to know, Barrett showed me the letters."

"What letters?"

"C'mon, Will. The recommendations he wrote on your behalf for Harvard, Yale and Stanford Law. I don't blame you, I knew you wanted to be a lawyer, to right great wrongs—"

"I never—" Will exploded. "I didn't—that's a lie. I never received recommendations from him."

"I saw them."

"Doesn't mean I asked for the letters. Or even wanted him to write ones for me." He jerked a hand through his hair. "Damn it, Finley. You should have said something."

She hugged her knees tighter, her head falling to rest on them. She could see so clearly now what she'd been blind to for most of her entire life. Of course Barrett had faked the recommendations, just like he and his campaign treasurer had faked the finance records sent to the Federal Election Commission. She, who prided herself on always being ten steps in front of others, had let Barrett string her along like a child's pull toy for years. Will was only confirming her worst suspicions. "I know that. Now."

Will exhaled, harsh and sharp. "I never went to law school."

She turned her head toward him. "What? That was all you talked about. I made sure Barrett sent the recommendations, despite our break-up. Why didn't you go?"

He made an impatient movement. "I—why didn't you join the State Department?"

"They turned me down." The memory still hurt, although it wasn't nearly as painful as the thoughts of Will over the years. "Barrett then offered me a role in his office. I stayed and worked my way up—and I earned those promotions by being very good at what I do. Why didn't you study law?"

He opened his mouth, then shut it and shrugged instead. "Things turned out okay."

"CEO of EverAftr? Yes. I'd say so." She tried for a smile, his refusal to answer her questions about law school cutting a little closer to the bone than she liked. "Surprised you named the app that. Since 'happily-ever-after' is nothing but a cute fairy tale for little children and the giant media companies after their parents' money."

"You don't believe that."

"You can't possibly believe otherwise. You're too smart."

Will's unreadable gaze searched hers. Then he turned

his head to stare into dying flames. "The name tested well. Marketing liked it."

With a start, she realized she hadn't expected him to agree with her. She wanted him to argue with her, to persuade her she was wrong. The fact that he didn't...

Well. Enough strolling down memory lane. Confession might be beneficial for her soul, but it was hell on her equanimity. She should return to her room. Her cold room. Alone.

She put the top back on the whiskey decanter and stood up. "This is where I say good night."

"Lee."

She froze, resolving to see a cardiologist when the road opened. Her continual rapid pulse couldn't be good for her health. "Yes?"

"I don't remember you believing 'happily-ever-after' was a myth."

The room was wreathed in heavy shadows. Hopefully, he couldn't see her face. Couldn't discern her naked yearning to turn back the clock fifteen years and tell Barrett where to shove his fake letters of recommendation. Wouldn't perceive just how much she regretted not having stronger faith in him, in their love.

But the past could not be rewritten. "I once bought into it," she said. "But I grew up."

He rose to his feet and stood next to her. So close, the tiny hairs on her arms vibrated with awareness. "I'm sorry," he said.

She creased her forehead. "For what? The breakup was my doing. This morning was my doing. I owe you more apologies than there were raindrops in last night's storm."

"For not convincing you I loved you for you."

An unfamiliar prickling sensation came from her nose. "You were convincing. I chose not to trust the evidence.

But thank you for the thought." On impulse, scarcely knowing what she was doing before she did it, she leaned up to kiss his stubbled cheek.

He turned his head at the last second. Her mouth landed on his.

Sparks ignited, setting her veins on fire. She opened her mouth, her tongue imploring his lips to open, plunging inside when he acquiesced to her demand. His tongue met hers, an intense dance of heat and pressure, and she was lost to the unique magic that was kissing Will. Her arms twined around his neck, her chest pressing into his as she tried to burrow closer, pull herself deeper into him.

A log fell in the fireplace with a loud crash. They broke apart at the sound. Finley looked up at Will from under her lashes. "Sorry, I didn't mean to break the truce."

"Don't apologize." Will's gaze reflected the flames dancing in the fireplace. His hands tightened on her waist. "I was a willing participant."

She licked her lips. They were swollen. She could still taste Will. "But you said in the paddock—"

"I'll repeat what I asked this morning. Is this what you really want or is it another game?"

She was about to faint from want. Her knees were soft with it. Her arms ached. Her sex throbbed, demanding more. Demanding him. "We're not meant for happily-ever-after. But for tonight, I want this. I want you."

"Tonight." His mouth closed over hers.

Ten

Will kissed Finley, storing up memories like so many precious gems. His near-perfect recall meant he would always remember this night, even as part of him still questioned if Finley was actually in his arms, her mouth hot on his, or it was a very vivid dream.

But nothing in his dreams ever approached the marvel that was kissing Finley now. They'd been relatively inexperienced kids that summer, not virgins, but still learning how to give and receive pleasure from a partner. Now, Finley's knowing lips and tongue gave as good as he gave. Desire ignited into an inferno, so hot, so fast, he didn't know if his senses would ever fully recover.

He trailed openmouthed kisses down her neck, over to her ear, wondering if her skin behind her ear was still sensitive. He licked and then ran his teeth lightly over the area. She gasped and shivered, pressing her belly hard against him.

He took that as a yes.

Her loose T-shirt was in his way. He bunched it up, running his hands over the curve of her abdomen, the indentation of her waist. It turned out his memory wasn't nearly perfect after all, for he'd forgotten how her skin glowed like luminescent silk, the way she shuddered when his fingers traced patterns up and down her spine.

She stepped back and pulled her T-shirt all the way off, revealing her breasts. His breath stuttered. Finley at twenty-one had been stunning. Finley now was…magnificent. Confident and aware of her power, a goddess by any measure. She knelt on the cushions in front of the fire, her gaze dark with invitation.

He didn't need to be asked twice. She leaned in to kiss him, placing his hands on her breasts, their weight and shape at once familiar but new. He set to learning them again, his fingers teasing one perfect globe then the other, pulling and rolling the tight, hard peaks the way she had once taught him to do. She collapsed against him, her breath coming fast and harsh.

Then she pushed him back, tugging his T-shirt over his head. Her thumbs brushed over his abs with feather-light strokes, dipping below the waistband of his sweatpants, lingering near but never quite touching his impossibly hard cock. He gritted his teeth, sweating with impatience, wanting her hand on him, her mouth, to bury himself deep and lose himself inside her, now. But also wanting this night to last forever.

How was this possible? After all these years, after numerous sexual encounters, and several girlfriends later—some of whom he cared for considerably—and he was about to come from just knowing the person touching him was Finley.

With supreme effort, he removed her hand and tugged

her to lie down beside him. Her yoga pants were an unnecessary barrier and he made quick work of discarding them, baring the dark triangle at the apex of her thighs. She sighed, her legs opening for him, her arms reaching. But he was a firm believer that turnabout equaled fair play. Keeping a tight grip on his self-control, he drew decreasing concentric circles from her rounded belly to the tops of her thighs, his fingers coming ever closer but never arriving at the tangled nest of curls. She writhed, her hips jerking, seeking.

"I concede," she panted, and rolled them both until he was on his back and she was looking down at him, black wings of hair falling to frame her face.

He'd never seen anyone more beautiful.

"Condom?" she asked.

The air escaped him. "In my bag. In my room."

She smiled, slow and sinful and full of promise. "Then we'll just have to improvise. I'm not letting you leave only to change your mind."

"Not going to happen."

"I know." She kissed him, her tongue lapping at his. Then she kissed her way down his throat, to his sternum, taking her time to lavish his nipples with wet, hot attention before raising her head to whisper in his ear. "Because I'm finally going to turn my favorite fantasy into reality."

Her hand grasped him then. Her fingers already knew how he liked to be stroked, what pressure to apply and where. His brain threatened to shut down. Her touch was too much for his nerve endings. She was too much. She watched him for a minute, her smile a mix of delight and sin, her hooded gaze shining. Then she lowered her head and took him in her clever, knowing mouth.

He wasn't going to last longer than zero point one three seconds. That wouldn't do.

He sat up, taking her off guard. Then he tugged her down on the cushions until it was her turn to blink up at him. "Was I doing something wrong?" she asked.

"No. Too much too right," he growled. Then he pulled her legs apart and buried his mouth in her wet heat, seeking her most sensitive spots. She screamed, a chorus of angels to his ears. He loved making Finley scream. He loved that he could still make her scream.

Her back arched. He held her steady, letting her know he had her, that it was safe to let go. He fell automatically into the rhythm he knew she liked best, using his tongue and fingers to coax and push and demand, until she broke and shattered in his grasp. His name was a chant on her lips.

Nothing, not even all the success of EverAftr, gave him the same sense of satisfaction as knowing he caused Finley Smythe to fall apart. He held her as she quieted, pulling the blanket she'd discarded earlier over them. Her chest rose and fell against him, her mouth lax against the side of his neck.

Her fingers enlaced with his.

His heart twisted. Out of everything they had just experienced, holding her hand felt the most intimate of all. Like she belonged there, by his side. Giving her strength to him, taking his strength for herself.

For tonight.

Morning sun teased Will's eyelids. He turned his head away from the source of light, resisting the temptation to open his eyes. What if last night really had been a dream? What if he woke up and Finley wasn't next to him?

They'd retired to his room, although not much sleep had been achieved. He should be bone-tired but exhilaration powered his nervous system. He hadn't felt this good upon awaking since…okay, fine. Since he and Finley had first slept together, all those years ago.

He reached out his hand, seeking the warm satin of Finley's skin. He encountered nothing but rumpled sheets. His eyes flew open.

Last night had been real. Her scent lingered, pomegranate and spice and sugar. The pillow next to his bore the imprint of her head. His body would forever be branded by her touch.

But where was she? He sat up, throwing back the covers that had cocooned them, and swung his legs out of bed. His sweatpants were…somewhere.

Finley laughed from the doorway. His heart clenched at the sight of her. She was fully dressed, wearing a fresh pair of jeans that clung to her hips and thighs and a blue flannel shirt that matched the sky outside the window. In her hands she carried a plate of what looked like peanut butter sandwiches. "I was hoping to serve you breakfast in bed, but you seem to be getting out of it."

He settled back on his pillow. "Serve away."

She sat on the edge of the bed next to him and handed him a sandwich. "Sorry for the monotonous menu. But surprise! I found a manual can opener. Canned salmon for lunch. Yum. Y'know, we should decide when we think the refrigerator is a lost cause and rescue some of the cheese before everything spoils. Knowing Nelle, I'm sure she requested some fancy, gourmet varieties to be stocked."

Finley was babbling. She only babbled when she wanted to divert someone—in this case, him—from having a serious conversation. He set the sandwich aside and tried to catch her gaze. "You're up early."

"Horses wait for no man. Or for any gender." She played with her sandwich but didn't take a bite. "You'll be happy to know both Trudy and Ranger have been fed and watered. In fact, I was thinking I might go for a ride. A horseback ride," she clarified with her familiar smirk. "Want to join me? Trudy is very sweet. I can teach you the basics, if you want."

If she thought they were going to turn the clock back to wary acquaintances sharing a house because they had no other choice, she was mistaken. Not after last night. "Tell me what's really going on inside your head, Lee."

She inhaled sharply. "You should know that I'm not fond of nicknames."

"Yes, you are."

"Yes, I *was*." She stressed the last word. Then she indicated the view from the window. "What's going on inside my head? I want to go riding. It's glorious outside. You should get up and see for yourself. California is spectacular after a winter rainstorm. The mountains are sharp and clear against the sky. The air is crisp—"

"Your head is going in circles about last night."

She raised her eyebrows in polite inquiry. "Oh? It is? You're that familiar with the contents of my head?"

"You're obsessing over what happened between us and if there will be a repeat. As I am. And I think there should be a repeat. As often as possible. If you want, of course."

She blinked at him, shock and not a little yearning written on her face. Then she turned away, her gaze focusing anywhere but on him. "Look, I know our situation must reek to you of a storybook. Two former lovers trapped together, old misunderstandings are discussed, dormant feelings combust, yadda yadda yadda, blah blah blah. But I don't do relationships. I don't do happily-ever-afters. And that's what your company sells. I don't blame you for internalizing your own marketing."

He held up his hands. "Whoa. Who said anything about a happily-ever-after?" Although, if he were honest with himself, the idea was more than a tickle in the back of his mind. "You're the one who mentioned mind-blowing, no-strings-attached sex. Can't fault a guy for being intrigued."

"Did you think that was what I was offering last night?" Her brows drew together, for a split second only, before her expression smoothed out. Then her slow smile reappeared. "Good. As long as we're on the same page." She held out her right hand. "I propose new truce terms. No-strings-sex until one of us is bored?"

He answered her by pulling her head to his, taking her mouth, demanding she open to him. She sighed and relaxed into him, her arms wrapping around his neck, her tongue seeking his. Something crashed to the floor. He didn't care. He had Finley back, and he wasn't going to let her use her words to create barriers between them again.

"The sandwiches—" she gasped.

"Only hungry for you." Her Western-style shirt was fastened with snaps instead of buttons, making it easy to rip open. Her breasts were encased in scraps of lace that enhanced rather than hid their perfection. He played with a tightly furled nipple, rolling it with his fingers, brushing the tip with his thumb, before leaning down to draw the sweet bud, lace and all, into his mouth. His cock throbbed but he ignored his insistent need. The more he kept Finley drunk on desire, the less time for her to come up with reasons to put distance between them.

Her hands came up to his chest, but she used them to push him away, insistent enough that he drew back. He shrugged off the disappointment threatening to crush him. "No?"

She shook her head. "Hell, yes. But fast. Hard. Now." She shimmied out of her jeans, revealing another scrap of lace just barely covering her mound. But before he could drink his fill of the tantalizing sight, her mouth was on him, pulling on his aching length, begging his full attention. He swelled to improbable dimensions in her warm, perceptive mouth, tormenting his most sensitive zones with pleasure so intense, he wasn't sure he would survive an orgasm.

Where was his recall of baseball statistics when he needed them for a distraction? He couldn't think. His neurons were replaced by nerve endings that could only feel. "Lee," he gasped. "Stop. Or slow down."

"If you say so." She released him with a smile, her cheeks flushed bright red, her breasts rapidly rising and falling. Last night, he'd thought Finley in the firelight was stunning beyond belief. But that vision didn't compare to Finley in the sunlight, kneeling on the bed, her gaze wide and wild. His chest constricted at her beauty. "But be careful what you wish for," she breathed.

She reached for a foil packet on his bedside table, one of the few remaining after last night. Without taking her gaze away from his, she rolled the condom onto his cock. Then she brushed the scrap of lace aside and guided him inside her.

His eyes nearly rotated to the back of his head. Then she bore down, burying his length even deeper in her wet, hot sex, and he was lost. The primal rhythm they generated together took over, as they moved in tandem faster, building the pressure higher. He circled his thumb around the sensitive cluster of nerves at her entrance and she screamed, shuddering as she bore down on him, demanding he not stay behind.

He let go and flew with her.

Finley collapsed on top of him and he cradled her close, smiling when her rapid breaths calmed into light snuffling snores. Languor weighted his limbs, but he fought the urge to drift into unconsciousness with her.

Pieces of the puzzle that had tormented him for years suddenly fell into place. They'd been young. Perhaps if they had met in their late twenties or thirties, they would have had enough perspective to weather interference by others. But they had been punch-drunk on love and each other, and neither had the worldly experience nor self-confidence to ask questions when the relationship went off the rails.

He didn't blame Finley, not now. Yes, she should have been honest with him. But he'd had his own run-in with Barrett—not over letters of recommendation, that was a damn lie—but they'd bumped into each other in the hallways of the Capitol. When Will eagerly introduced himself to the congressman, Barrett had given him a thorough once-over and silently put Will in his place, ignoring Will's proffered hand. Then Barrett had stepped past him and started a collegial conversation with Will's co-intern, the son of a Dartmouth dean.

The implication Will wasn't important enough to acknowledge, even with a handshake, still rankled. He hadn't told Finley after it happened because he didn't want to open up the possibility she would defend her stepfather. But he'd seen for himself the force of Barrett's personality. It would not have been easy for a young Finley to tell him no.

The more Will thought about Finley's words of the night before, the more he realized Barrett had manipulated them both. He'd played on Finley's fear of not being loved for herself. And he'd used Will's insecurity, that of a working class kid struggling to keep up with those born with the proverbial silver spoon in their mouths, to do so. Will would lay a hefty bet the only reason Finley didn't get the State Department position was because Barrett torpedoed her chances so she would come work for him.

But that was then. Now, there was no way Will would let another fifteen years go by without her in his life, much less fifteen minutes. And it wasn't just the sex, as astonishing as they were together. He'd missed *her*. Her intelligence, her snark, her charm—even when she'd tried to manipulate him.

She might want to think there weren't any strings attached, but he intended to fasten them securely before they left the ranch.

Finley snuggled closer, her legs entwining with his in her sleep. He yawned, reveling in the soft, warm weight of her. Maybe a nap wasn't such a bad idea...

His eyes flew open. He had a contract to star in a reality television series. Screenweb had already sent him their advertising concepts, built around the CEO of EverAftr using his own app to find a perfect match. But how could he search for a partner who fulfilled his ideal criteria when his perfectly imperfect match was in his arms?

Eleven

Finley walked into the ranch's main room, dressed for her morning horseback ride. In the last three days, she and Will had fallen into a routine: breakfast together, then Finley fed the horses before taking one of them out on the trails dotting the hills around the ranch. Will stayed behind, working on ideas for EverAftr until she returned to the house, then they foraged in the kitchen to make lunch. The rest of the hours were spent talking and making love until the sun threatened to make its appearance.

They had a lot of conversations to catch up on.

Will was already hard at work. He sat on one of the leather couches in front of the fireplace, scrawling intently on a yellow legal pad. She took a seat next to him and dropped a kiss on his cheek. "It's Trudy's turn to be ridden today, so I might be back a little later than usual. She likes to ramble."

Will frowned, still focused on what he was writing. "Be safe out there."

"Trudy knows this area like the back of her hoof. We'll be fine." She looked down at his pad. It consisted mostly of scratched-out words. "Doesn't look like you're making lots of progress on whatever you're doing."

He glanced up. "What?"

She pointed to his scribblings. "You've crossed everything out."

"Oh." He looked back at it. "Brainstorming. Not enough brain, too little storm."

She laughed. "You have a very big brain and as for storms…" She pulled his head to hers and kissed him until they were both breathless, the heat on constant simmer between them flaring into a supernova. "I see lightning, multiple times a night."

"Just at night?" he joked, rubbing his thumb over her lower lip.

"Don't push your luck. I've already complimented you." She smiled and kissed him again before sitting back. "What are you brainstorming? Maybe I can help. The horses can wait a few minutes."

"What do you know about television production? Specifically, reality TV."

She shook her head. "Not my area of expertise, unless we're talking media appearances on news channels."

His lips thinned, and he added to the scribbles on his page. "Right. The media. Forgot about them."

She narrowed her gaze. "Wait. You don't like movies—"

"I like them. I don't have the time—"

She waved his protest away. "So why are you asking about television production? TV is nothing but a string of mini-movies, even reality series. And if you don't have two hours for a film, you're not going to have ten or twenty-two hours."

"I do if the series is based on EverAftr."

She leaned back on the sofa. "Oh. Wow."

"The meeting in LA I missed thanks to the mudslide? It was with the streaming service that commissioned the series. To kick off the production."

"Is that what you're brainstorming? Ideas for episodes?"

"In a way." His lips pressed into a thin line.

"Let me see what you have—" She reached for the legal pad but he put it down out of her reach and turned on the sofa to face her.

"I have a better idea. Let's go on a date. A real date. Tonight."

If he was seeking a diversion, it worked. "A date? Tonight?" She laughed. "And go where? I think we've explored the house pretty thoroughly. Even the pool." The memory of just how they'd occupied themselves in the water caused a rush of heat to her cheeks. Who needed a working pool heater with Will around?

"Let me worry about that." He indicated the pad. "I need to work most of today. Pick you up outside your room at six?"

"You're aware I'm already sleeping with you, right? You don't need to woo me."

He raised his eyebrows. "Don't I?"

His question made her stomach flop, half queasy, half thrilled by a hope she dared not examine. She leaned up and kissed him lightly on the cheek. "You're being ridiculous, but I accept. See you at six."

"Wear something nice," he called after her.

She shook her head, laughing as she exited the room. Yes, he was ridiculous. But he was her type of ridiculous.

Giving him up when the time came was going to be difficult, but she'd manage.

By six o'clock, Finley's fluttering nerves had expanded from her stomach to her chest and down to her knees. Not even a galloping run on Trudy followed by a cold shower could calm down the roiling mixture of anticipation, dread, desire and pessimistic optimism that currently accompanied her every thought. Still, she dressed herself carefully for her "date," digging into her suitcase to find the dress she'd brought as a backup for Nelle and Grayson's rehearsal dinner. The long gown had been a gift from Nelle, an ephemeral blush pink concoction of silk and organza. It wasn't Finley's usual style, but Nelle had explained it reminded her of what a fairy godmother might wear—not the frumpy fairy godmothers seen in animated films, but the kind who made the impossible happen, like helping Nelle and Grayson find their way back to each other.

Finley had to admit the dress flattered her. She rarely wore pink as it tended to wash her out, but in the candlelight this shade made appear radiant. The neckline dipped low over her breasts, the fabric skimming her curves until the skirt flared out into layers of organza below her hips. She twirled in front of the mirror, and then laughed at herself. She was as nervous as she'd been as a twenty-one-year-old, waiting for Will to pick her up for the first time.

A knock sounded. She blew out the candles with some difficulty, her breathing already affected by anticipation of the night to come, and opened the door to reveal Will. He was hopelessly attractive in a dark blue suit that matched his eyes. In his hands he held a small bouquet of purple and gold pansies. "Only flower I could find in the gardens."

Her heart twinged. The date had just started and already he was finding chinks in her determination to resist any sentiment. "Thank you."

He offered her his left arm. "Shall we?"

She couldn't help her wide grin. "Of course. Lead on."

As they walked in silence through the now-familiar corridors, her fingers gripped the fine wool of his jacket. When they passed the living area, she looked up at him with surprise. "Will?"

"Almost there."

He led her out a side door she'd never used, and down a winding stone pathway. At the bottom of the slope, a one-story stucco cottage that matched the ranch house's architecture came into view. She stopped. "On the ranch map, isn't this marked as a private office?"

He smiled. "Reid had it built for Lauren. Off-limits to guests."

"Then maybe we shouldn't go inside."

Will nuzzled her cheek. "I'm not a guest."

He guided her to the cottage's front door, and then opened the wood and iron door with a flourished bow. "Welcome."

"Oh...my..." Finley stood transfixed on the doorstep.

The door opened into a large room that occupied the entire footprint of the cottage. The walls were lined with mahogany bookcases that soared from the terra-cotta-tiled floor to the high ceiling far above. At the far end, a spiral staircase provided access to a loft heaped with pillows. Lit candles were everywhere, their flickering light turning the space into an enchanted wonderland.

"I feel like I'm in *Beauty and the Beast*," she murmured. "All that's missing is a talking teapot."

Will glanced at her. "I don't remember a talking teapot in the fairy tale."

She blinked. "I'm referring to the film—or rather, two films. And a Broadway musical. You know what, never mind." She walked into the room, her gaze struggling to take everything in and store the details. "This is…stunning."

Will smiled. "I thought you might like it."

She gave him a mock glare. "I can't believe you held this out on me."

"Where do you think I was, that first day after we argued in the paddock? I came here to work." He took her hand and guided her to the middle of the room, where a small round table had been set with paper plates containing sandwiches. "If I'd been in the house, I would've finished what we started."

"I was too ashamed of my behavior to come out of my room. Now I wish I'd have looked for you. But if I'd found you in here, believe me, sex would have been the last thing on my mind." Her head was on a constant swivel, as she took in as many details as she could: the overstuffed wingbacked chairs upholstered in jewel tones. The massive oak desk in its own alcove. The stained glass windows reflecting the candlelight.

"In that case, we're going back to the house. Now."

"Oh no, we're not. When will I ever get the chance to dine in a place like this?" She leaned up and kissed him on the cheek. "Thank you. Even if the main course is rather familiar."

He handed her a glass of red wine. "But we have a damn good bottle of Margaux, thanks to Reid's wine cellar." He picked up his own glass and clinked it against hers. "Cheers. Here's to our second first date."

She sipped her wine, still taking in her surroundings. Or maybe looking around gave her an excuse to avoid the emotions shining in Will's gaze. Emotions she didn't dare name. Naming them would make the feelings real.

"I can't believe how many books are in here."

"Lauren has collected books all her life. Reid built this to store her library."

"But I thought the ranch wasn't their primary residence?"

"It's not. Which means Lauren rarely sees her collection." Will drank deeply from his glass. "May I interest you in an appetizer of canned pears?"

The table he'd set looked tiny to her eyes. They would be sitting very close together. Intimate. Her heart knocked hard against her ribs.

Silly to fear intimacy when she and Will were still clothed and vertical, especially since they barely kept their hands off each other over the past few days. But Finley was very careful not to confuse sex with love.

She enjoyed sex. It felt good, in much the same way a satisfying scratch of an itch did. She had fun and her partners did, too. But physical sensations were one thing. Emotions were quite another.

Tonight's dinner with Will loomed like an invisible line in the sand. If she stepped over it, she feared she would no longer be able to pretend there was nothing between them but a chemical reaction. Although, if she were honest, she'd admit she left that line far behind the night they spent in front of the fire.

"Do you mind if I explore more first?" She walked to the bookcase on the opposite wall, next to the alcove that held the desk. Putting as much space as she could place between them.

Above her head, first editions of Nancy Drew mysteries published over the decades occupied an entire shelf. To her left, she found a large section devoted to West African literature, and below that, histories of various Latin American countries written in Spanish. "I think I'd like your sister. What caused her to start collecting books?"

Will joined her. But his gaze wasn't on the shelves. He regarded her with longing and... Her cheeks filled with heat. "I'd rather discuss other topics than my sister," he rumbled. "Like us. What we're doing. And what happens after we leave the ranch."

Finley's pulse whooshed in her ears. She knew what would happen when they left the ranch. They would part. She would return to her messy, snarled life. Will would go back to earning accolades for running his successful company. That was the only possible outcome.

"I have a better idea." She leaned into him, nuzzling the side of his neck. "Let's forget the appetizer and go straight to the main course."

"You're that hungry for peanut butter?"

"No." She kissed him, her tongue seeking and finding his, igniting the spark that was never fully dormant between them.

He kissed her back, but when her hands ventured lower, he broke off the contact and stepped back. "Don't get me wrong. I like this. A lot. But I was hoping for a more traditional date. The kind where we talk first."

"Since when were we ever traditional?" She closed the distance he put between them. The silk of her dress did nothing to conceal her nipples, hard with need. And she wasn't the only one. The front of his trousers bore ample evidence.

"Lee—" he started, then stopped with a groan when her hands found what they had sought, stroking him through the fine wool.

"You're hungry, too," she whispered in his ear. "Don't deny it."

"I could never deny you. But—"

Through her peripheral vision, she spotted the desk. She hopped up on its broad surface. The flimsy organza of her skirt rode up. His gaze zeroed in on her bared thighs.

He always did have a thing for her legs.

"But what?" She made herself comfortable on the edge of the desk, leaning back on her elbows. If her skirt bunched even higher, revealing to Will she wore only the barest scraps of lace underneath the dress, that might have been on purpose.

"My laptop is behind you. Pretty much a dead paperweight now, but maybe we should…"

She glanced over her shoulder and then laughed. "Sorry, I didn't see it. You're right. Breaking your computer would be a mood killer." She slid off the desk and whispered in Will's ear. "But breaking the desk? I look forward to it."

She picked up the open laptop and handed it to Will, grabbing the file folder that was underneath. A printout fluttered to the ground. She bent down.

The hot glow winked out of Will's gaze. "I'll take that."

"Your hands are full—hey." She stood, examining the piece of paper in her hand. "This is a draft press release for your TV show. How exciting." She grinned at him before starting to read out loud. "*Finding EverAftr* is a reality television series where real-life singles use the highly successful EverAftr dating app to find a life partner perfectly matched to their personal strengths, weaknesses and desired attributes—"

"Lee. Stop. Let's have dinner. We need to talk—"

She waved him off. "The company's CEO, William Taylor—" she smiled at him "—is the star of the first season of eight one-hour episodes as he sets out on his own quest for his own happily-ever-after…"

She blinked. Hard. Then she blinked again. The text on the page remained blurry. Whoever printed the press release out needed to change the ink cartridge, because the rest of it was illegible. She took a shuddering breath, and the words swam into sharper focus. "...He'll be joined by six other people from across the United States, of all ages and from all walks of life, with only one question in common—can the world's most popular dating app really lead to *Finding EverAftr*?"

The room tilted on an axis before righting itself. Her hands were so numb, she almost dropped the printout. But her years of political training rescued her. She dredged up a bright smile and pasted it on her face. "Well," she said, affecting an airy shrug, "for the topic of your next brainstorm, I suggest finding a better writer for your press releases. I can recommend excellent PR agencies, but they're mostly based in DC. But I'm sure if you ask them for references—"

"This is why I wanted to have dinner. To tell you about the series." His hands clenched and unclenched by his sides. "And to tell you I've already sent word to the production company via Tim. I'm not going to be in it."

She laughed, a little too loud. "Why not? I might criticize the press release's style, but the content is fab. A tech CEO using his own service on camera for all to judge? It's a brilliant concept. People will be on the edges of their seats to see if EverAftr works for the man who came up with it." She stretched her grin farther. "Congrats. This is terrific stuff."

He grabbed the press release from her, crumbling it into a ball. "Yes, this is good exposure for the company. Otherwise, we wouldn't have agreed." He tossed the ball across the room. Turning back to her, he cupped her face with his hands. "But as for being in it... How can I, after the last few days?"

"Will." The floor threatened to fall from under her feet. Her vision blurred again, and blinking didn't clear it. "The last few days have been..." Now her voice was cracking. "They've been the stuff of fantasies. Believe me, I will make productive use of the memories when I'm alone. But we have a no-strings agreement—"

He kissed her. A gentle kiss, promising an unspoken future. A promise she knew he would not keep. Not because he didn't want to, but because she knew it just wasn't possible. "We did have one. But this is a date. You agreed to it."

She searched his gaze. For a brief second, she lost herself in his gray-blue depths, allowing herself to believe that they could be more, that they could leave the ranch and build a relationship despite any hurdles in their way. But even as she let herself imagine Will might be right, she knew it was illusory. She'd had a lifetime of experiences that proved love didn't conquer anything. Her mother had loved her father, but he'd abandoned her with an infant to take care of. Barrett had demonstrated over and over to her that relationships were transactional, nothing more. And yes, Finley had forced the fight with Will that led to their breakup, but they weren't confident enough in their feelings for each other to weather the first big storm that came along.

Once the road off the ranch opened, any possible future they had together would slam closed.

But in the meantime, they were still stuck on the ranch thanks to a literal storm. No need to ruin the time they still had together. What was the harm in humoring his fantasy? She was indulging in several of her own, after all. Fantasies like becoming accustomed to waking up next to someone she adored. Or having breakfast with someone who made her laugh just as easily as making her sigh with desire as a matter of course.

He'd come to his senses as soon as they joined the real world again. They both would.

"Okay." She smiled at him. "This is a date, so let's have dinner like you planned. And you can talk. I promise to listen."

He escorted her to the table, poured her another glass of wine and launched into the history of how he was approached to be on the series. She even laughed at some of his stories. But as Finley looked around the library, she decided it was just a room. A very pretty, delightful room, but it wasn't enchanted. And they may be currently trapped by forces out of their control, but she was not a princess. There wouldn't be a happily-ever-after for her once they were allowed to leave.

Twelve

Finley returned from her ride sore and exhausted, but from wrangling her thoughts instead of wrangling the horse.

The date last night had been a success…somewhat. Despite eventually finishing what they started on the library's desk and then retiring to Will's room for even more earth-shattering activities, she'd been unable to sleep. She'd slipped out of his bed earlier than normal and saddled Ranger, hoping a long gallop would help her sort through the thoughts bouncing around like multiple pinballs. Instead, the conflicting feelings warring for primacy only intensified, the pressure in her brain building to almost migraine levels, and her headache was not helped when she realized she'd let Ranger travel farther afield than she intended. By the time she pulled open the French doors that led to the breakfast room off the kitchen, she was ready for lunch and a quick shower—and only wished she could do both at the same time. "Will?"

He didn't answer her call. But there was something different about the house. The atmosphere seemed brighter, louder. There was a faint humming noise that hadn't been there before... And was that Will's voice? Was he talking to Tim on the CB radio? She followed the sound into the kitchen and froze with shock.

Appliances blinked blue and red lights. The ice-making machine in the refrigerator clanked. Copper and glass pendant lamps shone down from above.

The power had been restored to the ranch.

Will wasn't on the radio. He was on his cell phone. He caught her eye and gave her a smile and a thumbs-up, indicating the clock flashing "12:00" on the microwave. But she couldn't help but notice the deep furrows now creasing his forehead as he returned to his call. She acknowledged him with a wave, then ran/walked to the guest suite where she still kept most of her things. Her phone. She needed her phone.

She flew to the bedside table where she'd plugged her phone into the charger, just in case. The screen lit up. If she were prone to crying, she might have wept at the sight. She did do a little jig in place.

So many possibilities to choose from! She could read her email. She could go on the internet. She could call Sadiya—oh.

Her exultation fled.

She'd always been keenly aware their time at the ranch had an expiration date. The power company would restore electricity, the crews would clear the road and the bubble that had contained them would pop.

But now that the bubble had been breached, she realized she'd avoided planning her next steps. After all, the longer they stayed isolated on the ranch, the better for her. The claims in Erica O'Donnell's book would stay far away. She could ignore the ugly mess that was the remnants of a career she once loved.

She could let herself daydream about taking Will up on the future she saw shining in his gaze.

During her ride, she'd realized she was being selfish. He had a life, too. A life that wasn't knotted up with salacious rumors and tawdry scandals. A life of purpose, with people who depended on him. A life that deserved a partner who matched his strengths and complemented his weaknesses.

The life he was headed toward before a winter storm stranded him with her.

She unlocked her phone. The screen came alive with alerts for texts, missed calls and news articles. She was about to swipe and dismiss them in favor of calling Sadiya, but the top news alert caught her eye.

"Bombshell book from senator's wife promises dirt on insider trading, sex scandal."

She sank onto the bed. Erica O'Donnell's memoirs were no longer under wraps.

Sadiya answered on the first ring. "There you are! Are you back in civilization?"

"No. Road is still blocked. I checked on it while out for a horseback ride this morning. But the power is finally back, so I have a working phone."

"Great. Because we need to talk and I didn't want to leave this as a message with your ranch manager. There have been developments."

"I saw a news alert about the book. I haven't read the story, however."

"Don't."

Finley shut her eyes, her breath leaving her in one long exhale. "That bad, huh?"

"O'Donnell's book is mostly poorly written speculative fiction. Lots of scandalmongering not worth bothering with. No, I'm glad you called because the Justice Department has taken an interest in the insider trading claims. They've opened an investigation." Sadiya paused. "I spoke to my contact. They're being pushed for indictments. Doesn't matter who they find." Her tone carried a warning.

"Okay," Finley said slowly. "But what does that have to do with me?"

"Some of the allegations they're looking at... They involve companies your brother invested in."

"Grayson?" Finley caught her phone from hitting the ground at the last second. She put it back to her ear. "Grayson has nothing to do with this. He never spoke to Barrett about his work for this very reason—"

"I agree there's no fire there. But the O'Donnells are creating a thick smoke screen. Your brother ran for your father's seat in Congress before abruptly dropping out, despite being far ahead in the polls. He left the country just as Erica was shopping her book. And he's a well-known hedge fund manager with privy access to companies and their senior executives."

"He dropped out of the race for personal reasons! He left the country because he's on his *honeymoon*." Finley hissed the last word. "That is the flimsiest circumstantial evidence ever, and anyone with a brain—"

"I know that. You know that. You also know how the media likes their spin. There is a small but powerful audience out there who support Senator O'Donnell and would like to see him vindicated. The investigators are under pressure to look at all the angles. You're well aware how the game is played."

She was. She was quite good at it, too. But the last five days had cured her of wanting to play games.

She screwed her eyes shut. "So now they're going after Grayson?"

"Don't forget, you're still the ringleader. Grayson merely fed you information, which you then fed to the senator."

Finley scoffed. "Oh yes, however could I forget that. Because I'm the vindictive puppet master who not only led the insider trading ring, but I also set up the ring's members for the fall." She let out a shuddering sigh. "I can't even."

"Erica O'Donnell is skilled at making the media salivate." Sadiya sounded as disgusted as Finley felt. "I know this isn't the best news, but it's an investigation, not an indictment. They won't find anything."

"An investigation will darken Grayson's reputation. Which is impeccable, by the way, and deservedly so."

"At least the scent appears to be off you."

"Because they're chasing Grayson instead! He doesn't deserve any of this." Her fingernails left deep crescent impressions on her palm.

Sadiya was silent. "We're still trying to shut the whole thing down," she finally said. "There's a possibility it will go away."

"I received a news alert. On my phone screen."

"Right now, the media only possesses innuendo and blind items. O'Donnell's team hasn't named names publicly yet. The best thing to do is sit tight."

"I'm not going anywhere, so that shouldn't be too hard."

Finley finished her conversation with Sadiya and hung up. She flipped her phone over and over in her hands. The prospect of going on the internet had been soured for her. The last thing she wanted to do was to run into gossip sites breathlessly promising the arrival of scurrilous dirt from O'Donnell's memoir.

Staying in the guest suite was also rapidly losing its appeal. She needed to talk to Will—

No. She had not become emotionally dependent on sharing her thoughts with him. She merely wanted to impart a warning he should probably keep quiet about spending five days alone with a member of the notorious Monk family. His investors and shareholders who might not appreciate Will being linked to a DC insider trading scandal.

She'd last seen Will in the kitchen. Halfway there, she could make out his raised voice. She frowned. Will wasn't prone to loud displays of anger. He simmered on slow burn instead. Whatever conversation he was having, it wasn't a happy one.

As she entered the room, his words became clearer. "No! I refuse—" Will had his phone to his ear as he paced, his stiff, angry movements making short work of the vast room. "They can't cancel—"

He turned and saw her. Some of the ferocious energy leaked out of his expression, but he lifted a finger to excuse himself and then left the kitchen. The door to the outside patio slammed shut behind him, ensuring his conversation would remain private.

Great. Looked like their reentry to the real world wasn't going to be a soft landing for either of them.

Will's laptop was precariously perched on the kitchen counter. She walked over, intending to shut the lid and remove the computer to somewhere where it would be less prone to falling. An electronic song trilled from the speakers, announcing an incoming video call from his sister Lauren.

Lauren was one of the owners of Running Coyote and thus her hostess. It would be rude to ignore her, would it not? Plus, Finley had to admit she had some curiosity about Will's sister. He obviously cared deeply about her. And Finley wanted to store up as much data as possible about Will while she could. Her index finger hesitated over the laptop's trackpad, but then she clicked Accept on the call.

The attractive brunette Finley had seen with Will at Grayson's wedding appeared on the screen. She sat in front of a window, the curtains pulled to reveal a dark night sky punctuated with a recognizable city skyline. Lauren was in Tokyo.

"Hi," Finley greeted her. "I'm Finley. Will isn't available but I thought I'd take a message."

"Who did you say you are?" Lauren peered at her screen. "Wait—Grayson's sister, right? Of course. I hope you're enjoying the ranch."

"I am, very much."

"Sorry about Will barging in on your retreat. Nelle and Grayson said you badly needed some me-time. I hope staying with my brother hasn't been too onerous."

Finley kept her expression neutral. "I managed."

Lauren nodded. But there was a gleam in the other woman's gaze that told Finley she might not have been as successful at keeping a straight face as she had hoped. "Good. Listen, Reid has pulled every string he can to get the mudslide cleared as fast as possible. But apparently one of the earthmovers the local crews are using broke down. They're trying to get another one from Los Angeles, but the storm caused a lot of damage up and down the coast."

Finley nodded. "Tim suspected as much. He's done a great job keeping us informed."

"Tim's the best. Are you sure Will isn't available? I really do need to talk to him."

Finley glanced out the kitchen's picture window. Will was pacing, his eyes screwed shut in what looked like frustration. "He's on another call. I could try to interrupt him, but it seems important. I think it's about the Ever-Aftr television series."

"He told you about the series?" Lauren sounded surprised. "Great! So you know."

Finley wasn't sure what Lauren meant, but she wasn't about to tell the other woman that. "I know... It's a tremendous opportunity for him and EverAftr."

"And not just him. Could you take a message for Will after all? It's two in the morning here and I need to get some sleep, or I'd wait until he was free. Tell him Ji-Hoon was admitted to the hospital on Monday and released this morning. He didn't want to alarm Will, but I thought Will should be informed." She rattled off a phone number. "Will has Ji-Hoon's contact info, but just in case, that's the number where Ji-Hoon is staying in Los Angeles."

Finley made a note on her phone. "Got it."

"And tell Will not to worry. Ji-Hoon responded well to treatment. But between us, and the reason I want to talk to Will—I think being part of the series is the only thing keeping Ji-Hoon going. He's so excited to finally have his Hollywood moment." Lauren chuckled. "He said being a producer is better than being an actor. Now he gets to call the shots and crush other people's dreams. He was kidding, of course. But he's like a kid waiting for the candy shop to open."

"I don't blame him. Sounds exciting."

Lauren sobered. "Hopefully production will start soon, for his sake."

Finley nodded. "I'll give Will the message."

"Thanks." Lauren stifled a yawn with her hand. "It was great talking to you. Nelle mentioned you might do a little soul-searching while you were at Running Coyote. I hope the ranch helped you find what you are looking for. It helps me."

Finley's gaze returned to the window, zeroing in on Will as he still paced, his phone pressed against his ear. "Some things became clearer, yes. Thank you, and Reid, for letting me stay here."

Lauren laughed. "I wouldn't thank us, not after all you've been through. You'll have to return when the rains are less torrential."

"It was a freak storm. No worries." She and Lauren said their goodbyes and Finley closed Will's laptop. Her fingertips were still drumming on the computer's lid when Will reentered the kitchen.

Finley drank in his appearance. His navy shirt matched the dark rim outlining his irises. He'd rolled up his sleeves, revealing forearms tanned from helping her muck out the horses' paddocks. He'd exchanged his usual jeans for khakis, to her disappointment. But when he turned his back to her to retrieve a pot from a lower pullout drawer, she decided the khakis provided just as fine a view.

"Oatmeal?" He held up the pot. "I'm craving a hot meal. Anything hot."

"I will never eat a peanut butter sandwich again," she agreed. "I hope you don't mind me being nosy, but you seemed rather...perturbed...by your phone call."

"It was nothing." The pot banged on the stove. "Hollywood nonsense."

"It didn't seem like nonsense."

"It will work out. Just takes time, which we have. If I can't leave the ranch, the company can't start production."

"But they can cancel production?" she asked, remembering Will's barked words earlier.

He stirred the oatmeal, clanging the spoon against the sides of the pot. "That's their threat. They're concerned about the marketing if the show isn't built around me. I said they can market the show around real people using a real app to find real love."

"Not a bad description." She was impressed.

"The copywriter whose work you hated wrote that." He threw her an amused look, then began opening and shutting cabinets in a quest for something he couldn't find. "Where's the salt?"

She handed him the shaker, sitting in plain sight on the counter. "What did the production company say to that?"

"That I'm the only real person people will pay a subscription fee to watch using the app. Otherwise, it's not worth their investment." He turned off the heat and ladled the oatmeal into two bowls, handing her one. "Enjoy."

She held the bowl in her both hands, cupping her fingers around its warmth. "In other words, they will cancel the series if you're not in it, because Screenweb thinks the only viable marketing hook is the CEO of EverAftr using his own app to find his match."

He took his bowl into the breakfast room, sitting down at the table with its embroidered tablecloth and collection of cheerful pottery vases serving as a centerpiece. His spoon stabbed into his oatmeal. "We're still talking."

She took the chair opposite him, setting her bowl aside. "Before I forget, your sister called while you were on the phone. A video call, from Tokyo. I answered on your laptop. I hope you don't mind."

"You spoke to Lauren? What did she say?"

"Reid is trying to get the road cleared but there's a lack of equipment, just as Tim said." Finley leaned her elbows on the table, cupping her chin with her hands. She fixed her gaze on Will. "She also wanted to make sure you knew Ji-Hoon was in the hospital. He was released this morning."

Will's spoon stopped halfway to his mouth. He put it down, untouched. "What happened?"

"Lauren didn't say. But…" Finley hesitated. "I got the feeling she didn't think he could wait a long time for production to begin." She reached a hand across the table to Will. "Who is Ji-Hoon?"

"My mentor." Will pushed back his chair. "Would you excuse me? I need to phone Lauren."

"She was going to bed. But I bet she'll take your call if she sees it."

Will walked out of the room, his movements jerky instead of his usual fluid grace. Finley watched him go, then pulled her bowl of oatmeal toward her. The contents were cold. And too salty to eat.

Taking out her phone, she opened the web browser and entered "Will Taylor," "Ji-Hoon" and "EverAftr" into the search bar. Within seconds, she was looking at images of a younger Will—the Will who had occupied her memories for so long. He stood next to an older Asian man in many of the photos, their faces wreathed in smiles.

She clicked on the top link and started to read. It was a profile of Will, written for a business magazine shortly after EverAftr announced the company would be going public. She skimmed, looking for mentions of Ji-Hoon, and quickly found a paragraph quoting Will:

"If Ji-Hoon Park hadn't believed in me when I was struggling after college graduation, EverAftr wouldn't exist. Ji-Hoon was my parents' next-door neighbor. Then his commercial real estate business took off, but our families remained close. While I was growing up, he always

showed interest in my school coding projects. He's not a tech guy himself but he knew people in California from having worked in Hollywood as a young man. When he saw I was having a rough time, he made some phone calls. With his contacts, I landed an entry-level position in Santa Monica, a.k.a. Silicon Beach. Things took off from there."

Will had been in California after graduation? She didn't know that. She continued to read.

Things did indeed take off for Taylor. After leaving his job to strike out on his own, he developed a new process for hardware security and sold the patent for a cool million dollars. Other lucrative patent sales followed. But he never forgot his roots in the Chicago area. "I decided to move back to Chicago. I liked SoCal but I missed real pizza, y'know?" he said with a laugh. "And my sisters were complaining they couldn't find the right person using online services. Hookups, sure. But they were tired of constant first dates. They wanted to locate people serious about developing a relationship. Creating a dating app was the last thing on my mind, but Ji-Hoon pointed out it was just a matter of coming up with the right algorithm. He was my first investor. I owe everything to him."

Does Taylor use his own service? The handsome single CEO only laughed when asked—

Finley put down her phone. She'd read enough. Enough to know Will cared deeply about his mentor. And enough to recognize the television series would indeed be a success. The journalist wouldn't have asked if there wasn't public curiosity about the answer.

She drummed her fingers on the tablecloth. No matter how she sliced and diced the variables, only one conclusion could be reached.

Will's mentor eagerly looked forward to being part of the series but his health was precarious. The production company would only move ahead if Will was the main subject of the first season. Therefore, Will needed to be the star.

She must ensure he made it to Los Angeles and in front of the cameras. She had to disabuse him of his silly notions, such as he couldn't pursue his perfect match because he thought he had some sort of obligation to her…or worse, thought he had already found his lifetime partner.

And the clock was ticking on putting Will back on his rightful track, because she'd finally puzzled out what she needed to do once she left the ranch. If the O'Donnell camp was baying for blood to create a diversion from their own transgressions, she'd give it to them. She would dangle herself as bait, to draw any potential attention away from Grayson.

Creating a media frenzy was child's play for her. She'd make Erica O'Donnell look like an amateur by comparison. She knew exactly how to plant a story with enough ambiguous detail to make gossip columnists froth at the mouth. The only difference between this and the work she did as a political campaign manager was that now, she'd be the subject of her own innuendo.

The ranch had been an oasis. She would miss her time here desperately. But as much as she wished she could continue ignoring the outside world, it was time to be proactive. She picked up her phone again and scrolled through her contacts, punching the button to call when she found the right one. "Hey, CC, it's Finley Smythe. Sorry for the last-minute ask, but do you have any availability tomorrow? Can I run an idea past you?"

Long after sunset, Will walked into the living area to find Finley sitting on the leather sofa closest to the fireplace, the only illumination coming from flames on the hearth. She'd recently showered. Her dark hair was wet and slicked back and she wore a gray hoodie at least three times too big for her. With her legs curled underneath her, she looked like a college student about to burn the midnight oil.

Or a congressional intern, waiting for her date to arrive. His heart turned over in his chest.

"You don't have to sit in the dark now." He turned a nearby lamp on. "Look. Magic."

She smiled, but it didn't reach her eyes. "I've grown accustomed to not having lights. I think I prefer the dark."

He switched the lamp off and sat down beside her. She scooted over to make space, draping herself over the sofa's pillows. A low-energy Finley was unfamiliar to him, and his pulse thumped. "Do you feel okay?" he asked. His hour on the phone with Ji-Hoon learning about his latest medical setback was still very much on his mind. "Not coming down with anything?"

"I'm fine. Just a long day. Lots of excitement." She turned to him. "Finished all your calls? Did they go better than the one this morning?"

Bile rose in the back of his throat at the mention of the phone call. He didn't want the series to be canceled. He knew how much it meant to Ji-Hoon. But it wouldn't be honest to continue with the show's original concept. For one, his answers were all wrong. He thought he wanted a restful life, of low drama and high consistency. A life where he knew what he would be doing a year from now, five years, twenty years. A quiet life, controlled for as few surprises as possible.

Life with Finley would never be quiet. Predictability would be thrown out the window.

He couldn't think of anything better.

But first, he needed to get past her determination to

keep their current situation entanglement-free. "The last call was with the exec team at EverAftr. Different type of stress. More enjoyable. Were you able to reach everyone you wanted to talk to?"

"Yes." She kept her gaze focused on the drawstrings of her hoodie as she tied and untied them. "Why didn't you study law as you planned?"

Where did that question come from? He shrugged. "Three years of graduate school is expensive. I took a job instead."

"That's the only reason?" Her gaze searched his.

He rubbed his temple. "The idea lost its appeal. Decided to do something else."

"Did our summer have something to do with why it lost its appeal? Did I?"

"Why are you asking?" He shifted on the sofa so he could catch her gaze, but her eyes were unreadable. "As I've said previously, things turned out okay."

She leaned her head against the cushions. "I think you gave up your dream because someone or something made you feel small. So, you left Washington and politics, never to return. And I believe that someone was me."

"Lee." His beautiful, capricious and far-too-perceptive-for-her-own-good Lee. "If anyone made me feel bad about myself, that was my fault. I let them get to me."

"But it doesn't work that way, does it? We can't help but be affected by other people. We're human. We're social animals. We crave contact with others."

His eyebrows flew up to nearly hit his hairline. "I agree. But I'm surprised to hear you say it."

"Why?"

"You don't do relationships. No attachments." He stretched his legs along the sofa's length, and then tugged Finley to lie down next to him. After a moment of resistance, she joined him. The sofa was just wide enough for them both, Finley reclining half on, half off him. "I thought I'd never get you to acknowledge people need each other. Glad to hear you've finally come around."

He felt more than heard her chuckle. "I didn't say that. I said people can't help but affect one another."

He was certainly affected by her. But although his blood kindled as always at her nearness, he was content to hold her and listen to her words in the dark. "It's not the same thing?"

"No." She lifted her head. "Did I affect you so badly you gave up your dream?"

He tightened his arms around her. "It was my choice to give up on law school. Not your choice, not anyone else's. Mine. But if you're asking if you hurt me? Yes. The breakup hurt."

"I know." She kissed his cheek, then laid her head back on his chest. "If you hadn't been caught in the rainstorm and stranded on the ranch, you'd be working on the first episode of the series now, correct?"

He frowned. "Probably. Or getting close to it. But that ship has sailed. Why do you ask?"

"Just trying to figure something out."

"Like what?"

She shook her head. "Nothing important. Just idle curiosity." Her fingers began to trace a pattern over his shoulders, across his collarbone and back again. Feather-light, her touch trailed sparks in its wake. "This is nice, isn't it?"

"Very." The comfy sofa, the crackle and hiss of the fire and Finley curled up tight against him—he couldn't think of anywhere else he wanted to be. "But I'm still wondering what prompted this conversation."

She didn't respond with words. Instead, she kissed the side of his neck, her mouth hot and wet against his skin.

Her hands began to travel lower, finding the button of his waistband, the zipper of his fly. With a supreme effort, he sat up, gathering her to him so he could deposit her to sit next to him. She stared at him, her gaze wide with surprise. "What? Did I miss something? Was this a date, so there's an obligation to talk first?"

"You use sex when you don't want to have a conversation."

She folded her arms across her chest. "Really."

"In my observation."

She huffed. "Let's say you're right, which you're not. Most men would view that as a positive."

"I'm not saying it isn't. But not when you're obviously holding something back that is bothering you."

She rolled her eyes. "I can't believe you'd rather talk than have sex, but okay. Here's what I've been mulling all day. What's going to happen after you leave Running Coyote?"

"You mean when *we* leave."

"Fine. When we leave."

"We—" he stressed the word again "—will figure it out."

She shook her head. "Not good enough. You have a company to run. A TV series. You must have a plan in mind."

This was his fault for not letting her have her way with him as she intended. Served him right. But they needed to have this discussion, and the sooner, the better. The road wouldn't stay closed for long. "I do."

"Good." She nodded.

"Involving you."

Her nod came slower. "Okay."

"And me."

"Since it's your plan, I would hope so."

"Together. As we should have been all along."

She inhaled, but her arms remained loose by her sides. She didn't jump up and run. He considered that a win. "And the series?" she asked.

"Using the app on camera to find a romantic partner would be a lie. I have no desire to date anyone else." He leaned over and kissed her. She didn't respond at first. Then she sighed and kissed him back. He broke contact and held her gaze with his. "So. I won't do it."

She blinked, but not before he saw the shimmer of moisture at the corner of her eyes. "But what about your mentor? Ji-Hoon? Isn't he involved with the series? What if they decide the cost of production won't be worth their investment unless you're the star, and they pull the plug?"

He swallowed. Damned Screenweb executives, refusing to compromise. If they would only see reason. But the show wasn't canceled yet. Ji-Hoon could still have his Hollywood dream. "Yes, he has a producer credit. But I'm confident we can find a way forward."

"You're so optimistic. Which is not the same as realistic." She bit her lower lip.

He took her chin in his left hand, keeping their gazes locked. "There's only one nonnegotiable item. I want to be with you. I know we've been together only five days. But in some ways, it's been fifteen years."

He knew better than to mention love. Finley had made her opinion on the subject very clear.

But as she'd alluded to earlier, they affected one another. She'd focused on the pain of their past, but he chose to look ahead. *Affect*, after all, was the root of the word *affection*. And affection was just the start of what he felt for her. How he'd always felt.

Her dark eyes were wide, filled with an emotion he couldn't quite name. She pulled back from his touch, escaping into the shadows. "What if I told you I don't want the same thing?" Her voice was a thin whisper in the darkness. "Would you do the show then?"

"Then tell me." He threw his arms open. "Tell me you don't want me. Although your actions a few minutes ago said otherwise."

"Of course I want you. But what if it's only for a night? And we part forever the next day." Her voice grew stronger. "Would you star in the series then?"

"No. Because I'd find you the next night. And ask you to tell me again you don't want me." He grinned at her. "I'll take my chances on getting the same answer." He pushed up her sleeve to reveal her sensitive inner elbow, caressing the spot that always made her shudder. "I like my odds."

Her laugh became a voluptuous sigh. "Damn it, Will. I have zero self-control where you are concerned. Remember later, I tried to give you an easy out."

Before he could puzzle out what she meant, Finley had slipped off the sofa to kneel between his legs. She pulled his head down to meet hers and her tongue swept into his mouth as she tugged on his shirt, sending at least one button flying. But even as the heat and the pressure began to build, Will discerned a difference in their lovemaking. Her eyes remained open. Her movements were slower, more deliberate.

It was if she were memorizing every detail. As if this were truly their last night together.

Then her lips lowered onto their target, and he stopped thinking.

Thirteen

Finley was in Trudy's paddock when she heard the helicopter. She gave Trudy an apple, then buried her face in the mare's neck, inhaling the scent of dusty hay and warm horse. "This is it, girl," she whispered to the mare. "Wish me luck. Don't worry, I'll be back later for your supper."

She petted Trudy's nose, then walked over to the fence that separated the mare's paddock from Ranger's. The gelding's dark eyes watched her as she approached. "Don't give me that stare," she said, shining another apple on her jeans leg before holding it out for Ranger to munch. "This is the right thing to do. He's going to thank me for this, one day. He's going to look at his beautiful wife and amazing children and be oh so glad he didn't let a mudslide ruin his future."

Ranger tossed his head and snorted. "Yeah, I knew you'd take his side. You men stick together. But honestly, this is for the best."

The sound of rotor blades grew louder. She turned and watched as the MD500 copter came into view, descending until it hovered, looking for a good spot to land. Running Coyote had a helipad near the base camp, but it was on the other side of the mudslide. The helicopter's pilot finally settled on a flat stretch of the lawn below the pool.

She walked toward the house, steeling herself for what was to come. But before she could reach the door, Will came racing out. He grabbed her and placed her behind him, as if to shield her from whatever was in the copter.

"What the—where did that come from?" he shouted. "I'm going to go call Tim."

She stopped him from reentering the house. The rotors slowed, the wind died down and the noise subsided, allowing her to speak at a normal volume. "There's no need to call Tim. I hired the helicopter."

Shock froze Will's features. "You did what?"

"I hired it. A friend owns a helicopter sightseeing operation. I pulled in a big favor."

"But why?" Confusion filled his gaze, followed rapidly by hurt. "You're leaving?"

She hardened her heart against the pain in his eyes and shook her head. "No. I'm not leaving. You are."

He stared at her. "I don't understand."

"See the pilot exiting the cockpit? The tall Black woman? That's my friend CC." CC turned and helped a passenger out the door. "And the man—"

"Ji-Hoon," Will breathed. He turned to her. "You brought Ji-Hoon here? Why?"

She kissed him on his cheek, storing up the sensation of his unshaven stubble against her lips, pulling away before she was tempted to linger forever. "You're going to Los Angeles. This is goodbye."

"What? Lee, what are you doing?"

She swallowed. She had to get her words out fast. "Ji-Hoon and CC will reach us soon, so I'm only going to say this once. You must do the series. That was what you wanted. Your big goal. And then the mudslide interfered and caused a bump in your journey. But that's all our time here on the ranch was. An aberration. A detour. So—"

"Stop. Before you say something we'll both regret for another fifteen years."

She shook her head. She never cried. But for the first time in a very long while, she wanted to. "That summer, I listened to Barrett. I made you feel less than, because I thought our relationship was conditional, that you were attracted more to my family's status than to me. That calling us 'soul mates' was just a verbal trick, so you could get what you wanted." She sniffed. No, she wouldn't cry. "And because of that, you gave up on your dream career. I won't let you derail your life now."

She threw out her arms. "You want to settle down with a partner and start a family, or you would've never agreed to the series. So go find her, Will. Go find the woman you're meant to be with."

"No." His head shook, a blur too rapid to follow. "No. Because she's right here. And you know that. You might not like the word *love*, but that's what this is. That's what we have. That's what we always had."

She laughed. It was only a trick of her ear that made it sound like a sob. "We have good sex. We're compatible in bed. The last week was nothing more than two consenting adults, trapped without television or internet, who made the most of a bad situation."

"You don't believe that."

No. She didn't. But she needed him to believe she did. "Being with you was great. Really great. Best sex I've had in years, and I thank you for that. But you have a life and I have a life and it's time to stop pretending the real world doesn't exist. You have an obligation to the production company—"

His hands clenched. "You can't want me to be in the series. We spoke about this, last night."

Want was a strong word. It implied so many things. But ultimately, her wants were selfish. They didn't matter. Not when it came to his future.

She raised her chin. "If you ask me if I want you, I'll always say yes. But that's sex."

"It's more. I love you, Lee. And you love me. You're too stubborn to admit it."

He said he loved her. Her lungs couldn't get enough air. Funny, the one time she wanted strings wrapped tightly around a relationship was the one time that just wasn't possible. She couldn't hold his gaze any longer, or he might see how much she longed to say the words back.

So instead, she scoffed. "Hey, I'm flattered you think a week of great sex is worth throwing away millions of dollars and your potential future happiness, but one of us needs to be logical. You have a company. You have shareholders. The series is going to make them lots of money. People depend on you." She indicated Ji-Hoon, who was slowly making his way across the lawn toward them with CC's assistance. "And I have my own commitments."

His gaze narrowed dangerously. "Such as?"

She took a much-needed deep breath. "Preparing for an insider trading investigation, for one. Senator O'Donnell's wife has accused me of being the ringleader of the current Washington scandal du jour. The press will have the story soon."

Surprise mixed into the emotions rapidly cycling in his expression. "Insider trading allegations? You never said anything—"

"Why would I ruin the fantasy of the last few days with sordid details? But it's another reason why we must go our separate ways. Now, before the media catches on we spent the week trapped together at Running Coyote." She cut him off with a shake of her head. "I know how gossip works. You want attention for EverAftr and your series, but not that type of attention. The sleazy type does no one any good."

Through her peripheral vision she could see Ji-Hoon and CC coming closer. They would be in range to overhear her discussion with Will at any minute. She pulled out her last weapon, plastering a wide smile on her face and giving him an airy shrug. "We had a good run these last few days. But relationships based on intense experiences—like being stranded on a ranch thanks to a mudslide—never work." His gaze remained darkly incandescent without a glimmer of recognition. She knew he wouldn't get the film reference. Instead of annoying her, his refusal to learn pop culture history only reminded her much she lov—no. How much she enjoyed being with him. Which made her next statement even harder to say. "And so we move on to bigger and better things. I'll always remember our time here on the ranch fondly, but we're done."

He staggered, just a step, as the echo of the words she used to break up with him the first time resonated. She planted her feet, preparing to hold her ground. He would briefly argue with her, like he did fifteen years ago. But then he would turn angry, say things that would forever be painfully carved on her soul and walk away.

But to her shock, the fury drained out of his gaze, replaced by something like…pity. And deep, deep affection. He cupped her cheek with his hand and her pulse stuttered.

"You're scared," he said. "You're afraid someone will find you lovable, so you strike first and drive them away.

And I get why, now. Your father left. Barrett was an ass who taught you relationships were transactional. No one protected you so you protect yourself. And you protect others. Like me. You're doing this to protect me. Because you love me."

His words hit her heart like so many needle-nosed darts. Every cell she possessed wanted to run away from the truth, hanging in the air between them. His gaze kept her pinned in place, demanding she admit he was right.

He stepped closer, the wind carrying his scent to her, his hand on her cheek bringing warmth. "I can take care of myself. And if you allow me, I can help with the insider trading allegations. Give us time so we can find a way forward. For both of us."

For an eye blink, she allowed herself to relax into his touch. But while the picture he painted was very tempting, she knew what he proposed just wasn't possible. His optimism was no match for reality.

She pulled away, folding her arms as she called up her smirk. "A guy runs a dating app and suddenly he's an expert in human psychology."

He shook his head. "No. But I know you—"

"Oh, you know me. You know me better than I know myself, right?" Anger kindled in her belly, and she welcomed its glow. Anything to drive away the cold emptiness that threatened to consume her. "Sorry, unlike you I don't confuse orgasms with love. Now, CC will fly you and Ji-Hoon to Los Angeles—"

Sparks of answering anger lit his gray-blue gaze. "Ji-Hoon is ill. You shouldn't have pulled him into your scheme—"

"He was excited when I asked him, and his doctors gave permission. Someone must remind you what you have at stake here, and he's your mentor. I knew after our conversation last night you'd never listen to me."

"You're so afraid of future happiness you can't see—"

She waved him off, her hand oscillating rapidly. "What future happiness? Investigations and scandals? That's what I have in store. But you don't. I'm offering you an express pass to get back to the life you had planned before a freak storm stranded you here. Take it, damn it." She pushed past him.

He reached for her arm, his hand gently holding her bicep. "Unlike last time, I know what you're doing. You're trying to arrange all the pieces on your own. Don't walk away. Talk to me. Let me help."

She turned around. With supreme effort, she made herself look him in the eye. "Unlike last time, no one is manipulating me. I'm saying goodbye out of my own volition. Please respect that."

He dropped her arm, allowing her to pass. His gaze burned a hole through the back of her jacket.

She continued down the stairs of the terrace, her left hand outstretched in greeting as the newcomers reached her. She relaxed her expression into a grin, hoping her flushed cheeks would be attributed to the brisk February air. "Hi, I'm Finley. You must be Ji-Hoon. I hope you had a good flight. But of course you did. CC is a great pilot."

Ji-Hoon's handshake was firm, his smile warm and genuine. Finley liked him immediately. But his gaze was shrewd as he glanced between her and Will, still standing motionless on the terrace. Intuition told her the sooner she made herself scarce, the fewer pointed questions she might have to answer. "So!" She clapped her hands together. "I'll let you catch up with Will as he packs. CC, when do you need to take off for Los Angeles?"

"I'm leaving to refuel the chopper. I'll be back to pick

up everyone in, say, an hour?" She addressed Ji-Hoon. "You'll be good to go by then?"

"I'll be good, but it's not up to me." He turned to Finley. "What about you?"

"Oh, I'm not leaving. Not with you and Will." She laughed, a high tinkle that made her cringe inside as soon as it came out of her mouth. "I have to care for the horses until the ranch manager is able to take over. And speaking of the horses, I hope you'll excuse me. I need to give them their exercise. If I'm not back before you leave, it was lovely to meet you."

"The pleasure is all mine." The twinkle in his eyes diminished, but the warmth in his smile remained. "Thank you for the opportunity to spend quality time with Will before the chaos breaks loose."

"My pleasure. I know you have a lot of catching up to do." She threw a glance at Will, who stayed statue-still where she left him through the flurry of the arrivals. Finally, he came forward to thump Ji-Hoon on the back, shaking CC's hand.

His gaze continued to singe whenever he glanced at her, leaving smoking holes behind.

As Will escorted Ji-Hoon into the house, she escaped to the stable. She saddled up Ranger and then gave him his head, letting him take her wherever he wanted to go. She refused to look back at the house.

She wouldn't have seen anything, anyway. Her vision was too clouded by tears.

Will stopped packing, his attention caught by movement outside the window of his room. Finley was galloping away on Ranger without a backward glance. One thing was for sure: he was never coming back to the ranch, no matter how many times Lauren and Reid invited him. How could he when every square inch would remind him of her?

He turned back to his open suitcase on top of the bed and threw more clothes in it, not caring where they landed.

"That bad, huh?" Ji-Hoon asked from his chair in the corner.

"Afraid so." Will slammed the top of the suitcase closed and zipped it up. "What did Finley say when she called you?"

"She said the two of you had been trapped for almost a week and you would appreciate new company from an old friend."

Will scoffed and shook his head. "Nothing about the TV series?"

"Just that you were working on ideas. She made it sound like you were eager to catch up on lost time, which is why she suggested I fly up here." Ji-Hoon shrugged. "I would never say no to a helicopter ride from Los Angeles to Santa Barbara. The scenery is breathtaking."

Will pushed the suitcase to the side and sat down on the bed, catching Ji-Hoon's gaze. "I can't be the subject of the series. But if they can't build the marketing around the CEO of EverAftr using his own app to look his partner, Screenweb will probably cancel production. I don't want to disappoint you."

Ji-Hoon nodded. "Well, being a TV producer would have been fun. I was looking forward to having dinner at Spago—is Spago around? It was all the rage in the eighties. Everyone in the industry went there."

"Still popular, I hear."

"There you go. But I don't have be a TV producer to have a meal, do I?"

"Pretty sure anyone with a reservation can eat there."

"Good. Then that's the plan. We'll go to Spago. The rest is gravy."

Will's gaze was caught by a sparkle of gold from under the bed. He bent down to retrieve the object. It was Finley's shoe from the night they had their date in the library.

Man, his chest hurt. His ribs were simultaneously too tight for his lungs but too big for his heart, bouncing painfully around the cavernous space. He looked up at Ji-Hoon. "Should I stay, try to talk more sense into her? Or should I go?"

Ji-Hoon raised his eyebrows. "I don't know. I just met her. Her friend CC is very nice, however."

Will carefully put the shoe on top of the chest of drawers. "I know why she's running away. I don't know how to make her stop."

"Probably shouldn't make her do anything."

"Bad choice of words." There was a sharp pain below his sternum. No matter how he shifted, it would not go away. "I love her. I've loved her since I was twenty-one."

"Twenty-one...hmm. So, she's the woman you met during your internship in DC." Ji-Hoon regarded him. "You were very hurt."

Somehow, today both did and didn't hurt as bad as the first breakup. "I was much younger. I had less perspective then." *Damn it, Lee.* He wished they'd had more time. More time to show her how much he cared. More time to prove to her that what they had was the stuff poets declaimed and songwriters sung about. But even if they'd been trapped on the ranch for a century, it might not have been enough. Finley's defenses were high and deep. "But I don't feel awesome now, either."

"Unrequited love is painful."

Will shook his head. "It's not unrequited. I'm positive of that. But things are...complicated." The allegations she alluded to still stunned him. "You lectured on real estate at the University of Chicago's business school. I don't suppose you know anyone there who's an expert on insider trading?"

"Insider trading? That is a complication."

"Finley isn't a rule follower." The memory of climbing over a fence to enjoy a midnight assignation in a private Washington garden flashed through his head, and he smiled. "But a crook? No."

"Then I suppose the question is, how do you uncomplicate things?"

Will stared out the window again. Finley was long gone, disappeared into the brush-filled hills. "She asked me to respect her decision."

And he received the impression that if he stayed and tried to talk more sense into her she would only stonewall him further—using heavy stones with very sharp edges. He turned to Ji-Hoon. "I'll return to Los Angeles with you. Give her one less complication to worry about."

The last week had been an intense maelstrom of emotion. He understood why she was determined to put space between them.

Plus, she wasn't wrong. He did have responsibilities and commitments. Big ones, with people's livelihoods riding on them. They required his attention.

But he wasn't walking away for good. Not this time. The mistake he'd made fifteen years ago was to not demonstrate to Finley that his love for her was deeper and stronger than her doubts about herself.

He'd give her the room for which she asked. But not enough that she would be lost to him for good. He hoped.

Fourteen

Finley pulled back the curtains, just the tiniest fraction, to check on the setup for the press conference. The stage of the auditorium at Sadiya's law firm held a long table with two chairs behind it: one for her, centered in the middle, and one next to her for Sadiya. Microphones and recorders were already arranged at the front of the table, while cameras on tripods lined the back wall. Some people were milling about, conversing in groups of two or three, but most of the seats facing the stage were empty. Which was as expected since she wasn't scheduled to face the media for another thirty minutes.

She let the curtain fall back into place and faced her sister-in-law, who was shaking her head. "I can't believe you played the 'I'm breaking up with you for your own good' card," Nelle said. "You and Grayson—what is with you two? He did the same thing to me." She pointed to the wedding band on the fourth finger of her left hand. "Here's a hint. That excuse doesn't stick."

Finley resumed perusing photos on Nelle's cell phone. Nelle and Grayson had returned from their two-month extended honeymoon several weeks ago, having had such a good time in Kenya that they added other African countries as well as a good swath of Europe to their itinerary. But when they touched down in San Francisco, Finley had been busy closing her DC apartment. She'd sublet it after Barrett was indicted, believing she would eventually return to the Hill in some capacity or another. Finally, she'd decided to permanently relocate back to California. Easier to wait for the other shoe to drop with family nearby.

But harder to erase her memories of Will. Every time someone mentioned Santa Barbara, or Napa, or driving down the coast, thoughts of him flooded her being. She missed him even more than the first time they parted. Regret was a painful companion.

Her only consolation was knowing she'd made the right call and Will was back on his intended path. She'd found Screenweb's press release announcing the start of production while scrolling through the internet shortly after she left the ranch, late at night when she couldn't sleep.

At least the sticky morass of Erica O'Donnell's accusations kept her mind somewhat occupied and not constantly dwelling on Will. O'Donnell's memoir had sold at auction for a sizable sum and had been rushed to the printer. While the book had yet to hit the stores, juicy excerpts had been leaked all over the mediasphere.

Today's press conference was part of Finley's plan to keep the media's attention focused on her and off any allegations that might come Grayson's way. When Nelle heard about the event, she volunteered to keep Finley company backstage until Finley and Sadiya went in front of the cameras. Finley accepted, both to keep her nerves at bay and to assuage Nelle's persistent curiosity about Finley's stay at Running Coyote in person, a conversation she had avoided until now.

She held up Nelle's phone so Nelle could see what she was looking at. "Why didn't you update your social media more often while you were in Kenya? Some of these shots are amazing."

"You should see the pictures Grayson took with his SLR camera... But you're trying to change the subject. Why on earth did you break up with Will like that?"

"My situation is not comparable to what happened between you and Grayson." Finley started counting on her fingers. "One, Grayson has always been a hopeless romantic, although I have no idea where he got it from. Certainly not from hanging out with me. Two, you had a fairy godmother, if I do say so myself. Not to take full credit, but I had something to do with your reunion. Three, it's a stretch to call this a breakup when we spent less than a week together—can you really break up after a handful of days? Four, I didn't do it for his own good. I did it because it was the right thing to do."

Nelle regarded her. "Uh-huh," she deadpanned.

Finley mock-rolled her eyes at Nelle and gave the phone back to her. "Thanks for coming. I appreciate it."

"Grayson is on his way."

"I'm concerned about Sadiya. She should be here by now." She checked her own phone. No missed calls, texts or voice mails.

Nelle placed a gentle hand on Finley's arm. "You've got this. The press conference is a walk in the park for you."

Finley examined her fingers, looking for flaws in her new manicure. Always important to look one's best when facing a firing squad of journalists. "Sadiya and I have a pretty good strategy. I hope she gets here soon."

She started to pace. They were expecting a full house, thanks to Erica O'Donnell's recent appearances on TV talk shows to promote her book. The noise grew louder from the other side of the curtain as time ticked down.

She and Sadiya planned to issue vague statements, backed with innuendo, to make it appear as if Finley did indeed have knowledge of the insider trading scheme. By indicating there might be blood in the water, the media sharks would be drawn to circling her while the investigation was ongoing. Finley wasn't concerned the investigators would uncover anything; there was nothing to find. But enough tantalizing inconclusive statements would be dripped to keep all eyes tightly on her. And off anyone else.

No matter the outcome of the investigation, after today her professional reputation would be ruined even more than it already was. It was a consequence she was prepared to face. And it was yet more proof that she'd made the right decision at Running Coyote. If she and Will had continued their relationship, the stench would be on him, too. It always carried over. She was in this predicament in the first place because the stink of Barrett's scandal made her an easy target for Erica O'Donnell's accusations.

Loud, excited conversation began to buzz from the other side of the curtain. The scrape of chairs and the sounds of people scrambling to leave the auditorium were easy to identify. Finley and Nelle exchanged confused looks. "What's going on out there?" Nelle asked.

The two women were about to pull back the curtain to see for themselves when Sadiya swept into the backstage space. Her dark brown eyes sparkled. "Change of plans, everyone!"

Finley whirled about. "You're here! What change? Why are people leaving?"

"Oh, a few will stay behind to get your reaction." Sadiya handed Finley an electronic tablet. On the screen was a headline in big, bold capital letters: "GAME OVER FOR SEN. O'DONNELL, WIFE." Underneath, the sub-headline read, "Feds indict former Washington power couple for selling government secrets, insider trading."

Finley looked up. "When did this happen?"

Sadiya gave her a smug grin. "Just now. Literally hot off the presses."

"Does this mean what I think it means?" Finley didn't dare allow herself to hope. Hope was flimsy and led to crushed expectations.

"It means the O'Donnells were hoisted on their own petard. They went to their dark web friends to falsify transactions so Erica's accusations would stick more firmly. But what they didn't know? The friend they approached to hack into various accounts to cover their tracks was working undercover for the FBI."

"Wow."

"It gets better. The Securities and Exchange Commission can take months, even years to investigate allegations. But your case received priority. That's the reason why I was late. I was pushing to get an answer as to what we could reveal at the press conference. My contact said they knew you and your brother were in the clear weeks ago, but they wanted to give the feds time to finish their dark web investigation and not tip off the O'Donnells. Timing worked out perfectly, I must say."

"We were cleared weeks ago?" Finley tried closing her mouth. It only fell open again.

"Unofficially, yes, but it wasn't confirmed. Officially,

no, not until the indictments could be announced. I didn't know, either, until today."

"I can't believe the investigation was over so fast."

Sadiya shrugged. "It seems someone likes you. My contact said you should thank someone named Ji-Hoon Park for the expedited investigation. Apparently, he knows one of the SEC unit chiefs from their days lecturing together at the University of Chicago."

"Wait. Grayson was under suspicion?" Nelle broke into the conversation. "And you knew?" She turned to Finley, balling her fists on her hips.

"I…" Finley blindly reached out her hand, seeking a chair, a wall, anything to keep her propped upright. Ji-Hoon interceded on her behalf? How did he… Will must have said something. But…why would he…

"You knew?" Nelle repeated, dark clouds brewing in her gaze. "Fin, you should have told us. I couldn't figure out why you insisted on putting this display on for the media, but now I get it. You're doing that thing again, where you try to manufacture outcomes without letting the people affected know."

"Hey, everything turned out okay," Finley said.

"That's not an excuse! You may have all the good intentions in the world, but you can't continue thinking you can manipulate your way out of every situation on your own. Stop treating the word 'help' like it's one of the bad four-letter words."

Finley shivered at the echoes of Will's last words to her in Nelle's accusations. Was that what was she doing? Manipulating others?

Like how Barrett manipulated her?

Affecting the people she loved, but to their detriment?

She had always suspected she and Barrett were alike. But she didn't have to be like him. Perhaps if Barrett had asked for help, confided in the people who loved him, he wouldn't have turned to fraud to maintain appearances.

There was a lesson in there, somewhere, for her.

She turned to Sadiya. "What do I do next? I was preparing myself to be a punch line on late night talk shows for months to come. You ruined my plans."

"Make new ones." Sadiya shrugged and looked at her watch. "Ready to go face the media? Or whoever is left?"

"Can I have a minute?" Finley tried to collect her thoughts. But they had scattered far beyond her reach. As soon as she pinned one down, another struggled loose and flitted away.

Ji-Hoon had called in a favor for a woman he barely met. He must have done it because Will asked him to. But why? She'd all but told him to stay out of her life. Sure, she said what she did to give him his future back, but still. As Nelle just said, intentions were not excuses. And when she'd returned to the ranch after her long ride on Ranger to find every trace of his presence gone, she thought he'd taken her words at face value.

She'd expected her relationship with Will to return to the status quo of the past fifteen years: radio silence with zero contact. That's what she'd geared her heart up to anticipate. Those were the walls she'd built around her expectations. And yet...

She took out her phone, clicked on her email app and scrolled down.

An invite sat in her inbox, from an email account with a Screenweb address. She opened it for the first time since it arrived ten days ago. It contained an offer for a VIP all-access pass to the launch party for Screenweb's summer series, to be held in LA in one week's time. *Finding Ever-Aftr* was listed among their new debuts.

The attached note read simply, "Since you were so insistent that the series go forward, I thought you might like an advanced look at the first episodes. Please arrive by 7:30 p.m. Will."

Before she could do the cowardly thing and delete the entire email, she clicked Accept on the invite. She owed Will and Ji-Hoon her thanks for the expeditated investigation in person. Besides, she'd told Will to go out and find his perfect match. She was glad he'd listened. She only prayed it wouldn't be too painful to witness how happy he was without her.

But a slender candle of optimism remained lit, despite all her efforts to snuff it out. Perhaps hope wasn't as fragile as she thought. Will wasn't cruel. He didn't send her the invite just to rub a new relationship in her face. He must have another reason for wanting her there. Whatever his motivation may be.

She grabbed Nelle's hand. "I'm sorry. You were right. Someone once told me I protect others because I didn't have much protection growing up. And as a result, I also do all I can to push people away, to not let them in. I should have told you and Grayson. We're lucky my scheme to draw all the attention didn't blow up in our faces. I promise, next time I'm accused of nefarious dealings, you two will be my first call."

She turned to Sadiya. "I'm ready. Let's go kick some media butt."

Palm trees swung high overhead but didn't block the bright Los Angeles sun. The rays beat down on the red carpet, which rolled from the street to the entrance of a hip, trendsetting downtown hotel. Will sucked in a breath as the door of his limousine was opened. Ji-Hoon exited from the car pulling up behind him. They met where the carpet began. "Do you think she'll show up?" Will asked his mentor.

"The Screenweb publicist said she RSVP'd," Ji-Hoon reminded him. "I did just receive a beautiful thank you basket for allegedly helping to nudge along the SEC investigation. But my phone call wouldn't have moved the needle."

"Speaking of the publicist, here she is." Will smiled as a young woman approached, dressed in the obligatory black suit worn by young Hollywood execs despite the unseasonably warm late May afternoon.

The publicist greeted him and Ji-Hoon, and then spoke into her headset. "Secured the talent. Walking now."

"Talent," Ji-Hoon whispered to Will. "Finally. I'm talent."

The publicist turned to Will and indicated a small stage halfway down the red carpet, surrounded by a banner of repeated Screenweb logos printed on a white background. "The step and repeat is just ahead. You'll take some photos, but most of the press is gathered upstairs on the pool deck for the party. At six o'clock, the president of Screenweb will make a few announcements, and we'll roll the teaser footage from the new series. *Finding EverAftr* is scheduled to be last. After that, you'll take some questions from journalists, and then you're free to mingle with the guests. There's a VIP area for when you need an escape. Are you ready?"

Will's gaze searched the crowd gathered to watch the celebrity arrivals. He was far from the biggest name at the presentation and most of the people ignored him in favor of another new arrival, an aging screen legend making a comeback in a historical drama series.

Finley was nowhere to be seen.

"Lead on," he said to the publicist, affecting a smile he didn't feel.

Will posed in front of the banner, feeling somewhat foolish, but didn't trip over his own feet while walking on the rather lumpy red carpet, which he considered a success. Ji-Hoon thoroughly enjoyed his time bantering with the photographers, and even stole attention away from the movie star.

They were whisked up in a hotel elevator that opened directly onto a rooftop pool deck, which had been reserved exclusively for the event. A well-stocked bar occupied one side of the wall next to the elevator, while clear glass railings outlined the rest of the desk. Wide-screen high-definition monitors were attached to poles dotted around the venue, ensuring the cocktail-attired guests had an unobstructed view of the Screenweb promos running on a constant loop. The skyscrapers of Los Angeles provided a spectacular backdrop.

Ji-Hoon rubbed his hands together as they stepped on the deck. "I'm going to find a nonalcoholic cocktail and schmooze. Want to take bets on when the first guest goes into the pool?"

"With luck, after I'm back at the corporate apartment." Will grinned. No matter what happened, he would always be glad Ji-Hoon had enjoyed his time working with Will on the series.

"So, nine thirty." Ji-Hoon made a note on his phone, then tossed Will a wave. "Ciao, as they say in the industry."

"You mean Italy."

"You have much to learn about this town, my friend." Ji-Hoon plunged into the crowd.

Once Will was alone, he turned his back on the view to take in the guests. The deck was filling rapidly, the guests dressed in anything from sharp, European-tailored suits to khaki shorts topped with Hawaiian-print shirts, while others wore sequined dresses verging on ball gowns or even ripped jeans and tank tops. He recognized some people. Eduardo Cabrillo, the star of ScreenWeb's breakout sword-and-sorcery fantasy series, was unmistakable with his waist-length hair. And the beautiful woman with the glowing ebony skin could only be Amanda Gbeho, currently appearing in a perfume ad on billboards all over LA. More than once, Will squinted at someone and almost approached them to ask if they had gone to high school together, only to realize the person he was staring at had played the next-door neighbor on Lauren's favorite sitcom or had been a featured player in a film an old girlfriend had dragged him to.

Thinking about films made him recall Finley's teasing admonishments regarding his lack of movie knowledge. He tensed, his stomach rebelling against the champagne he'd tasted in the limo only to leave the glass mostly untouched. All these famous faces packing the party, but the one face he wanted to see was nowhere to be found.

The music wafting through the speakers stopped, and the president of Screenweb stepped onto the low dais at the far end of the pool deck, the setting sun casting a golden glow over the scene. Will continued to watch the crowd, his gaze zeroing in on the elevator whenever it opened to spill out more guests, as the president introduced one new summer series after another.

Then the theme song they'd chosen for *Finding Ever-Aftr* began to play. Will dragged his attention back to the stage. His heartbeat thudded in his ears, a dull ache.

She hadn't come to the party.

The president caught Will's eye and motioned him forward, taking the microphone off its stand as Will approached. "Folks, I'm going to mix things up for our last great series. Instead of listening to me describe it, we're going to let you hear directly from someone intimately involved in the show. And when I say intimate, I mean it." He chuckled along with the audience's knowing laughter. "Without further ado, here's the CEO of EverAftr and the executive producer of our new series based on the globally popular app, Will Taylor!"

Will's feet carried him toward the dais, moving on autopilot. He thought he'd braced himself for the disappointment he'd experience should she not show up, but the crushing agony as his optimism died an excruciating death was beyond his limited imagination. Still, he shook the president's hand and took the microphone from him, pausing for one moment to deeply inhale and push down his heartache.

Then, from out the corner of his eye, he saw someone pushing through the crowd. The person beelined toward the stage, bursting through the first row to stand directly in front of him.

Finley.

Her dark hair was longer, the ends softly curling around her shoulders. She wore a plain blue dress but what the silky fabric did to her curves was anything but simple. Sophisticated but hinting at immeasurable pleasures in the dark; her outfit suited her to a T. Her golden brown eyes were wide with apology, her cheeks flushed pink.

He'd never seen anyone more beautiful, including at tonight's party filled wall to wall with photogenic celebrities.

She mouthed, "Sorry I'm late," followed by a roll of her eyes and the word, "traffic."

He wanted to laugh. No, actually, he wanted to sing. Or perhaps dance. And those two activities had never crossed his mind as things he should do before. Now he understood why people liked musicals. If he could belt out a song about how seeing Finley made him feel, he would.

The Screenweb president raised his eyebrows in Will's direction, and the publicist threw him a confused look. Right, he was supposed to be talking, not staring at the vision that was Finley, here, almost within arm's reach. He brought the microphone to his mouth. He wouldn't deliver a song, but he hoped his words would find a responsive target—namely, her heart.

"Hi," he said, ostensibly to the crowd but he could only see one person. "You may be familiar with a dating app called EverAftr—" He waited for the crowd's applause to die down. "Good. I see you've heard of it. When Screenweb approached us about creating a series based on the app, they had a certain pitch in mind—me. Specifically, they wanted me to use the app, alongside six ordinary people from across the United States, all of us searching for a long-term romantic commitment. I guess they thought America would be entertained by watching a boring software engineer like myself try to find someone who'd agree to date him."

The audience laughed again, except for Finley. The color had leeched out of her cheeks. But her gaze remained fixed on him.

"And yes, I'm a believer in EverAftr, the dating app. I created EverAftr when my sisters complained they were having a hard time meeting potential life partners, and somehow I got them to agree to be among EverAftr's beta testers. Now Lauren is married to her husband, Reid, and Claire is married to her wife, Berit. So, when Screenweb approached me with the idea, I thought, why not? I'm also a big believer in happily ever after—the concept, that is."

Finley dropped her gaze. Her head swiveled from left to right, as if she sought the nearest exit.

He hurried on. "Here's the thing, though. I created EverAftr for people who had yet to meet their partner. People hoping that somewhere there was a perfect match for them. And no dating app can promise its users they will find love. Or that they will be with the person they met though the app in one year or ten years. But I stand behind EverAftr's track record of happy customers. Soul mates do exist."

Finley started to back into the crowd behind her, before turning and weaving her way toward the elevator. Any second now, and he would lose sight of her in the sea of people packing the pool deck.

"Which is why I'm *not* a user of the EverAftr app. I was lucky. I found my match a long time ago. But we lost each other until recently."

Finley paused, her back to him so he couldn't see her expression.

"And that got me to thinking. What if EverAftr could be used not only for people who haven't met their partner yet, but also to reunite couples who parted but might want a second chance? I spoke to Screenweb about my idea, and they agreed. So, I'd like to present to you clips from *Finding EverAftr* and its companion series, *Finding EverAftr: The Second Time. Finding EverAftr* will debut this summer, and if all goes well, *The Second Time* will come out this fall. Fortunately for the viewers, I will only be on camera as the host."

Finley turned around. She slowly made her way back to standing in front of the stage again.

He smiled at her. Just her. The rest of the crowd melted into multicolored mist. "I may not get my happily-ever-after. Life is complicated. You can want someone but give them up because you think that's best for them. Or maybe the other person doesn't want the same things as you. And I respect that."

Finley remained statue-still. But her dark eyes shimmered in the setting sun.

"But I want her to know I love her. I never stopped, despite trying. I resented how we broke up the first time. I didn't understand the pressures she faced. But since we met again, I hope she knows my thoughts and plans have been with her in mind. She alone is the reason why I'm here on this stage." He took a deep breath, willing Finley to listen, to hear not only with her ears but her heart. "Once upon a time, I didn't fight for her. I didn't convince her she was not only loved, but beloved. But I'm fighting for her now." He put the microphone back on its stand, his gaze never leaving hers, hoping she could read in his eyes what words were too inadequate to express. "You are very much loved, Lee. I love you."

Her hand came up to cover her mouth. Her chest rose and fell under the clinging silk of her dress.

"So." He finally pulled his gaze from Finley and motioned to the nearby technician in charge of running the video. He spoke into the microphone. "Enjoy the sneak peek of *Finding EverAftr*."

The audience, who had been so silent during his speech he could hear the pool filters hum, broke into boisterous applause and Finley was swallowed by the mass of people pushing toward the stage to shout questions at him. The Screenweb publicist tried to grab his attention. The president of the streaming service, his face wreathed in smiles as he no doubt anticipated the scores of press articles that would be written about Will's speech, held out his hand for a hearty congratulatory handshake. Ji-Hoon, standing by the side of the stage to watch the footage, gave Will two thumbs-up.

Will ignored them all. He strode off the dais. He had one focus: Finley. Ji-Hoon followed him, keeping those who would intercept Will at bay as he parted the crowd, looking for his target.

He found her standing alone in a far corner, her back to him, her face turned to the nearby skyscrapers.

"Lee?" Maybe this had been a bad idea. Maybe a public declaration of love had been the wrong move. But she didn't believe him when it had just been the two of them on the ranch. How better to show her he meant what he said than for his words to be witnessed by hundreds of people, many of whom carried cameras and video recorders? "Are you angry?"

She spun around. Her face was wet with tears. "Of course I'm angry. You made me cry. I never cry." Then she threw her arms around his neck and pulled his mouth to hers. "You realize your speech is about to go viral on every single media platform, don't you?" she whispered against his lips.

"I'm confused. Does that mean you're angry or not?"

She laughed and shook her head. He tears continued to fall. "Only at myself, for breaking up with you twice. What a fool I am."

"Hey, don't talk that way about the woman I love." He smiled and kissed the damp path on her cheeks. "I meant every word."

She sniffled and nodded. "I know. And I'm so sorry, for everything. For the original breakup, for the second breakup, for not trusting you when you said we could find a way forward. Can you forgive me?"

"Always." He smoothed back a lock of her hair. "And you were right to push me on my commitments. I was about to walk away from the contract. That would have been a bad, costly decision."

She smiled, the sparkle in her eyes returning. "Two series, huh? Not a terrible compromise."

"I had to agree to host and reduce the license fee for using EverAftr's name. But they liked the second-chance idea almost better than the original concept. Thanks for being my inspiration."

"Anytime. And thank you for telling Ji-Hoon about the O'Donnell mess. I assume you've heard the news?"

"About the indictments? Yes. Congratulations on being in the clear. I hear your press conference was a bust, however."

She laughed, but then sobered. "I almost screwed that up, too, by not informing Grayson and Nelle about my plan. For so long, I thought I had to arrange everything by myself, or it would all fall apart... And I was good at it. I was a damn good chief of staff and campaign manager."

"I know. Because I know you. You're smart and competent and you care about the people around you."

"But everything became a transaction. There had to be winners and losers. Nothing was freely given. And that was comfortable for me, because that's all I knew." She sighed. "I'm sorry it took me so long to see you were right. I was scared. Of us. Of our future. Of how...big... you make me feel."

"Big?"

"Like I take up space of my own. That I can just... exist, and that's enough. I'm not used to taking up space. I squeeze my way into other people's spaces instead. When I should be letting others in." She shook her head. "I'm not making much sense. You scrambled my brain with that very public speech of yours." She smiled at him, open and genuine. "I'm pretty sure people in Madagascar are watching clips of you speaking right now."

"Let them. And if the clips are wiped off the internet,

I'll give the speech all over again on our fiftieth wedding anniversary." He took her chin in his left hand, gazing into the warm brown eyes he adored so much. "You matter, Lee. Not your family, not your job, not even your ability to pull strings and play games to protect the people you love. You. And I love you."

"I love you, so much." She moved to kiss him, but he pulled back, just a half-inch.

"And if a relationship based on an intense experience doesn't work, we can always base the relationship on sex." He grinned at her.

Her eyes widened. "You...you watched the movie *Speed*! You really do love me."

Then her lips were on his and they sank together into the kiss, the lights of Los Angeles swirling around them and creating a shimmering world for two.

Fifteen

One year later

Finley Smythe loved weddings. Especially when they were her own. And especially when they were spur-of-the-moment Las Vegas weddings presided over by an Elvis impersonator. She and Will were second in line, but it would soon be their turn.

"Ready to begin our happily-ever-after?" she asked the groom, handsome in a pair of board shorts topped by a T-shirt that read, "If Lost or Drunk, Return to the Bride." Her own T-shirt read, "I Was Told I'm the Bride."

They were in Las Vegas to attend the country's largest wedding trade show. Both TV series had become so successful, Screenweb had asked for a third. Finley came up with *Finding EverAftr: Saying I Do*, featuring the weddings of couples who united on the previous series, and the streaming service executives jumped at it. Will had bowed out of hosting yet another series—he had an actual company to run, after all—but Screenweb loved Finley's presence on camera. This trip was to tape interstitial footage to be shown between scenes of the couples' weddings.

And when in Vegas…

"You can't believe in that fairy tale," Will said, his expression straight. "You're too smart."

"I have it on very good authority such a thing exists." Finley adjusted the oversized pink tulle bow decorating her hair.

"On whose?"

"On mine. And I'm going to prove it to you, every day." She flung her arms around his neck.

He smiled, laughter and love spilling from his gaze, and pulled her closer. "I think you mean we're going to prove it to each other."

"For ever after."

"And ever after."

* * * * *

COMING
SOON!

We really hope you enjoyed reading this book.
If you're looking for more romance, be sure to
head to the shops when new books are
available on

Thursday 3rd
March

To see which titles are coming soon, please visit
millsandboon.co.uk/nextmonth

MILLS & BOON

THE HEART OF ROMANCE

A ROMANCE FOR EVERY READER

MODERN

Prepare to be swept off your feet by sophisticated, sexy and seductive heroes, in some of the world's most glamourous and romantic locations, where power and passion collide.

HISTORICAL

Escape with historical heroes from time gone by. Whether your passion is for wicked Regency Rakes, muscled Vikings or rugged Highlanders, awaken the romance of the past.

MEDICAL

Set your pulse racing with dedicated, delectable doctors in the high-pressure world of medicine, where emotions run high and passion, comfort and love are the best medicine.

True Love

Celebrate true love with tender stories of heartfelt romance, from the rush of falling in love to the joy a new baby can bring, and a focus on the emotional heart of a relationship.

Desire

Indulge in secrets and scandal, intense drama and plenty of sizzling hot action with powerful and passionate heroes who have it all: wealth, status, good looks…everything but the right woman.

HEROES

Experience all the excitement of a gripping thriller, with an intense romance at its heart. Resourceful, true-to-life women and strong, fearless men face danger and desire - a killer combination!

To see which titles are coming soon, please visit

millsandboon.co.uk/nextmonth

LET'S TALK
Romance

For exclusive extracts, competitions
and special offers, find us online:

f facebook.com/millsandboon

🐦 @MillsandBoon

📷 @MillsandBoonUK

Get in touch on 01413 063232

For all the latest titles coming soon, visit
millsandboon.co.uk/nextmonth

JOIN US ON SOCIAL MEDIA!

Stay up to date with our latest releases, author
news and gossip, special offers and discounts, and
all the behind-the-scenes action
from Mills & Boon...

 millsandboon

 millsandboonuk

 millsandboon

It might just be true love...